FRACTAL

ARUN RAJAGOPAL

PROLOGUE

Twenty-Six Years Ago
Somewhere on the North African Coast

After seven days of harrowing travel across the desert, Mariama Ndiaye felt a wave of relief when she glimpsed the sea for the first time since leaving home. Shrouded by the morning fog, the formless gray expanse came into view as the bus crested the final dune. Her family had embarked on their journey into the unknown, and this desolate spot on the North African coast was the terminus of the first leg.

The bus lurched down the gravel track toward the coastline, raising a cloud of dust as it ground to a halt beside a dilapidated dock. As the rising sun penetrated the fog, shafts of light revealed the vast body of water that stretched as far as she could see, where water and sky blurred together on the horizon. A lone seagull pierced the morning gloom with a screech as it sailed over the dock, scanning the water.

Stiff after the long night's ride, Mariama stood and stretched. She nudged her brother awake. Her mother, already alert, was busy shoving their belongings into a worn bag. Mariama gathered her sleeping two-year-old son and followed the stream of refugees as they disembarked.

A wave of apprehension swept through her as she gazed at the single boat tied to the rotting timbers. That fragile vessel was to carry her and her family across the sea to an uncertain future. She and her mother exchanged a glance, a silent acknowledgment of an unspoken truth.

There was no turning back.

As soon as the last passenger disembarked, the bus rumbled away, leaving only silence, the boat, and the waiting sea. Her mother gave her a reassuring nod and whispered:

"Léegi ci loxo Yàlla la nekk." (It's in God's hands now.)

The boat was larger up close, but its condition did little to inspire confidence. Faded blue paint peeled away in strips, streaked with rust where bolts bit into the hull. Near the waterline, stringy algae and knobby barnacles clung to the exposed wood. The boat looked like it could hold twenty people, yet forty eager and anxious souls crowded the dock, jostling to climb aboard. Within half an hour, the vessel lurched away from shore, the motor emitting a labored rumble as it pushed into the gray expanse.

On their second day at sea, the journey took a desperate turn. Out of the haze, a speedboat appeared, leaping across the waves. It pulled alongside, and the pilot of their boat shouted a few hurried words to the two men in the speedboat before jumping into the smaller craft. In seconds, it sped away, leaving the refugees abandoned and in disbelief. Shouts of anger broke out, but soon the shock gave way to the grim realization that they had no choice but to continue.

There was no turning back.

One man reached a tentative hand toward the controls as others murmured words of encouragement. The compass showed they were heading in a northeasterly direction, and they clung to that heading, praying for salvation. Rations were scarce; each refugee received only a meager portion of food and water. Mariama cut back on her share so her son and brother could eat more. The unspoken dread of running out of food hung over them like a dark cloud.

The condition of the boat added to the refugees' despair. The hull creaked and groaned as it crested every wave, as though threatening to split apart. There was no toilet, so sanitation meant perching on the edge of the deck while hanging on to a strap for balance. By the ninth day—or perhaps the tenth, Mariama had lost count—hunger and fear boiled over when a man struck a woman who had taken something to eat. He shouted something unintelligible and pulled what the woman held, tearing it from her hands. She screamed and clawed at his face in retaliation. Mariama pulled her son closer to her chest, heart pounding.

Then it got worse.

A storm erupted as dark clouds surged from the south, the sea rising to meet them. There was no chance of outrunning it. A rogue wave slammed into the boat, hurling it skyward. It perched on the crest, teetering as the timbers shrieked in protest. For one suspended heartbeat, they balanced on the edge of a watery cliff. Mariama's stomach dropped. She saw the towering wall of water, and they all knew they were about to die. She clutched her son and brother, shouting for her mother to hold on, her cries lost in the chorus of terrified screams.

A teenage girl lost her grip and slid over the side. Her arms flailed as she hurtled down the wave, her scream piercing the storm. She turned and looked up at the boat. Her terrified face seared into Mariama's memory as she sank beneath the foam and disappeared in a cloud of bubbles.

For a moment, the boat teetered, as if trying to make up its mind about tipping over. The creaking intensified, this time followed by a crack from a seam. Then the Hand of Providence intervened. A wave rose in the opposite direction, colliding with the rogue surge. Almost as quickly as it had risen, the sea flattened, and the boat righted itself. The squall passed as suddenly as it had come. The refugees huddled together, trembling with relief. An unnatural silence fell as the wind died, and they realized the engine had stalled. When the sun broke through the retreating clouds, Mariama heard only the grief-stricken sobs of the girl's mother, pierced by the screech of gulls emerging from hiding.

A sudden shout cut through the silence.

"Piit! Ab gaal!" (Look! A ship!)

On the horizon, a naval vessel appeared, angling toward them. A blue-and-white flag climbed the mast as it slowed, engines rumbling before shutting off fifty yards away. Figures moved across the deck. A rope ladder unfurled, slapping against the waves, while a sailor gestured for them to approach.

They maneuvered their boat close and lashed it to the ladder. As the refugees clambered aboard, Mariama felt a wave of gratitude, but it faded when she met the sailors' eyes. No smiles. No warmth. Only blank, disapproving stares.

They don't care about us. They're only here because they have to be here.

The refugees huddled on deck as a sailor passed out blankets and bottled water. The sailors used cards with pictograms to explain the situation. This was a Greek naval vessel, which would take the refugees to the island of Lesvos for intake and screening. The refugees would live at a camp while the authorities processed their cases. Most would be sent back.

Mariama listened, heart sinking.

Maybe... maybe they will let me ask for asylum.

Moria Refugee Camp, Lesvos, Greece

Three months later, Mariama sat outside her makeshift shelter, staring across the camp. Frayed tarps snapped in the wind, clinging to poles and scraps of wood. Beyond the fence stretched coils of barbed wire and cameras. The lines etched on her young face told the story of despair. They had given up everything, scraping together the family's savings to pay a smuggler, only to end up here. The alternative, staying in the slums of Senegal, had been worse. At least, that's what they told themselves.

Life inside the camp was crushing. The sheer number of migrants crammed into the camp meant fewer resources for each migrant. A single television offered some respite from the boredom, though most programs were in Greek. Power blackouts were frequent, and the nights grew bitterly cold. Out of desperation, refugees chopped down trees for firewood.

When her son fell ill, Mariama's despair deepened. It started with a runny nose, and by morning, he had a high fever. The camp's only clinic opened for a few hours each evening, staffed by foreign volunteers. Mariama was grateful that one of them spoke French. For three nights, she cradled her son against the cold, pressing a damp cloth to his burning face as the fever rose and fell. On the fourth day, it broke. Relief washed over her.

She practiced a single phrase in English: "You have asylum papers?" Each time she approached camp staff, she repeated the well-worn phrase. But to no avail. The asylum process dragged on at a glacial pace, while the days were filled with monotony and indifference. On rare occasions, a staff member, usually a woman, offered a smile and greeting.

Then one morning she was summoned for what she thought was an asylum interview...

"Your name is Mariama?" The man at the desk spoke English like it was not his native language.

"Yes," she replied in broken English.

"Surname?"

"Ndiaye." She spelled it carefully in French.

"Where from?"

"Senegal."

He did not ask how she had crossed from Senegal to North Africa to board a boat. He typed on the keyboard without making eye contact.

Mariama studied him. Mid-thirties, black hair, two days of stubble, an aquiline nose with thin lips. His head bobbed as he pecked at the keys.

He looks like a bird.

She looked around the bare, sterile room, with nothing to suggest it was his office, more like a medical exam room.

"You are how old?"

She snapped back to attention.

"*Pardon? Dix neuf.* Nineteen."

"And you have a two-year-old son?"

"Yes."

"Any problems when… uh, pregnant with him?"

"No."

"Where is the boy's father?"

"I not know. Maybe still in Senegal."

"You are not married?"

"No."

She frowned.

"Why you ask these question?"

The man ignored her and continued with his list.

"Anyone else from your family here?"

"Yes, my mother and brother."

"Can your mother… uh, take care of your son if needed?"

"Yes."

Mariama frowned, her voice rising.

"Why you ask these question?"

The man ignored her again. She hesitated, then repeated the phrase she had practiced so many times, a tinge of hope creeping into her voice.

"You have asylum paper?"

He finished typing her details, then turned to a questionnaire. He swiveled in his chair and made eye contact for the first time. His aquiline nose, sharp in profile, now seemed like a thin plate stuck to his face. Mariama resisted the urge to feel her own fleshy, rounded nose.

But he said nothing about asylum.

"Are you healthy?"

"Yes."

"I will read list of medical problems. Tell me if you have any of these."

He read off a list of medical conditions, most of which she did not understand. She shook her head or shrugged her shoulders at each one. When he finished, he stacked the papers in a neat pile, set down his pen, and steepled his fingers. After a long pause, he picked up the phone.

Mariama watched in silence as he spoke in a language she could not follow. He nodded, listened, then hung up and turned back to her.

"This is not asylum hearing," he said. "We have an offer for you. If you agree, you and your family will receive permanent residency in Greece. You will not be sent back to your country."

Mariama's breath caught. She stared at him, not following what he said.

"Not asylum hearing?"

"No. This is a medical checkup meeting. And we want you to do something for us, something to earn your freedom and stay in Greece."

Her voice was wary.

"What you want me to do?"

"There is a wealthy man in Greece. His wife cannot carry children. We want you to carry his child as surrogate."

Mariama stared, uncomprehending. The phrase "carry his child" twisted in her mind. She realized the literal translation of the phrase was not what this man wanted.

"You want me... to carry baby?"

"Yes."

Then recognition dawned and horror spread across her face.

"No! I not want to be with this man!"

She shoved her chair back, and it tipped over with a crash as she backed toward the door.

"Wait," the official called. "You do not understand. You do not have to be with this man."

Mariama froze, hand on the doorknob.

"No?"

"No, please sit. I explain."

She set the chair upright and perched on the edge, looking at the official with suspicion. She flicked a glance at the door, getting ready to bolt again.

"This is medical procedure," he continued. "We make the baby outside the body, then put it inside you. You stay in a special, safe place, not in the camp, for nine months.

Your mother takes care of your son and brother. All you do is grow baby inside."

He patted his stomach.

"Then we take it out. Finished. You and your family get permanent papers. Free to live anywhere in Greece."

Mariama's mind reeled.

"Make baby outside? How you make baby outside? And how you put it inside?" The technical aspects of *in vitro* fertilization were beyond her comprehension.

"Difficult to explain. But you make baby without having to be with the man. You only carry it. And you and your family get freedom."

The word "freedom" hung in the air as she leaned back, staring at the official. She thought about their perilous crossing, the girl lost to the sea, the hopelessness of camp life, and her son's illness. The offer of freedom and permanent residency status was appealing and too difficult to turn down. Now there was a way out—for all of them.

She sat upright.

"Okay."

Nine Months Later

The first contractions were mild, creating small waves that rippled like stones tossed into a pond. A dull tightening spread through her belly, fading before she awakened. She grunted, shifted, and tucked the pillow between her legs.

"Kii di nekk plus de suba." (This will be over tomorrow.)

The bedside clock glowed red: 11:50. Ten minutes later, the numbers rolled over to midnight. At that exact moment, the first proper contraction struck, hard as stone. Pain rippled across her body, and her belly clenched until her breath caught in sharp gasps.

Mariama bolted upright, hands pressed to her abdomen, chest heaving in and out in quick gasps. The contraction eased, and she exhaled through puffed cheeks, sweat dripping down her face. She snatched a washcloth, dabbing her glistening face and neck.

"*Benn bi dafa metti.*" (That one hurt.)

The fan hummed, blowing warm air over her. She clicked it higher, letting the steady stream cool her flushed face. As she eased back into the pillows, her mind drifted. Back to the camp. Back to the boat. And to the screams of the girl lost in the storm, a memory that still haunted her dreams.

Off the Coast of Lesvos, Greece

A small boat chugged through the narrow channel connecting the crescent-shaped *Kolpos Geras*, or Gulf of Yera, to the Aegean Sea. The sole passenger sat at the stern, gazing at the shoreline, trailing his hand in the dark water as the sun sank behind the sea. Dots of light flickered across the hillsides. Ahead, the gulf opened in a wide arc.

At the wheel, the pilot squinted toward the right shoreline and adjusted course.

"Almost there," he called.

The man in the back nodded, withdrew his hand, and stuffed a few belongings into his bag. Minutes later, a blinking light appeared on shore, and the pilot guided the boat toward it. The pilot cut the engine, and it burped to a halt as the boat drifted against the dock. A rope appeared from the dock. The pilot grabbed it and secured the boat. He turned to the passenger.

"Welcome to Greece," the pilot said with a bow.

The passenger rose, stretching his lanky frame, nearly brushing the boat's roof. He slung his bag over his shoulder and climbed ashore.

A car waited with its lights off. As he approached, its parking lights flicked on, and the back door swung open. Inside, a man sat, his face half-lit.

"Dr. Mbaye," the man said.

The newcomer leaned down—a flash of teeth in the dim light.

"We meet again. Welcome, welcome." The man smiled. "Climb in."

Dr. Mbaye slid into the back seat as the driver stowed his bag.

"Comfortable trip?"

"Yes," Dr. Mbaye replied. "Thank you. Better than crossing the sea any other way."

"Good, good," the man murmured as the car made its slow ascent away from the dock.

"How is Dr. Diop?" asked Dr. Mbaye.

"Fine, fine. He has been here for months. The first phase went well."

"Good. I look forward to helping finish the project."

"Yes. And as you speak Wolof, the girl will trust you more. We want her... cooperative for this last step."

"Of course," Mbaye said.

"Good, good. Then we are all set. And the timing of your arrival is perfect. She has gone into labor."

Throughout the night, Mariama's contractions came and went, leaving her with only a restless sleep. She was already awake when a knock sounded at the door.

Eleni, the young nurse who had cared for her over the past few months, entered, pushing a wheelchair. Beside her stood a tall man Mariama had never met. Both wore dark red hospital scrubs.

"Good morning, Mariama," Eleni said.

"Hello, Eleni," Mariama replied with a wary glance at the stranger.

"Mariama, this is Dr. Mbaye."

"Subag jàmm," Dr. Mbaye said. *"Na nga def?"* (Good morning. How are you?)

Mariama's eyes widened.

"You speak my language?"

"Yes," he replied. They continued in Wolof.

"I am Dr. Mbaye, the anesthetist. I hear you're having contractions. You probably didn't sleep well, but this should be over soon."

"That is good," Mariama said. "I am ready for this to be finished."

"No breakfast today," Eleni said.

Dr. Mbaye showed her picture cards illustrating a cesarean section. Mariama's son had been born naturally, so this was going to be a novel experience. She ran her tongue over her dry lips in nervous anticipation, looking at the cartoon illustration of the incision.

"Looks like it will hurt," she murmured.

"Only later, for a few days," he assured her. "During the procedure, you will feel nothing. We will give you an injection in your back."

He held up another set of cards showing a spinal block. Mariama touched her lower back.

"Here?"

"Yes. Don't be afraid. It's quick and not painful. Ready?"

"Yes."

Mariama climbed into the wheelchair. Eleni pushed her into the adjoining room, opening the door with her hip.

Mariama felt a wave of heat as she entered the room. Just inside stood an infant bed under twin rows of orange lights fixed to a frame. Resuscitation equipment that resembled doll toys lay on one side.

Eleni noted Mariama's puzzled look.

"Infant warmer," she explained.

Another man stood by a table of surgical instruments. He turned and waved.

"Hello, Dr. Diop," Mariama said.

"Hello, Mariama," he replied warmly. "Ready for this to be over?"

"Oh yes. Are you doing the surgery?"

"But of course. Everything looks wonderful. All your checkups were fine. This should be routine."

From his accent, Mariama knew he was African as well, but not Senegalese.

Eleni parked the wheelchair and guided Mariama onto the operating table. Activity surged around her. Eleni wrapped a blood pressure cuff around Mariama's arm, clipped a red-light sensor to her finger, and fitted nasal prongs that streamed cool oxygen into her nose.

"Oxygen," Eleni said.

Next, she helped Mariama roll onto her side and pull her knees to her chest.

"This will push your back out," Eleni explained.

Dr. Mbaye moved around to Mariama's back. Mariama felt liquid swab her lower back as the cuff tightened.

"Hold still," Dr. Mbaye said. His fingers probed, then came a sharp prick. Mariama winced but stayed steady.

"That's the worst of it."

A warm rush spread through her legs and abdomen. When Eleni and Dr. Mbaye rolled her onto her back, her legs already felt sluggish. Soon she realized she could not move them at all. Testing with her finger, sensation faded below her chest until it vanished just above her navel.

Dr. Mbaye's eyes crinkled behind his mask.

"Don't worry. In a few hours, everything will be back to normal."

Eleni and Dr. Diop returned in gowns. Eleni cleaned Mariama's belly, then lifted a blue drape with Dr. Mbaye to block her view.

"Ready?" Dr. Diop asked.

"Please proceed," Dr. Mbaye nodded, and the procedure was underway.

Mariama heard clinking instruments and felt tugging at her abdomen. She heard a gush of liquid splatter on the floor, and a moment of panic surged through her. She felt her breathing quicken.

Is that my blood?

Dr. Mbaye injected something into her IV, and calm washed over her. She closed her eyes, sighing with relief. She let her thoughts wander, relieved that this ordeal was almost over.

Moments later, a newborn's cry interrupted her thoughts. As automatic as any new mother's reflex, she felt tears streaming down her face.

My baby, she thought, as she realized this was the first and last time she would see this infant.

Eleni carried the tiny, dusky-pink bundle to the warmer, cleaned and swaddled it, then tucked it under the glowing lights. Mariama sniffed and turned her face to the ceiling. Dr. Mbaye dabbed the corners of her eyes, and she managed a smile.

The steady beep-beep of monitors filled the silence while Dr. Diop closed her wound. Mariama's thoughts drifted to her son and younger brother, and to dreams of land and freedom. She wondered if they would allow her to buy a piece of land.

I can live off the land...

Suddenly—

Whang!

The muffled metallic crack echoed like a firecracker inside a tin can. Mariama looked up to see Dr. Mbaye drop like a marionette with its strings cut. She glimpsed a flash of crimson where his throat met his chin as his arms jerked at the shoulders. He crashed to the ground.

A second and third *whang* sounded. Dr. Diop and Eleni collapsed, the young woman managing to start a scream before it was interrupted in mid-breath.

A man in black stepped around the drape. A balaclava masked his face, leaving only his eyes visible. A wave of terror slammed into her as he loomed over the operating table, gun in hand.

"No, no!" she cried, thrashing, but her body lay paralyzed below her chest. She flung her head from side to side, crazed with fear.

The man seized her chin, squeezing her cheeks until her lips puckered into an "O." She winced, staring into those blank, merciless eyes.

Xët yooyu. (Those eyes.)

The man placed the muzzle of the gun against her temple and pulled the trigger.

Whang.

ONE

Present Day
Dallas, Texas

"Vic, stop!"

Samantha Arnsson, known as "Sam" to her friends and relatives, yelled at her son. Someone had left the pool area a moment ago, and as the safety gate swung shut, little Vic sensed his opportunity. With a squeal of delight, he bolted through the opening, one floatie slipping off his elbow as he dashed toward the deep end of the pool.

Jick Arnsson, Vic's uncle, reacted first. He rolled off his lounge chair, vaulted the security fence, and caught the giggling toddler just as he reached the pool's edge. He grabbed the back of little Vic's life jacket and hoisted him off the pool deck as little Vic's legs continued to churn like two pistons. With his free hand, Jick scooped up the fallen floatie and exited the pool area, nudging the gate shut with his heel. He deposited little Vic next to his mother.

"Energetic little turd," Jick muttered. "He would have been fine, though, even if he had tumbled in."

"I know," Sam said, eyeing the missing floatie. "But he lost one."

"That was a good save," Quin said from his lounge chair, where he lay next to Sam. His daughter, Gabrielle, a young girl with dark curls, sprawled at his feet.

"Maybe we should wrap this up soon," said Jick. "I think we've been here about an hour, and I'm sure little Vic will start getting cranky soon. I remember Vic Sr. always did when he was hungry..." His voice trailed off.

Sam fished in her bag and pulled out two wrapped cookies. After peeling the wrapper off one, she handed it to Vic, who plopped to the ground and started nibbling. She handed the second cookie to Gabrielle.

"Here you go, Gaby," she said.

Sam reached into her bag a second time and pulled out the bottle of sunscreen. She eyed her companions' coffee-colored skin.

"You two are lucky you don't need to slather this on constantly like I do."

"I hardly used sunscreen in Jamaica," Quin ventured. "Probably should have."

"Same here," Jick said. "I grew up here in Dallas, and being half-Indian, sunscreen was always an afterthought."

Sam's thoughts flickered to her thoughts of the past. She had been married to Jick's younger brother, Vikram, or Vic, before his shocking murder two years earlier. Soon after his death, Sam had discovered she was pregnant and a few months later, little Vikram Jr. was born. The surreal chain of events that had led to Vic's murder and Jick's untethered life seemed like a distant, fading nightmare. Sam had finally begun taking cautious steps to move on with her life.

Quincy "Quin" Duncan was part of that new beginning. A colleague from work, he was a widower raising an eight-year-old daughter. Born in Jamaica, he had moved to the United States as a teenager. Only a faint singsong lilt of his Jamaican accent remained. Sam and he had developed a friendship at work, and over the past few months, it had blossomed into something deeper.

Two lounge chairs sat side by side, and Sam and Quin stretched out together. Vic Jr. and Gabrielle sat in a patch of shade next to Sam, munching on their cookies. Jick reclined in a third lounge chair, angled toward the pair. The adults sipped their drinks as the afternoon sun dipped behind Jick's condo.

"So, Jick," Sam said. "I haven't been here for a while. Been spending more time with Quin. What's new with you? You're looking buff."

"I joined a gym and a Krav Maga club," said Jick. "I've been keeping busy working out and sharpening my martial arts skills."

"Good for you," Sam said. "Everyone needs a hobby. Haven't you been doing Krav Maga for a while?"

"Yes, but this is more intense. I'm trying to get to level four."

"Interesting," Sam said. "Hopefully, you won't need these skills. Unless you get involved in another adventure."

"What happened?" Quin asked.

Sam and Jick exchanged a glance.

"Oh, nothing much," Jick said with a dismissive wave. "Just an attempted mugging when I was in Albuquerque. I got the upper hand on the attacker and fought him off."

"Fought him off, eh?" Quin said. "I'd have just handed over my wallet."

"So would I," Jick said. "But I was with someone, and we had a few drinks. Maybe that's why I was brave. Regardless, my Krav Maga training came in handy, so it turned out well."

Jick changed the subject.

"I've also been studying locksmithing."

"You want to be a locksmith?" Quin asked, puzzled.

"Not really. It just seemed interesting. It's one of those skills that is useful, but you never know when you might need it. I'm thinking of learning a musical instrument too. Maybe learn Spanish. I have a lot of free time."

"Good for you again," Sam said. "Staying busy will prevent your brain from getting rusty. Especially with how much you drink." She winked.

Jick flashed her a withering look. She winked again.

"Are you planning to do any traveling again?"

"Not sure. I probably will. My last round of traveling didn't go so well, remember?"

"What happened?" Quin asked.

Damn. Shouldn't have said that.

"I met someone, and we spent some time together. But it didn't work out, so I came back home. And there was the mugging. Overall, not a great trip."

"I hear New Mexico is beautiful. I haven't been there."

"It is," Jick said. "Many interesting and unique things to see and do."

Quin did not ask any further questions. Jick changed the subject again.

"I thought Quin had two 'n's at the end."

"Quinn does," Quin said. "But my name isn't Quinn with two 'n's. It's short for Quincy."

"Quincy? Your parents named you Quincy? Were they trying to get you beaten up at school?" Jick needled.

"My mom liked the TV show 'Quincy.' It was an old TV show with Jack Klugman as a medical examiner."

"Oh, okay. That makes sense. Quincy was a good show. But most doctor shows on TV are so ridiculous."

"How would you know?" Quin shot back. "And how do you know about Quincy? You must have been, what, five when it was out?"

Damn. Shouldn't have said that either.

"My mother watched old TV shows too. I caught a few episodes."

Sam interjected with a change of subject.

"What are you driving now, Jick? I thought I saw an old Mercedes in your parking spot."

"It is an old Merc. I don't like new cars. They're all pixels and plastic, which I guess today's generation likes. I want actual switches, knobs, and a genuine wood dashboard any day. I can't imagine sliding my finger along a touchscreen to adjust the air conditioner."

"I didn't realize you were so passionate about cars," Sam said.

"I guess as I've gotten older, I've grown nostalgic. And the build quality of older cars was better."

"What are you talking about?" Quin asked. "You're younger than me by at least a decade."

"I just like classic cars," Jick said.

Sam jumped in with another deft subject change.

"Ever been to Hawaii, Jick?"

"Yeah, once, years ago."

Jesus, when was that?

He had gone with his former wife, Dorothy, about a year into their marriage. They had gone to Honolulu and spent a week on the North Shore, soaking in the famous Hawaiian hospitality. Now it felt like a distant memory, already cracked and fading around the edges like an old photograph. So much had happened in his life in the intervening years.

"Why do you ask?" Jick inquired.

"Just wondered if you might be interested in a visit. It could be fun to look around."

Sam smiled at Jick.

Did her smile just end with another wink?

Jick chose his words.

"I guess it would depend on what you want me to 'look around' for," Jick put the words in air quotes.

"Who said anything about me wanting you to look around?" She feigned indignation.

"I know you well."

"Fair enough," Sam said with a grin. "Let's go to my place, and we can talk about it over dinner."

They folded their lounge chairs and stacked them against the pool fence. Little Vic lodged a mild protest at having to leave but was in the early stages of tuckering out and left with little fuss.

"That sounds good. I'll have a quick shower and head over."

Quin and Sam left with Gaby and little Vic.

"Gaby and I are not staying for dinner," Quin said as he drove Sam home. "Her grandparents are coming for a visit, so we're heading to the airport. I'll see you at work tomorrow."

"That's too bad," Sam said. "I planned to order Indian food."

"Oh, man," Quin said. "I love Indian food. Jamaica has a sizable Indian population, and the Indian food there was fantastic. There are some great Indian restaurants around Kingston. Maybe next time.

"Callie's parents called last week and asked if they could visit on short notice. The accident left them as devastated as I was. We've done our best to stay in touch, for Gaby's sake. I think they know at some point, something will probably change in my, our, family situation, but I want them to always be in Gaby's life."

"Absolutely yes," Sam said. She paused for a moment and then asked Quin a gentle question.

"What happened if you don't mind my asking?"

"I don't mind. It's been a few years, and I guess life goes on. It was just one of those random things that came like a bolt out of the blue. Who was it that said 'Life is what happens when you're busy making other plans?' A car accident. It was a lady who ran a red light because she was late for work. That's it. Callie was killed, and the lady who hit her was hurt badly enough that her life will never be the same."

"I'm so sorry," Sam said.

"I've slowly moved past it. I used to feel terrible for Gaby, but kids are resilient. She's tougher than I ever imagined."

They arrived at Sam's house. Quin carried little Vic into the house, exchanged a quick smooch with Sam as he and Gaby departed. Sensing little Vic was fading for the evening, Sam hurried through his dinner and put him to bed just as Jick arrived.

"What did you bring?" Sam asked, eyeing the bottle.

"For after dinner. It's a South African port."

"Sounds good. I just ordered Indian food."

"Excellent."

Jick glanced around.

"Where's Quin?"

"He had to go to the airport. His in-laws, Gaby's grandparents, are arriving today."

"What happened to Quin's wife?"

"Funny you ask. It came up in a conversation when he drove me home. It was a car accident. One of those random things you don't see coming. Gaby was only two when she died."

"Kids are usually quite resilient. I'm sure she'll do fine."

"That's what Quin said."

"So, what's the story between you two?"

"He works with me. We're not in the same department, but our offices are on the same floor. He has been interested in me for quite a while. He asked me out, I don't know, almost a year ago, and I said no. It was still too soon. He waited until I was ready. I guess I was kind of frozen in indecision but finally said yes."

"He seems like a good guy."

"He is," Sam agreed. "I resisted for a long time, still felt guilty about Vic."

"It's okay. It's been two years. Vic would have wanted you to be happy. And little Vic likes him. And Gaby too."

He eyed Sam.

"You look good, Sam. For a while there, you looked ragged. When I got back from my little adventure in Vernon, I thought you looked almost wiped out."

"I'm much better now. I must admit the last two years were brutal. And then, when Vic Jr. came along, not having Vic around..." She broke off with a shuddering sigh.

"When little Vic started crawling, I watched these videos about childproofing the house. The reality is quite a bit more involved. It's amazing the number of things that kid can put in his mouth or stick his fingers into. He is quite the inquisitive and energetic little troublemaker. And I love him to pieces. And I keep wishing Vic could have seen him, and I keep realizing that part of my life is over..."

"And life goes on, right?"

She looked at her arms, rotating them under the light.

"You know, Jick, time is remorseless. And implacable. But you found a way to cheat it, didn't you?"

"Maybe in the short run. But there was an enormous price to pay. And speaking of which, we need to keep our guard up when discussing the past around others."

"Yes, we should. We almost slipped up in front of Quin."

She poured two glasses of wine, and they clinked glasses.

"How do you feel now, two years later?"

"Great. Younger. Stronger. But in a weird way, I seem to be aware of how different I am from before. I am aware of how I act differently now, doing things I would never have dreamed of as a physician."

"Such as?"

"Well, going around like a vigilante, for one. In the old days, I would have run from dangerous situations and called the police. I feel fear, but also a sense of recklessness. I don't think I care as much if something happens to me. Could I be depressed? An interesting tradeoff. I feel younger and stronger but ripped away from everything in my previous life. I'm the same person. But my environment has changed. And that has made me, for better or worse, behave differently."

"Don't say that. You're my only family on Vic's side."

"I'll be careful," Jick promised. "I guess I rely on my sense of trying to anticipate events. So far, it has worked out. But a year before everything happened, I was a physician working in a routine job at a hospital in Dallas."

"Life happens, right?"

"I guess."

"Did you ever think of moving out of Dallas?"

"Yes," Jick said. "And I might. Dallas is a big city, but there's always a chance I may run into the only person who may recognize me. I don't know what I'd do if I ran into Mireille. I've changed a lot in two years, but she may still recognize me. I left Dallas to wander around the country, and things didn't work out. Then I came back, and I've been pretty much staying around this neighborhood, lying low. Even this Krav Maga thing makes me a little nervous."

"Why?"

"Because Mireille was also into it," Jick said. "I know the chances of her coming to my gym are remote, but you never know."

"Well, we may be able to get you out of here for a while," Sam said. "Enjoy a few weeks of island life. May do you some good."

Jick studied her inscrutable face.

"I can hardly wait."

TWO

Twenty-Eight Years Ago
Los Angeles, California

Two years before Mariama Ndiaye's ill-fated journey to Greece, and half a world away, George and Sherryl Sturgis lounged by their pool. The Southern California sun seemed to sink into the deep end of their infinity pool as the end of the pool merged with the reflection of the Pacific Ocean.

Sherryl was about to comment on its appearance when George made a proclamation that caught her off guard.

"I want a son," he announced, swirling his drink.

"I want a baby too. And we have been trying for a while," Sherryl said. "Maybe we should see someone."

"As long as it's a boy," George said.

"Why, George? Why does it have to be a boy?"

"A boy can carry on my name, my legacy. After this most recent deal I just completed, I want to create something, anything, with the Sturgis name so it lasts forever. And a son can carry on that name."

Sherryl sighed. She was used to George's strong-willed nature.

"Okay, George. Maybe we should see someone," she repeated.

Three weeks later, George and Sherryl Sturgis sat in a doctor's office. George drummed his fingers with impatience as he looked around the room.

A money tree plant with a braided trunk sat next to a window, and on the wall, a framed poster bore the letter "A" next to which someone had scrawled "Roll Tide." Another poster, this one an autographed glossy picture of someone in a Western-style embroidered shirt, hung on the wall next to the scarlet "A." The famous person had scribbled "To George, from George" with a thick black Sharpie. Judging by the cowboy flair of his appearance, George guessed he was a country singer.

The diplomas bearing the doctor's credentials read like a Who's Who of prestigious institutions. Berkeley, Stanford, UCSF.

California guy, George thought.

The view from the doctor's office on the seventh floor stretched westward, where a ribbon of dark blue ocean blurred into the horizon. George craned his neck as a plane swooped in and vanished behind the skyline as it touched down at Los Angeles International Airport.

The door opened, and the doctor entered. He was of medium height, with slicked, grey-streaked brown hair, and a retro mustache that looked straight out of a 1970s-era adult movie. A short-cropped salt-and-pepper beard rounded out the look.

Looks like he escaped from a 70s stag film. Christ, that mustache...

He walked over to George and Sherryl with a dazzling veneer smile, hand extended.

"Mr. and Mrs. Sturgis?" he said. "I'm Dr. Jones. George Jones. The less famous one."

The joke landed flat, and the Sturgises looked at him with blank stares. He shook Sherryl's hand first.

"Pleased to meet you," Sherryl said. She regarded him with frank interest.

"Country singer," Dr. Jones said. He pointed at the picture with the "To George, from George" inscription. "I met him once. Never mind. I guess y'all are not country music fans."

Not a California guy.

Dr. Jones sat at his desk and flipped the chart open. As he thumbed through the chart, he glanced at George and Sherryl.

"Y'all from around here?"

"Yes." A one-word answer from George.

"San Diego," Sherryl said.

"Me, I'm from Alabama," he offered with a grin. "We call it God's country."

He glanced at George.

"You're a George, too," he commented. "Our parents had good taste in names."

This quip did not generate a response either.

I don't like this guy.

Dr. Jones noticed their lack of response to his quips and switched to business.

"Right," he said. "I reviewed your questionnaires. Looks like you have been trying for a while to have a baby, with no success."

He licked a finger and flipped through a few pages.

"You may not know this, but the Jones-Gibson fertility clinic is the best in California, if not the entire western United States. We handle the most challenging fertility cases and have the best success rates. You've come to the right place."

"Dr. Jones, I don't need a sales pitch," George cut in.

"Right," Dr. Jones said. "Let's get started. Tell me about how long you've been trying, whether there is a history of difficulty having children in your family, your medical history, etc. I'll jump in with questions for more details, and we'll get a big picture to plan our next step."

For the next thirty minutes, George and Sherryl Sturgis talked, recounting bits of their medical history. Dr. Jones scribbled notes while they talked, interrupting now and then for clarification. At the conclusion, he placed his pen down and leaned back.

"We'll order a few tests like blood tests and an ultrasound of your uterus...," he looked at Sherryl, "and schedule a follow-up in a couple of weeks. Today's visit will be brief. We'll have a better game plan then."

"Couldn't we have done all the tests first," George asked, "then just schedule one visit?"

"Right. It's better to do a brief 'meet and greet' first," Dr. Jones said. "For this quick initial consultation, I don't bill for it. If you decide not to proceed, you won't see a bill. Your health insurance doesn't cover this anyway, so we just do a bundled bill for everything. Jocelyn, our finance coordinator, can discuss this with you."

George opened his mouth to say something about his time being just as valuable but decided against it.

"Okay."

As they drove away from the clinic, George glanced at his wife.

"I didn't like him."

"I thought he was pretty good-looking," Sherryl said.

"He looked like an aging pornstar. And he was so smarmy. Like a car salesman."

George snapped his fingers.

"You know who he reminded me of?"

"Who?"

"Burt Reynolds. That character he played in Boogie Nights. He was either a porn star or a porn filmmaker. I can't remember. We saw it a long time ago."

"I barely remember it."

She eyed the papers Dr. Jones had given them.

"Let's at least do the tests he's recommending, George. I want a baby, and we're not getting any younger."

"Agreed. And I need a son to carry on my legacy."

Sherryl looked at her husband. She said nothing.

Two weeks later, George and Sherryl Sturgis sat in Dr. Jones' office again.

"Heard any George Jones songs yet?" he asked as he came into the office.

"No," Sturgis said in an icy monotone.

"Right, sorry," Dr. Jones said. "Let's discuss the results."

He clicked through a few screens on his computer and drew his brows together.

"We may have found the reason you've had so much difficulty conceiving. It's not good news."

George frowned as Sherryl turned to look at him.

"What's wrong?"

"The analysis of your sperm reveals some abnormalities that would make it very difficult to father any children the usual way," Dr. Jones said. His accent had become more professional, businesslike.

Sounds less Southern.

"Perhaps even impossible," Dr. Jones continued. "Both the morphology and the absolute counts are abnormal. We could do in vitro fertilization with your sperm and your wife's eggs, but only if we could get a sperm sample that would work."

They stared at Dr. Jones, uncomprehending.

"What does that mean in plain English?"

"It may be impossible for you to conceive. But the chances are not zero. Very low, though."

The doctor handed George a sheet of paper.

"These are your labs," he said. "You can see the numbers printed in red. That one," he leaned across the table and tapped a number, "is quite low. Low enough that we would question the efficacy of even doing in vitro. But I have achieved success in the past and I am willing to try again."

George's face cycled through a few emotions and settled on anger. He raised a fist to pound the table but at the last instant, caught himself. The clenched fist landed with a soft thump on the table.

"But this is impossible!" he said, raising his voice. "There is nothing wrong with my sperm."

Sherryl looked equally indignant.

"There is nothing wrong with my George," she said with some emphasis, putting her hand on his arm. "George is..." She left it hanging and stared at her husband.

"Maybe there's something wrong with the testing? Should we repeat the tests?" Sherryl asked.

Dr. Jones looked startled by this collective outburst. George Sturgis' expression had changed from anger to a cold, blank stare.

Obvious who calls the shots in their relationship. But boy, does she enable him. And he's an odd one...

"I'm sorry, sir, ma'am," Dr. Jones said. "These things happen. As I said earlier, you have come to the right place. If there is any clinic that can help you solve your dilemma, we can."

George's blank stare was gone, and his expression softened. "I must have a son. An heir to the Sturgis name. My legacy."

Dr. Jones frowned.

"I don't think we're quite at the level of made-to-order babies. We can certainly tilt the odds in one direction, but even if we did our best, we cannot guarantee a son."

"I am about to create a research foundation, Dr. Jones, the Sturgis Longevity Institute, whose purpose it will be to explore how long the human body can live, with proper modifications to the environment. I must have a son to carry on my legacy."

"We'll do our best," Dr. Jones said.

This guy is quite the narcissist. And a megalomaniac.

He looked at Sherryl.

"Which brings us to our second problem. Even if we can successfully create an embryo, we would then need to implant it. We did the ultrasound of your uterus. Your uterus has a structural abnormality known as a bifid uterus."

"What's that?" Sherryl asked.

"The normal uterus is round and a little elongated."

He held his hands up like he was cupping a small ball with both hands.

"Yours is wider at the top..."

He separated his hands at the top.

"And it has a dividing line down the middle..." He folded the tips of his fingers down. "...so it looks like a little heart. Each half is smaller than normal. Of course, you can carry a baby, but it is riskier. Since we already have some, uh, challenges with your," he glanced at George, "sperm count and maybe difficulty getting a good sample, to maximize the chance of success, I would suggest y'all consider a surrogate."

"A surrogate?"

"Yes, your egg, your sperm, implanted in a willing host. It's common, done all the time, and it may reduce all the uncertainty. And it's 100% your genes. It's where we have had the best results in couples where both husband and wife have a less-than-ideal situation. The last thing we want to do is go through all the effort, not to mention the substantial expense, and have a miscarriage before viability."

"Is that the only option?" George asked.

"Well, no. But it is the best option and gives us the best chance of success."

"We need to think about this."

"Of course, of course. Today's visit was to go over the results. And...," Dr. Jones looked at George, "I won't bill this visit either. Just the cost of the tests you did. Let me know how you want to proceed, and we can go from there."

"Let's get out of here," George said.

Dr. Jones slid a brochure across the table.

"This brochure explains the different procedures we do here. I've circled the one that I think offers the best chance of success. If you want to move ahead, give me a call."

They rose from their chairs and left, George leading the way in a brisk stride and Sherryl scurrying after him. She turned and looked at the doctor with a resigned "not sure what to do next" expression. As they drove away from the clinic, Sherryl avoided looking at her husband.

"This is impossible," he said again. "A disaster. I must have an heir. A son."

"A daughter would be fine, too," Sherryl put in. "As long as it's a healthy baby."

George turned to her with a glare.

"I want a son."

They turned south on the interstate. George was silent and brooding during the hour-long drive. As soon as they reached home, George poured himself a couple of fingers of whiskey on ice and threw himself in a lounge chair by the window.

"I'll have some too," Sherryl said.

George stared for a moment, then strode to the bar and poured a drink for his wife.

"Shall we do the in vitro thing?" Sherryl started the conversation.

"I need to think about it. Leave me alone for a while."

Sherryl reached for the remote and clicked on the television.

"Turn that off. I can't think with that noise. Just, I don't know, go for a walk or something."

Sherryl turned the television off.

"Okay, I'm going for a swim."

Sherryl strolled out of the house, made her way past the tennis court, and down to the pool. Their pool guy, Alejandro, had finished earlier that day, and swimming conditions were perfect. She lowered herself into the water and stared at the coastline over the infinity edge.

As she swam laps, she thought about the appointment earlier in the day. It had been a blow to her psyche that she had an abnormality in her uterus, but the hammer blow was ten times worse for George. She finished swimming laps and went back to the house. She noticed the car was gone.

"George," she called. No answer.

George arrived home an hour later but said little to her. He spent the next few days moody and distant, saying little. He would disappear on brief trips and provide no details.

"George, what are you doing?" She had asked on one occasion.

"Nothing, just doing a lot of research into various options for having a baby. I'm thinking the in vitro thing may be the way to go. With a surrogate."

"Like Dr. Jones recommended?"

"Yeah, sure. But I'm not sure we should do it here."

"Why not? Isn't that clinic the best?"

"That's what he says. I need to do some more research into this."

After a few more weeks of enduring his distant behavior, she awakened one morning to find George standing by their bedside. Wearing a big smile on his face, he carried a tray with coffee and bagels, which he placed on Sherryl's bedside table. He took both of her hands in his.

"Honey, how would you like to go to Greece?"

THREE

Athens, Greece

George and Sherryl Sturgis sat in the doctor's office. George tapped his fingers on the desk as he studied the room.

I'm getting a feeling of déjà vu.

Except this time, the diplomas all bore the doctor's credentials in the unfamiliar letters of the Greek alphabet, and the large window faced a cityscape of irregular red roofs that stretched into the haze. If he craned his neck to the right, he could just glimpse the edge of the Acropolis.

George approved the décor; typically austere and European, square, no-nonsense furniture and sleek, elegant fixtures. There were no personal touches, such as signed celebrity pictures.

I already like this guy better than Dr. Jones.

Sherryl fidgeted with nervous anticipation. George, grim and focused, turned to his wife with a blank, piercing stare.

"Stop fidgeting. The doctor will come in when he's ready."

"I know," Sherryl replied. "But I'm anxious. And I'm still a little jet-lagged. Maybe I drank too much coffee this morning."

As she spoke, the door opened, and a tall, distinguished man in a white coat entered.

"Hello, I'm Dr. William Pappas," he said in accented English. "Thank you for coming to the clinic today."

He carried a file that he flipped open as soon as he sat. He peered at George and Sherryl over his glasses.

"Do you speak Greek?" he asked George.

"Den miláo polý elliniká." (I don't speak much Greek.)

Sturgis switched to English.

"I used to speak it a lot better," George said. "Our last name was Stavridis when we emigrated to the United States. Living in California, I didn't keep in touch with the language much."

"No matter," the doctor replied. He turned to Sherryl. His eyes roved over her obvious Northern European features.

"And I presume you do not speak Greek either."

Sherryl shook her head.

"Well, then, English it is."

His English sounds like there's a little British sprinkled in.

As if reading George's mind, the doctor said, "My mother is English. My father is Greek. I spent many summers in England."

"I see," George said.

"So," the doctor tapped the file. "I have reviewed the records you sent from your clinic in California." He pronounced it *Kah-lee-fornia*.

"You already know the results of your testing. It does not look too good, but I believe we can help you."

George and Sherryl exchanged a glance.

"I would recommend a procedure called intracytoplasmic sperm injection," Dr. Pappas said. "I won't get too technical. It's basically what Dr. Jones recommended."

He looked at Sherryl.

"I know many women want to experience the entire birthing process, but in this case, enlisting the help of a surrogate would be the proper course of action."

Sherryl glanced at George. Before she could answer, George surprised her as he chimed in right away.

"Of course we should use a surrogate. That would be fine."

Dr. Pappas tapped a pencil on his desk.

"But I am curious about one thing. Why here in Greece? If you don't mind my asking, why not do this in California?"

Sherryl looked at her husband, unsure of what he would say.

"Two reasons," George said. "First, it's a lot less expensive. Something like thirty or forty thousand cheaper. Second, I'm Greek-American. I figured if we're going to do this, I could do it here where the medical care is just as good."

Both the doctor and Sherryl seemed satisfied with the answer.

"Okay, I'll go over the details, and we'll get started."

Two weeks later, Dr. Pappas sat at his desk, reviewing and signing off patient charts. The phone rang; it was his receptionist.

"Mr. Sturgis is on the phone, Doctor. He would like to speak with you."

"Sturgis," Dr. Pappas paused. "Oh yes, the American couple who were here two weeks ago. Yes, I'll take it."

Dr. Pappas waited for the call to be put through.

"Good morning, Mr. Sturgis," he said.

He listened to George Sturgis for a minute.

"Sure, that's fine. There's no rush," Dr. Pappas said. "I'll wait to hear from you in March."

He listened for a few seconds.

"I understand. Yes, it is costly, even if we do it here. That's fine. Let me know when you and your delightful wife are ready."

Dr. Pappas placed the phone in its cradle and frowned.

"So eager to have a child," he mused.

What an odd couple.

North San Diego County

In the weeks following their appointment with Dr. Pappas, George Sturgis seemed reluctant to decide on whether to proceed with *in vitro* fertilization in Greece. Sherryl tried to engage the topic in conversation, but George brushed her off.

"I thought you wanted to get this started as soon as possible," Sherryl complained one day.

"I do, I do," Sturgis said. "But I have a few other matters. Business matters. I'm traveling out of the country on a business trip."

"Where out of the country?"

"Europe."

"Why?"

"I'm working on some new deals that should make us a lot of money. I won't be gone long. Probably a couple of weeks. And then when I get back, it will be March. We can go to Greece then."

"Where in Europe are you going?"

"Probably Greece."

"Greece? Aren't we going there in March anyway?"

"Yes, but this is business. I'm working on some deals. Then we'll go to Greece to make a baby."

Sherryl had learned not to question George's business ventures.

"Okay, whatever you think is best."

Luxury Villa, Aegean Coast, Greece

George's business trips lasted longer than expected, but a year later, the arrival of the baby was imminent. Sherryl Sturgis stopped pacing and stared out of the large window of their villa. Her husband had rented an opulent residence that overlooked the Aegean Sea. Gentle waves lapped at the ribbon of sand stretching in both directions. Under the midday sun, the pale beach sand looked almost white. A few fishing boats shimmered in the distance, and a foghorn bellowed as a departing ferry crawled away from the coast.

Once again, she glanced at the road winding along the shoreline.

Nothing.

Her eyes shifted back to the shrinking ferry. An idle thought flashed through her mind.

Turkey is over there, I think.

She resumed pacing, then stopped at the window again.

They should be here any minute now.

An almost empty glass of white wine perched on the sill. A ring of water had condensed around its base. Sherryl downed its contents, refilled the glass, and concentrated for a moment to center it on the watery circle. Her hand shook.

I'm so nervous. Hope everything went well.

Her thoughts returned to the events of the past year. They had flown to Greece shortly after George returned from his European trip. He had been jubilant about the business deals he struck, thus paving the way for a stress-free trip to Greece to move ahead with their plans. The doctor had gone over the details, and they had signed up for the procedure. Sherryl endured nearly three weeks of hormonal treatments, followed by the uncomfortable vaginal ultrasound procedure to harvest the eggs.

I wish we could have done this in America, but George is right. It's cheaper here, and he is Greek. Still, I would have liked to carry the baby.

She pressed her lower abdomen. She did not understand what the doctor had said about the shape of her uterus.

A bifid uterus?

She continued pacing. Today was the arrival day for the baby. And George had said he would go alone. Which surprised and disappointed Sherryl, but this was George, and this was the way he wanted it. She was used to his ways. So she waited, restless.

She wondered for the hundredth time why they had not arrived yet. She leaned out of the window and looked to the right. No car yet. But she saw a woman appear around the corner, with three children in tow. Each child sucked on a lollipop.

Looks like a mom with three kids. And in a hurry. Wonder if she had them natural. Bet she doesn't have a bifid uterus.

The woman looked harried, and the children seemed to have difficulty keeping up with her brisk pace. One child was in the middle of a full-blown tantrum. As they passed Sherryl, he sat on the ground and refused to move. The mother turned and yelled at him, waving a finger. In retaliation, he pulled the lollipop out of his mouth and flung it in the dirt.

The woman snapped. She grabbed the boy's wrists and hoisted him off the ground. As he swung in the air suspended by his wrists, she started whacking his bottom like she was beating dust off a rug. Sherryl heard the woman yell at the boy in Greek. The child wailed, but when she let him go, the tantrum subsided. He sat on the ground, made a few convulsive gasps as the sobbing abated, and then pointed at his lollipop in the dirt. She said something to him, and he stood, quiet and sullen. He trotted obediently behind her and his siblings.

Sherryl stared after them. She realized she had balled her fists. She thought about running out of the house and confronting the mother.

Bitch. You don't know how lucky you are to have three kids.

But the group continued up the road and disappeared around the bend. She glanced at the road and froze. A large black car appeared around the bend.

They're here!

She rushed downstairs and opened the back door, staring at the driveway in eager anticipation. The car turned into the driveway and stopped under the porch. She spotted her husband in the back seat. A car seat was attached to his left. He unbuckled the seat and lifted it out.

Sherryl gasped at her first sight of the squirming bundle. The blanket had pulled to the side, and a pink foot emerged.

"He's beautiful!"

George beamed at his wife.

"Isn't he!"

Sherryl gazed at the baby and clasped her hands together against her cheeks.

"I still can't believe it. He's perfect." She cocked her head at the baby. "You know, I think he looks a lot more like you."

George carried the baby inside and placed the car seat next to the loveseat. They both sat marveling at their little bundle.

"Our son," George said.

"How did it go?" Sherryl asked.

"It was fine. No problems."

"And the surrogate? She's okay?"

"Yes."

"I'm glad. Such a long road for us to get here, probably a longer road for her. All I had to do was suffer through that, what did they call it, egg aspiration? You had the easiest part, right George? Naughty boy." She giggled at the thought of his simple contribution.

George smiled faintly but said nothing, his gaze fixed on the baby.

"What shall we name him?" Sherryl asked. "We haven't really talked about names."

George held his hand out, caressed the baby's cheek with the back of his index finger.

"I christen thee... Phoenix," he said.

Sherryl Sturgis looked at her husband.

"Phoenix?" she asked. "Why Phoenix? George, that's such an unusual name. How about a few other choices? Like Harold, after my father. Or even a Greek name from your side of the family."

"I like Phoenix. The phoenix is a symbol of immortality, of regeneration and rebirth. He will carry on my legacy."

He turned to his wife and stared at her. She looked at his expression, knowing his strong-willed personality. The personality trait that had made him such a business success. She managed a wan smile and a sigh.

"Okay, George, we'll name him... that."

"I'm glad you agree."

Phoenix joined the conversation with the sound of a wet fart, followed by a protracted squelch. George and Sherryl stared at each other. Sherryl burst out laughing.

"Was that what I think it was?" Sherryl asked.

"I think so."

"I have a diaper bag ready to go," Sherryl announced with some pride.

Sherryl produced a colorful bag festooned with cartoons of various animals. She pulled a snap open, and a changing pad unfurled.

"I've read books about how to do this," she declared.

She fumbled her way through the first diaper change as George hovered, offering no help. When she was done, she picked up the bundle and beamed at George.

"Good," George said. "Now let's go home."

FOUR

Present Day

Sam dabbed her mouth and leaned back in the recliner. She pressed a button, and the footrest extended with a soft whine. A glass of port sat within easy reach on the end table. She had already fed, changed, and tucked Vic Jr. in his crib. Curling her toes, she stretched her legs out and took a generous sip as she glanced at Jick with a ghost of a smile.

"That dinner was amazing," Sam said.

"It sure was," Jick agreed. "I am so relaxed now."

"You can stay in the guest room if you want."

"I just might. I haven't slept there in years."

He thought back to the last time he had stayed in the guest room. Vic's murder had been fresh in his mind and for several nights, Jick had replayed Vic's last comment in a recurring nightmare, "Oh God, please don't...", followed by the sound of the gunshot that ended his brother's life.

Jick snapped back to attention as he realized Sam had been speaking to him.

"Sorry, what did you say?"

"Daydreaming?"

"Just zoning out. I thought back to the last time I slept in the guestroom."

Sam did not inquire any further. She leaned forward.

"Let's talk about Hawaii," she said. "We have an assignment for you. Or, more precisely, *I* have an assignment for you."

Jick resisted the urge to ask her who "we" was. Previous attempts at finding out the identity of Sam's employer had been in vain. He realized she worked for one of the alphabet soups of various security agencies in the government.

He swirled his port and took a sip.

"O-kay," he said. "What's up?"

"It's a missing person case."

"You remember what happened last time I embarked on a missing person quest."

"That wasn't an assignment. You met Brenda and the relationship was great, not to mention the sex. Helping her find her missing sister was natural and chivalrous. And it came with perks. I'm sure you didn't expect it to turn into a bloodbath."

Jick grinned.

"That's a pretty blunt assessment. About as subtle as a sledgehammer. But you're right, and it was quite an adventure."

"This assignment is different. It may come to nothing. In fact, it's likely that it will come to nothing. You'll just have a great vacation in Hawaii on the government's dime."

Jick topped off their glasses.

"This port goes well after Indian food," he remarked.

"I'm no connoisseur, but this South African stuff is good."

"Okay, fire away. What's the assignment?"

"First, some background. As you know, I'm a data analyst. That's a catch-all term for online snooping. We monitor internet traffic, financial transactions, physical travel, etc. All we're looking for using various algorithms is anomalies. We don't keep any of the collected data, so there are no privacy risks or identity theft risks for the person being surveilled. No harm, no foul."

"I'm not sure about that. Should the government be conducting these types of operations without proper legal review, you know, like getting a warrant when they suspect something?"

"We're not investigating actual crimes," Sam countered. "So, at this stage, there's no warrant needed. This is more of a 'see something, say something' type of operation. After all, we tell the general population the same thing, to report anything suspicious. Think of this as the same thing, but a digital version. If we identify a potential trouble spot or something that needs further investigation, we bump it up to the next level. Then the legal process kicks in."

"I see. So where do I come in?"

Sam sipped her port as she glanced at the baby monitor. The green lights that strobed to sounds were off. The only sound was the reassuring background hiss from the speaker.

"Almost eight months ago," she began, "we sent one of our people, a Honolulu-based investigator named Alicia Kehaulani Rogers, to the Big Island of Hawaii for a preliminary investigation. She arrived on the Big Island, checked into her room at the Hawaiian Orchid resort, and was there for four days. On day five, by all accounts, she drove somewhere, parked her car, and went for a walk by herself. She did not return from her walk and has been missing ever since."

"What was she investigating?"

"We can't tell you too many details. But the overall case can be summarized as follows.

"Starting more than a year ago, give or take, we noticed shipments of materials that could be used for a specific and possibly shady purpose. Whoever sent them used small packages to avoid drawing attention. All these shipments went to a shipping company in Kona. The same company paid for all the shipments and from there, a private truck took the shipment somewhere."

"That's it?"

"No. A few months into the shipments being sent over, a scientist with a history of questionable research in the same field moved to the Big Island from California."

"What questionable research were you worried about?"

"Cloning."

Jick was about to take another sip. He stopped and looked at Sam.

"Cloning?" Jick's tone was skeptical. "Cloning what?"

"Humans."

"You've got to be kidding me." He gave her a look somewhere between disbelief and amusement.

"You think there's someone in Hawaii who wants to clone people?"

"It's not as outlandish as it sounds. Have you heard of the Honolulu Technique?"

"Sounds like a dance move. But I'm guessing it isn't."

"No, it's a cloning method. Here's a synopsis. Have a look at the first highlighted section."

She slid a paper toward him. Several sections appeared highlighted in yellow. Jick scanned the first passage:

Dr. Teruhiko Wakayama at the University of Hawaii developed The Honolulu Technique. In this method, starting with a somatic cell, the nucleus is carefully extracted. In another cell, this time a stem cell, the nucleus is removed and the nucleus from the somatic cell is injected. The egg is bathed in a special chemical solution and cultured. The cell, now with the transplanted nucleus, begins dividing until an embryo forms. It is then implanted into a surrogate and allowed to develop to maturity.

Sam pulled another paper out of a folder.

"Do you remember Dolly, the sheep that was cloned?"

"Yes, that was years ago. I remember reading about it."

"Here's another paper. Dr. Wakayama and Dr. Ryuzo Yanagimachi improved the technique by giving scientists more precise control over the process, thus resulting in much higher yields.

"So, you see? Researchers in Hawaii have been involved in the world of cloning. So, it's not that outlandish to suggest that this could be going on in Hawaii."

"Hmm, I always visualize Hawaii as a languid island paradise that runs on so-called 'island time,' with beaches and mai tais. I admit I'm a little surprised you think there may be an underground cloning lab."

Jick emptied his glass and helped himself to another splash of port.

"Well, this sounds straightforward. You want me to go there and see if there are clones wandering around. And if I find any, should I go full 'Rick Deckard' on them?"

"Who's that?"

Jick grinned and winked. "He's a character in a sci-fi novel from the late sixties, 'Do Androids Dream of Electric Sheep?' And in the movie *Blade Runner*, which was based on the novel. Harrison Ford played him."

"I know who Harrison Ford is. And I've heard of the movie. Just haven't seen it."

"Rick Deckard is a bounty hunter. His job is to find and kill 'replicants,' who are bioengineered humans similar to clones."

Sam frowned.

"No, I do not want you to go 'full Rick Deckard' on anyone. All I want you to do is retrace Alicia's steps and see if anything turns up."

Jick leaned back in his chair.

"I wonder if there are any wild geese in Hawaii."

"I'm not following."

"You know, so I can chase after them." He grinned at Sam.

"Really, Jick." Sam frowned again.

"All right, all right, I'll be serious. I'm blaming the port. So, did your investigator find anything interesting?"

"We don't know. She went missing before filing any reports. Without evidence of criminal activity, we didn't put anyone under surveillance. If this was a false alarm, a 'nothing burger' in today's vernacular, there was no need to sully the targeted person's reputation."

"I'm sure someone notified the cops?"

"Of course," Sam said. "Alicia had notified the concierge desk that she would be gone all day and return in the evening. When she didn't return, the hotel staff alerted the authorities right away that same evening. By morning, they mobilized canine units, volunteer patrols, and aerial surveillance. The authorities also checked her cell phone records and credit card transactions. They found nothing."

"Where do I come in?"

"I want you to go to Hawaii to look for Alicia."

FIVE

Eighteen years ago
Big Island, Hawaii

Phoenix was seven when he first felt the urge. A year earlier, the Sturgis family had moved to Hawaii, settling into a large house in Kailua-Kona on the Big Island. They had enrolled their son in a private school, but the first few weeks of first grade were rough. Phoenix struggled to make friends, so his mother, hoping to encourage socialization but against Phoenix's wishes, invited his entire class to their house for his seventh birthday party.

At first, he did not know what the urge was. But he knew he liked it, from the first sensation, a thrill of anticipation, followed by a euphoric rush, then a strange calm. It began after a stressful afternoon on his seventh birthday...

At three o'clock, about a dozen classmates gathered at his house, dropped off by parents grateful for the three-hour reprieve. All the children wore swimsuits for the water-themed party. After depositing presents by the door and kicking off their shoes, they clustered in the family room where his mother had assembled various activities.

For the next hour, the house and yard exploded with the cacophony of boisterous activity. Phoenix's mother had rented an inflatable bounce house, and in small groups, they took turns jumping and tumbling. Other kids ran and slid on a water slide that George had laid out on the grass.

"Let's get them tired out," Sherryl had said earlier to George.

After ninety minutes of non-stop activities, George served pizza followed by Sherryl bringing out ice cream cups and birthday cake.

The birthday cake was a sugar-fueled spectacle. Instead of plastic decorations, the cake decorator had used various chocolates and candies to sculpt an artistic masterpiece of a Hawaiian scene: palm trees, leis, turtles, and beach. Sherryl carried it in, her face glowing in the candlelight as seven candles flickered. Everyone sang "Happy Birthday" as George hovered over a video camera. Phoenix listened to the calls to blow out the candles. George and Sherryl watched the kids gorge on cake and ice cream, followed by Phoenix opening his presents.

"Wow, Phoenix, that Hot Wheels is awesome," one boy exclaimed as Phoenix tore off the wrapping.

Phoenix looked at the collection of presents with indifference. Hot Wheels cars and action figures of popular characters meant little to him. One toy was a memory game, a battery-operated circle with multicolored lighted buttons that flashed in sequence. One of his classmates had activated it and it emitted a series of harsh electronic beeps while the lights flashed. Phoenix felt a throb, and he squinted, rubbing his temples.

After opening all his presents, his mother prompted him to thank everyone. Phoenix only wanted the day to end. Relief washed over him when the doorbell rang; it was the first parent arriving to collect their child. Twenty minutes later, the last child left. Phoenix closed the door and exhaled a long sigh.

Three hours of sensory overload had left him drained. His mind buzzed, worn raw by the constant stimulation. He slipped out into the garden and sank behind a woodpile. This tucked away area in the garden's corner was a refuge, a quiet corner where Phoenix could enjoy the solitude. He sat on the ground, knees bent, idly twirling a dried twig. His eyes closed as he savored the tranquility; he leaned against the stacked logs.

A tickle brushed his knee. Opening his eyes, he saw that a dragonfly had landed there. Its iridescent wings moved in a slow rhythm, a gentle up and down cadence. Phoenix stared at it, mesmerized by the rainbow hues glinting off its wings. As he watched the hypnotic up-and-down motion of the wings, he felt an urge wash over him.

His fingers tingled as he reached for the dragonfly, approaching from behind. The dragonfly did not move. He extended his thumb and index finger in a pincer-like fashion. The dragonfly still did not move. As soon as he grasped the rear wing on the right, it panicked, and its fluttering intensified. The up-and-down motion of its wings became a blur as it tried to escape. Phoenix did not let go. He pinched its rear left wing with his other hand. Now it was trapped, its front wings fluttering helplessly.

He pulled his hands apart, and the right wing tore free. Heart pounding, breath quickening, he held it by its body and pulled off its left wing. Still clutching the hapless insect's body, he tore away the front wings. He let go of the dragonfly and watched it spiral to the ground. He stared at it, transfixed by its helplessness in the presence of his power. Its long, slender body curled and straightened as it lay mortally wounded. Phoenix lifted his foot and brought it down on the wounded dragonfly.

Leaning against the woodpile with eyes closed, a beatific smile crossed his face...

By his mother's estimation, the birthday party was a success. Even her husband, normally of a stern and no-nonsense demeanor, seemed uncharacteristically lighthearted. He swam with the children, took part in the games she had arranged, and laughed and joked with the children.

This is a side of George I don't see often. I like it... Sherryl thought.

By six o'clock, the parents had collected their children and gone. Phoenix's mother exhaled a sigh of relief as the door closed behind the last departing guest.

"High five." She held up her hand, and George slapped her palm.

"I liked that," he said. "All the kids called me 'Uncle George.'"

"It's such a Hawaiian custom," Sherryl said. "Everyone's an uncle or aunty."

"I like that," George said. "Uncle George. I can be Mr. Sturgis when I'm on business and Uncle George to Phoenix's friends and the local community."

"Our first birthday party in Hawaii. I thought it was wonderful. I'm glad we moved here."

"I'm glad we moved here too. It is nice here," George agreed. "And it's a nice place for Phoenix to grow up."

His tone shifted.

"But I'm not sure I like Kona, though."

Sherryl frowned.

"What's wrong with Kona?"

"Too hot, too much vog. When you look out over the ocean, the sky is never bright blue. It always has that hazy, faded bluish-grey tint. I looked at some oceanfront properties last week."

"You did?"

"Yes," George said. "And they all had the same thing in common. Each house had a lanai with a magnificent view of the ocean. Each house also had the same view of the faded grey-blue sky. And with Kona now becoming a tourist hot spot, every parasail charter, manta ray expedition, snorkeling trip, or dinner cruise seems to go past our house. So much for privacy. Plus, cruise ships dock regularly in Kona, and there are hordes of tourists swarming the town."

"But I like it here," Sherryl protested.

"You'll like it even better where we may be going."

"What? Where are we going?"

"Oh, nowhere far. Still here on the Big Island. There's a nature reserve off the highway toward North Kohala, just past Kawaihae. Gorgeous greenery and lush forests. The state set aside part of it for residential lots. The lot at the very top just came on the market. It's the best lot and I think it's at least twenty acres. Gorgeous sunset views every night, milder weather, and it borders the nature reserve. Incredible privacy. The only thing missing is the sound of the ocean and for that, we can get an oceanfront condo here as a second home."

"I don't know about this."

"I already bought the lot."

Sherryl blinked. "What?"

"I'm sure you will like it."

Sherryl stared at George's determined face. The smiling, cheerful birthday party demeanor had faded, replaced with his more usual blank stare and the "I've-made-up-my-mind" expression. She sighed, knowing there was no use arguing.

"What about Phoenix?"

"What about him?"

"He's made friends."

"He's seven, Sherryl. He'll be fine. There's a private school nearby, only an hour away. If he has any close friends, you can always arrange a playdate. But I don't think he's made many friends anyway. I thought he looked a little stressed at the party."

Phoenix entered the kitchen. His mother thought he looked pale and tired. George departed for his office.

"Are you feeling okay, sweetie?"

"Yes, Mom," he said. He avoided her gaze. "I'll be out in the garden."

He walked out into the garden as Sherryl tidied the kitchen. She turned off the birthday music, savoring the sudden silence.

Later, George wandered back into the kitchen. He pulled a beer out of the fridge.

"Don't stress about this lot," George said. "I bought it because it was a great deal, and it wouldn't have been around for long. We're not in a rush to move."

"Oh, okay," Sherryl said, relieved. "I thought you wanted to move right away."

"No, I'm still too busy with work. But I would like to get out of Kona at some point."

"Can I go see it?"

"Of course. I'm closing the deal in a couple of weeks. Want to drive up there now?"

"Sure."

George looked around the kitchen.

"Where'd Phoenix go?"

"He said he wanted to go out to the garden. I think he's a little worn out from the stress of the party. He doesn't do well around so many people."

"I know," George agreed. "I was like that as a kid. I think I'll go talk to him. Did you see where he went?"

"Past the pool," Sherryl said. "Probably near that woodpile in the corner. He likes to sit there."

"I'll go get him, then we can go see the lot."

George walked past the pool and approached the woodpile. Without making a sound, he peered over the edge. Phoenix sat on the ground, leaning against the wood, facing away from him.

Phoenix held a dragonfly by both wings. As George watched, he saw Phoenix pull the helpless insect apart. Phoenix dropped the insect on the ground, raised his foot, and smashed it.

George watched without making a sound. An expression flickered across his face for a split second. He shut his eyes.

I didn't think he would do that...

Then his eyes snapped open as he stepped back, turned, and went back to the house, a worried expression on his face. His wife was in the kitchen.

"Was he there?"

George nodded. Sherryl noticed his expression.

"What's wrong?"

"Nothing," George said. "He's just sitting there. Looks like he's meditating."

"He probably needs a little downtime. I'm sure he'll be in soon. I'm looking forward to seeing this lot you're so excited about."

Almost on cue, the back door opened, and Phoenix walked in.

"You feeling better, sweetie?" his mother asked.

"Yeah, Mom, I'm feeling a lot better now."

SIX

Present Day

"You want me to go to Hawaii and look for Alicia?"

Before Sam could answer, the baby monitor crackled. A line of green lights flashed, then faded as Little Vic whimpered in his sleep and rolled over. The green lights turned off, and the reassuring background hiss resumed.

"Probably had a dream about swimming," Sam said.

"Or passed gas," Jick suggested with a grin.

"Yeah, that too."

"So, to get back to the case. Why now, after eight months? I doubt I'll find anything else that the police wouldn't have after all this time."

"I guess I feel a little guilty since I gave her the assignment. We identified something that may have been a reason for concern, and I sent her to investigate."

"What happened to the investigation?"

"Well, it sort of faded away. Got put on the back burner. Then, last week, we identified another shipment. Same shipping company, same payer."

"What was in this shipment?"

"Some type of holding tank."

"A holding tank?"

"Yes, a large tank from some aquarium supply company. But a tank big enough to hold, among other things, a body."

"Come on, Sam. Just because a tank can hold a body doesn't mean it will."

"I know. As an isolated shipment, not a big deal. But when you add it to the list of other shipments, it may be worth checking out."

"Since she didn't file any reports, you don't even know if she found anything."

"Nope. Hang on a second."

Sam fished out her tablet and swiped through some screens. She turned the tablet to Jick.

"This is a picture of her."

Jick saw a young woman, probably late twenties to early thirties, slender, straight black hair, with part-Asian features.

"Hawaii's such a melting pot she could be from anywhere along the Pacific Rim. I'll get some hard copies of this picture for you.

"Her father is Caucasian; he was a soldier stationed at Schofield Barracks near Honolulu years ago; he's retired. Her mother is a native Hawaiian. They live in Kihei on Maui now. I spoke to them via a video call after Alicia went missing. She was their only child. Her mother looked devastated. Maybe that's part of why I felt a bit guilty."

"Hmm," Jick let out a noncommittal grunt.

Sam reached into her bag and handed Jick a thumb drive.

"This contains all the information about her travels during those four days she was there. Mostly cell phone records, car rental agreement, airline ticket info, etc. All I want you to do is take a deep dive into everywhere she went in those four days, talking to as many people as possible. I know after this long; it would be easier to find the proverbial needle in a haystack, but just do your best."

"What's the name of the guy she was investigating?"

"We would rather not say. As I said, this investigation may come to nothing. If so, there's no need to drag his name into this. The file will be closed and purged, and that's it. I mostly want you to retrace her movements around the island, not chase suspects."

"But you said there was another recent shipment."

"Yes, there was. And if we think it bears further investigation, we'll send one of our people. You're not officially part of this. Honestly, Jick, this is mostly just for my peace of mind.

"Go there, enjoy yourself, see if you can uncover anything, and let me know. The most likely scenario is that she went on a walk, probably had an accident, and may have been killed. If that's the case, we may never know. All we can hope is that she didn't suffer."

"Why didn't you send me to find her earlier, like after one or two months? I still don't get why now, after eight months?"

"Earlier, it was still an open investigation," Sam said. "For the first couple of months, the police were still investigating. Then the case went cold."

"Okay, and?"

Sam sighed and looked at Jick.

"I guess you know me too well. Okay, there's a little more. Alicia has a boyfriend and a kid. She was widowed a couple of years ago. When she went missing, her son had to go live with her parents. I know what they're going through, you know what I mean? Young, widowed, with a kid. Her mother emailed me a few weeks ago. She wanted to know if there had been any progress in finding Alicia. She said she couldn't believe Alicia was really gone and had a very difficult time accepting it. I couldn't tell her the case had gone cold because we had no leads and had stopped looking. I felt a little guilty and decided on the spur of the moment to ask you to do a search. So, I told Alicia's mother we were still looking. Just a little white lie. And then, this recent shipment happened. And I figured I owed it to her and to this investigation to take one last look."

"I see."

Jick fished his wallet out and extracted the driver's license.

"Not to change the subject, but something's been on my mind," Jick said.

"What's that?"

"After my last adventure, you pointed out that my fingerprints were all over that compound. And I went racing back to burn the whole place down."

"I remember."

"How do we know that won't happen again?"

He studied his hands.

"If I uncover criminal activities, and there is a body count, I can't go around torching buildings every time."

Sam smiled at him.

"You don't have to worry about that. Your fingerprints match your identity now. Still, you should be careful."

"Wow, whoever you work for must be pretty influential."

"It's all about national security, Jick."

"I'm sure it is. All right. This sounds harmless enough. And I haven't been to Hawaii in a long time. This could be fun."

"And if you meet a woman in a bar there..." Sam grinned and left it hanging.

SEVEN

Twelve Years Ago
Big Island, Hawaii

The urges had grown stronger. Phoenix kept to himself, doing just well enough in school to avoid scrutiny or trouble. His house, like most houses in Hawaii, was built on posts and a crawl space extended under the entire structure. In one corner, shielded from view by pipes, Phoenix had made himself a hideout. His parents were unaware of the mousetrap he kept down there.

His mousetrap was a simple five-gallon bucket with a drop-down trapdoor, concealed beneath a curved plastic shroud. Lured by the peanut butter smeared under the shroud, mice would scamper up a ramp, noses twitching, and step on a trapdoor. The trapdoor would pivot open, and the mice would tumble through.

The trap itself was "humane." What Phoenix did afterwards was not. The cruel methods he invented to kill the mice soothed his urges. And the dirt floor made it easy to hide the evidence.

Sherryl Sturgis glanced at the caller ID with a sinking feeling. The incoming call was from Phoenix's school. Phoenix had struggled in his transition from middle school to being a freshman in high school. Trouble seemed to find him more often and fights had become more frequent. With a sigh of resignation, she picked up the phone.

"Hello. Yes, this is she."

A flood of words poured from the other end, interrupted by Sherryl's interjections of "He did what?" and "Oh my gosh." By the end of the call, she agreed to go to the school at once.

Thirty minutes later, she sat in the principal's office. Phoenix slouched beside her, silent, fidgeting with his fingers. Across from them, the principal folded her arms.

"This is a difficult situation," Mrs. Lee began. "Phoenix got into a fight. Several students witnessed it. Even though it was probably the girl's fault, there was no reason for him to have lashed out while holding a pencil."

"How bad was it?" Sherryl asked with a tinge of apprehension.

"She was stabbed over her eye but luckily, it missed her eye. Her parents are furious and threatening legal action. We realize you and your husband are strong supporters of Hawaii education, but we have no choice. Phoenix is suspended for seven days. I strongly suggest obtaining professional help for him to deal with his anger management issues, at the very least."

"Yes, whatever you say," Sherryl said.

On the way home, there was a strained silence in the car. Phoenix tried to avoid looking at his mother and stared out the window.

"I'm going to tell your father when he gets home," Sherryl finally said.

"Yes, Mom."

They stopped at a red light. A herd of goats had clustered in the brush next to the intersection. As Phoenix stared at them, he felt an urge wash over him. It released some of the pent-up tension from the events at school. He shut his eyes and leaned back in the seat.

As soon as they arrived home, Phoenix escaped to his hideout.

I need to do this. I need to...

He opened his mousetrap and peered inside. Four pairs of pink eyes stared back at him for a moment, and then the mice scampered around the bucket in a blind panic. He reached in and pulled one out by its tail. He pulled out a pair of shears and opened and shut it a few times. A smile crossed his face...

When he was done, he leaned against the beam in the crawl space. The urge had passed. He looked at his handiwork and, for the first time, looked away. Then the need to look away passed.

I needed to...

Later that day, George Sturgis sat at his desk, listening to his wife's narrative about what had happened in school.

"Some girl teased him, and he stabbed her with a pencil?"

"Yes. And the school suspended him for a week. They're recommending he see a child psychiatrist for help with anger management."

Sherryl's eyes welled with tears. Her voice trembled.

"What's wrong with him, George? Why does he have these anger issues? No one in our family has these problems."

George slowly shook his head. He fixed a blank stare at his wife.

"No, no one does. I don't know about having him see a child psychiatrist. That would be difficult."

He rose from his chair.

"I'll go talk to him. What we need here is more doctors."

"Phoenix, time to wake up," Sherryl yelled from downstairs.

"Coming, Mom," Phoenix answered.

Like most fourteen-year-olds, Phoenix hated getting out of bed in the morning. He particularly hated going to school. He lay in bed, staring at the ceiling, dragging out the inevitable.

"Phoenix, come on!"

He rolled out of bed, pulled on a pair of jeans and a T-shirt, and ran a brush through his hair.

His mother had prepared a plate of scrambled eggs and toast. As he sat at the table, she picked a sizzling skillet off the stove and slid three sausage links on his plate. Phoenix speared one with his fork. A faint hiss escaped as a brownish liquid leaked out and pooled on his plate.

"Be careful, son; that sausage is hot."

He tore a piece of toast and dabbed the brownish liquid. *Blood.*

As he waited for the sausage to cool, his thoughts wandered toward the sausage's origins.

It's pork. Pigs. There are plenty of pigs on the Big Island. Now that would be fun...

"What, Mom?" He blinked, realizing she had been talking to him.

Sherryl frowned at her son.

"I don't want a repeat of what happened yesterday. You're suspended from school for the rest of this week because of it. Do you understand?"

"Yes, Mom," Phoenix said, sounding meek.

"You're going to wake up every morning this week like it's a normal school day. And you're going to help me with chores around the house. The school has sent home all the work you're going to do this week. If you do your chores and schoolwork well, you can have some playtime in the afternoon. Understand?"

"Yes, Mom."

Phoenix spent the next few hours helping his mother with chores. In the afternoon, he disappeared back into his hideout...

Sherryl Sturgis stood in the midday sun, cradling the garden hose. She adjusted the nozzle to a fine mist setting and played it over her flower garden. A rainbow shimmered in the mist over her plants as fine droplets clung to the waxy surface of the petals, sparkling like precious stones. Stepping around a large sunburst begonia, she reached for the hanging pot nearby.

She wore a wide-brimmed, dark green gardening hat with a matching gardener's belt. The side pockets held a pair of gloves and pruning shears like pistols in a holster.

Moving closer to the house, she made sure she had properly watered the flowers that ran along the base. With a practiced flick, she whipped the pair of shears out of its holster and leaned forward to clip a stray stem.

Then she wrinkled her nose as a noxious odor assailed her nostrils. She took a quick step back.

"Yuck," she recoiled. "What is that smell?"

She leaned close to the house and sniffed. The smell seemed to seep from the crawl space under the house. Bending down, she peered through the small opening between the slats but saw nothing out of the ordinary.

She straightened and looked around the garden. In the distance, she could see one of their hired hands.

"Kimo," she called. "Come here. Tell me if you smell something."

Kimo strolled over, pulling off his gloves.

"Lean down toward the crawl space. Something smells bad down there."

Kimo leaned in toward the crawl space.

"Yes," he replied. "Maybe something is under the house, yeah? Something died there? Probably a rat. Didn't they put rat poison down there?"

"I don't think so. But it could probably use it."

"I go look," Kimo said.

On the far side of the house, a trapdoor led to the crawl space. Kimo pried the trapdoor open and propped it open with a stick. Standing next to a bush, he took off his hat and draped it on a branch. He put his gloves on, and Sherryl watched him drop to his knees as he disappeared into the crawlspace. She stood by the open trapdoor, hands on her hips, listening to his shuffling in the dirt. Then she heard a sharp exclamation.

"I found something!"

She heard him scrambling back in a hurry. As he emerged from the crawl space, his lips were pursed together. His face was pale and queasy, and he looked like he was about to lose his lunch. He staggered out holding a bucket. He set it on the lawn and stepped back, reaching for his hat.

"There's something very bad in there, Aunty."

Sherryl's stomach tightened. She had to look. She gently slid the lid back, and it toppled off. A moist and fetid stench emanated from the bucket, almost overpowering her in its intensity. She took a careful peek inside the bucket. Her gut muscles twitched as a sour acid taste gurgled into the back of her throat from her stomach. She swallowed and stepped back, eyes watering.

"Oh my God," she said.

As George pulled into the driveway later that evening, he was surprised to see Sherryl through the study window, watching him head to the garage. He was more surprised to see Sherryl's worried expression as she offered him a drink.

"Here," she said, offering him one.

"What's going on?"

"We need to talk."

George settled behind the desk as Sherryl paced the study.

"Earlier today," she began. "I was watering the begonias and smelled something awful. Kimo crawled under the house and pulled it out. You're not going to believe what it was."

George scrunched his face and wiped his eyes. He exhaled heavily, as if he already knew what she was about to say.

"What was it?"

"A bucket. A bucket full of mice! Some were dead, cut into pieces. There was a pair of scissors in there, too. With a mouse skewered on it."

"Shears," George corrected.

Sherryl stopped pacing.

"What do you mean 'shears?'"

"There were garden shears in the bucket, not scissors. Just looked like a pair of rusty scissors."

Sherryl stared, uncomprehending, for a second. Then she realized what George had said.

"You knew about it? Whose are they?"

She could not accept the obvious answer.

"Phoenix's, obviously."

"Wait, what... you knew?"

"I discovered it about a month ago. Same thing, the smell. I confronted him about it. At first, he denied it. When he realized he couldn't lie his way out of it, he admitted they were his. He said he had these urges."

"George, this is sick. Sick! Some of those mice were still alive, traumatized, I'm sure. These are the types of kids who become killers and psychos when they grow up. How could you keep this from me?"

"I didn't want to worry you. I hope it's just a phase he'll outgrow."

He stared into the distance.

"Or learns to control."

"George, there was a mouse stabbed through with those... shears. The two blades stuck out of its side! It must have died a horrible death."

"It's no worse than some mousetraps you can buy at the hardware store. Have you ever tried to pull a mouse off one of those sticky pad traps? Or listened to one drown in those bucket traps? Killing is always ugly. It's just sometimes necessary." His voice trailed off.

"That's not the point, George. He's torturing animals! Shouldn't we have him see someone? A psychiatrist? A therapist? Especially after what happened at school with that girl. What if he's slowly turning into... something worse?"

"No," George said firmly. "We'll keep a close watch on things and see how he does. I really hope it's just a phase he's going through."

Sherryl's eyes welled with tears.

"Our son needs help, George. I think we should have him see a child psychiatrist."

"I said no," Sturgis said with finality. "We'll see how he does. Where is he?"

"His one-week suspension is over. He went to school."

"Okay. I'll talk to him this evening."

Phoenix lay in bed, staring at the ceiling. He shut his eyes and breathed in until he could not take in any more air, then *whooshed* it out. His door creaked, and his father stepped in.

"Hi, son."

"Hi, Dad."

George got straight to the point.

"Earlier today, your mother discovered your stuff under the house. She's very upset."

Phoenix stared at his father but remained silent.

"We talked about this last month, remember? You need to be more careful and not leave things where someone can find them."

"How did she find it?" Phoenix said meekly.

"The smell. I told you last month, you're supposed to bury everything right away. What happened?"

"I don't know. Probably didn't do it good enough."

"Good enough? You left everything in the bucket. Next time, make sure you hide everything properly. Immediately."

"Sorry, Dad. Yes, Dad."

George returned to his desk and slumped in the seat. His face reddened as a wave of anger swept over him.

"Damn it, damn it!"

He balled his fists but did not slam the desktop. He leaned back and studied his hands. The slight swelling in his joints, the early signs of chronic sun damage to his skin, the thickening of his nails, all signs of aging.

He clicked open his email thread to re-read an email from earlier in the day. His namesake longevity institute's director had advised him they were still losing money and very little of their research and wellness protocols had generated any income.

And now, Phoenix.

"This kid is supposed to carry on my legacy?"

He rubbed his eyes.

"Damn it!"

EIGHT

Since the incident with the discovery of the mouse horror show in the crawl space, Sherryl had turned an uneasy blind eye to whatever Phoenix did. There were no other episodes of noxious odors, but Phoenix still had a habit of disappearing for prolonged periods, especially after school. Sherryl had tried to talk to her son but got nowhere. And her husband was not willing to discuss it any further.

"I think it's time we moved out to Wao Kele Estates," George announced one summer day.

The first time George had mentioned moving, Sherryl had resisted. Now she was more agreeable about the move. George had done well, they had money to spare, and after all these years of living in Kona, she was ready for a more relaxed life in the cooler elevation of the verdant nature reserve.

"I'm okay with it."

"Getting that land at Wao Kele was an incredible investment. I was always too busy and didn't have time to move. Now I can tie up everything with my work and probably retire soon. Not bad, eh, at fifty. And Phoenix's transition to high school has been a challenge. Maybe a change of scenery will do all of us good. We can put him into that private school in Waimea."

"Maybe you're right. Phoenix may have some difficulty at a new school, but the change of scenery should help."

"And," George continued. "Guess what. There's a one-hundred-acre parcel next to our lot. It's state-owned land, has no easements and is worth very little. I negotiated to buy it; they agreed with the condition that we don't develop it."

"That's wonderful," Sherryl said. "A hundred acres of forest land just for us."

"Let's meet with an architect and get started."

After reviewing several top architectural firms, George settled on one of Honolulu's top high-end architectural firms. The deciding factor was the architect's Greek surname, Katsaros. George wanted a house that reflected his Greek heritage.

The frustration with the financial state of his longevity institute bubbled over in his choice of a self-aggrandizing name for the house.

"Sturgis Mansion," he mused. "Located in Sturgis Estates."

The house would have a modified Greek look, adapted to suit its location in Hawaii. It would have an "oikos," or central courtyard like many Greek homes, but would also have a semicircular lanai that faced the ocean, supported by pillars that flanked either end. The exterior would have plenty of natural stone and brick, and the extensive use of columns harkened back to George Sturgis' Greek roots.

The house would sit on a slab, unlike their house in Kona with the crawl space that concealed Phoenix's grisly hideout. Phoenix resisted at first, especially when he realized the house did not have a crawl space. When he realized how much land there was around the house, especially in the undeveloped state land that his father had bought, his reluctance faded.

"Sherryl, I need to go on a business trip. I'll be gone for a month," George announced one day.

"A month?"

"Yes, I'm wrapping up work, so this is my last trip. After that, it's nothing but fun in the sun."

As George wrapped up his work, Ms. Katsaros oversaw construction while Sherryl kept up to date with Phoenix's schoolwork. Over the ensuing months, despite a few frustrating delays because of logistical issues and "island time," construction moved along. The house was completed three months behind schedule, and they breathed a sigh of relief when the county inspector issued a "Passed" final inspection.

On move-in day, after the movers left, George, Sherryl, and their son sat on the lanai, gazing at the view. From their vantage point, the ocean sparkled like gemstones scattered on a navy-blue rug. The ground in front of the lanai had been graded in anticipation of the lawn that was to be put in soon. A shallow retaining wall at the far end of the lawn marked the edge of the eventual infinity edge of the pool. The afternoon sun lit the red earth, casting a warm glow over the house.

"Beautiful," George said.

"Wow, those whitecaps are something," Sherryl remarked. "The ocean never looked this beautiful in Kona."

"No, it sure didn't. Everything had that washed out gray look. We should have done this years ago. And do you feel how it's a little less humid and cooler here? What do you think, son? Like our new place?"

Phoenix was a little morose in the days leading up to the move.

"Looks alright," he said with a shrug. "Can't hear the ocean here."

"No, we can't," George said. "But we are planning to buy a small oceanfront condo, probably at a resort like the Hawaiian Orchid."

"I guess I got used to falling asleep to the sound of the waves."

"Change is never easy, son. Your Dad and I felt this was the best time to move. Your new school is great. It's a small, private school, and the teachers will spend more time to make sure you're learning and keeping up."

"Okay, Mom."

Phoenix eyes drifted to the forest.

"All that is ours too, right?" He pointed at the former state-owned parcel.

"Sure is," George said. "It stretches to the edge of the reserve, where the forest ends and beyond. There's a fence and a gate on the far side, where the forest ends. On the mauka side, it ends at the bluffs and on the makai side, it's not fenced. I'm planning to put a fence there, so we'll enclose it on three sides, and the fourth side borders our house. You can go exploring all you want. Just don't get lost."

"I think I'll go for a walk now," Phoenix said, already eager.

Maybe I'll see a pig.

"Don't be gone too long," Sherryl said. "We'll have an early dinner when you get back."

Phoenix stepped off the lanai and headed to the forested parcel. Pushing some fronds out of the way, Phoenix stepped into the forest. He walked in a straight line through the trees, catching glimpses of the ocean through the thicket of trees.

After walking for fifteen minutes, he came to a clearing. A waist-high boulder was a natural seat, so Phoenix perched on top, enjoying the sounds of nature. He shut his eyes and started imagining what he could do in this secluded land. As he was about to jump off the rock to head home, a sound caught his ears.

Something is in the bushes.

He slid off the rock, being careful not to make a sound, and crouched behind a bush. Nothing happened for a few minutes, then he heard the same sound. A rustle, loud enough that whatever made the sound was big. And it was coming closer.

Bigger than a cat.

Then he saw it. A few yards off to his right, on the mauka side of where he hid, a pig ambled into view. Phoenix stared at the animal with rapt attention. Its snout twitched as it snuffled in the bushes. As it foraged away from him, three piglets came into view, one squealing at its mother. The squealing piglet darted under its mother like it wanted to be fed. The mother ambled in a circle like she wanted to find a place to lie down.

Phoenix held his breath, enthralled by the spectacle. He shifted his cramped position as he stared at the porcine family, imagining future scenarios.

The mother pig let out a loud sneeze, and Phoenix jumped. He took a step back, and his right foot stepped on a twig.

Crack.

The sound may as well have been a gunshot. In a flash, the pigs bolted, crashing through the brush in their hasty flight.

As the sounds receded, Phoenix stood and stretched, continuing to stare at the spot where the pigs vanished. As he turned to head back to his house, he smiled in anticipation of returning to his land.

My place.

When he returned, his parents were still on the lanai.

"Did you enjoy your walk?" Sherryl asked.

"Yeah, Mom, I loved it. I saw a pig too. With three piglets. It's so peaceful in the forest, quiet except for bird sounds. I think I'll make it my place."

"Your place?" Sherryl smiled.

"Well, not *my* place, just a place that I can go play."

"You mean your playground?" George asked.

"Yes. My playground."

Sherryl flashed an uneasy glance at her husband, recalling Phoenix's activities under their Kona house. She stood.

"I think I'll get dinner ready." Sherryl excused herself and went into the house.

"Son, you can use that land as your 'playground,'" George said. "But nothing outside the playground, you understand?"

"Yes, Dad," Phoenix said. "I love that place."

Five months after George returned from his monthlong business trip, he announced he needed to go to the airport to meet someone.

"Sherryl, I have decided to hire an assistant."

"An assistant? What for?"

"I've done lots of business deals, and I made a lot of money. I need an assistant who can also watch over us, you know?"

"You mean... like a bodyguard?"

"Bodyguard, and general fixer."

Sherryl's brow furrowed.

"You're not in trouble, are you, George?"

"Heavens, no. This is a guy I met on one of my business trips. He lives on the island and needs a job. The perfect candidate."

George returned two hours later from the airport. Sherryl looked out the window to see him step out of the car with a towering Hawaiian man, broad-shouldered and built like a bodybuilder.

Sherryl opened the door to greet them.

"Sherryl, this is Thaddeus," George announced.

Sherryl reached out with a tentative hand. Thaddeus shook her hand and gave a respectful bow.

"Aloha," he said.

The next few years blurred into Phoenix's uneasy passage through adolescence. He limped through high school, withdrawn and difficult, his last three years a jagged ride of ups and downs.

It was Sherryl who bore the brunt of it—meeting with the principal about Phoenix's behavior while George was away. At home, she tried to ignore what unfolded under her nose, especially since George preferred silence to confrontation. Together, they chose willful blindness, letting their son vanish for long stretches into the forest he called his "playground."

On one occasion, George returned home to find Sherryl sobbing in his office.

"What's wrong?" he asked.

"We have to go to the police station and bail him out."

"What did he do?"

"I don't know. But he's under arrest at school."

Once again, the couple found themselves bailing their troubled son out of trouble.

On the Big Island, George was the proverbial big fish in a small pond. His influence and his money smoothed over Phoenix's missteps, whether with the police or the school board. Once, when the school nearly expelled Phoenix, a last-minute donation from George to the fundraising drive bought his son another chance.

Somehow, Phoenix scraped through to graduation. The day itself felt anticlimactic, but both George and Sherryl exhaled with relief that he had crossed the finish line at all.

College was never on the table. Phoenix remained at home, drifting between idle chores and long, solitary walks into the woods. Sherryl no longer questioned him; his need for isolation was a battle she had given up fighting. Life settled into a fragile, uneasy routine.

Until a few years later, on a warm summer afternoon, when George went scuba diving with friends.

And their lives were upended...

NINE

Present Day

Jick's clamshell suitcase lay open on the bed. He stood by the bed, holding a shirt in each hand. After a moment of indecision, he tossed one into the suitcase and put the other aside to wear on the flight.

I'll pick up some Aloha shirts there.

On the bed beside him, a foam pillow in the shape of a fluffy letter "C" lay in a pile of items for his carry-on bag, alongside his toiletries and shoes. As he debated what else to put into his carry-on bag, his doorbell chimed.

Quin stood at the front door, holding a black case about the size of a toiletries bag.

"Good morning," Jick said. "Come on in. There's coffee in the kitchen."

"Thanks. Finished packing?"

"Almost. We can leave in about half an hour."

"Got room for an add-on?"

Jick eyed the black case.

"What have you got?"

"Sam and I talked this morning. We figured if you needed to do any surveillance when you're there, we could give you one of our motion sensor cameras. Beats having to stay in one place for hours. Let technology do the work."

He set the case on Jick's coffee table.

"Why on earth would I want to do any surveillance? I'm just going for a long walk to follow Alicia Rogers' path. And spend time on the beach, enjoying Uncle Sam's hospitality."

He grinned at Quin.

"Maybe so," Quin said. "But this is just in case. Better to have it and not need it, ya know, than need it and not have it."

"How does it work?" Jick asked.

"Let me get some coffee first."

"Help yourself."

Quin returned a minute later with a steaming cup and set it on the coffee table. He undid the clasps and flipped open the lid.

"Since you're familiar with medical jargon, do you know what digital subtraction photography is?"

"More or less."

"There's a similar technology using the same concept in surveillance. In basic terms, a stationary camera aims at a fixed spot. At some preset interval, it takes a picture. Then, say, three seconds later, it takes the next picture and compares it to the previous one. If the pictures are the same, when you subtract one from the other, there's nothing left.

"Now, what happens if a person walks across the field of view? When it subtracts one picture from the next, the only difference between the two images is the person. If the difference is big enough, it sends an alert. You can program it to ignore small things like feral cats, rustling leaves, or clouds."

"This is like digital subtraction angiography. I've used it before when looking at, for example, contrast uptake in blood vessels."

"You have?"

"What I meant is, I've seen it done in procedure rooms. Digital subtraction is used to look for blood flow, uptake of contrast, etc. I sometimes get to watch doctors to familiarize myself with their practice, so I can help set up their practices."

"Oh, okay. The primary unit is this camera," Quin continued, pointing to a small device about the size of a pack of cigarettes.

"You'll notice the lens is recessed to prevent sunlight reflecting on the glass, but that narrows the field of view.

From a distant vantage point, that shouldn't be a problem. Just aim it at your target."

He took out a small rectangular plate about the size of a thin paperback novel. Quin angled it and its metallic surface sparkled with rainbow-colored specks.

"This is the solar panel. Aim it toward the sun. The western side of the Big Island gets plenty of sunshine. It plugs in here," he pointed to the power input port on the camera. "It's weatherproofed and pre-programmed. Just set it among the rocks somewhere or use this clamp to fasten it to a tree. Once it's all set up, press this button," he pointed to a button on the housing, "and this little green dot lights up. That's it. If it sees anything that is worth reporting, it automatically saves it to a thumb drive. Every so often, you swing by and swap out the thumb drives."

"Pretty straightforward," remarked Jick. He tossed the case into his carry on.

Thirty minutes later, Quin dropped Jick off at the airport.

TEN

Two years ago
Big Island, Hawaii

"It's a beautiful day," Sherryl said as she gazed out the window. "It was super windy yesterday, but today looks great. In other words, a perfect day for golf. Got any plans, George?"

She sipped her coffee and stared at the ocean. On windy days, from their elevation, the ocean looked like a rumpled navy-blue blanket with whitecaps resembling tufts of whipped cream. Clouds scudded along from the north. Today, the blanket was smooth, and the clouds were still. The glassy surface of the pool mirrored the clouds, so they looked like they kissed the ocean from the infinity edge.

George looked up from his tablet.

"Slow news day," he remarked. "Actually, yes, I had planned to go scuba diving if the weather cooperated. And it looks like it has. I'm going with Chief Williams and a couple of his friends. We're heading out to Kailua Bay."

"That sounds like fun," Sherryl said. "I'm going golfing with my ladies' group, probably at Mauna Lani."

Neither one wondered what Phoenix had planned for the day. Phoenix kept to himself, and they assumed he would wander around in the hundred-acre parcel that adjoined their property.

After breakfast, George set off on the hourlong drive to Honokohau Marina, where he had rented a slip. As he pulled into the parking lot, he spotted Chief Kalani Williams in conversation with two other men. One looked vaguely familiar, but he could not place the name. The other was a stranger.

"George," Chief Williams said as George disembarked from his car. "Great day for scuba diving, yeah?"

"It is," George agreed.

"George, this is John Sampson; you may have recognized him. He had my job before me. He retired a few years ago. You may have seen him on TV?"

"Oh yeah, I thought you looked familiar."

George shook his hand.

"And this," Chief Williams, nodding at the other man, "is Bill Viola. An old friend visiting from Honolulu. He's a personal injury attorney."

Probably a sleazebag, George thought as they shook hands.

Bill Viola looked part Native Hawaiian, with black hair swept straight back, thick glasses, and an expression that looked like a perpetual grimace.

George unlocked his private locker and pulled out his equipment. His private boat, the *Kaimakea*, or Glorious One, was already ready for departure. The captain waved to the assembled group.

"Come on down," he called out. "We are ready to go."

Ten minutes later, the captain navigated the boat out of the harbor. Then he increased the throttle and thirty minutes later, they arrived at the scuba site. George Sturgis and his three companions perched on the edge of his boat.

"This is a nice boat," Bill Viola remarked.

"Thanks," George said. "I got it a year ago. I've gone out a few times to scuba dive. There are many great sites. We can do this area first, then go further down the coast if we want."

"First time I've scuba dived on the Big Island," Bill admitted. "You would think that being a Hawaiian and living here, I would have come out to the Big Island more often."

"You must be very busy," George commented.

"I am. But I gotta keep working. That's what happens when you collect ex-wives."

George grinned. "How many you got?"

"Two. And my wife and I have four-year-old twins."

He looks like he's sixty. Four-year-old twins?

"You'll be working for a long time."

"Damn right. But there's plenty of personal injury business. Not to sound immodest, but my practice is one of the most successful in the state."

"Strictly personal injury?"

"That's plenty. You'd be surprised how often insurance companies and big corporations try to weasel out of paying justified claims."

The men had already changed into scuba gear. The captain jabbed a button, and a telescopic mast with a fluttering red-and-white "Diver Down" flat rose toward the sky. As soon as the captain gave the go-ahead, Sturgis held his mask with one hand and the back of his head with the other. He leaned back and fell into the water as his companions followed, all swimming with powerful strokes as they descended to the depths of Kailua Bay.

A movement far off to the left caught Sturgis' attention. His companions had not noticed it and continued to swim toward the bottom. Sturgis veered away from the group and headed toward the moving object.

Reef shark?

After following the object for a few minutes, it changed direction and headed toward him. A jolt of adrenaline coursed through him as he realized it was a shark. It swung its tail briskly, then held still as it glided through the water like a miniature submarine on the prowl.

I better not move.

He hung motionless, barely breathing, as it swam past him. Another jolt coursed through him as its tail thwacked against his leg. He realized it had zero interest in him as it turned once again, indifferent to his presence, as it swam away in lazy strokes. George swam after it in hot pursuit but realized it was futile. After a short burst of strokes of its tail fin, the shark zipped away and soon disappeared into the murk.

George turned his attention to the reef, marveling at the view. The multicolored coral and marine vegetation seemed to stretch into infinity as it faded into the background. Colorful fish darted around and then disappeared in the blink of an eye into the coral. One inquisitive fish bumped into Sturgis' leg and then darted for cover behind a coral that resembled a castle turret.

It looks like a medieval cityscape.

The light was clear and strong under the pristine conditions, illuminating every detail. He swam over the cityscape, looking down at the "streets." He marveled at the sight of colorful schooling fish that darted in unison through the reef like they shared one hive mind. Time drifted by as he relaxed in the tranquil depths. He glanced at his diving watch and realized he needed to head back to the boat. As he surfaced, he noticed none of his companions were in sight.

Wonder where they went.

He scanned the bay and realized he had swum a good distance away from the boat. A muffled high-pitched whine that kept increasing in volume attracted his attention. He wiped the seawater off his mask and looked around, noticing that his swimming buddies had swum back to the boat. One of his companions had noticed him reaching the surface and began waving frantically, making downward gestures for George to resubmerge.

George realized with a sudden shock the sound was the whine of a fast speedboat. And it headed his way. Tearing through the water in tight S curves as it bore down on him, George caught a momentary glimpse of the pilot.

Before George could swim out of the way or dive back under the water, the boat slammed into him with a sickening thud. A bright flash of stars exploded in his vision, and a warm gush ran down his face as the world went dark around him.

ELEVEN

Sherryl Sturgis and Phoenix sat in the waiting room, staring at the doors that led to the operating rooms. Each time the doors whooshed open, they looked up, expectant. Honolulu's busiest trauma center was a beehive of activity. They said little, each immersed in their own thoughts. After the unexpected and shocking phone call from the Coast Guard about a boating accident, the rest of the day had been an exhausting ordeal of rushing to the emergency room, watching George being loaded onto a gurney as the first responders rushed him to a local airport, then hurriedly arranging flights and transportation to Honolulu. George's assistant, Thaddeus, had been invaluable in organizing things as Sherryl fluttered helplessly, unable to deal with the calamity. And Phoenix had retreated into a shell, unable to cope.

A surgeon emerged from the operating room and went to another waiting family.

"Everything went well," he said to the eager group. "He should be in the recovery room in about fifteen minutes."

Phoenix glanced at the door to the operating theater as it whooshed shut. He turned to his mother.

"Do you know how much longer, Mom?" he asked.

"How would I know?" she snapped. "I only know what they told me five hours ago, that it would take four hours. Hopefully, any minute now..."

On cue, the operating room door swung open, and another surgeon entered. She glanced around the room and approached Sherryl and Phoenix.

"Mrs. Sturgis?"

"Yes." She shook hands with Sherryl and Phoenix.

"Hi, I'm Dr. Kawahara," the surgeon said.

"How is he?"

"He's doing okay from a surgical standpoint," Dr. Kawahara said. "He made it through the operation, and it looks like he'll pull through."

Sherryl exhaled a sigh of relief.

"Oh, that's great," she said. "I don't know what I would ever do without my George."

"There's more," Dr. Kawahara continued. "It's not all good news. Unfortunately, the damage to the area of the brain called the frontal lobe was extensive. He will need weeks, maybe months, of rehab."

Sherryl and her son looked at each other.

"Another thing, and this could be important. The part of the brain that was damaged controls what we call 'executive functioning.' It helps us make decisions and understand the consequences of our actions. This area of Mr. Sturgis' brain sustained a lot of damage, so I don't know what kind of person he will be until he heals."

Dr. Kawahara paused for a moment and then continued in a soft voice.

"It could be difficult."

Sherryl's eyes welled with tears.

"I don't understand."

"His personality may be different," Dr. Kawahara said. "I'm sorry. We did our best. He'll live, and he should be functional. But I won't lie to you. There may be some bumps in the road with his rehab and when he finally gets to go home."

Sherryl continued to look confused.

"Can we see him now?"

"Not right now. I want to watch him overnight in the ICU, so he'll go straight from the operating room to his ICU bed. They have visiting hours. Check at the ICU desk in an hour."

"Okay, we'll do that," Phoenix said.

"Before I go, one last thing. To prevent spinal fluid buildup and to keep the brain from swelling, we had to put in a small device that shunts, or diverts, the spinal fluid to other parts of the body."

Sherryl stared at Dr. Kawahara with a blank expression. She turned to Phoenix. Dr. Kawahara noticed the look.

"Not to worry," she said. "Basically, what it means is we had to put in a small tube under his skin that carries that fluid into his abdominal cavity."

Sherryl's eyes widened.

"A tube that runs through his body?"

"It's tiny and not noticeable. He will have a small object implanted under his skin on top of his head. It's a valve that allows us to access the tube if we need to. This whole thing, the access port and tube, is called a VP shunt. He won't even know it's there."

"Oh, okay. Thanks. Thanks Dr. Kawahara," Sherryl pumped Dr. Kawahara's hand.

"You're welcome. He's in excellent hands, and I'll keep checking on his progress."

Dr. Kawahara left Sherryl Sturgis and her son looking at each other.

A week later, George Sturgis lay in a bed in a private room in a rehabilitation facility. The TV was on, but his attention was elsewhere. A plate of unfinished breakfast sat on a bedstand. He reached for a bagel with slow determination, his hand somewhat unwilling to follow his commands. His hand shook as he picked up the bagel, navigated it to his mouth, and took a bite. He put it back on his plate and picked up the fork. His Portuguese sausage had been cut into bite-sized pieces; he speared a piece and brought it to his mouth.

"That's pretty good, honey," Sherryl Sturgis said from the doorway.

George turned to find his wife and son watching him.

"Come in, come in," he said.

Sherryl parked herself in a chair while Phoenix perched on the window ledge.

"How are you doing, Dad?" he asked.

"Pretty good," George said. "They've had me walking a lot. I'm having to relearn plenty of things, but I can still talk. That's good. The headaches aren't too bad."

Sherryl beamed at him.

"Hand me that mirror," George said, pointing to the washstand.

Reaching out with a shaking hand for the proffered mirror, he brought it to his face to study his reflection; the sight stopped him cold. His hair was gone, shaved clean. A long C-shaped incision stretched across his scalp, stapled shut. A second, smaller C-shaped scar marked the side of his head, the two together resembling a crooked cedilla. Beneath the smaller scar, a bump jutted up like a stack of coins under his skin. Curious, he felt it, noticing its firm contours and a soft spot in the middle. The skin felt numb and rubbery. Sherryl watched him.

What did they do to me?

"That smaller scar is from the tube Dr. Kawahara said they had to put in. I didn't understand what she said, but I think it moves some brain fluid to somewhere else in your body."

"That bump is a valve," Phoenix added. "The soft spot is where they can inject things like dye if they need to take pictures."

George went back to studying his face. He tilted his head in the mirror. His slightly tinted glasses cast a shadow across his face, lending him a strangely sinister look.

"Those staples will come out in a couple more weeks, I think," Sherryl offered.

"I look so goddamn different," he muttered.

"It's so good to see you making so much progress, George," Sherryl said. "What a crazy week it's been. I don't think I'll ever forget the phone call from the Coast Guard. And I couldn't have done anything without Thaddeus' help."

George gave a faint smile.

"We should adopt Thaddeus as our hanai son. We have known him for three years, and he has been a great assistant. He's like family anyway."

"I think that's a wonderful idea," Sherryl said. "I wasn't sure about him at first, but now..."

George tried to smile again, but the effort twisted into a wince. His eyes grew blank.

"Anything new with the investigation?"

"The Coast Guard people called yesterday. I didn't understand everything. The boat that hit you belongs to someone named Robert Hardy. He wasn't on the boat; his son and some friends had taken it out. One of the son's friends was piloting the boat when you were hit. Boy named Caleb Jonathan."

"I hope they arrested and charged him."

"I don't know about that. They didn't say."

"Did you call Darren?"

"No, it slipped my mind."

"Don't worry. I'll call him."

George suddenly flushed red, then broke into an odd giggle, clamping his lips shut before bursting into a loud snort of laughter. A surprised look swept over his face.

"George, what's wrong?"

"I, I don't know," he said, holding his sides. "I don't know... why I'm laughing."

Phoenix jumped off his perch and hurried over, a frown on his face.

"Dad, what's wrong?"

"Not sure. We were talking about Darren, and when I said I would call him, I wondered what I would call him. Ambulance chaser? Shyster? Liar? Bottom feeder? All perfect names for a lawyer. And it was funny, I think."

Phoenix and Sherryl looked at each other.

"Darren is our attorney, George," Sherryl reminded him.

"I know, I know." George stopped laughing and wiped his eyes. "And I couldn't help it. See? I can't help it."

His expression twisted into another grimace. He held a tissue to his face and made a sound.

"Are you crying?" Sherryl sounded incredulous.

"No, I mean, maybe," George said as another sob wracked his body.

After a minute of sobbing convulsions, the episode passed. George dabbed his face with tissues as he looked at his wife.

"What the hell was that?" he said.

He held his head.

"All that laughing and sobbing is making my head hurt."

Sherryl and Phoenix exchanged worried looks.

"Next time Dr. Kawahara comes around, I'll ask her," George said.

"You're not in the hospital anymore, George. We're in a rehab facility. Dr. Kawahara won't be seeing you until you follow-up with her, which is in about two weeks when they take out the staples."

George sank back into his pillow.

"Call her office. Leave a message. I need to know what's going on."

"I'll try," Sherryl said.

Phoenix and Sherryl Sturgis left an hour later. An orderly from food service stopped by and with a cheerful grin, deposited a lunch tray by his bedside. George lifted the lid, stared at the insipid offering, and lowered the lid. He had no appetite. He lay back against his pillows and felt the incisions again.

I wonder if this numbness will go away.

He pressed both incisions with gentle pressure. No pain. He held up the mirror again and turned his head from side to side.

That is going to be one big goddamn scar. I could have died...

Random thoughts and feelings went through his head. He stifled another round of giggles, and his face reddened at his inability to control the laughter.

And if I had died, then what? Everything I built would be in the hands of Sherryl and Phoenix...

He shut his eyes, took a few slow deep breaths to steady himself. Without intending to cry but unable to control himself, he felt tears squeezing out the sides of his eyes.

The tears trickled down the sides of his face and collected in his earlobes. He pulled some tissues and dabbed his ears.

I need some other options...

TWELVE

Phoenix lay in bed, stunned by the transformation he had witnessed in his father. The sudden change in his father's behavior, and his inability to control it, shook Phoenix's sense of balance. He craved the safety and security of his own house and his playground. He left the rehabilitation facility with his mother and asked her if it was all right for him to return home. His mother had agreed, and Phoenix caught the next flight home.

He arrived home and went straight to his bedroom. Later that day, armed only with his shears, he went for a walk in his playground. He skulked through the bushes, pausing, hoping for a pig or a feral cat. But after an hour of fruitless hunting, he gave up and returned to his room.

What had his mother said?

Caleb Jonathan. That's his name. The person who hurt Dad.

His father, who was discharged from the hospital after several surgeries from his boating injury. His behavior had changed, and he was no longer the same Dad. And maybe never would be.

Phoenix searched online for Caleb Jonathan. There was only one on Hawaii Island, and Phoenix was sure it was the right person. He found a social media post about Caleb starting a new job at the Seaview Grill.

Caleb's trial for injuring his father was set to begin the following week. Phoenix planned to watch, to learn everything he could about one Caleb Jonathan. Thoughts churned through his head about what to do with that information.

His earlier quest for a pig had ended in failure. But there were bigger and better targets. As he lay in bed ruminating, his breathing quickened. He held his shears and with his eyes shut, traced a slow sideways figure eight in the air, like a conductor leading an orchestra. He smiled as he felt a rush of excitement...

Although the trial was not televised, as a member of the plaintiff's family, Phoenix could log in to watch the proceedings from the privacy of his bedroom. On the screen, he saw his mother and father seated beside their lawyer, Darren Snead. His father sat slumped in a wheelchair, waving feebly to the jury. Though he could walk, George had chosen to appear weak and infirm. Somehow, he'd even assembled a cheering section in the gallery.

A panel of jurors sat to the right of the bench. The jury trial was George's demand. The trial was already under way.

"This is bullshit!" He heard his mother yell at the judge.

"Order in the court!" The judge banged his gavel and glared at Sherryl Sturgis. "You are not being addressed by the court. One more outburst like that and I'll have you removed."

There was a rumble from the assembled audience. Sherryl turned to look at their attorney. Darren placed a cautionary hand on her arm and shook his head. The judge admonished the audience to be quiet, or he would have them removed as well. Phoenix watched in rapt attention from home.

"I'm sorry, Your Honor," Sherryl said.

"Continue," the judge said to Sue Levine, the attorney representing Caleb Jonathan.

"Yes, Your Honor," Ms. Levine said. She rose and faced the jury.

"As the court is aware, Hawaii law requires that scuba divers display a diver-down flag to mark the diving area."

She clicked a button on a handheld remote as she walked to a large monitor. A red flag with an angled white stripe appeared on the screen.

"Mr. Sturgis' boat, the *Kaimakea*, displayed such a flag. The court is also aware that vessel operators in the vicinity must operate at a 'slow-no-wake speed' within two hundred feet of a diver-down flag."

She clicked the button, and a copy from the State of Hawaii Revised Statutes replaced the diver-down flag.

"This is the text of the law from the revised statutes. We do not know if this happened because the *Pomaikai*, the vessel that hit Mr. Sturgis, was *at least* four hundred feet away."

She clicked the button. A satellite picture of Kailua Bay appeared on the screen.

"This is the location where the *Pomaikai* struck Mr. Sturgis." Ms. Levine flicked a laser pointer on. A red dot played over an "X" on the map.

She pointed to two black spots with numbers inscribed alongside.

"And these two markers are GPS coordinates from the *Pomaikai*. GPS trackers are now standard equipment on all seagoing vessels."

She pointed to a blue dot with inscribed numbers.

"And this is the location marker for the *Kaimakea*."

"As the court and the members of the jury can see, the distance between the *Kaimakea* and where the *Pomaikai* struck Mr. Sturgis is four hundred and thirty feet. Therefore, the *Pomaikai* was not bound by the 'slow-no-wake speed' clause of the law."

She clicked the button again.

"As the court is aware, the law also states that divers must not surface more than one hundred feet away from their flag in ocean waters. This is the text of the law from the revised statutes."

She waved the handheld remote at the screen.

"The evidence is clear that Mr. Sturgis surfaced in open waters beyond what Hawaii law stipulates. He surfaced in the direct path of the *Pomaikai*, and there was simply no time for Mr. Jonathan to react. Therefore, although the defendant regrets the injuries Mr. Sturgis sustained, criminal liability for his injuries cannot extend to Mr. Jonathan. This was simply an unfortunate and unavoidable accident."

As Phoenix watched the proceedings on his computer, he felt his breathing quicken. His father sat in his wheelchair, a piteous, crestfallen expression on his face. Phoenix watched as his mother jumped to her feet.

"This is bullshit!" exclaimed Sherryl Sturgis again. A murmur rumbled through George Sturgis' cheering section. George turned to them with a weak wave.

Darren Snead put his hand on her arm and once again admonished her, this time with a glare and an angry "Shhh!" It was too late.

"Bailiff!" the judge thundered. "Remove Mrs. Sherryl Sturgis from the court."

"No, no, please," Sherryl shouted. "I'll keep quiet, I promise. Please let me stay with George."

The bailiff approached Sherryl Sturgis and made a polite gesture asking her to stand, pointing to the door with an outstretched palm. Sherryl Sturgis glared at Sue Levine and Caleb Jonathan before storming out of court. The jurors recessed and reconvened a short thirty minutes later.

"Jurors, have you reached a verdict?" the judge asked.

"Yes, Your Honor," the foreperson of the jury said. He handed the bailiff a folded sheet of paper.

The judge cleared his throat. He motioned for everyone to stand. Sturgis made a weak motion with his hand toward the jury and remained seated.

"For the single charge of reckless endangerment, it is the decision of the court that Mr. Caleb Jonathan is not guilty."

Caleb Jonathan leaned back in his chair. His cheeks whooshed out in a relieved sigh, and a huge smile broke out on his face. Phoenix stared at the video in shock. He hit the "Pause" button, and Caleb Jonathan's triumphant grinning face filled the screen. Phoenix logged off and leaned back into his pillows, clutching his shears.

THIRTEEN

Present Day

As the plane descended, Jick gazed at the green patchwork-quilt panorama of the Big Island of Hawaii. Irregular squares of farmland stretched across the land like patchwork, stitched together by rows of trees. In the distance, the quilt bunched and folded as ancient cinder cones, now cloaked in green, jutted from the earth. The same lush fabric also draped over the mountainsides like a tablecloth. Here on the northwestern coast, there were no beaches, only cliffs that plunged into the ocean where waves crashed against the rocks.

As the plane banked to the left and pointed south, the landscape underwent a dramatic change on the western side. The terrain was just as hilly, but the lush green gave way to sparse, brown terrain. The divide from the wet to dry side was so sharp it looked like someone had drawn a straight line along the crest of the mountain range.

Not as much rain on this side.

As the plane continued its descent, Jick noticed an unexpected large patch of greenery spreading down the hillside on the dry side. It looked incongruous, like a golf course in the middle of a desert. Somehow, even though it was on the dry side, it seemed to attract enough moisture to maintain its verdant appearance. It looked like a large square, petering out to match the surrounding dry terrain near a highway.

A climate anomaly. Looks like an interesting microclimate area. It must be hundreds if not thousands of acres. I wonder if there's a stream running down the middle. Or maybe it just rains a lot.

As the plane descended over the western flanks of the Big Island on final approach, the edges of the quilt disappeared into barren earth and then morphed into dark grey-black fields of craggy lava.

Landing in Honolulu wasn't like this, Jick thought, recalling his one previous trip to the islands.

The plane swept low over the edge of the shoreline. Jick glimpsed a flash of golden sand as the plane streaked over a beach near the airport, followed by rushing black lava rocks as the plane touched down. As the plane rolled to the gate, Jick gathered his belongings and reactivated his phone; he sent Sam a confirmatory text.

The plane stopped on the tarmac, and Jick saw boarding stairs being towed to the plane. As he disembarked, he was pleasantly surprised to notice that the airport had no jetways. He stared at the gaping maw of the plane's engine as he clattered down the metal stairs. Orange-vested personnel directed him to the terminal. He felt the first prickle of sweat as the late morning sun beat down on him and the thick, muggy air clung to his clothes.

Like stepping into a sauna. Good thing I packed shorts and a T-shirt in my carry-on.

He dragged his sleeve across his forehead as he waited by the baggage conveyor belt. He bought a bottle of cold water that was three times as expensive as it should have been.

But worth every drop, he thought, as he quaffed it.

As he waited for his bags, he scanned the names held up by the airport greeters; he noted with mild dismay that none said "Arnsson."

Maybe the driver's running late.

The baggage carousel clattered to life and after a brief wait, he scooped his bag off the conveyor belt. He looked at the greeters; still no one waiting for him.

Damn.

He sighed as he dug through his carry-on for the travel information packet. He dialed the resort number and after two rings, a man's voice answered.

"Howdy, pardner, how are yew?" The accent was such an over-the-top exaggerated Southern accent that Jick was taken aback.

"Uh... excuse me?" Jick said. "Is this the Hawaiian Orchid resort?"

"Naw, suh."

"Sorry, I must have the wrong number." He moved his thumb over the phone's screen to end the call.

"Now hold on. Is there really such a thing as a wrong number?" The Southern accent disappeared.

"What?"

"I said, is there really such a thing as a wrong number? There's nothing wrong with my number. Maybe you were meant to call me. Maybe it was written in the stars."

Jick was amused by this man's genial nuttiness.

Welcome to Hawaii. What a colorful character. I bet a shrink can find a DSM diagnosis for this guy.

Jick played along with the conversation for a while longer.

"What's your name?"

"I'm your Uncle George."

"Uncle... George?"

"That's right, son. Uncle George. That's what everyone calls me. What do they call you?"

"Jick."

"Jake?"

"J-I-C-K." Jick spelled it out. "A childhood nickname."

"Oh, I see."

"That's what everyone calls me. I just arrived in Hawaii and tried to call my hotel. They were supposed to have a car waiting. What's with the fake Southern accent?"

"Your caller ID said your area code was from Dallas. Figured you were Texan."

"I see. You're right. I am."

As he talked to the eccentric Uncle George, Jick saw a man running toward the baggage claim area. Probably

Hawaiian, untucked colorful aloha shirt stretched over a protuberant belly, crisp black trousers, black shoes, and a name tag clipped to his shirt pocket. Everything about him said "Hotel Staff."

Maybe that's my driver.

The man carried a placard, which he tucked under his arm as he stuffed his phone into a pocket. As he arrived at baggage claim, he waved the placard above his head in a frantic gesture as he scanned the passengers. Jick noted with satisfaction that "Arnsson" was the name stenciled on the placard.

"Sorry, gotta go. My ride just got here."

The accent returned.

"That's fine, son. Welcome to Hawaii. Hope you have a nice stay."

FOURTEEN

Two Years Ago

Sherwin Smith bounded out of bed on graduation day. After a quick shower, he stood in front of the mirror and studied his reflection. He towel-dried his hair, then patted his afro-textured hair into place, wincing at the number of hairs that pulled free in his brush. He stared at the brush in dismay.

I'm too young for my hair to start falling out.

A quick shave, a splash of aftershave, and he was ready. He slipped into a crisp white shirt and dress slacks, followed by his silver crucifix necklace and a tie.

He tucked his necklace under his shirt as he went downstairs to the kitchen. His mother stood by the counter, whipping eggs for an omelet. Her blonde hair was tied in a ponytail, and she blew a few stray strands off her face as she continued beating the eggs. She glanced at him.

"Wow, Sherwin, you're already showered and dressed."

He pushed his thick glasses up the bridge of his nose.

"I can't wait. I'm ready to finish college and move on."

She served the omelet, and they sat together at the breakfast table.

"This is good," he said after a few bites. He looked at his mother.

"What's wrong, Mom?"

"Oh, nothing," she said as she wiped her lower eyelid with the back of a finger. "I wish your Dad was still here."

"Yeah, me too."

Harold and Jane Smith had adopted Sherwin when he was a toddler. His father, Harold, had unexpectedly passed away two years earlier, one of those "sudden cardiac death" moments no one sees coming. One minute, he had been sitting on their riding mower, head bobbing under an oversized hat as he crisscrossed their lawn, and the next minute, he had tumbled off. The mower plowed through a flower bed and into the pool. Sherwin's mother heard a loud noise and looked up to see a cloud of smoke rising from the pool. His passing was shocking and final.

"Are you still planning to move to LA?" his mother asked.

"Not yet. I was going to tell you about it. I'm postponing job hunting for a while."

"Oh. What are you going to do instead?"

"I'm going on a trip. To Africa."

"Africa?! Why Africa?"

"I've always wanted to see the place. The home of my ancestors."

"Africa is a big place."

"Oh, I know. There's a youth hostel program in West Africa, and I'm exploring just that area. I'll fly into Dakar, go on some guided trips for students, and then return home. It's affordable since we're staying in youth hostels, and mostly for students."

"I guess now is a good time. How long are you planning to be gone?"

"Not too long. Probably a month."

"Have you also been job hunting? Weren't you planning to move to LA?"

"Yes. I applied as a lab assistant at a company called Gene 6 Therapeutics."

"Where else?"

"That's it, for now."

"Why only one place? Shouldn't you apply to a few places?"

"I thought this place looked interesting. I'll send out more applications as soon as I get back. Besides, they already called me for an interview."

She sighed.

"Okay. Just be careful."

"I will."

After breakfast, Sherwin went back to his room. His computer was still open on the Gene 6 website. He spent a few minutes surfing their website. He scrolled through staff biographies, stopped to re-read one, then shut his computer to finish getting ready for graduation.

George Sturgis sat at his desk, his cane propped against the polished wood desktop. He had returned home weeks ago and had endured what he called "hell" in rehabilitation. He had been awaiting the trial of "that little shit", as he called Caleb Jonathan, and had been apoplectic with rage at Mr. Jonathan's acquittal.

His gait and balance had improved. Much to his annoyance, he still had bouts of unexplained laughing and crying. Dr. Kawahara had told him he had a condition called *pseudobulbar affect,* an unfortunate side effect of his brain injury. She had told him it may improve over time, or he would just have to learn to live with it. She had prescribed medication for the condition, but it had not yet made a significant difference.

He picked up his phone and dialed a number.

"Darren Snead, please," he said to the receptionist. "It's George Sturgis."

"I'll let him know. Please hold for a moment."

After a brief pause, Darren took the call.

"George, how are you doing?" Darren said. "How's the rehab and everything else going?"

"Fine, I think. The last few weeks have been brutal, but I'm finally back home. And I'm pissed. Which is why I called."

"I expected you to," Darren said. "Tell me why you're pissed. I can guess. But I'm sorry there's not much to do from a criminal liability standpoint."

"I know, I know," Sturgis said with some impatience. "I want to know if we can go after Robert Hardy, the boat owner. He let that damn kid go out with his son unsupervised."

"Caleb Jonathan is an adult, and he has a license to operate the boat. Sure, from a civil standpoint, we can go after him. You stand a better chance of winning. But it's still not guaranteed. It's a big ocean, and sometimes accidents happen."

"We'll see what a jury says," Sturgis said.

"A jury trial? I was thinking of a settlement from Hardy's insurance."

"That's shirt buttons, Darren. I want a jury trial."

"That will be expensive."

"If you can't do it, let me know, and I'll find someone who can. Maybe someone from Honolulu."

"George, you know I would help you, but I'm not a personal injury guy."

"Do you think someone else could have done a better job at the trial travesty I just went through?"

Darren Snead was silent.

"I don't know," he said. "The letter of the law is pretty cut and dried. And Sue Levine is a real ball buster, from what I've heard. And experienced in court."

"Maybe I'm wasting my time," Sturgis said. "Maybe I should just call that guy Bill Viola."

"Who's Bill Viola?"

"Some personal injury attorney from Honolulu. I've met him once. He was with us that day when Caleb Jonathan ran into me. Looked like a real sleazebag. Probably the perfect kind of lawyer I need."

Darren Snead stayed silent.

"I'll think about it," Sturgis said.

He hung up and stared at his phone. He opened a browser window and started perusing Bill Viola's website.

"This guy looks good," he said out loud. His site mentioned Bill Viola was in practice by himself and specialized in several areas, including personal injury and, as a smaller slice of his practice, Native Hawaiian rights.

"Time to call Mr. Bill."

Bill Viola checked his calendar and glanced at the clock. On cue, his assistant stuck her head in the door.

"Almost time for your ten-thirty," she said.

"Thanks, Momi."

He logged into his camera on one screen as he opened the appointment information screen on the other.

"George Sturgis," he read. "Where have I heard that name?"

"You know him? He called two days ago; said it was urgent. I checked our client base. There were no conflicts, so I scheduled him for today."

Viola frowned.

"Oh, yeah, now I remember. It's that guy we went scuba diving with months ago. He got badly hurt. We pulled him out of the water. Kalani Williams told me he made it. I guess he must have been in rehab or something. I wondered how he was doing."

At ten-thirty on the dot, George Sturgis logged into his computer. Bill Viola stared at the screen, shocked at George's transformation. The hair was gone, replaced by a prominent scar that went across the front of Sturgis' head.

I bet I know why he called.

"George," Bill said. "Long time, no see. And you look quite... different."

Sturgis looked grim.

"Glad you noticed," he said. "That's why I called."

For the next half hour, Sturgis outlined everything that had transpired since the boating accident, sprinkled with several choice comments about his opinion of Caleb Jonathan, as well as Robert Hardy, the boat owner. Viola said nothing, busy scribbling notes as Sturgis spoke at length. Finally, the narrative was over, and Bill Viola leaned back in his chair.

"Wow, you've been through hell," he commented. "I didn't follow-up on the details of what you had been through after me and the others pulled you out of the water. Chief Williams told me you had made it. You have been through a lot. All I can say is, holy shit."

"Glad you feel the same way," Sturgis said. "So, what can I do?"

"What do you want to do?"

"Sue him. They acquitted the little shit who did this. I want to sue the boat owner and the little shit, too."

"I'll look up the details of the criminal case. From a civil standpoint, this seems to be pretty cut and dried," Viola said. "Mr. Hardy had a duty, as the owner of the boat, to make sure anyone operating his vehicle had the proper training and license. If Mr. Jonathan had a license, then it depends on whether Mr. Hardy 'should have known' this could happen. If he should have known, then maybe we can argue that his actions directly caused your injuries through his negligence. And you suffered obvious injuries as a result."

"Good," Sturgis said. "Let's sue him."

"Hold on a second. All this takes time. If you want to move forward, Momi will draw up an agreement, set up a trust account, and you'll need to fund the retainer."

"How much?"

"Ten thousand."

"I want to move forward," Sturgis said.

"Okay. And I will personally handle the case."

"Thanks," Sturgis said. "Oh, and I want a jury trial."

Viola arched a brow.

"A jury trial? That's a little irregular this early, but if you insist, sure, we can do that. Settlements are quicker, easier, and less expensive. Like I said, it's obvious that Mr. Hardy is liable for your injuries."

"I want a jury trial," Sturgis said.

"Your injuries were very severe. Life-changing. I'll do some research into Mr. Hardy's background. I think you'll be pleased with what we find."

"That's what I hoped to hear."

"We'll be in touch."

The dinner rush at the Seaview Grill had tapered off, and only a handful of tables remained occupied. The patrons at

Caleb Jonathan's tables had departed, and he had finished tidying up his space. His manager had already doled out his tips in cash.

"Wanna take off early?" his manager asked. "It's just twenty minutes to quitting time and we can handle the closing."

"Sounds good. I think I will head out then," Caleb said.

"How are you holding up?"

"Better. It's been a rough few weeks. Could have been worse."

"Don't do something stupid like that again. Jesus, Caleb, that was Uncle George you hit. You're lucky you got off with a slap on the wrist for operating that boat."

"It was an accident. I didn't mean to hit him. Besides, he was way away from his boat. Like they said in court."

"I know. I'm talking about operating the boat at all."

"You know it wasn't my idea. I just went out with the guys, and the boat belonged to Tony's dad. Could've been any of us."

"I get that. But you're not used to something that big. And you're very lucky the dad sprang for that lawyer. I know he did it to avoid his liability, but you had no business driving the boat if you didn't know what you were doing. You should have been more careful."

"Yes, yes, I know. Stop riding my ass."

"As both your uncle and your boss, I can chew your ass out if I want to. But go on home."

"Thanks."

Caleb sauntered out of the restaurant and headed to his car. He beeped open the door and climbed in. And frowned.

"Weird. Feels like it's sagging in the corner. Hope it's not a flat."

He climbed out of the car and flashed his cellphone flashlight around the tires.

"Ah, shit."

He stared in dismay at the front-left tire. He debated walking back to the restaurant and asking his uncle for a hand. The car was on level ground, and it would not take long. He decided to do it himself.

He placed the jack under the front left jack point and loosened the lug nuts. The car creaked as he cranked it higher. As the tire lifted off the ground, he heard the crunch of gravel behind him. He stopped cranking and glanced around. He saw a man walking up to him, his face in darkness under the visor of a baseball cap.

"Need help?" the stranger asked.

FIFTEEN

Phoenix drove to the restaurant and parked on the far side, where employees parked. He had already spotted the target vehicle. A dozen cars dotted the lot, but his eyes stayed fixed on one. He reached into the bag and extracted his favorite instrument, the shears.

Slipping out of his car, he moved casually across the gravel lot, heading for the target vehicle. The front left corner of the car was in darkness as the dim cone of light from the light affixed to the corner of the building petered out. Phoenix crouched, pressed the sharp tip into the sidewall, and drove it home. A soft hiss escaped from the tire as the corner of the car sagged toward the ground. He stood, pocketed the shears, and strolled back to his vehicle. Once inside, he settled low in the seat and waited.

Fifteen minutes later, a young man pushed through the restaurant doors. Phoenix watched, and his face creased into a smile as the figure stepped into the light.

Caleb Jonathan.

Caleb walked to the car and climbed in. Something must have felt off as the young man climbed out just a few seconds later. He turned on his cell phone flashlight and stared in dismay at the flat tire.

Phoenix watched the man place his phone on a rock, aiming it at the tire. He placed the jack under the car and cranked the end of the car off the ground. As Phoenix watched him, a thrill of anticipation coursed through him. He had never done this before. His breathing quickened as he turned the shears in his hand, focusing on the glint in the dull light. Then he climbed out of his car, tucked the shears in his waistband, and walked to where the man crouched by the tire.

"Need help?"

Caleb Jonathan glanced at Phoenix.

"Aw, thanks, brah, I got this."

Phoenix moved fast. As Caleb turned back to the tire, Phoenix pulled the shears out of his waistband. As Caleb grunted with exertion against the tire iron, Phoenix reached around his face, clamped his hand across his mouth, and with a brutal thrust, drove the shears into his chest.

Caleb's eyes went wide. He bit down as hard as he could on Phoenix's hand. Pain lanced through Phoenix's palm. He muffled a scream and, in blind rage, stabbed again and again—chest, gut, neck. The steel punched through flesh until the tips split the skin on the far side of Caleb's throat.

Caleb's vise grip on Phoenix's hand loosened, and he let go of Phoenix's hand as he toppled sideways, twitching. Then he gave a final wheeze and lay still.

Phoenix stood over him, panting, blood hot in his ears. He looked at Caleb's figure and was unsatisfied at the lack of blood; most of it was trapped inside. His own blood looked like poorly applied lipstick smeared on Caleb's mouth.

Phoenix smiled as he felt the urge wash over him, dulling his throbbing hand for the moment. No one had come out of the restaurant. Then he ran back to his car, jumped in, and sped away into the night.

Sturgis leaned back in his chair, satisfied with the call with Bill Viola.

I'm going to sue that bastard for everything he's worth.

He smiled with a sense of savage satisfaction as he evaluated the potential financial windfall. He did not need the money but felt a need to get some measure of retribution for his injuries. A knock at the door interrupted his thoughts.

"Come in."

Phoenix opened the door and stepped in. As he closed the door, George noted his hand shook, like he had drunk several energy drinks. And a bandage wrapped his left hand. He parked himself in a chair, jittery, eyes bright.

"Hi, Dad," he said. "Whatcha doin'?"

Sturgis tilted his head.

"Nothing, just browsing. You all right?"

Phoenix leaned over the desk.

"Yeah, fine. Must have had too much coffee this morning. I couldn't sleep last night."

He examined his father's open browser window.

"Personal injury attorney. Bill Viola. Trying to sue someone, Dad?"

"Robert Hardy. He's the boat owner. He should not have let his son and those other kids take his boat out. I'm still pissed about the first trial. I can't believe they let Caleb Jonathan walk."

Phoenix grinned at him. Then his expression changed to a blank stare.

"What's up?" Sturgis asked. "And why is your hand bandaged?"

"Glad you asked. Caleb Jonathan... I took care of him. Want me to take care of Robert Hardy, too?"

"What?"

"Caleb was our problem. I took care of him."

Sturgis' eyes narrowed. He stared back at Phoenix.

"What are you talking about?"

"I killed him." He hissed out the words in an undertone, like a soft whisper.

The blank stare disappeared, and Phoenix grinned at his father again.

"You did what?" Sturgis almost shouted as he leaped out of his chair. He tottered to the right, forgetting his balance problems. The cane slipped as he jabbed it on the floor. He grabbed the edge of his desk, steadying himself as he sank back into his chair.

"Do you realize what you've done? The reason I'm looking for personal injury attorneys is because I plan to sue them. I could have gotten a huge payout. But now, thanks to you, that may be in jeopardy."

"Like you need the money, Dad," Phoenix said, sullen.

"That's not the point!" Sturgis shouted. "They need to feel the pain of losing their money. Losing something important. They took away my life! And the court did nothing."

"Didn't you feel like doing it yourself?"

"Maybe. But Jesus, Phoenix, you don't go around killing people who piss you off. You use the courts to settle disputes. That's what courts are for. You only kill when it's absolutely necessary..." His voice trailed off.

"I thought it was necessary," Phoenix looked aggrieved. "I thought you would be happy I took care of the problem for you."

"When did you do it?"

"Yesterday evening."

"What did you do?"

"Stabbed him."

Sturgis froze, staring at his son.

Jesus, I bet he used those shears...

Phoenix held up his wrapped hand.

"And he bit me."

"Did anyone see you?"

"No."

"You sure?"

"Yeah."

"Don't ever do something stupid like this again," Sturgis said.

He leaned back in his chair, thinking hard.

"Phoenix," he said.

"What?"

"Don't tell your mother and never mention this again. Ever. You understand?"

"Yes."

"And I'll repeat it, don't ever..." he paused. "...ever do something like this. If you're caught, you'll spend the rest of your life in jail. No more doing anything you enjoy. Understand?"

"Yes."

At least I can still sue Robert Hardy.

"And under no circumstances are you to do anything to Robert Hardy. Understand?"

"Yes." Phoenix looked meek. "Sorry, Dad. I was just caught up in the moment. I watched the trial. He was laughing after he won. I... I must have lost it. Okay, I won't do anything like this again."

He left Sturgis' office. Sturgis stared after him as he closed the door.

"Shit. Maybe Sherryl was right. Maybe we should've had him get therapy."

He touched the scar on his head. The edges were smooth without the staples, but the scar still felt like a ridge of bumps.

"He's getting worse. I need to come up with something. Fast."

The following morning, Sturgis sat at his desk, deep in thought over his conversation with his son. His phone rang, interrupting his thoughts.

"Hello."

"Good morning, George, Bill Viola."

"Good morning, Bill. What's the good news?"

"I'm afraid it may not be good. I looked over the final verdict and reviewed the judge's findings. And it looks like Mr. Jonathan has a license to operate the boat. What that means is, this was an unfortunate accident, but it may be difficult to attach liability to Mr. Hardy. Of course, Mr. Jonathan could be found civilly liable, but he does not have any significant assets. Mr. Hardy has a generous liability insurance policy with coverage for injuries. The best outcome may be to get a settlement from his insurance company, which they may agree to because you're a high-profile client and they would want to avoid a spectacle."

"I still want a jury trial."

"I would not recommend it. If you want to move ahead, we can. It will be expensive. We may win if the jury is sympathetic, but it is almost guaranteed it will be overturned on appeal."

Sleazebag.

"Okay, let me think about it."

Sturgis placed the phone on its cradle.

"Shit."

"Who's next?"

It was Tom, the pathology assistant, who posed the question to Dr. Willard Grosvenor, associate pathologist at the Hawaii County medical examiner's office.

Dr. Grosvenor studied his screen.

"Caleb Jonathan," he read out. "Male, age 26, stabbed to death in a restaurant parking lot. It was that homicide last week."

"Oh yeah, I heard about it."

"Let's get started."

Thirty minutes later, the body lay on the autopsy table under the sterile white lights of the examining room. Dr. Grosvenor tied his gown in the back and leaned over the body of Caleb Jonathan as he pulled on a pair of gloves.

"Jesus, the number of times he was stabbed..."

Multiple small puncture wounds riddled the torso. Most were on the right side.

"A lot of these are on the right side," Tom observed.

"It's unlikely his assailant stabbed this many times from the front. He may have been restrained from the back and stabbed repeatedly. Could have been more than one attacker. I hope they catch the guy. This kind of thing doesn't happen here."

He peered closer to the neck. He gently turned the head from one side to the other.

"Hey Tom, take a look at this."

"What do you see?"

"See this stab wound on the right side of his neck?"

The small oval hole was plugged with dark blood.

"It's small. Kinda looks like a raisin squashed against his neck."

"Colorful description, but yeah, it does look like a raisin smushed into his skin. Didn't bleed much."

"What about it?"

"It's one entry wound on the right but two exit wounds on the left."

"How do you know it isn't three separate wounds?"

"Years of experience. Unlikely he would be stabbed once on the right, then the attacker switches hands, and stabs twice on the left? I've seen this pattern before. It's usually when someone is stabbed with a pair of scissors."

"A pair of scissors?"

"Yes. The blades were slightly open and diverged as the killer drove them through his neck. By the time they exited on the left side, they emerged as two blades."

Dr. Grosvenor stepped on the foot pedal and leaned toward the microphone as he started his dictation.

"Penetrating wound noted on the right side of neck, oval, approximately one centimeter. Two exit wounds noted on the left side, also one centimeter, suggesting a diverging path of twin blades, most likely a pair of scissors..."

He took his foot off the pedal.

"Let's collect our swabs from the surface and get started with the dissection."

"Sure thing, Doc."

"There's some blood on the lips," Dr. Grosvenor said as he gently pried open the mouth. He angled his overhead light for a better look.

"Hmm, interesting."

"What is it?"

"Take a look at the back of his mouth. See anything unusual?"

Tom peered into the open mouth.

"No, looks pretty normal."

"Exactly. Looks normal. And no contusions around his mouth either. Which means he wasn't punched in the mouth. Which means the blood around his mouth is not his. He probably bit his attacker."

"Damn, you're right."

"I bet whoever attacked him surprised him from the back, clamped a hand around his mouth, and stabbed him. Poor kid put up a fight and bit the attacker. Who probably freaked out and kept stabbing him over and over."

SIXTEEN

Present Day

Jick ended the call with a shake of his head and slipped the phone into his pocket. He waved to the portly driver, who ran over with an apologetic expression.

"Sorry, sir," he said, extending a damp hand. "I'm Kaipo, the driver for Hawaiian Orchid. There was a traffic jam on the Queen K highway. They always doing roadwork."

Jick shook the outstretched hand and watched as Kaipo dabbed his forehead with a handkerchief.

Everything is damp and sticky here.

"No problem. I haven't been waiting long. Watch my bag for a minute; I'll duck into that restroom and change into shorts."

After Jick changed, Kaipo led him to a parked black SUV. The Hawaiian Orchid logo, a stylized magenta orchid with a golden lei draped over it, was emblazoned on the front doors. Jick climbed in and shut his eyes for a moment, turning his face from side to side in the blast of cold air. Kaipo loaded Jick's bag in the back and climbed into the driver's seat.

"Good flight?"

"Yes, very little turbulence."

"Very good," Kaipo said. "The resort is 'bout thirty minutes. If you need something, sir, let me know. The cooler next to you has complimentary drinks. Please help yourself."

He swung the SUV into the thru-lane and crawled to the airport exit. He made a left turn onto the Queen Ka'ahumanu Highway and headed north.

"First time here?"

"On the Big Island, yes. I came once before many years ago. But only to Honolulu. The Big Island is a little different from what I thought."

"How so?"

"I didn't think the west side was so dry and rocky."

"That's just here. If you go north to Waimea and cross over to the wet side, it looks way different. Lots of green, forests, farms, rain."

They drove on for a few miles in silence. Jick opened a bottle of cold water.

"You here on work, yeah?"

"Well, supposedly. But I plan to treat this trip like a vacation. I have some work to do, but I also plan to do some touristy things, maybe go to the volcanoes. How did you guess I was here on work?" Jick did not elaborate on his work.

"They gave me a business account to bill the ride. And you traveling alone. So, I figured you here for work."

"I'm a medical consultant," Jick said. "I'm just here to check out practice locations."

"We need doctors," Kaipo nodded.

"Are you from around here?"

"Yeah, I'm a local. Born and raised Hilo side."

Then Jick mentioned the errant phone call.

"You have some colorful characters here in Hawaii."

Kaipo flashed a glance over his shoulder at Jick.

"You just got here. Meet someone at the airport?"

"No. I tried to call the hotel when you weren't there. Called a wrong number. Some weird guy named Uncle George. He wanted to keep talking to me about how there's no such thing as a wrong number."

Kaipo eyed Jick in surprise.

"You call a wrong numbah and talk to Uncle George?"

"You know him?"

"Never met him. Lots of people know about Uncle George. He's lived here for a long time. Throws parties at his house or on the beach all the time. Everyone from the mayor down knows him. The cops treat him good too."

"Is he rich?"

"Yes. He lives in a big house somewhere north, as you head to Kohala. That's the far northern area. Just him, his wife, and a son. Son is supposed to be *lōlō*."

"Lōlō?" Jick queried.

"Crazy," Kaipo grinned at Jick as he twirled his index finger next to his face. "Nuts. He used to come to town with aunty and uncle. They say he stays in the house most of the time now."

"What does he do?"

"I guess nothing. He don't come to town no more so no one knows."

SEVENTEEN

Eighteen Months Ago

David Finlayson pulled into the parking lot at Abe's Family Diner. This was his weekly "TGIF" ritual, treating himself to breakfast at Abe's every Friday morning before work. The hostess greeted him with the easy familiarity of a regular.

"Good morning, Mr. Finlayson. Your usual table?"

"Good morning, Natalie. Yes, please."

"His" table was in the corner that afforded the best view of the bustling freeway. It also faced the east, and the changing weekly pattern as the sun rose behind the buildings led to spectacular sunrises. Today, the sun was behind the Gene 6 building, where he worked. From his elevated perch, the morning sun cast a bright glow at the base of the obelisk-shaped building.

Looks like it's about to lift off.

As he ate, he spotted a familiar face. It was Sherwin Smith, the new lab assistant they had hired a few months ago. Finlayson waved to him, and Sherwin came over to his table.

"Good morning, Mr. Finlayson," Sherwin said. "First time here. Just heading in to work early, so I thought I'd try it."

"I'm a regular here. Every Friday, like clockwork. My routine. And call me Dave."

"Mind if I join you?"

"Not at all. Have a seat."

Sherwin settled into his seat.

"You've been here what, three months now? How do you like it so far?" Finlayson asked.

"Great. I already feel at home. And I enjoy working in the lab."

"That's good."

The waitress stopped at their table. She handed Sherwin a menu.

"Coffee, sir?"

"Oh yes, please." He eyed the menu. "And the 'American Special' breakfast. Over easy on the eggs, with sausage."

"You got it."

After a few minutes of silence, Sherwin ventured a question to Finlayson about his background.

"How long have you been here? You have an unusual background for this place. Physics, then biophysics?"

"It began with a love of maths. I love maths, the patterns, the numbers, the order."

"Maths?"

Finlayson smiled.

"I'm English," he said. "We say 'maths'."

"I'm not good at accents," Sherwin said. "I figured you were from either England or Australia."

Finlayson put on a look of mock horror.

"Carful. It's considered an insult to be confused for an Australian."

Then, seeing Sherwin's alarmed face, he added, "Just joking."

He sipped his coffee.

"Well, my love of mathematics began with a trip to the museum when I was very young. I must have been twelve, and my class had taken a trip to the local natural history museum. I saw a fossil labeled 'Ammonite.'"

"An ammonite? Those spirally shell things?"

"They're not shells. And yes, those spirally things. The ammonite was iridescent and seemed to sparkle in its display case. It looked like a rainbow trapped behind glass. But it was not the color that fascinated me. It was the spiral pattern."

"The lowly ammonite mollusc lived and died some sixty-five million years ago, leaving behind a collection of fossils of breathtaking mathematical geometry. You should take a closer look at it. Each segment increases in size as it progresses outward in a swirl. The display case had a description of the maths behind the pattern. And I was hooked."

Sherwin Smith looked a little nonplussed. He opened his mouth to say something, then closed it. Finlayson continued.

"Do you know what a Fibonacci sequence is?"

"Uh, yes."

"They converge on *phi*, the golden ratio. Know what that is?"

"Yes."

"That golden ratio exists in so many things in the universe. From lowly ammonites, all the way to spiral galaxies. And in the local grocery stores, when you look at the pattern of spirals in Romanesco broccoli. The Fibonacci sequence, the golden ratio, the pleasing symmetry; the greats throughout history knew about all of them.

"DaVinci knew about it. He incorporated the golden ratio in the Mona Lisa and the Vitruvian Man."

"Vitruvian Man?"

"You know, the da Vinci drawing of a man in two superimposed positions. It's supposed to represent ideal proportions. And the golden ratio is there! Can you believe it?"

Sherwin's breakfast arrived.

"Can I get you anything else?"

"No, thanks."

As Sherwin dug in, Finlayson resumed the narrative, his voice full of excitement. Sherwin took a bite of his breakfast as he listened to the fervor in Finlayson's voice.

"Well, these are examples of fractals, order from chaos, patterns of self-similarity of increasing complexity that form as organisms grow."

"And that's how you ended up here?" Sherwin asked.

Finlayson took a bite of his breakfast.

"Sort of. I started doing research into the kinetics of cell reproduction, the negative feedback loop between availability of resources and population growth. Know what I mean?"

"Kinda."

"You know that equation. When resources are plentiful, populations thrive. As resources dwindle, there is a negative feedback loop, and populations shrink. The so-called 'logistics map' is an equation that beautifully illustrates this."

"Oh, yes, I have heard about it. And you're doing research in this field with cells?"

"Yes."

"What does that have to do with ammonites?"

"It doesn't. At least not directly. But it's all connected. Fractals, symmetric spirals, the logistics map."

"So, what do you do with cells?"

"I'm working on a way to replicate cells up to a certain point, then stop. Making perfect little copies. Sort of like fractals in a biological sense."

"Why would you want to do that?"

"Sherwin, if I cloned a sheep, all I would get is a clump of cells with the same DNA as the original, right?"

"Yeah."

"What if I could speed it up to a certain point, then stop?"

"What if you could?"

"Then I could make a perfect little copy of the original."

"I still don't get the point of doing that."

"It's just a very fascinating field of research."

Finlayson took a bite.

"Have you ever thought about cloning a human?"

Finlayson finished chewing.

"Why on earth would I want to do that?"

"Oh, I don't know. One would think a cloned human would represent a 'human fractal,' right? A smaller replica of the original."

"Wouldn't be the same. Even if the genetic makeup was identical, epigenesis would separate the original from the clone. Not quite the same thing."

Sherwin waited for Finlayson to continue.

"Clones are just genetically identical copies. But they're separated by time. For example, if I cloned you, Sherwin, even though the clone would have your identical genome, it would grow up in a different era, with different epigenetic influences. In other words, not really you. But what if you could clone yourself, then step on the accelerator, so to speak, until the clone catches up to you, then stop. And maybe, just maybe, transfer your knowledge to the 'human fractal.' Wouldn't that be something?"

Sherwin frowned.

"Seriously?"

"Immortality, right?"

"Is that what you're working on here?"

"Oh, heavens no. I'm just doing research on cells."

"By the way, that segues into our next topic," Sherwin leaned back. "Are you ready for today's huddle?"

"What about it?"

"You better be going. You're the guest of honor."

"What? I am?" Finlayson blinked. "Why?"

"It's about your work. You know, with the logistics equation. And your work with cells."

"I didn't know that."

"It's probably on your calendar."

David Finlayson sat at his desk, staring at his screensaver. A blue stripe that looked like a stock ticker streamed across the bottom of the screen. Numbers streamed across the blue stripe as a paisley-shaped pattern mushroomed onto the rest of the screen. Every few seconds, the image would zoom in, displaying the same symmetry as it continuously zoomed in like a funhouse infinity mirror. Then the stripe would clear, the paisley pattern would vanish, and a new set of random numbers would start streaming as a new pattern bloomed on the screen and started zooming in. The kaleidoscopic pattern had a hypnotic quality, and Finlayson stared at it, chin cupped in his right hand. He had a never-ending fascination with fractals, especially the Mandelbrot fractal. He rolled his mouse button over the pattern, and the pattern vanished, replaced by a paper he had been working on.

A knock at the door interrupted his reverie. Without waiting for an answer, the door opened, and Sherwin poked in his head.

"Time for the huddle. See you there in a few."

The door closed and Finlayson leaned back with a sigh. He did not want to go to the huddle, the office term for a morning team meeting. These meetings were tedious and run by corporate stuffed shirts, so he had zero interest in the proceedings. But it was a requirement of his job as a senior scientist at his biotechnology firm. He jiggled his mouse just as the screensaver reappeared, and the fractal pattern disappeared. The stylized G6 logo of his company, Gene 6 Therapeutics, appeared on the screen. He opened an earlier presentation, reviewed its contents, and clicked it shut with another sigh.

Coffee in hand, Finlayson strolled to the meeting room and sat in one of the back rows. A screen at the front of the room displayed the agenda for the meeting. His research was the first topic of discussion. After a perfunctory greeting, his boss began the meeting by recognizing Finlayson's work.

"Dave, we would like to take a moment to recognize your contribution to the field of cellular reproduction."

Finlayson shifted in his chair and mumbled his appreciation.

"Thanks, Warren."

"This could be a game-changer in the areas of tissue injury and wound-healing. Would you like to take a few minutes to explain to the rest of the corporate folks, in layman's terms, what the research involves?"

"I don't have a prepared presentation, so I'll just wing it."

"That's fine."

Finlayson opened his presentation, took a deep breath, and began.

"In population growth studies, as a population grows, there are restrictions inherent in the environment. Think about the growth of any animal species. As it grows, there is greater depletion of resources and eventually, the population levels off and then decreases. Later, when the availability of resources exceeds the population, the population grows again. The entire process is self-limiting. The logistics map is such an equation. Depending on the growth rate, there is a negative feedback loop. Everyone following so far?"

A few heads nodded.

"I theorized this could apply not just to entire populations but to cells, too. In other words, if you control the environment around clumps of cells, you can watch cells grow to a specific point and then stop."

"What's the use of that?" someone asked.

"Imagine the practical applicability. You have a wound, a fresh incision in the skin. Now imagine you can apply something to it, a combination of nutrients and a source of power, sort of like electrodes applied to either side of the wound. Now imagine you check back in twenty-four hours and the wound is completely healed. You turn off the power, stop giving the cells additional nutrients, and everything goes back to normal. The cells are back in their natural environment. Except you have a wound that has healed in twenty-four hours."

He paused for a moment to let it sink in. The room went silent. Then someone whistled.

"Wow, David. You can really do that?"

"That's what I'm working on. It's mostly maths at this point. I have been experimenting with cell cultures, making copies of clumps of cells. As I control what goes into the cells, they make smaller clumps of nearly perfect symmetry, almost like growing organic crystals. Then the process stops, and the cells grow normally, in a random pattern. Obviously, for wound healing, it's a little more involved. I would need to talk to experts in the field about newer things, like the various membranes, synthetic skin, local nutrients, etc. Underlying all of this would be my contribution, to make the actual cells reproduce faster."

Someone else chimed in.

"Hey Dave, what if someone did that to a whole person? Can they speed up the aging process?"

Finlayson paused.

"No."

"But theoretically, it's possible, right?"

"Why would anyone want to do that? What possible reason would someone have to want to age faster? No, they can't speed up the aging process. But for local uses, like on wounds, it has limitless possibilities."

Finlayson sat down.

"Any questions?"

"Just one." It was a young man sitting in the opposite corner, arm raised.

"Mr. Finlayson, how do you plan to safeguard the intellectual property? Planning to file for patent protection?"

"I'll let Warren handle that one," Finlayson said. "By the way, I don't know you. Are you new here?"

"No, I'm a guest, invited by Mr. Sachs." He nodded at Warren. "I'm a journalism student."

Finlayson sprang out of his seat.

"A reporter?"

He sprang to his feet and almost glared at Warren.

"Why the hell is there a reporter here?"

"He's not a reporter. He's studying journalism. We're impressed by what you've done so far, Dave. Not a big deal. He's a friend of my son, and he wants to be a reporter. He wanted to do a little write-up for one of those news aggregator websites."

Finlayson turned to the man.

"Get the hell out of here! And don't publish anything about what I said."

Warren intervened.

"Dave, what has gotten into you? This kind of story is great PR for the company. There's no reason we can't do a little puff piece about this."

"I'm just a private person. The last thing I need is publicity, interview requests, and all of that. I prefer to be left alone. And it's still too early in the research. We don't need this publicized just to turn into a clickbait article on some website. God, I hate this social media stuff."

"We can talk about that later." Warren nodded at the young man. "You can go now."

Two months later, Finlayson sat at his desk. Against his wishes, the reporter had published a glowing article about Finlayson's research. For weeks afterwards, a sense of dread filled Finlayson's days. There had been a small flurry of interview requests, and Finlayson had batted them away. Then the feeling faded, and he had sunk back into a welcome feeling of obscurity.

Until the phone rang one day...

EIGHTEEN

Twelve Months Ago

"Hey, Sherwin, got a minute?"

Sherwin Smith took a swig from his third energy drink of the day. He looked up from his desk and saw David Finlayson standing at the door. Sherwin's desk sat in a corner of the lab; his workstation was to the right with a lab stool alongside. It was late in the day, and everyone else had gone home.

He gestured toward the stool.

"Sure, what's up?"

Finlayson parked himself on the stool and stared at Sherwin, deep in thought. He placed his palms on his thighs, lips pursed, frowning. He opened his mouth to speak, hesitated, then closed it.

"Everything okay, Dave?"

"Yeah, I was just thinking about a project I've been asked to take part in."

"What kind of project?"

"It will involve taking time off from work."

"How long?"

"Probably about a year."

"A year! Wow, that's quite a long time. And why are you telling me about it?"

"I'm thinking about taking it. And I need a capable assistant. You're good, very good. You've only been here a short time, and you have already mastered a lot of skills."

"I just started this job. I can't afford to quit or take time off."

"I talked to Warren already. I've been here a while and have quite a bit of seniority. If you agree to join, it will mean unpaid time off from this job, but the person sponsoring the project would double your money."

"Is this something illegal?" Sherwin looked askance at Finlayson.

"No, this could be groundbreaking stuff. You would have to sign a non-disclosure agreement, though."

"No problem. So, what's the project?"

"We're going to set up a lab just like the lab here. All the research I've been doing here with accelerated cell growth. But it will be for a private client."

"You're sure this is not something illegal."

"Yes, quite sure. All we're going to do is set up the lab. A private client saw the article about me that the journalism student published about my research a few months ago. Remember that? At the time, I wasn't too thrilled about the publicity. I think I've changed my mind."

"What happened?"

"In Hawaii, there's a big push towards sustainable farming and locally grown stuff. This client wants me to do a little research to see whether my technique will work on plants. If it does, it could lead to accelerated growth and therefore, much better crop yields."

"So, you're going to Hawaii? For a year? To grow plants?"

"Yeah. After the lab is running, you can leave. I'll stay for a few months longer to finish up."

"Is the part you're going to do later something illegal?"

"Sherwin, stop asking questions. No, it's not illegal. We're doing research on plant biology. The hard part is getting everything set up. Once that's done, you can head back home."

"Who's the client?"

"His name is Sturgis. George Sturgis. He lives in Hawaii."

"Sounds great."

"Yes. You get an all-expenses paid trip to Hawaii for about a year, a doubling of your salary, and then come back to your job."

"And you're sure Mr. Sachs is okay with this?"

"Yes, I talked to him already."

Finlayson held out his phone.

"This is a picture of the client. George Sturgis."

Sherwin's eyes widened, and he stared at the picture in amazement. He leaned back in his chair. He could hardly believe his luck. A year in Hawaii, more money, and a guaranteed return to his old job. His hand shook as he put his energy drink down.

A few weeks later, Finlayson and Sherwin Smith touched down at Kona International Airport on the Big Island of Hawaii. After collecting their bags, they spotted a man holding a placard with Finlayson's name. They walked to a nearby private lot where a Cadillac Escalade stood, with darkened windows and engine idling. The driver stashed their bags in the back and held the back door open for them to climb in. Sherwin stared at the figure of George Sturgis sitting in the back seat.

"Welcome to Hawaii."

The Escalade purred in silence, heading north along the Queen Kaahumanu or "Queen K" highway. Sherwin sat in the third row. Sturgis turned to look at Sherwin.

"So, you're Sherwin," Sturgis said.

"Yes, sir," he replied. "Sherwin Smith."

"David speaks highly of you."

"Thank you, sir."

"He says you're one of the brightest lab assistants he has worked with."

"Uh, thank you again."

The conversation petered out for a few minutes. Then Sherwin ventured a question.

"What is this project we're supposed to do?"

"Later, later," Sturgis said. "First, we get you settled into your condo, then we go to the place we're setting up as the lab. You have to sign some paperwork, a non-disclosure agreement, then we will discuss things."

The conversation petered out again. Sherwin ventured another question.

"How long have you known Dr. Finlayson?"

Sturgis turned to Sherwin. His eyes lingered for a moment before he answered.

"Not that long, maybe a few months. I read about his research and felt it would be a good idea to explore further. I offered him a financial incentive he couldn't turn down. And here he is, and here you are."

"I know I didn't want that kid reporter in the room when I talked about my research," Finlayson said. "But there was one benefit. I met George Sturgis."

"I'm curious to find out more. Now I'm getting excited," Sherwin said.

The car turned left onto the road that led to the Mauna Lani. Sherwin gazed out the side window, looking past the outline of Sturgis' face. The black lava fields provided a stunning backdrop to the manicured green foliage and rainbow of flowers. He allowed his gaze to drift between the blur of colors and Sturgis' face. He focused on Sturgis' head.

Sherwin could not make out whether Sturgis was bald or kept his head shaved. He wore dark-framed glasses that darkened in the sun, giving his face a sinister appearance. A prominent scar ran across the top of his head, with a smaller comma-shaped scar attached to its left side.

That's quite a scar. Wonder what happened to him.

The car turned into a driveway and parked next to one of the condos.

"Here's your home for the next few months," Sturgis announced.

The driver helped unload their bags. After half an hour to refresh from their long flight, the four piled back into the SUV. They turned left on the Queen K highway as they made their way to the small village and shipping port of

Kawaihae. The driver turned into a small neighborhood just off the highway and stopped outside a small house set apart from the rest of the neighborhood.

"Here we are," Sturgis announced. "Welcome to the lab."

The driver held the door open and then settled into the driver's seat to wait. Sturgis stepped out, carrying a briefcase, and led Finlayson and Sherwin to the back door. A large oval gas tank with 'Propane' stenciled on its side sat on a concrete pedestal. A yellow pipe led to a generator that nestled against the windowless back wall of the house.

"It's quiet here," Finlayson observed. He glanced around the neighborhood. "And private."

Sturgis unlocked the door, and they stepped in. A rush of cool air spilled out. Lab benches lined two walls, and there were piles of unopened shipping boxes everywhere. The lighting was an antiseptic white from rows of fluorescent lights that adorned the ceiling. Blackout curtains prevented any outside light from filtering into the room.

"Wow, this is quite a setup," Sherwin commented.

Finlayson eyed the stacks of boxes.

"Looks like we have some work to do."

Sturgis pulled out a stool and parked it next to one of the benches. He opened the briefcase and pulled out a sheaf of papers.

"Let's go over this stuff, Sherwin, and we'll get you signed on," Sturgis said. "Then we can go into details."

Sherwin glanced at Finlayson.

"Did you sign all of this already?"

"Yes," Finlayson said. "I've been working with George for a few weeks."

Sherwin glanced from Finlayson to Sturgis, shrugged, and started reading the non-disclosure agreement.

"Looks straightforward enough."

He signed the document and handed it back to Sturgis.

"Okay, son, here's what we would like you to do..."

The car dropped Finlayson and Sherwin at their condo. After they had finished unpacking their suitcases and finished an early dinner, Finlayson announced he was going to bed early as he was exhausted from the day's travel.

"Yeah, me too," Sherwin said. He hesitated, then added, "But can I ask you something first?"

"Sure."

"What are we doing here?"

"What do you mean?"

"Sturgis said we're going to set up a lab just like your lab back home."

"That is correct."

"For what? Is this guy really into growing plants better? Seems like a silly idea. I get the sustainable farming bit. But it looks like he's spent quite a bit of money in the lab so far. I don't see how he'll get his money back or make a profit."

"Sherwin, your job is to set up the lab. That's what I need you for. Some people have more money than sense, and they can afford to indulge 'silly ideas.' So, we'll do our best to see if my idea of accelerated growth works on plants. Imagine growing crops in just a fraction of the time it normally takes. If it works, he could make a lot of money. If it doesn't, it's probably money he can afford to lose. Regardless, there's quite a financial windfall for both of us.

"Setting up a lab is a lot of work. Too much work for me. Don't ask any more questions. Once we get everything set up and running, you can leave."

"I just don't understand why a private citizen would go to this much expense to set up this lab. But okay, I'll help you set up the lab."

"That's the spirit, my boy." Finlayson clapped him on the shoulder. "Now let's unpack and get some rest."

NINETEEN

Present Day

The big SUV continued lapping up the miles as it cruised north on the Queen K highway. Cargo trucks slowed their progress, and Jick found himself clutching the seat when Kaipo swung into the oncoming lane to gauge the distance so he could pass. He eyed the drinks cooler.

Too soon for a drink? Nah, not the way he's driving.

He opened the cooler and helped himself to a beer.

"So, this Uncle George's, uh, *lōlō* son just stays at home all day and his dad throws parties on the beach?"

Kaipo shrugged.

"Is this Uncle George a good guy?"

Kaipo shrugged again.

"He been here for years. Sometimes people talk story about him. They say he was a good businessman. I guess you gotta bust a few heads to be good. He got hurt pretty bad few years ago. Boating accident. Now he mostly throws parties, and everyone treats him good. Even the cops."

"You already said that about the cops. Makes it sound like there could be some corruption around him."

Kaipo glanced at Jick and replied with another shrug.

"You know how it goes. We a small island. You got money, you can make things happen. And Uncle George got money." He held up his hand, rubbed his thumb and forefinger together.

Jick jumped when Kaipo slammed his palm on the horn as he swerved. A white convertible had made an illegal left turn in front of them. Kaipo's last-second swerve avoided an accident by inches. Jick noticed the driver of the convertible flash a sheepish grin and a wave as he finished his turn. Jick caught a glimpse of someone in the passenger seat.

"Tourists," Kaipo murmured under his breath.

"Anytime you see a convertible here in Hawaii with two people in the car, they tourists," he said. "It's like a mainland dream, go to Hawaii, get a convertible, drive around."

"I'm a tourist too," Jick reminded.

"But you here to work, yeah?"

"Yes, but I'll do some touristy things."

"Most tourists are okay. Some are bad, cause lots of trouble. Some tourists are from countries where they drive on the left. I worry about this road. It's a two-lane highway and has no lights. It's tough when the flights arrive after dark and the tourists got to drive their rental cars to the resorts on this road."

"Why no lights?"

"The telescopes," Kaipo said. "We got telescopes on Mauna Kea, so they don't allow lights in many places. No lights on the highways."

"Maybe a few more road signs then?"

"You said it, bruh."

A few miles later, Kaipo pulled into the left turning lane. Jick saw the familiar Hawaiian Orchid logo in gold letters fastened to a wall made of black lava rock. As Kaipo turned left, Jick noticed that in a wide swath across the impenetrable black lava field, the terrain gave way to a swath of cultivated paradise. Colorful orchids grew out of niches formed in the rock wall. A shoulder of vibrant emerald-green grass flanked either side of the road, its texture so smooth it could have doubled as a putting green. A ribbon of impossibly colorful ground orchids studded natural crevices in the lava rock where the grass met the lava field. Palm trees lined either side of the road; between the palms, alternating red and white bougainvillea bushes waved like pom-poms. Further down the road, the palm trees gave way to trees with branches that formed a speckled canopy over the road. Bright purple and white orchids clung to the trees, adding a splash of color along the trunks.

"Beautiful," Jick murmured. "The colors are unreal."

"They did a good job with the landscaping," Kaipo agreed.

Kaipo turned into the porte cochere and stopped next to the main entrance. He unloaded Jick's bag, and Jick pressed a tip into his hand.

"Thank you, sir," Kaipo said. "By the way, I also drive for a rideshare service, so if you need anything, here's my number."

He fished a card out of his pocket and handed it to Jick.

"Thanks," Jick said. "I probably won't, though. The people I work for have supplied a rental car that is being delivered here this evening. It was more convenient than picking it up at the airport."

"Hope it's not a convertible," Kaipo grinned. "Those things are only good on the paved roads. And we got lots of steep roads that are gravel."

"I guess I'll find out later today."

"Keep my number if you need anything. Mahalo."

Jick remembered that "mahalo" meant thank you. Kaipo walked him to the concierge desk, then flashed him the shaka sign as he bade goodbye. Jick flashed the sign back.

I'm in Hawaii.

"Hello, Mr. Arnsson," the concierge smiled at him. "Here is your key; you're already checked in. Room 412. Your car will be delivered this evening. Would you like help with your bag?"

Sam sure knows how to set up a luxury experience. Our tax dollars at work...

"No thanks, I can manage."

Jick found his way to his room. He let himself in. He noted with satisfaction that housekeeping had turned on the air conditioner.

He opened the curtains, and a dazzling vista of the shimmering ocean greeted him. He squinted at the swaying palms and golden sand stretching toward thatched cabanas and a beachside bar.

I could take a picture of this and put it on a postcard.

Jick turned away from the magnificent view with some effort. The minibar beckoned. He ignored it for a few minutes as he unpacked his clothes.

After arranging his clothes in the drawers under the TV set, he opened the minibar, surveyed the contents with satisfaction, and helped himself to a chilled chardonnay.

"Here's to Sam. And Uncle Sam." He pointed his glass at the vista outside his window.

I'll have a quick shower, then a little snooze. I bet the sunsets are gorgeous from this room. Or from down on the beach.

TWENTY

Jick's "little snooze" extended until five o'clock. He awakened, stretched, and glanced out of his hotel window. The sun was a radiant orange orb suspended a few inches above the horizon. On impulse, Jick extended his thumb and forefinger to arm's length and squinted at the sun between his fingers. When it looked like he pinched the sun between his fingertips, he took a picture with his phone. He texted it to Sam, captioned with "beautiful sunset, palm trees, beaches, drinks. Now why am I here again?" He attached a laughing emoji picture and hit the send button.

First day here, I'm going to enjoy the sunset and have dinner on the beach.

He took the elevators to the ground floor and made his way to the beach. As he stepped out onto the beach, he stopped to survey the layout. In front of him, the water's edge was about fifty yards away. Blue and white lounge chairs and cabanas dotted the sand. Crisscrossed tiki torches lined the edge of the area reserved for hotel guests. To his far left, a rock grotto framed one side of a kidney-bean shaped pool. More tiki torches lined the top of the grotto, and a platform for jumping into the pool had been shaped into the rock. He could hear excited squeals from teens jumping into the water, punctuated by the occasional whistle from the lifeguard.

On the right, several cottages artfully hidden among the trees were also part of the resort. Their staggered arrangement preserved a view of the ocean while maintaining privacy. A paved stone path with lava imprints wended its way through the trees, dotted with knee-high pathway lights. The entire area exuded a relaxed ambiance. Jick sighed and headed to a lounge chair.

He found an unoccupied lounge chair close to the water, which was good, but also closest to the pool and the squealing teens, which was not so good. He sprawled on the chair, tipped his hat forward and absorbed the sunset from behind dark glasses.

Absolute paradise.

A woman in beige shorts and a starched white shirt stopped at his cabana. Jick estimated she could be in her late forties. Streaks of gray pushed through her touched-up roots in front. Years of sun exposure had weathered her skin, giving her face a toughened grace. Her name tag had the familiar Hawaiian Orchid logo under a stick-on label that read "Lenore."

"Beautiful evening," she remarked. "Looks like we're going to have a fantastic sunset today."

"Excellent," said Jick. "Not a bad first evening here."

"Welcome to the Aloha State. Can I get you a drink?"

"Since I'm in Hawaii, I'll start with a top-shelf Mai Tai."

"Good choice. The Hawaiian Orchid is known for our great Mai Tais. Best on the island. Do you want to see our happy hour menu? Ends at five-thirty, so you can order for another ten minutes."

"Sure."

She handed him a menu. He ordered coconut shrimp and *furikake* fries. She tapped his key card on a scanner and handed his card back.

"Done," she said. "I'll be right back."

Jick settled back in his chair and gazed at the sun. It had taken on a deeper orange hue as it inched closer to the horizon. A few seagulls swam over the ocean in lazy arcs, their silhouettes etched in sharp focus against the setting sun.

Now that was a picture postcard moment.

From his vantage point on the beach, he could see beyond the rock grotto and down the expanse of the beach. He saw a large canopy tent pitched in the distance. About a half-dozen young men milled around, unfolding chairs, setting up tables, and assembling audio equipment on stands. A generator sat at the edge of the beach where the vegetation began. One man began unfolding tripod legs topped with light fixtures. Two tiki torches flanked the entrance.

Probably a wedding party tonight. How could it not be with this setting?

He stretched and curled his toes, allowing the sand to sift between them.

I could get used to this.

His server returned with his drinks and happy hour snacks.

"Here you go," she said. "One top-shelf Mai Tai and your *pupus*."

"My what?"

"*Pupus*. Hawaiian for snacks, finger foods."

"Ah, got it."

Jick pointed his thumb toward the canopy tent.

"Looks like a wedding party this evening."

"No, that's a private party. There's a rich guy on the island who sometimes throws parties for his friends. They call him Uncle George. This is one of his parties. That's Arcturus Beach; the locals call it Hokule'a Beach, which means 'Our Star of Joy.' It's a public beach, as all beaches are in Hawaii."

Jick turned to look at the preparations.

"So that's one of Uncle George's parties. Maybe I'll drop in. It will be amusing to meet him."

"Do you know him?"

"No," Jick said. "I landed at the airport today and called the wrong number while waiting for my ride. An eccentric guy who called himself Uncle George answered."

"Wow, what a coincidence. Gotta be the same guy. They say he's nice but a little nuts. A few years ago, he was involved in a boating accident. The whole thing was tragic."

"That's what my driver said. What happened?"

"He was out boating with some friends. He had a nice boat, a fifty-footer, sleek, fast." She paused and looked at Jick. "Are you into boats?"

"Uh, no."

"Doesn't matter. But if you want to go on a boat ride when you're here, like maybe a sunset cruise or dinner cruise, my husband runs a boat charter. Full service, catered dinner. Here's his card."

She fished a business card out of her pocket and handed it to Jick.

First an offer for a rideshare, now an offer for a boat charter. Wonder if the hotel knows their staff solicit guests for side business...

As she continued her story, Jick gazed at the sun and let out a contented sigh. The orange sun was almost a dull blood-red, looking like it was half submerged in the waves.

"Oh, sorry, let me finish my Uncle George story. Anyway, so he's out boating with friends and Uncle George is in the water. A bunch of kids are in a smaller boat and come speeding too close to where Uncle George is scuba diving. The boat hits him and knocks him out. He almost drowns, but the others pull him out."

"Did he get badly hurt?"

"Yes, it was bad. They had to medevac him to Honolulu. I heard one of the boat's propellers cut open the top of his head in the front. The doctors saved his life, but they say he was never the same afterwards. In some ways, better. They say he's nicer now and insists everyone call him Uncle George.

"He tried to sue the teen, the boat owner, and I don't know who else for his injuries, but something happened in court, and they dismissed the case. I think they said he went too far from the boat so the kid who hit him wasn't liable. It was all in the news for a while."

"What's his real name?"

"Uncle George's? I don't know. I just know of him as Uncle George.

"Anyway, in a weird twist, a few weeks after Uncle George returned home, the kid who was piloting the boat when it hit him was killed."

"How did that happen?"

"He was stabbed outside a restaurant in Kona. We don't have many murders on the island, so it made the news. And because he was the kid who hurt Uncle George."

"They ever find out who did it?"

"I don't know. I don't think so. That story didn't stay in the news long."

"Didn't they suspect Uncle George? You know, if he was maybe angry enough that he had been hurt by this kid and the kid didn't get punished enough?"

"They probably did. People talk story sometimes. But Uncle George is harmless, you know? He wouldn't have done nothing. Most likely, the kid was into drugs, and something bad went down. There's lots of drug use here."

Jick looked around at the beach, the ocean, and the soft glow of torches.

"Here?"

"You'd be surprised."

She looked over her shoulder at the ocean.

"Oh, I'm sorry! Did I spoil your sunset?"

"No, not at all," Jick assured her with a smile. "I had a great view and watched it while listening to your fascinating story. Besides, I'm here for a few days, and I'm sure there will be plenty more sunsets to enjoy."

He glanced at Uncle George's party.

"Now I feel like I should go over and say 'Hi' to this Uncle George. What a small world."

TWENTY-ONE

The swells lapped over the setting sun as it sank into the ocean. As it disappeared, radiant orange fingers of light streaked through breaks in the clouds. Jick slurped the last of his Mai Tai and downed the last of his pupus.

The nap helped, but I am one tired puppy. I'll just go say 'Hi' to this 'Uncle George' guy and then hit the sack.

Jick walked past the tiki torches and rope stanchions marking the boundary of the Hawaiian Orchid and strolled across the sand to Uncle George's party. As he neared the canopy tent, the first strains of music reached his ears.

Sounds like island music tonight, of course.

He stopped a few yards from the canopy tent and surveyed the guests, trying to guess which was Uncle George. It was obvious.

About a half-dozen round tables flanked the perimeter of the tent on three sides. On the fourth side, speakers stood on pedestals with an open area in the middle for dancing. At one table toward the front sat a man dressed in a white suit. A Panama hat sat in front of him, and a polished wood cane topped with a brass knob leaned against the table edge. His glasses had a slight tint; the flickering reflection of the tiki torches in his glasses gave him an oddly whimsical appearance.

Geez. That's Uncle George? He looks like a cross between the Penguin and Uncle Fester.

A woman who Jick assumed was Uncle George's wife sat to his left; on the right sat a man in a police uniform. Standing a few feet away from Uncle George, leaning against one of the tent supports, was a man-mountain of a

Hawaiian. He looked like he was about six foot one tall and about half as wide. He scanned the arriving guests, arms folded across his chest. His arms sported an intricate pattern of tattooed lines that, from a distance, resembled a row of knife blades lining both arms. His hair hung down to the top of his shoulder and the overall appearance said "bodyguard." His eyes met Jick's for an instant and then moved on.

He looks like he could bench press a Volkswagen.

Jick walked to the tent entrance, where a man stood holding a guest list.

"Name?"

"I'm not an invited guest," Jick said. "I just wanted to say 'Hi' to Uncle George. Is that him?" He pointed at the man in the white suit.

"Yes, but this party is only for invited guests."

Jick smiled.

"Okay. But give him a message from me, if you don't mind. Tell him, 'Maybe you're right, there's no such thing as a wrong number.' Let's see if he gets it."

The man frowned.

"What is this about?"

"Just tell him. Let's see what he says."

The man eyed Jick with suspicion for an instant, then said, "Wait here."

He walked to the table where Uncle George sat and murmured a few words. Uncle George looked up at the man, startled, and then at Jick. He motioned for him to come over. As Jick walked to the table, Uncle George got to his feet with some effort. Jick appraised him as he walked over to where Uncle George stood.

He reaches my chin.

"Jick?"

"In the flesh," Jick gave a slight bow and extended his hand.

"What a small world. I just checked into the Hawaiian Orchid, and here you are, having a party right next to where I sat on the beach."

"You see?" Uncle George burbled with excitement as he grasped Jick's hand. "There's no such thing as a wrong number, is there? We were meant to meet."

He took off his glasses, polished them with a cloth, and placed them on the table. His eyes twinkled at Jick.

"Have a seat." He pointed to the seat to the left of the woman. "Let me get you a drink. What will you have?"

"Oh, nothing. I just came to say 'Hi.' I'm pretty jet lagged, so I'm going to hit the sack."

Jick surveyed his host. Uncle George stood about five-four, with no hair on his face or head, except for his eyebrows, piercing dark eyes, and the most prominent feature, a scar on his head. The shape and contour of the scar intrigued Jick.

That transverse scar looks like he had a craniotomy for a right frontal lobectomy. Probably where the propeller hit. The surgeon did a good job. I figured his head would look like he'd been fed into a meat grinder. The little scar looks like he probably has a VP shunt.

"Sit, sit. Most of the guests aren't here yet anyway."

He motioned at the woman on his left.

"This is my wife, who is Sherryl."

Odd way to put it. Maybe it's his brain injury.

Sherryl was a woman in her sixties, perfectly coiffed reddish hair with gray roots, a pale complexion with watery blue eyes. Her skin bore evidence of her many years of living in the sun, although it appeared she had had some cosmetic work done in years past. She held her hand out to Jick, who clasped the tips of her fingers in a gentle handshake.

"Pleased to meet you," she said.

"Likewise." Jick dipped his head in a slight bow.

"And this," Uncle George motioned at the man in the police uniform. "This is Chief Kalani Williams, Hawaii County chief of police. I contribute to the various law enforcement charities, so Chief Williams makes it a point to come to my parties."

Jick leaned forward and waved to the police chief.

"So, my wrong number friend, what brings you to Hawaii?" Uncle George queried.

"Just a brief vacation. I've been in Dallas for a while, and it seemed like a good time for a break from the hustle and bustle of the big city. Oh, good observation on the Texas connection."

"What do you do?"

Jick thought his tone was a little direct.

He's used to being obeyed. And I bet no one says 'no' to him.

"I'm a medical consultant. I help young doctors set up offices."

"That's great, great. I hope you're here on an assignment because we could sure use more doctors here on the Big Island."

"No, sorry, this trip is just for pleasure."

"You should have a drink, just to help you unwind from your long trip."

He waved the bartender over and then looked inquiringly at Jick.

I guess he won't take no for an answer.

"A glass of red wine."

The bartender listed the choices, and Jick chose a Cabernet Sauvignon. The bartender nodded and walked back to the bar. Jick looked at the menacing man leaning against the tent pole.

"What's that guy's name? Oddjob?"

Uncle George looked at Jick in astonishment, and his face broke out in a smile. His face turned red as he tried to suppress a laugh. Jick saw tears at the corners of Uncle George's eyes as his stomach heaved and twitched. Then he could not hold in his laughter, and Uncle George broke out in an explosive laugh.

Sherryl looked a little vexed. Jick frowned.

It wasn't that funny.

"Are you okay?" Jick asked.

"He's fine," Sherryl said. "He does that sometimes. Started after an accident he was involved in."

The giggling continued, and Uncle George's face contorted as he tried to suppress his laughter. Then his body convulsed as he dissolved in tears, sobbing into his napkin. After a few moments, he stopped.

"Yes, I'm fine," he sputtered. He dabbed his eyes with a napkin. He folded the napkin against his nose and honked into it as he cleared his sinuses. One of the staff brought a new napkin and discreetly removed the soiled one.

"Sometimes I can't help it," he said. "The tears, the laughter. It just happens. But that was funny."

"My comment about Oddjob?"

"I love the James Bond reference!" Uncle George exclaimed. "At your young age, I'm glad your generation enjoys the old Bond classics.

"And yes, his name could be Oddjob," he said, as another giggle burst out. "But it's not. That's Thaddeus. He's our hanai son."

He motioned Thaddeus over to the table.

"Hey, Thaddeus," Uncle George said. "Did anyone ever call you Oddjob?"

He giggled again.

Thaddeus stared at Uncle George and Jick.

"No, Uncle George."

Thaddeus returned to his position by the tent support.

"Like Oddjob, Thaddeus is my bodyguard. And all-purpose assistant. And hanai son."

"I am not familiar with that word. Did you say 'hanai' son?"

"It's an old Hawaiian custom. A family informally adopts a child from another family. Usually because the adopting family has better financial or other resources."

"So, he's not legally adopted?"

"Not in the Western sense. But in the Hawaiian sense, yes."

"Did you adopt him as a child?"

"It doesn't matter. He's my hanai son now."

Jick glanced at Thaddeus again.

"He's Podagee," Uncle George offered.

"Another word I'm not familiar with."

"You know, Podagee. His family is from Portugal. De Silva."

"Oh, you mean *Portuguese*."

"What I said. Podagee."

Jick saw him turning red-faced as another giggle was about to burst out. Uncle George was able to suppress it by blowing his nose. He dabbed his eyes and folded his napkin.

There is something wrong with this guy. Now I'm curious about that head injury.

"George wasn't like this until his accident," Sherryl said, mentioning the accident again.

"What happened?" Jick asked.

"He was in the ocean swimming, and a careless person recklessly operating a boat ran into him." Sherryl turned to her husband with a look of sympathy.

Sherryl spent the next ten minutes extolling the virtues of her husband and all his accomplishments. Jick paid half-hearted attention.

Looks like Uncle George calls the shots in their marriage...

Uncle George looked at an arriving guest over Jick's shoulder.

"It's David," he said. "And Sherwin's with him."

"David, over here," he beckoned.

A white-haired man, mid-sixties, walked over to them, favoring his right leg. A young black man, who appeared to be in his twenties, accompanied him.

"David, this is Jick. He's a medical consultant. You're a science guy. You guys should have a lot in common. Have a seat."

It sounds like a command, not a request.

David sat at the table. The young black man sat next to him. Jick thought David looked a little uncomfortable. He reached over to Jick for a perfunctory handshake, avoiding eye contact.

"Hi, Jick," he mumbled.

Jick shook his hand, keeping his gaze on him. After a momentary glance at Jick, he focused on the flower arrangement on the table.

Wonder what's bugging the guy.

Jick tried to break the ice.

"Science guy?" he inquired.

"I'm a biologist and biophysicist," David replied. "I mostly crunch numbers on a computer now."

"Do you do research?"

"No, not anymore. I used to." He offered no details.

"I live in California. I'm just here for a few months helping Uncle George with a project."

He nodded toward the young man who had arrived with him.

"Oh, this is Sherwin," he said. "He's my assistant."

Jick looked at Sherwin. He saw a slender young man with an already receding hairline. Sherwin blinked rapidly, like someone not used to wearing contact lenses. Jick noticed marks on either side of his nose from years of pushing glasses up his nose. A crucifix hung around his neck on a silver chain. He looked just like what Jick would have imagined a lab assistant should be. Jick reached out and shook his hand.

"Pleased to meet you."

Looks like he just started wearing contacts. Wonder what kind of project they're working on.

"What kind of project are you guys working on?" Jick asked.

David looked at Jick for a moment before looking away.

"Plant biology. We're trying to grow more efficient plants."

"Oh, I'm a medical consultant. That's human biology," Jick said. "I guess we don't have that much in common."

After a few more minutes of forced conversation, David excused himself. He and Sherwin went to mingle with other guests and then settled at another table.

"Looks like Pavel's done with paddle-boarding," Uncle George remarked as he stared at the ocean.

Under the dimming light, Jick saw a man pull his paddleboard onto shore. He trudged through the sand; one of the staff handed him a robe as he ducked under the canopy.

"Hi, Pavel," said Uncle George. "Have a seat."

Jick noted a tall, well-built man, probably early fifties, with short-cropped blond hair and blue eyes that flickered in the light from the tiki torches, lending his eyes a tiger's eye appearance.

And speaking of Bond villains...

"Pavel, this is Jick. Jick, this is Pavel."

As they shook hands, Uncle George patted the man on his back.

"Pavel is another assistant," Uncle George said.

"Pleased to meet you," Pavel said. It came out "plissd to mitt you."

"Likewise," Jick said.

Sounds Eastern European. Russian? Pavel's a Russian name.

Jick surveyed the party trappings and turned to Uncle George.

"What do you, or did you, do before?"

"I was a businessman, real estate tycoon, and entrepreneur," Uncle George threw his arms out in an expansive wave of his hands, like he was about to embrace the world.

"Impressive," Jick said. "I guess you're retired, so you can enjoy the company of your friends with parties?"

"You said it," Uncle George said.

"I live in the biggest and most expensive house on the Big Island. Not that I'm trying to impress you."

What a narcissist. A legend in his own mind. I guess with his brain injury, especially in his frontal lobe, he probably has some issues with filters.

"But it's far away, up north on the island," Uncle George continued. "It's easier to host parties closer to Kona. And it's better on the beach, don't you think?"

"Yes, definitely," Jick said. "But thanks for letting me intrude on your hospitality. And thanks for the wine. I just stopped by to say 'Hi' and I've had a long flight. I think I'll head back to the hotel."

"You're welcome to stay as long as you want. It's nice to make new friends."

"I really should get going."

"Sure, pardner," Uncle George grinned with his fake accent. "Nice meetin' yuh."

As Jick rose from the table, he glanced at the man mountain again. Once again, their eyes locked for an instant.

"That's Thaddeus," Uncle George said. "He takes care of me."

He already told me that.

"'Bye, Thaddeus," Jick said, waving at the big man.

Thaddeus glanced at Jick for an instant and looked away. No response.

Interesting evening with some colorful characters. Haven't even been here a day yet.

TWENTY-TWO

The next morning, Jick sprawled in a cabana, savoring his first day in Hawaii. He was still on mainland time and had awakened at four. Having nothing to do until the restaurant opened, he had set up his laptop on the hotel's Wi-Fi and installed the virtual network from instructions Quin had provided him.

The sun rose behind him, painting the beach in streaks of bright light as it shone through the palm fronds. By eight o'clock, the waves sparkled, and the first gaggle of resort guests made their way to the beachside bar and grill for breakfast. Jick sighed with contentment as he speared a piece of Portuguese sausage.

Delicious. I don't remember eating this last time I was here.

After finishing his breakfast, he leaned back, clasping his hands behind his head.

Should I do it? Mimosa? Bloody Mary?

He eyed his empty coffee cup.

Or more coffee?

The Bloody Mary beat the other contenders. He signaled for one and leaned back, surveying the other beachgoers, the stand-up paddleboarders, and a couple of distant yachts anchored offshore. When the Bloody Mary arrived, a reddish powder adorned the rim. The server noted his inquiring glance.

"Hawaiian Bloody Mary," he said with a smile.

"What's the powder? Not salt," Jick observed.

"*Li Hing Mui*," his server said. "Local Hawaiian dried fruit, powdered. It's both salty and sour. Goes great on a margarita or Bloody Mary."

Jick took a lick of the rim.

"Nice flavor," he remarked. "I could get used to this."

He swirled the drink with the celery stick and took a sip.

Ohhh, that's good.

Eight-thirty rolled around, and Jick eyed his empty Bloody Mary glass.

"Another?" His server appeared at Jick's elbow.

Jick resisted the impulse. He rolled off the chaise and stood.

"No, maybe tomorrow. But it was great."

He signed the bill and made his way to the elevator.

Time to get to work. Been awake almost five hours.

He went back to his room and pulled up a chair at the desk. He booted up his laptop with the thumb drive Sam had given him protruding from its side. Jick perused the first batch of its contents. As he read through the files, a clearer picture of the events of eight months ago formed in his mind.

Alicia Rogers had checked into the Hawaiian Orchid, and for the first three days, she had driven around Kawaihae, North Kohala, and had traversed the Kohala Mountain Road loop. Multiple pages of cell phone records mapped her travels as she crossed cell boundaries. Between the cell phone records and GPS tracking, Jick had a reasonable idea where she had gone. On day three, she stopped in Kawaihae for two hours.

Kawaihae's not a big town. Wonder what she did there for two hours.

On day four, her phone pinged from a scenic lookout on the mountain road where she had spent some fifteen minutes. She had stopped at the scenic lookout once before, when she had traversed the Kohala Mountain Road. Then nothing.

Wonder why she stopped there twice.

The thumb drive contained several other files that were locked out by password access.

Those must be files with personal information about the subject. I shouldn't need those for now.

On the day she disappeared, she had parked her car on the Akoni Pule Highway, which led from Kawaihae to North Kohala, in a parking lot next to a trail that led to the coastline. None of her belongings were in the car. Cell reception must have been poor in this area, as there were no pings from the lot where she had left her car. The pings resumed after she had made her way further north and looped through Hawi. There were no pings anywhere else on the island.

It doesn't look like she drove around the entire island, just the north loop. I'll focus on that scenic lookout, Kawaihae, and the lot where she left her car. This shouldn't take too long.

Jick spread a large map of the Big Island on the bed next to him. He leaned over and drew an "X" where they had discovered Alicia's car. Then he drew an "X" over the scenic lookout and over Kawaihae. The three "X"'s formed a triangle. He leaned back and surveyed the entire island. The line connecting the scenic lookout where her phone last pinged to the spot where her car was found traced a line through a wooded section of the Big Island, an incongruous patch of verdant forest on the otherwise drier side of the island.

"It's that green area I saw from the plane. Must be a microclimate area," Jick mused. "Everything around that area is dry as a bone. I wonder if Alicia tried to survey that from above and below."

He loaded a contour map of the area. The microclimate forest looked like a series of natural terraces with a valley that formed a gentle slope down the side of the mountain.

Maybe that somehow allows precipitation to get trapped. Or maybe incoming ocean breezes funnel into that valley and condense into clouds carrying rain.

A few widely spaced houses dotted the forest along the lower elevations. All were on the left side of the valley, the north side. The upper elevations and the right side of the valley, the south side, were labeled "Wao Kele Nature Reserve." The scenic viewpoint where Alicia stopped twice was above the upper elevations of the reserve.

Three-fourths of that lush area is a nature reserve. The rest looks like about a half-dozen lots. Bet it's a pricey subdivision. Maybe I'll check out the nature reserve. Looks like a nice place for a hike.

He clicked open a file marked "Receipts." It contained credit card records of transactions from Alicia's credit card. On the day she went missing, she had stopped at a bar and grill in Waimea for lunch. He studied the phone data and noted that she had been in Waimea for about an hour.

Might be a suitable spot to ask questions.

He folded the map, gathered his laptop, and made his way to the concierge desk.

"Your vehicle is here," the concierge said.

After a quick signature on the rental agreement, the concierge handed him the keys and pointed to where his car was parked. He noted with satisfaction that it was a hardtop silver Jeep.

But the last time I drove around in a Jeep looking for a missing woman, it didn't go so well...

He set off in the Jeep, turning left as he exited the resort. The highway headed north through dry scrubland, with the black lava slowly changing to an earthy, weathered red. The vegetation was dry and scraggly, with few trees. He was surprised to see a herd of goats perched on rocks alongside the road. Some grazed on the highway shoulder, unfazed by the speeding cars.

He arrived at a T-junction and took the right turn, heading toward Waimea. He noted a distinct change in vegetation with the rapid change in elevation, with desert-like scrub and desert cacti disappearing in favor of grass and pastureland.

Wow, desert cactus in Hawaii... who knew?

As he headed into Waimea, his ears popped as he passed the two-thousand-foot elevation sign. Soon, the pastureland gave way to trees and flowers.

This is amazing. Going from cactus to grazing pastureland to trees in just a few miles...

As he reached the outskirts of Waimea, he spotted the left turn onto the mountain road. He had ascended almost twenty-five hundred feet in a short ten miles. As he ascended toward the nature reserve, a mist rolled off the top of the surrounding hills and descended on the road. Intermittent patches of fog painted a layer of moisture on his windshield. He swallowed to relieve the pressure change, marveling at the rapid change in temperature.

This is quite something. Thirty minutes ago, I was lying on the beach enjoying a Bloody Mary...

He reached the scenic viewpoint and pulled into a parking area wide enough to accommodate a half-dozen cars. On this blustery morning, only a few cars had pulled onto the shoulder next to the "Scenic Viewpoint" sign. Jick felt his Jeep being buffeted by the stiff breeze as the wind whistled around the crevices in the door frame. He glanced at the outside temperature gauge.

Sixty?! Sheesh. It was eighty at the resort!

He pushed the door open against the wind, regretting not having brought something long-sleeved to wear. The fog had lifted, but a faint misty drizzle made conditions worse.

He saw a sign with "Wao Kele Nature Reserve" next to a dirt road that meandered down the hillside. A sign describing the scenic viewpoint flapped against a wooden post. The scenic viewpoint was on Kohala Mountain, one of the five volcanoes that formed the Big Island. On a clear day, the other four volcanoes were visible from this spot.

Not today.

Jick moved to the edge of the scenic viewpoint, braced a pair of binoculars against a rock, and scanned the nature reserve. From his vantage point, he could make out little other than a large patch of forest that disappeared down the hillside to the lower highway. Further down the slope and closer to the lower highway, he could make out patches where the forest had been tamed into landscaping. He could not see any houses from his position. A stiff gust fluttered his shirt, and he shivered. His view through the binoculars deteriorated in seconds as the mist coated the lenses.

This is hopeless. No hike today. Freaking colder than I thought it would be in Hawaii! Feels way colder than sixty. And the wind!

Jick climbed back into the Jeep. He turned the heater on at full blast for a few minutes and rubbed his hands together in the warm air. The nature reserve sign looked like it was about to detach from the post.

Wonder what Alicia did up here. Maybe I'll come back when it's sunnier.

A red and white hat blew across the front of his car, and he spotted a woman in hot pursuit. He glanced to his left and saw a man struggling with the convertible top of a Ford Mustang. The woman stomped on the hat and then tucked it under her arm as she struggled back to her car. As she and her companion struggled with the convertible roof, the wind whipped her skirt into an immodest position. The woman let out a shriek as she pulled the skirt down with one hand while struggling with the roof. The couple eventually latched the roof shut and tumbled into the car. Jick chuckled and shook his head.

Tourists.

He made a note of the nature reserve's hours and then set off on the mountain road back to Waimea.

I'll check out the other end of the nature reserve from the lower highway. Should be warmer down there, anyway...

He drove back to Waimea to visit the bar and grill Alicia had stopped at for lunch. He pulled into the parking lot and eyed the amusing restaurant. It looked like a local hangout called "Uncle Waldo's Lanai" and a local brewery called The Big Isle Brewski had joined forces. The single building looked like two buildings fused together. The left side was colorful in a garish way, with faux thatched Hawaiian-themed décor. All the neon beer signs in the window were of the brewery that formed the right half of the building.

Jick went into the restaurant side since Alicia had had lunch there.

Too early for lunch.

The greeter at the door asked him if he wanted a table for one.

"Uh, no," Jick said. "I wanted to see if the manager was available for a quick minute."

"Sure, hang on a second," the young woman said. "Let me see if Waldo is available."

There's an actual Uncle Waldo?

A jovial man in his mid-fifties pushed through the swinging door to the kitchen. He wore a Hawaiian-themed apron with two dolphins that appeared distorted from being stretched over his protuberant abdomen. He wiped his hands on his apron as he approached Jick.

"Aloha, what can I do for you? I won't shake hands; my hands are greasy."

Jick noticed a hint of an accent.

"Oh, no problem. I had a quick question. You see many people here, so you may not be able to help me. I'm looking for a missing person. She ate here about eight months ago. I was hoping something might have happened during her visit here that stands out."

Jick showed the manager the picture of Alicia. Uncle Waldo studied it and shook his head.

"No, sorry," he said. "She looks like any of several customers we get here daily."

"That's what I figured," Jick said. "Are you from around here?"

"Midwest. Wisconsin." It came out *Wis-cahn-sin*.

"But been here twenty years. Still a cheesehead."

Jick smiled.

"I could tell you were from somewhere in the Midwest. Well, thanks. If you don't mind, I'll just show this to the bartender and whoever's out here. Maybe I'll get lucky."

"Sure, go ahead."

Neither the bartender nor the greeter recognized the photo. Jick pushed the door open and stood in the parking lot, admiring the swirling mists that rolled over the hilltop on Waimea's northern side. He climbed back into his Jeep.

This is not going to work. No one will remember her after this long.

TWENTY-THREE

Jick left Waimea and drove back toward Kawaihae, once again marveling at the rapid transition from verdant pastureland to dry desert in just a few miles. Instead of heading back to the resort, he carried on into Kawaihae and then turned right to head to North Kohala. After a few miles, he saw a road that turned toward the lush area on the right.

This is the only major road to the microclimate forest, so this must be it.

He turned right and headed up the mountain. He found himself in a valley with a seasonal stream running along the right side of the road. The base of the valley appeared to be in perpetual dampness. He noted a slow trickle of water, and patches of moss adorned most of the rocks on either side of the stream. The right flank of the valley was steeper and narrower than the left. On the left, the valley was flatter with several natural terraces suitable as building sites. As he meandered his way up the road, he encountered an occasional driveway on the left. He stopped at each gate to get a quick glimpse of the house, but nothing was visible from the road. All the lots featured well-manicured lawns and immaculate landscaping around curved driveways.

Very private. I can't see any signs of the houses.

Jick stopped and got out of his car for a quick survey of the area.

Not only do they have a fantastic ocean view, but they also have a splendid view of the rainforest.

Although the left side of the valley was not as steep, it was wider, and the terraces afforded an excellent ocean

view. Compared to the manicured left side, the lush
vegetation on the right side of the valley looked like an
untamed forest.

A high-pitched whine interrupted his thoughts, and he
felt a sting on his left cheek. He swatted at a mosquito in
vain as he jumped back into his Jeep.

I guess the mosquitoes like it down here too.

As he drove higher up the nature reserve, the trees were
shorter, and he noticed more sunlight filtering through the
trees.

*Probably fewer mosquitoes at the higher elevation.
This is amazing. Hard to believe just a few miles back, it's
desert. And about a mile up the hillside, it's rainy and foggy.*

He made a mental note of six properties that lay along
the left side of the valley. The last driveway came off at the
top, where the road widened into a cul-de-sac. The ornate
gate on the left graced a stamped concrete driveway with a
central cobblestone pattern reminiscent of old Europe.
Flanking the cobblestone pattern was a border, also of
stamped concrete, with a swirly Hawaiian lava pattern. A
plaque with brass numerals was affixed to the stone
gatepost.

*These people have the best house. Or at least, the best
gate and driveway.*

On the right, a dirt road meandered up the hill. As Jick
turned onto the dirt road, he noticed a sign pointing to a
hiking trail.

*This must be the bottom of the nature reserve. I should
have come here first.*

He drove up the dirt road. Within fifty yards, the road
ended in a dirt parking lot. He spotted a wooden sign in the
shape of an arrow affixed to a tree, pointing to a trail that
disappeared up the hillside. He parked under a tree and
climbed out. A faint rustle high in the trees betrayed the
wind but at ground level, the air was almost still. He noted
with satisfaction that the temperature was seventy-two.

*Now that's what I'm talking about. It is nice here on the
leeward side.*

Jick grabbed his binoculars and water bottle. He set off along the trail, which meandered into the nature reserve and up the right side of the valley. After about a quarter-mile of mostly gentle uphill hiking, during which he met no one else on the trail, he came to a natural clearing. A wooden bench, looking the worse for its years of sun exposure, sat along the edge of the clearing. He perched on the bench and gazed at the ocean, admiring the view. He paused, took a swig of water, and surveyed the terrain. The trail continued further up the hill.

Probably continues back up the hill to the main entrance.

The view was spectacular. The Pacific Ocean shimmered in the midday sun as a few lazy clouds drifted by. Toward the northern part of the island, which Jick had read was the windier tip, high clouds skittered toward the west, painting a white swath across Maui.

Wow, this is beautiful. I best most tourists don't make it this far down. And it seems like no one uses this trail.

He took another swig and then peered through his binoculars. He was still on the left side of the valley, but at this elevation, both sides of the valley had merged into a shallow pan. The cleft through which the seasonal stream ran was smaller and difficult to spot as it had curved away from the developed side of the valley. From his vantage point, he could see five of the six properties. The lowest property, closest to the road below, was not visible.

The house closest to him, the only property on the cul-de-sac, seemed to be the most opulent.

Looks like a Greek-inspired design.

He noted the house was on a shallow bluff with a semicircular lanai, or patio, downstairs and a matching veranda upstairs, both of which promised spectacular ocean views. He noted several pillars along the left side and what looked like an open, or partly open, central courtyard. A plush green carpet of lawn stretched toward the ocean. An infinity pool sat on the side closest to the road.

I bet the view of the ocean from the pool is quite something...

On the *mauka,* or away from the ocean, side of the house, a curved driveway led to a T-junction. The left fork swept through a porte cochere and looped back to the driveway. The right fork led to another building, most likely the garage. A covered breezeway lined with a dense hedge led from the house to the garage. Behind the garage was a storage shed built against the bluff.

Some serious money there...

He trained his binoculars on the other houses. They were smaller than the house on the cul-de-sac but boasted the same meticulous landscaping. There were no signs of activity from any of the houses.

As he lowered his binoculars, a movement caught his eye. At the base of the valley, two vehicles had turned onto the road. The first was a white delivery truck, followed by a Ford Mustang convertible.

I bet it's tourists in the Mustang.

He wondered if it was the same couple who had lost their hat.

Maybe they had the same idea I did.

The truck disappeared around the curves in the road. After a few minutes, Jick noted it had made its way to the top of the cul-de-sac as it appeared on the driveway of the house. At the T-junction, it turned to the right and stopped in front of the garage. Now he had a clear profile view of the truck. It was a standard sixteen-foot box truck, white with no other markings. There were no DOT numbers on the passenger door. A faint beeping echoed up the valley walls as the truck turned around and backed close to the garage. There were no markings on the driver's side either.

The convertible was nowhere to be seen.

Two men jumped out of the cab and went to the back of the truck. Two men came out of the garage as the driver rolled up the cargo door of the truck. Jick caught a glimpse of white hair and a red baseball cap from the men in the garage. Jick watched as one of the men extended the loading ramp. He saw a large box emerge from the back of the truck, guided by one of the men.

Looks like a coffin on steroids...

The container was about seven feet long and four by four feet square. As the container rolled down the ramp, Jick noticed a logo painted on the side of the container. The men rolled the container into the garage and acknowledged delivery with a signature. Jick watched the delivery men climb back into the truck and leave.

Jick watched the proceedings with mild interest. As he leaned back on the bench, he frowned. The logo on the container looked familiar, but he could not place where he had seen it before.

That wasn't a grand piano. Maybe a sideboard for their dining room...

The white-haired man in the red cap walked into the main house. Jick finished his survey.

As he was getting ready to leave, Jick heard voices, and a man and a woman appeared. They were dressed like tourists and carried a small backpack. Jick noticed the familiar red and white hat on the woman's head.

"Hi," he said. "Looks like you discovered the lower entrance to the reserve too."

"Good day," the man said. "Were you up there at the main entrance?"

His "Good day" sounded like "Good Eye."

He sounds Australian. Hope he knows how to drive on the right side of the road...

"Yes."

"It was bloody cold up there. I'm surprised more people don't check out this end of the reserve."

"I know, right?" Jick said. "I was up there and almost froze my butt off."

"And I almost lost my hat," the woman said.

"I noticed you chasing after it up there," Jick grinned.

"Yes, good thing it didn't blow over the edge. This end of the reserve is much nicer. And calmer. On a clear day without wind, I bet it's beautiful up there, though."

The couple took a swig of water from their backpacks, exchanged a few more pleasantries, and set off on the trail.

Jick loped down the trail back to his Jeep. It was well past lunchtime, so he stopped at a restaurant in Kawaihae for a delicious seafood lunch washed down with a couple of Mai Tais.

After lunch, he planned to do a little exploring around Kawaihae to familiarize himself with the layout and try to understand why Alicia would have spent two hours here.

It did not take long, not even half an hour. Other than an industrial harbor and port, and a main street with a handful of restaurants and shops, there was not much else. Jick cruised around some of the residential areas, but nothing stood out. He debated making inquiries at some shops in the area but decided against it.

She was here once, for two hours, eight months ago. Maybe she just had a long lunch.

Those were good Mai Tais...

He finished his survey of Kawaihae and headed back to his resort.

"Enough work for the morning. Let's see what else is on Alicia's thumb drive."

TWENTY-FOUR

Jick helped himself to a bottle of chilled Chardonnay from the minibar in his room and sat at the desk.

A Bloody Mary for breakfast, two Mai Tais at lunch, and now wine. Oh, what the heck, I'm on a working vacation... time to call Sam for a quick update.

He did a quick calculation in his head. Five hours ahead meant it was about eight o'clock.

Hope little Vic's in bed...

Sam answered on the second ring.

"Jick!" she exclaimed. "How's things? You've been there a couple of days. Hope you're having fun. I guess you haven't made any progress in the search, but that's not a big deal. Like you said, it's a bit of a wild goose chase, anyway. Alicia has been missing for eight months."

"I'm doing great. I read over your notes and mapped out where she went on her last day from cell phone records. No leads yet.

"On her last day, she went from a scenic lookout on a mountain road to a spot on a lower highway. Those two spots are just a few miles but a couple of thousand feet apart in elevation change. There's a microclimate that looks almost like a rain forest even though it's on the dry side of the island. Looks like a big green splash against a khaki-colored background. There's a few high-end homes in the area at the lower elevation, up to about fifteen hundred feet, on the left side of the valley. From there to the scenic lookout, which is about three thousand feet in elevation, it's all nature reserve."

"Doesn't sound like there's much to go on."

"I did a quick hike and scanned the houses there. Nothing much to see. I stopped off at a restaurant where she had lunch, but the staff there didn't remember her. Not surprising after all this time.

"Tomorrow I'll hike down the dry side from where they found her car, down to the ocean. I don't think there are any trails as such, but maybe I'll spot something. If that's a dead end too, I don't know what else to do. I guess I could look at those case files, but I don't think I'll have a flash of insight that the cops haven't already checked out."

"Just do your best. I'll feel better we left no stone unturned looking for Alicia."

"Will do. Hey, how's little Vic doing?"

"He's a handful, but he's a great handful. I can't imagine life without him, Jick."

"Me too. He's a great kid."

"I wish Vikram could have been here with us, Jick. I look at little Vic sometimes, and he's such a clone of Vic it's uncanny. He looks like Vic with a splash of cream. Know what I mean? I was just the incubator to grow the little booger."

Two years later, Jick still felt a lump in his throat.

"Yeah, Sam, you and me both. I wish he could have seen little Vic."

After a few more minutes of chitchat, Sam said goodnight to Jick.

The next morning, Jick repeated the routine from the previous day. He loaded his Jeep with his water bottle, binoculars, and snacks. Expecting a much hotter day since this hike was toward the ocean along the drier and rockier side of the highway, he packed extra water in a small backpack.

He drove past the turnoff to the Wao Kele reserve and the neighborhood he had surveyed the day before. A mile further, he arrived at the spot where Alicia's car had been found. A paved parking lot with six parking spaces adjoined the highway on the ocean side. He spotted a sign marked

"Scenic Overlook" attached to a short, black chain-link fence. Jick saw a blue and white sign with "Shoreline" and "Public Access." A gravel trail sloped toward the ocean.

Jick parked his Jeep and climbed out. He tightened his chinstrap as he surveyed the *makai,* or toward the ocean, side of the highway. He turned and looked uphill toward the nature reserve. The line demarcating the border of the nature reserve and the drier terrain was visible. He could barely make out the two lowest houses. He turned back and surveyed downhill toward the ocean.

"Let's see if Alicia wandered down here," he said to himself.

He set off toward the ocean. He passed a few scattered houses, but none looked suspicious. Half an hour later, he had completed the half-mile trek from the highway to the cliff edge. The going was arduous; he stumbled and skinned his right knee against a small outcrop of *aa*, the rough-textured lava that he had clambered over.

I can't imagine Alicia coming down here.

He lay on his belly and peered over the edge, wincing as his skinned knee brushed against the ground. Some twenty feet below him, waves crashed against rocks as they eroded the shoreline, pounding the rocks with the patient persistence of millennia. Every half-dozen waves, a larger wave would crash onto the rocks. The water was clear, and he could see small flecks of yellow as fish darted around the submerged rocks. Small black crabs darted toward the water and then skittered back under the larger waves. The hypnotic, soft cadence of the waves reeled him in for a few minutes and he lay still, eyes closed. Then he stood and perched on the edge of a rock shelf as he poured some water on his knee.

He noticed an opening between the rocks that looked like a trail that led further north along the coast. Setting off along the trail, he clambered over rocks for a hundred yards until it petered out among rocks. He spotted the ruins of an ancient Hawaiian village in the distance and decided he would do a quick survey. As he entered the ruins, he realized he had entered a back entrance of a state historical park. He could see a few cars parked uphill.

He walked around among the ruins for about thirty minutes, exploring each building for any signs suggesting Alicia's presence.

Conceivably, she could have come here. Interesting place.

The village sat on a shallow bluff that was almost at sea level. He walked to a rectangular stone structure built along the water's edge.

Bet they stored their outriggers here. Easy to launch from this spot.

He took a few swigs of water as he surveyed the ruins and mulled questions in his head.

Could she have come here? Why would she? And if she did, did she have an accident? Foul play?

The warm ocean breeze whipped around the village. One building had the remnants of a tattered thatched roof, bleached from years of sun exposure. A few pieces of straw detached from the building and swirled upward in a cloud. He peered inside the building. Other than a few heavy stones that formed a circle in the middle of the room, there was nothing else. He scraped the dirt in the circle with his foot.

Probably used for a small fire.

A pair of beady eyes peered at him from behind a rock. Then, in a moment of panic, a black and white blur darted out from behind the rock and streaked away.

Feral cat. This is hopeless. If she made it down here, there's no way to know.

He trekked uphill to the parking lot. A faded sign read "Visitors Center" but it was closed. He peered in through the window. It looked like the visitor's center was closed for good. A bulletin board held a few faded posters about the history of the village. The public restrooms were also padlocked, but three portable toilets were in the corner of the parking lot.

Looks like this place lost its plumbing and electricity.

He placed his hands on his hips and surveyed the landscape. There was nothing to suggest any connection to Alicia's disappearance.

Looks like this wild goose chase is staggering to its conclusion.

He started the trek back to his Jeep.

As he approached the highway, the nature reserve came into view. He stopped for a water break under an *ōhi'a* tree. He dragged his sleeve across his mouth and dropped the bottle into his backpack.

He glanced at his cellphone. No signal.

Wonder why Alicia was here. There's nothing here except the nature reserve and those few houses.

He reached the Jeep and climbed in, tossing his backpack on the back seat. He turned the engine on and aimed the cool blast from the air conditioner at his face.

Amazing how hot it is here and how cold it was at the lookout.

He mulled over his next step. Six months ago, Alicia had parked her car at this very spot and then disappeared. With nothing to investigate on either side of the highway, he wondered if she had been kidnapped from this spot.

If she was kidnapped, not much I can do. She'll just join the legion of missing persons who are never found. But, we are on an island. No way to get her off the island easily.

As he ratcheted the Jeep into drive to head back to the hotel, a thought struck him.

Crap. Forgot to look at Alicia's thumb drive. Got distracted by talking to Sam and by the booze...

TWENTY-FIVE

Back in his hotel room, Jick flipped his laptop open and loaded the next set of files on Alicia's thumb drive. He grabbed a bottle of a random white wine from the minibar, unscrewed the top, and settled at his desk. Within a minute, his laptop connected to the hotel's Wi-Fi.

Let's see why Alicia was so interested in the nature reserve. Maybe I'll start with county tax records.

After a brief search, he discovered the Hawaii County property tax website and used the map search feature to zoom in on the neighborhood below the Wao Kele nature reserve. The county website had some details of each property, including owner info, tax history, appraised values, and history of previous permits. He jotted the names and tax identification numbers on a piece of paper.

Next, he focused on the area he had just explored, near where her car was found. There were ten houses scattered on lots on a bluff overlooking the ocean. The Hawaiian village he had explored was further up the coast.

I doubt these properties are important. Maybe I'll investigate these later if I need to.

He emailed the information on the six lots next to the nature reserve to Sam and then called her.

"Aloha, Sam. Got a minute?"

"Aloha, huh? Sounds like you're enjoying Hawaii life." Jick heard her chuckle. "Sure, what's up?"

"Not much, just a quick update. I drove around Kawaihae, went up to the scenic lookout Alicia went to, and to the spot on the highway where her car was. Nothing. Just an old Hawaiian village that's now a state park. A few tourists, and that's it. I even asked the guy at the restaurant in Waimea where she ate. Nothing. I wasn't sure what to do next, so right now, I'm looking at the county website for info on the properties below the nature reserve. There are only six properties, and they're all on huge twenty-acre parcels.

"I just emailed you a list of those six houses. There's not much else to go on. Want to do a quick search on the owners and call me back?"

"Think these properties are important?"

"I don't know. I have nothing else to go on. She spent some time at a scenic overlook above these lots, and her car was in a lot below these lots. Maybe there's a connection."

"Okay, hang on a few minutes."

Time for another vino. Pinot this time?

Half an hour later, Sam called.

"Jick, we need to talk. One of the houses in that neighborhood near where Alicia's car was found is owned by an entity called 'Sturgis Trust.' Sturgis is the name of the guy we asked Alicia to investigate."

Jick whistled.

"That is interesting. Looks like she was already surveilling your person of interest. Which house was it?"

"Hang on a second. Let me look at a plat map.

"Looks like a house that comes off the cul-de-sac at the top."

"Oh, that one. Yeah, that house is the biggest in the neighborhood. The lot backs up to a shallow bluff. It's shaped like a shelf with what must be the best ocean views. It is also the most private location. On the other side of that house, it looks like all forest."

"Yes. She hadn't filed a report, so we didn't know what she had been up to when she disappeared. Besides, we didn't suspect anything criminal per se going on with this guy. This was mostly supposed to be a scouting and checking-up kind of investigation."

"You think the investigation and her disappearance could be connected?" Jick asked.

"It's possible. What did she do down there by the highway that could be related to the investigation?"

"Maybe it's time to fill me in on more details."

"Yes, let's do a video call. I'll loop Quin in, too. After we go over everything, you can decide if you want to investigate this or not. I don't want to risk losing you too, especially if this turns out to be something bigger."

"All right. But now I'm interested. And you know me, I always try to anticipate what could happen and plan for it."

"Yes, yes, I know. But you can't plan for every contingency. Give me a minute and I'll call you back with a link for the video call."

"Sounds good."

Jick hung up and leaned back.

Time for more Pinot.

A minute later, Jick received the link, and the video call opened on his laptop with two windows displayed.

"Hi, Quin," Jick said.

"Hi, Jick. Enjoying Hawaii?"

"Oh yeah, it's great. Already had quite a few Mai Tais. Probably a half-dozen, but who's counting? And the minibar in the room is great. I'm loving Uncle Sam's generosity. Although, in the true spirit of Hawaii, I guess I should say a big 'mahalo' to Aunty Sam, too."

Jick grinned and winked at Sam.

"All right, guys, let's get to work," Sam said.

Jick thought back to his reconnaissance visit to the neighborhood.

"You know, Sam, yesterday I said I didn't see anything in that neighborhood. That wasn't entirely true. There was a minor issue with that place. I didn't mention it because it didn't seem significant at the time.

"A delivery truck showed up when I was scanning the houses. The main house connects to the garage through a breezeway. The delivery truck backed up to the garage, and they unloaded a big box shaped like a coffin on steroids. It was probably six or seven feet long and about four feet square."

"What do you think it may have contained?"

"No idea. Could be anything from an enormous bathtub to a sideboard for their dining room. Not sure why they would deliver it to the garage, though."

"Oh, hang on, guys. I hear little Vic. I'll be right back."

Sam stepped away from her camera and went to check on Vic. With the camera pointed at the inside of her office and through the door, Jick could see the familiar hallway that led to the kitchen and living room. Jick reminisced about the number of times he had visited when his brother was still alive. He still visited, more so now that little Vic was around, but the memories still bubbled to the surface every time he set foot in the house. Sam had been an exceptional foodie and the aroma of various dishes she had experimented with would permeate the house. Staring at that familiar hallway brought back many fond memories. Since Vic's death, with just her and now little Vic in the picture, her cooking had tailed off. Jick hoped she would resurrect her cooking hobby someday.

"I'm going to grab some coffee," Quin said.

A minute later, both returned to their desks.

"The case seems to have taken an interesting twist," Sam remarked.

The sound of a spoon clattering against a ceramic saucer came through the speakers. It was from Quin's cup of coffee.

"Meanwhile, back in the year one..." Jick sang.

"What?" Quin asked.

"Oh, nothing. The sound of the spoons against the saucers made me think of a song. Just the start of a song by Jethro Tull. It's called 'Skating Away'. Before your time..."

"What do you mean 'before your time?' You're younger than me."

There was an awkward pause.

"I grew up with songs from the sixties. That's all. I sometimes feel older than I am."

Quin grinned.

"Don't rush it, my man. First your old Mercedes, now music from the seventies. You're only, what, thirty-five? Enjoy it. Forty-five is worse."

Sam changed the subject. She clicked on something, and her screen appeared on Jick's computer.

"Let's get back to the subject at hand. Jick, this is the case we asked Alicia to investigate."

The first screen on the slideshow had the word "Subject1:" followed by "Georgios Stavridis (George Sturgis)." The next line had "Subject2:" followed by "David Finlayson."

Sam started her narrative.

"George Sturgis is a retired businessman, a multimillionaire who has lived on the Big Island of Hawaii for thirty-plus years. Originally from Greece, his birth name was Georgios Stavridis. At a young age, the family emigrated to the United States. When he turned eighteen, he changed his name to George Sturgis. He married Sherryl Ivanson, and they have one son."

Her pointer hovered over "Subject2."

"David Finlayson is an English biologist and biophysicist who has lived in the United States for most of his life. He had been in academia years ago but left to work in industry. He did research on cellular division in a field that could have led to human cloning. There are obvious ethical issues surrounding any type of cloning, let alone human cloning. It isn't clear why he left academia, but his research may have taken him close to cloning humans. He did not make tenure and eventually left the academic world to take a position at Gene 6 Therapeutics as a research scientist. From what we know, he has lived in California for many years."

She paused for a sip of coffee and continued.

"Those are the facts regarding the principal subjects. Now for some character information on Sturgis.

"When he was a businessman, he had a reputation for being ruthless to his competitors. His ruthlessness was probably not an undesirable personality trait, as studies have demonstrated that successful CEOs tend to have psychopathic tendencies anyway. Once or twice, he had some white-collar brushes with the Securities and Exchange Commission over shady dealings. He had to cough up a couple of hefty fines.

"There was one case in which he defrauded investors in his company by filing false reports with the SEC. He was siphoning funds from his company to fund an entity he had created called the Sturgis Longevity Institute. It didn't end well."

"What happened?"

"I guess he's obsessed with longevity. Anyway, the institute didn't do well, and one of the investors, who had lost a considerable sum, kept harassing him at his office. Sturgis couldn't tell the police because he didn't want his fraudulent scheme discovered. Want to guess what he did?"

"What?"

"Hired a local thug to rough up the guy. Not a smart thing to do. Both Sturgis and the thug were arrested. Sturgis got thirty days in jail, and the thug, who had a previous criminal history, got six months."

"Wow, a successful businessman and he resorted to this?"

"He's supposed to be a supreme narcissist. Maybe he has problems with impulse control too."

"So, he's a narcissist who lacks impulse control. I guess it explains the grandiose, self-aggrandizing title of the institute. And had a brush with the law that resulted in a month in jail. So what?" Jick interjected. "He did his time, is retired, and lives in Hawaii with his family. What did he do to trigger an investigation by the government? Parenthetically, I'll just assume you guys work for the government even though you've never told me." He winked at the camera.

Sam's expression did not change.

"I'll continue," she said.

"About a year ago, Finlayson left his job and moved to the Big Island of Hawaii. A lab technician at his company also went with him. They leased a luxury two-bedroom condo at a resort called the Mauna Lani. Guess who paid for the lease."

"Sturgis?" Jick asked.

"Not directly. A holding company that is affiliated with him paid the lease. And the truck that receives the shipments I mentioned earlier is owned by the same holding company. Also, the same holding company signed a lease for a small house in Kawaihae. It's just a few miles up the highway from the Mauna Lani resort where Finlayson and his assistant stayed."

"A small house in Kawaihae?" Jick mused. "Maybe that's what Alicia was investigating. She was there for two hours. I drove around there; there's not much, certainly not enough to take two hours if it was just driving around. Maybe you should tell me where it is, and I can do some snooping around."

"When Finlayson and his assistant arrived in Hawaii," Sam continued, "one of Sturgis' people met them at the airport. You're probably wondering why Finlayson was already under surveillance."

"You're a mind reader," Jick said. "Yes, that is exactly what I wondered. Here's a guy who quits his job and moves to Hawaii. Maybe he stays with friends, maybe he has family, but no. Somehow, you guys know that Sturgis, or this holding company, paid for his lease, and that Sturgis' people met them at the airport. So, do tell me, why was he already under surveillance?"

"Because in the weeks leading up to Finlayson quitting his job, there were those mysterious shipments of materials to Hawaii Island that could be used to set up a laboratory."

"Let me guess. Finlayson ordered them?"

"Yes."

"And it triggered an alert because you were concerned Finlayson would clone a human?"

"No," Sam said. "It's because he then bought a ticket to Hawaii. That's why he was already under surveillance."

Quin chimed in.

"The materials that were ordered in small shipments that looked like they were designed not to draw attention could be used to, yes, set up a lab to start cloning."

"This is such an outlandish discussion I don't know what to say. You think this guy Sturgis hired Finlayson to make a clone? Why on earth would Sturgis want to clone a human?"

"We don't know. He's supposed to be a supreme narcissist. Maybe he wants to live forever. Wouldn't be the first time a megalomaniac has done crazy things to take a stab at immortality."

"Oh, I see. You're assuming Sturgis wants to have *himself* cloned?"

"It's one possibility."

"I still don't get the 'why' part," Jick said. "You said he already has a son. It seems like a lot of effort to go through, not to mention the risk of getting caught. And why would Finlayson agree to such a thing?"

"Again, this 'association' between buying certain things and having a cloning scientist move to Hawaii is not definitive proof of wrongdoing," Sam said. "That's why we decided to just do a quick survey and see if there's anything there. Alicia disappeared and did not file a report. Now, it turns out her car was next to a neighborhood in which the subject lives."

She smiled.

"Notice I didn't call him the 'primary suspect.'"

Jick shot a baleful look at the camera.

She clicked her mouse through a few other links.

"This is a picture of George Sturgis."

Jick's eyes widened as his eyebrows shot up in astonishment.

It was a picture of Uncle George.

TWENTY-SIX

Jick continued staring at the picture on the screen. There was no mistaking Uncle George, although the picture was a few years old. He had thinning hair but had not shaved his head and had no scars and no glasses. But there was no mistaking his identity.

"I know this guy," Jick blurted out.

The speakers on Jick's laptop let out a piercing whine as both Sam and Quin said, "You know him?" in unison. Jick fumbled with the volume slider.

He recounted his experience on his day of arrival with the errant phone call.

"Later in the day, I noticed a party being set up next to the beach where I'm staying. According to the server, he's into throwing parties. Everyone knows him as 'Uncle George.' He seems to be a harmless old man, a bit eccentric. I would say he's only about five-foot-three, so I wouldn't be surprised if he had, or still has, 'small man syndrome.' From the scars on his head, he has obvious evidence of a previous brain injury. It looks like he had a frontal lobectomy and probably needed a VP shunt."

"A VP shunt?" Quin asked.

"Ventriculoperitoneal shunt. It's an implanted device to regulate pressure inside the brain by moving spinal fluid out of the brain."

"How do you know so much about medical stuff?"

"I work as a medical consultant on the side, helping recent graduates set up their practices. So, I need to be familiar with the jargon."

Quin bought the explanation. Jick looked at the picture of Sturgis again.

"We spoke for quite a while at his gathering on the beach. He's an odd duck, probably because of the brain injury. At one point, for no reason, he started giggling and then sobbing, all over a silly joke I made about his bodyguard."

"What did you say?"

"I asked him if his bodyguard's name was Oddjob, from the old James Bond movie Goldfinger," Jick explained. "That's it. He almost doubled over, giggling and sobbing. It was quite odd. I vaguely remember reading about it in..."

Shit. Almost said medical school. Have to remember the company and not let my guard down.

"...a magazine article somewhere. I'll look it up."

"Reading about what?" Quin asked.

"A brain injury where it's difficult to control emotions."

Jick returned to the chief topic being discussed.

"About this cloning thing. What triggered this? Uncle George is just like you imagine an eccentric uncle would be. He's wealthy and shows it with his parties and personnel. The limo driver said it was just him, his wife, and a son. Why on earth would someone in his position, or any position for that matter, clone a human?"

"No reason," Sam said. "It looked suspicious, that's all, especially after Finlayson showed up."

Jick had a thought.

"What does this Finlayson look like? Got a picture?"

"Hang on a second," Sam said.

A few clicks later, a picture of David, the biophysicist at Uncle George's party, appeared on the screen.

"It's him," Jick said. "I met him too. He was at that gathering on the beach."

He stared at the picture and the shock of white hair.

"Wonder if he was one of the guys who met the delivery truck. He was white-haired..."

"I'm glad you met him because your overall first impression is important," Sam said. "If you think this guy is harmless and we're barking up the wrong tree, we can wrap this up quickly. Alicia is probably gone. I guess we'll never know what happened to her. Do you think there are any other angles to investigate? This is an unofficial investigation that I started because I wanted to take one last look before closing this case, just for Alicia's sake. If you think there's nothing left to look over, we're done."

Jick ruminated for a moment.

"No, that's about it. My first impression of Uncle George, as he calls himself here, was positive. Overall, he's a nice guy. He even adopted a local guy as a hanai son and is helping him and his family. Now, to be fair, that guy he adopted looks like a thug. But I shouldn't assume that based on his appearance."

"What's a hanai son?" Quin asked.

"An informally adopted son. It's an old Hawaiian custom. Having said that, there were a couple of odd things. For example, that hanai son looks like he could twist anyone into a pretzel. Even though I shouldn't judge by his appearance, he looks like he could have been a criminal. Also, Finlayson seemed a little stressed about something. I may be wrong. He could be one of those guys who's on the spectrum somewhere and socially a little inept. He also had an assistant with him, which makes me wonder why he needs an assistant in the first place. And..."

"Go on."

"Remember that delivery I mentioned? Now that I know Uncle George is George Sturgis and what your suspicions were in sending Alicia there, in the context of suspicious shipments, I thought the logo on the delivery container looked familiar."

"It did?" Sam's eyebrows shot up.

"Yes. It slipped my mind earlier," Jick said.

As he recalled the logo on the container, Jick suddenly recalled where he had seen the logo before. He looked at the two open windows on his computer with Quin and Sam.

Can't almost slip up again.

"Let me think about this a bit more. In the meantime, was there another recent delivery that your spy network was tracking? And was it delivered yesterday?"

"We'll check."

"Okay, I'll call you if I think of something about that logo."

"Hmm, okay. I guess we should continue investigating this a little more."

"Set up that camera somewhere where you can see the house for a few days," Quin suggested. "Maybe scout the place long-distance for a while."

"Not a bad idea," Sam concurred.

"I will do that," Jick said.

They ended the video call. As soon as the call ended, Jick phoned Sam.

"Sam, I know where I saw that logo before. It was in the operating room when I worked as an anesthesiologist. It's from a well-known hospital equipment company, and it was on the operating room table."

"That's interesting," Sam whistled. "Why would Sturgis get a delivery from a hospital equipment company?"

"I guess I need to do a little more snooping."

"Okay, be careful."

As he disconnected the call, a knock at the door interrupted his thoughts. It was a member of the front desk staff.

"With apologies, sir," he began. "We have this wing of the hotel, these ten rooms," he pointed from Jick's room down the hall, "scheduled for a water shutoff so we can do some plumbing maintenance tomorrow. The person who gave you this room didn't know about it. If you're going to be out for the day, the water could be back on by the time you get back. But things sometimes move slow here. If you want, at no cost, we can upgrade you to a room upstairs. Bigger room, better view."

"Shoot, how can I pass up that deal?" Jick smiled at the man. "Okay, I'll take it."

The man grinned at him.

"Figured you might. I already got your key card ready."
He handed Jick a key card. "Room 518. One floor up, that
way." He pointed in the opposite direction.

"I'll have someone move all your personal items to the
other room. We'll get it set up just like this room. Very sorry
for the inconvenience."

And I bet it has a fully stocked minibar.

TWENTY-SEVEN

Jick's new room at the same resort was one floor higher and three rooms closer to the bar and grill. He unpacked his belongings and settled by the window. A glass of red wine had already found itself attached to him. The setting sun perched on top of a palm tree.

Nice. It's going to set right behind that palm.

As the setting sun sank into the palm fronds, for a few minutes, each frond emitted radiant fingers of light. Then the light faded into embers as the sun settled into the ocean. The palm tree was outlined with an orange halo.

Wow, those colors!

Jick sighed with contentment.

A Mai Tai, dinner, a couple more glasses of wine, shower, bed, in that order.

The following morning, Jick checked his camera to make sure everything worked. He loaded the camera and some refreshments into his rental vehicle.

The weather looks good today. Probably like this every day!

Sam had sent the address of the small house in Kawaihae rented by Sturgis' holding company. Jick planned to stop there for a spot of reconnaissance before proceeding to the clearing.

The address led Jick to a neighborhood that sprawled on top of a shallow bluff overlooking Kawaihae harbor. A series of parallel cul-de-sacs extended from both sides of a central road in a layout that resembled a leaf pattern.

The first cul-de-sac on the right-angled away to accommodate a natural contour in the ground. As a result, houses on that cul-de-sac would not have an ocean view and of the half-dozen lots on that road, five remained vacant. A small house built on a lot at the end was the only house, and that isolated house was the house Sturgis had rented.

Jick parked at the mouth of the cul-de-sac and frowned. The location of the house meant great privacy as there were no neighbors nearby, but it also meant that a stealthy approach would be impossible. Jick drove to the next cul-de-sac and parked, stepping out of the Jeep to survey the neighborhood.

A small dog began yapping at him from the front yard of the nearest house as the front door opened. A woman, stooped with age and holding a four-pronged aluminum cane, emerged onto the lanai.

"Kai, come here," she called out to the dog.

"Aloha," Jick said with a wave.

"Aloha. Can I help you?"

"I hope so," Jick replied. "I'm looking for a young woman who went missing here on the Big Island a few months ago. She may have visited someone in this neighborhood. May I show you her picture?"

"Sure."

Jick watched her start a slow struggle to climb down the four steps in front of her house.

"Wait there," Jick said. "I'll come over."

"Mahalo. I got bad knees."

The dog started sniffing around Jick's ankles as he walked over to the woman.

"He won't bite," she said. "He just likes to look mean."

An ankle-biter that doesn't bite.

Jick looked down at Kai, who let out an obliging growl as Jick made his way to the woman. He held out the camera picture and swiped through a few pictures of Alicia. The woman studied the pictures with a frown.

"No. I can't say I seen her. Or if I did, I don't remember. My thinking not as sharp as it used to be."

"No problem," Jick said. "Let me ask you another question. That house over there," he pointed toward the house he was investigating, "the one on the first turnoff. Do you know who owns it?"

"No, I don't. Whoever owns it don't live there. Sometimes I seen people going in and out and I figure it's a short-term rental. They got those all over the island. It's not a good house because from back there, there's no ocean view."

She pointed to the shimmering ocean beyond the harbor.

"We got a beautiful ocean, and we get great sunsets here," she said. "From that house, they mostly got a view of the mountains. That's how come the other lots are still empty. They got to come around to see the ocean or go to the harbor. I don't think they gonna build any more houses there."

"Have you seen any cars or people recently, like in the past few months?"

"Yeah, a few months back, a couple of trucks were there. Looked like delivery trucks. I figured someone was moving in but now I don't think so. There is a car that goes there now, but whoever lives there don't come out and talk. So I don't know."

"Okay, thanks for the info, Aunty. Aloha."

Jick looked down at the dog.

"Aloha, Kai."

The dog growled in response but did not follow Jick back to his Jeep.

Jick sat in his Jeep to ponder his next move. Finally, he decided on a direct approach. There was no reason to suspect anything out of the ordinary. He turned his Jeep around and made his way back to the house. He parked by the curb to survey the house and noticed right away that all the front windows had blackout curtains.

He walked up to the front door and paused. He noticed a faint sound from somewhere in the back of the house.

There's a generator in the backyard.

There was no doorbell. He knocked on the door and took a step back. After thirty seconds, he knocked again. No response.

"Hello," he shouted. "Anyone home?"

There was no perimeter fence, so Jick walked around the side of the house and peered into the backyard. Two double-wide windows were on the side wall, and the back of the house had one window and a solid door. Blackout curtains hung on all the windows, and a propane tank that looked recently installed sat on a concrete slab, connected to a modern generator padlocked inside a metal cage.

"Hello," he yelled again. "Anyone home?"

No answer. He tried to twist the doorknob on the back and was not surprised it was locked.

Jick took a deep breath and sighed.

Nothing else to do here.

As he turned to head back to his Jeep, he noticed a small, white, half-moon shaped object attached to the soffit at the back corner of the house. His eyes widened.

Shit, security cameras.

As he hurried back to his Jeep, he noticed a similar half-moon object attached to the front soffit. He climbed into his Jeep and sat staring at the house, pondering the deepening mystery.

Sturgis rented this place. And it has security cameras and blacked out windows. I wonder why. Maybe there is something going on. But cloning?

He started the engine and headed out of the neighborhood, arriving at the clearing shortly afterwards. He took out his binoculars and surveyed the valley to identify a suitable spot to set up his camera. A chest-high rocky ledge about ten yards from the clearing, on the opposite side of the trail, seemed an ideal spot. He clambered over to the ledge and set his camera case down.

Less chance of being discovered.

He looked back at Sturgis' house. Squinting along the ledge, he noted with satisfaction that it offered a direct line of sight to Sturgis' house.

A little closer would have been better, but this should work.

The camera was almost in line with the tree line, so if he ducked as he approached the ledge, no one from the house would see him. The camera angle pointed a few degrees west of true north, so there was no chance of sunlight glinting off the lens, and the solar panel could collect adequate sunlight. There was a remote chance another hiker would stumble across the camera, but that was a chance he would have to take.

He positioned the camera so it was hidden from anyone in the clearing and aimed it toward Sturgis' house. He powered it on, verified the direction in the viewfinder, and stepped back.

Perfect.

He went back to the clearing and sat on the bench. It creaked in protest but held. He leaned back and took a second, more detailed look at Sturgis' house.

The garage building, or whatever the second building's purpose was, nestled against the shallow bluff with a storage shed squeezed alongside. A waist-high hedge ran the length of the breezeway connecting the main house to the second building. A gap in the hedge allowed access to the breezeway. The roof tiles from the main house flowed through onto the breezeway and covered the second building as well.

That could be the garage. Or a workshop. Or a lab...

He juxtaposed his video meeting with Sam and Quin against his phone calls and meeting with Uncle George.

This whole thing is weird. Cloning?

He laid his binoculars on the bench and pulled a protein bar and bottled water from his backpack. After finishing his snack, he walked back toward his Jeep. Just before he reached his vehicle, he made an impromptu decision to hike along the perimeter of Sturgis' property. He walked past his Jeep and a few yards before reaching the cul-de-sac, veered off to the right and between the trees. He made his way through the thick undergrowth, stumbling on the uneven ground.

I'm glad there are no snakes in Hawaii.

A short distance ahead, he could see the perimeter wall. Then he changed direction, keeping the same distance from the wall, as he reconnoitered the perimeter.

The first thirty minutes were useless. With the perimeter wall being as high as it was, he could see nothing beyond. There were no lights or cameras mounted on the perimeter wall. The ground sloped upward toward the bluff, and the walk became more strenuous. He paused for another swig of water and plodded on. As he approached the bluff, the slope became too steep to walk, let alone continue building the wall. The wall stopped at a pillar and from that point on, for the last ten yards, it was a simple chain-link fence that was almost too steep to walk up to. It ended in a series of anchors embedded in the stone wall of the bluff.

Jick did not walk any farther. He was closest to the garage building and did not want to risk being seen. He focused his binoculars on the fence. One end was anchored to the pillar; the free edge of the other end was cut to match the contours of the bluff. A series of six anchors, orange-brown with rust, held the chain-link fence against the bluff. The top of the fence had broken loose from the anchor and flapped against the rock. Jick skulked between the trees and slid down the slope to the wall. He peered around the edge of the pillar.

The garage building was some sixty feet away. One side of the shed abutted the bluff, and the adjoining side snugged against the garage. There were no windows in the garage, but Jick could see large vents on its roof. He could discern the breezeway hidden behind the hedge, and in the distance, he could see the back of the main house. There was no activity.

As he scanned the house, a bird screeched close to him, and he jumped. He felt a sudden sense of apprehension as a thought struck him. He looked around where he stood, scanning the hillside behind him and the forest he had walked through. A few scraggly trees dotted the hillside leading up to the scenic viewpoint as the forest gave way to the rocky bluff wall. An abandoned bird's nest lay draped over a branch of the nearest tree.

Where's the security? No cameras, dogs, perimeter lights? No trip wires?

After scanning the property for a few minutes, Jick decided he had seen enough. There was nothing going on at the house. He peered through the binoculars, but as close as he was to the house and garage, the binoculars added nothing of value. He sighed and turned away.

This whole thing is a wild goose chase. A few days of camera surveillance and that should do it. If there's nothing there, I'm going home.

Thaddeus sat at a desk, staring at a bank of monitors. Next to one monitor, a red light started blinking. Something unusual had registered on the monitor and the software had flagged it. He clicked on an icon on his desktop to select that monitor, and as he turned a roller wheel mounted on his keyboard, the image zoomed and lost focus. Then the image of a man with his back to the camera sharpened into focus. The image swayed with a gentle rocking motion as the branch the camera was affixed to rose and fell with the breeze. Tucked inside a bird's nest for concealment, the nest partially obscured the lens.

I gotta fix that.

The mystery man peered through the fence where the perimeter wall ended near the bluff. Thaddeus moved a joystick to keep the back of the man's head centered in the field. The man lifted his binoculars to his face and surveyed the main house. Then he turned to leave.

Thaddeus froze the image as the man turned; he zoomed in on his face. The slight rise in his eyebrows was the only sign he recognized the man who had paid Uncle George a visit at the beach.

He saved the image and reached for the phone.

TWENTY-EIGHT

Sturgis put the phone down. Thaddeus had called, wanting to meet him right away. He said it was urgent. Sturgis tapped a pencil on his desk, frowning. Moments later, there was a knock at the door.

"Come in," he said.

Thaddeus entered. He got straight to the point.

"That man who came to you at the beach, that one you said was a wrong numbah. I just seen him on the security camera."

"What? Which one?"

"The mauka one, where the wall ends. He stood outside the fence looking in with binoculars."

"You sure it's him?"

"Yes, I saved the picture. Log into the security camera and look at the saved pictures."

Sturgis clicked his way to the picture. He frowned and tilted his head as he looked at it.

"You're right; it is him. He's just a random wrong number. Or is he? Did he mean to call me? Couldn't be, it wasn't my number that he called me on. Why the hell is he here outside my fence? I need answers, Thaddeus. I need to know who he is, what he's doing here, who sent him, and why. We can't do anything... yet."

"Yes, sir."

Sturgis leaned back in his chair. Then he jerked upright with a start. Thaddeus gave him an inquiring look.

"I just thought of something. Let's see if my suspicions are right."

Navigating through various links, Sturgis started typing on the keyboard, rolling his mouse around. Then he stopped and his face reddened. He pursed his lips together but could not stifle an angry giggle.

"Damn it!" He pounded his desk. "I hate this."

He pulled a cloth out of his desk drawer and pressed it against his face, taking a few deep breaths. The episode of giggling passed.

"You okay, sir?"

"Yes," Sturgis said. "Take a look at this."

Thaddeus walked around Sturgis' desk. A frozen image of a man was on the screen.

"Same guy," Thaddeus said.

"Yes, same guy."

"Which camera?"

"The one at the lab. Earlier today."

Thaddeus' eyebrows rose.

"This is no good," he said. "He was at the lab earlier today, and then he come up here."

"We need to bring him here and have a talk."

"Yes, sir."

Sturgis squeezed his eyes shut as he massaged the bridge of his nose.

"Think of something, Thaddeus."

"Why not invite him to your next party? He say he know a lot of doctors. Few drinks, get him talking. Maybe ask him to come here so we can talk about ways to bring doctors here."

Sturgis stared at Thaddeus. Then his face broke out in a smile.

"Thaddeus, you're a genius. That's a great idea. We'll have Uncle George talk to 'Jick the medical consultant' and we'll see what he's up to. There's no way he's just a medical consultant. We can't risk any screw-ups this late in the game, and we can't draw attention here if someone sent him. We need to bring him here; we have a room for him."

"Yes, sir."

As Thaddeus left the room, Sherryl Sturgis walked in.

"George, I need to talk to you."

"I think this is where we turn right."

Leo Truong wrenched the steering wheel of the rented Ford Mustang convertible in a sudden jerk, and the car lurched onto the dirt road, kicking up red dust as it scrabbled for traction. The road curved up the hillside and disappeared around a bend. Green patches of grass and scrub replaced the reddish-brown dirt.

"Are you sure this is the right turnoff? I didn't see a sign," his wife, Amy, asked.

"I looked at a map. Hawaii Island has a bunch of dirt roads everywhere. On the map, this road leads to the nature reserve from below. The nature reserve is up there." He pointed up the slope and to the right, where an expansive forest covered both sides of a valley.

"The guidebook also said the main entrance is from a scenic viewpoint higher on the mountain. This road isn't even on the map. Why did we go this way?"

"It is on the map; it's marked as a dirt road. I figured this would be a great place to hike. We can do a loop through the nature reserve in a couple of hours, see an unknown corner of the reserve that most tourists don't go to, and be back at our hotel for a late lunch."

"There's no cell coverage here," Amy said, checking her phone.

"Listen, Amy Truong," Leo said with a grin. "I like the sound of that. Amy Truong." He let the name roll off his tongue.

She flashed him a withering look.

"I could have kept Nguyen," she muttered.

"I'm glad you didn't."

Around the next bend, the smoother gravel road petered out, and they bounced over bumps and potholes.

"This is ridiculous," Amy complained. "We need to turn around."

"We can't here," Leo said. "Let's just go a little more and next time we see a wider area, I'll turn around."

The road ended at a closed farm gate. The gate was about six feet high, constructed of metal tubes painted bright red. Twin strands of barbed wire twisted around the top tube, and a green and white sign hung off the middle tube. Leo slowed the car to a stop, and they climbed out to survey the terrain beyond the gate.

"Looks quiet and scenic there. I read somewhere that in Hawaii, the locals keep farm gates closed to prevent animals from going out, not to prevent visitors from going in. The gate's not locked, so I vote we go through," Leo said.

Amy pointed at the sign.

"What does 'Kapu' mean?"

"I don't know."

"What if it means 'keep out'?"

"I would think if it did, they would write it in English too, to make sure there were no intruders. It wouldn't make sense to write it just in Hawaiian. 'Kapu' is probably the brand name of the company that made the gate."

"And there's barbed wire around the top. What kind of animals do you think could be in there?"

"It'll be fine."

"What if it's some kind of wild animal sanctuary? You know, with predators?"

"You worry too much, Amy...," he paused with a grin, "...Truong."

"I don't know about this, Leo."

"Oh, come on, we're in Hawaii. Stop stressing."

He unlatched the gate and pushed it open. He climbed into the car and eased it through the opening, waiting for Amy to close the gate and climb back in. Amy's face displayed hesitation as she shut the door. He gave her a reassuring pat as they pushed on along the dirt road.

A hundred feet down the road, they came to a natural clearing. Ahead, the scrubland they traversed ended abruptly at a wall of trees marking the start of the forest.

"There it is. The nature reserve."

Leo swung the car around and parked.

"This is perfect. We hike up the road until it ends, then do a quick loop in this quiet corner of the nature reserve, and head back to the hotel."

Amy looked around. The view from this spot could have been on a postcard. The ocean shimmered in the distance; the forest seemed to exhale a cool breeze in front of them, and a few high-flying birds hovered motionless, wings outstretched in the stream.

They donned wide-brimmed hats, stuffed water bottles and sunscreen into a drawstring backpack, and set off. After a hundred yards of hiking in the sun, they came to the edge of the forest.

"This is neat. And weird," Leo said. "The land doesn't look any different, but suddenly there are tall trees everywhere. Feels like we're entering a rainforest."

They continued their hike. The dirt road ended at the edge of the trees, and they chose the path of least resistance as they made their way through the trees.

"Should we mark our way in, so we don't get lost?" Amy asked.

"Mark our way with what?" Leo replied. "Stop worrying. All we have to do is turn around and walk in a straight line. We can always use the ocean and the slope of the ground to figure out the right way."

They pushed deeper into the forest. Amy realized the ground had natural undulations, and it was not obvious which way was straight back to the car. She also realized she could not see the ocean anymore. She felt a twinge of concern.

"Leo, I think we should stop."

"What, why?"

"I can't see the ocean, and I don't know the way back to the car."

He swung around to face her.

"If we go any further, we're going to get lost. And I'm a little hungry. I want to leave. What's wrong?"

As she spoke, Leo's expression had changed. The ground sloped upward behind Amy, and something behind Amy had caught his eye. She turned to look.

It was black, furry, about the size of a large dog, and its gentle swaying motion against the tree trunks had drawn Leo's attention. In the dim light under the canopy, it resembled a punching bag hung off a branch.

"What the hell?" Leo took a step toward it.

"Wait, what is it?" Amy took a step to stand behind Leo.

Leo drew in a sharp breath.

"It's a pig! It's one of those wild pigs that's supposed to be all over this island. Looks like it's caught in a trap."

A rope around its neck led to a higher branch off which the animal hung. As it swayed, flashes of sunlight traced bright lines along its body, illuminating its paws, its head, its torso. Its tongue protruded out of its mouth and lolled to the left. The pig's face was matted and red, and its eyes were closed. The ends of its paws were also red, and streaks of red ran down both sides of its head. Amy realized the sensation climbing up her belly was a horrified revulsion as she realized what someone had done to this unfortunate animal.

"Oh my God," she whispered. "Leo. It's not a trap."

"Wait here." Leo took a step over some rocks and clambered closer to the animal.

He reached out with a shaking hand and touched the animal on its belly. The animal began a sudden series of violent jerks at the end of the rope, thrashing like Leo's finger was a cattle prod.

"It's alive!"

Leo let out a yell and stepped back. His right foot slipped on a rock that was slick with something that had leaked out of the animal. He lost his balance as his foot wedged into a tight space between two rocks. He fell with his foot pinned between the rocks. His right ankle twisted in an unnatural direction, and he felt something snap. His shriek of pain eclipsed his surprised yell as he toppled to the ground.

"Leo!" Now it was Amy's turn to shriek.

"I'm okay, I'm okay," he said as beads of sweat started pouring down his face. "Ah, shit, that hurts."

He pulled his foot out from between the rocks and let out another yell.

"Something's broken. I can tell," he rasped, gritting his teeth in agony.

He pulled himself to his feet, placing his entire weight on his left foot. It was no use. Just the act of standing with his broken foot suspended in the air was agonizing. Amy offered him a supporting shoulder, and they tried to take a few steps toward the car.

"Do we have anything to make a splint?"

"Amy, grab one of those branches and let's see if we can tie it to my ankle with the cords from the backpack."

They tried for about fifteen minutes, but none of the branches worked. And the cord was too short to be an effective tether for the splint. They gave up and Leo sank to the ground.

"There's only one thing to do. Amy, you go and get help."

"I am not leaving you here," Amy said firmly.

"Amy, listen. Our phones don't work, and I can't walk back to the car. You have to go. Drive down to the highway and call 911. Then drive back up here. You should be back in a couple of hours."

"This honeymoon is turning into a nightmare."

Phoenix trudged through the forest, heading home. He loved these outings in the woods. Smiling as he re-experienced the pleasure of satisfying the urge, he closed his eyes and leaned against a trunk. Tomorrow, he would go back to finish what he had started. The pig was fine where it was; it wasn't going anywhere. And if it didn't make it, there were always more pigs...

A loud shriek interrupted his daydreaming, and he jumped. He looked around. The shriek came from the direction of the pig. But it wasn't the pig. He turned and ran toward the shriek, holding the handle of the shears tucked in his waistband in a comforting grip...

TWENTY-NINE

Sherryl Sturgis closed the door and pulled up a chair by the desk, worry etched on her face. George tapped his pencil on the desk and looked at her. He said nothing.

"George...," she began.

"What's up?"

"There was this thing on TV I just saw. One of the local reporters did a special on unsolved murders in Hawaii. Today's episode was about the Big Island. I guess we don't have that many that go unsolved. They covered only three murders in the last ten years that were still unsolved. That's pretty good, isn't it?"

"Get to the point, Sherryl."

"You remember when you got hurt in the boating accident?"

"How could I forget? And it wasn't a boating accident. It was a reckless kid who should have been charged with attempted murder."

"One of the unsolved murders they talked about on that show was that kid."

"Yes, I knew someone killed him," Sturgis said. "I don't care. Why are you bringing this up now?"

"'Cause they went into some information about it. They said he had been stabbed over and over. They said he had been stabbed in the neck. And they said they were certain he had been stabbed with scissors."

Sturgis said nothing.

"Just like what Phoenix did with those mice that I told you about five years ago."

"Where are you going with this, Sherryl?"

"I'm asking myself, could it have been Phoenix that killed that kid?"

"No way," Sturgis said.

"How can you be so sure? Could he have been mad at that kid because you were hurt? You were mad when they didn't give that kid a stronger punishment for almost killing you. Could Phoenix have killed the kid as revenge for hurting you?"

Sturgis said nothing.

"George, I think we need to tell the police about this, yeah? He's our son and I don't want anything bad to happen to him. But if he killed someone, we can't keep it to ourselves."

"Sherryl, we will not talk about this with anyone. Is that clear?"

"I don't get why you're being like this. You didn't want therapy for him when he was growing up. You said it was just a phase. Now he's an adult, and it may be too late."

"Calm down, Sherryl. You watched a TV show. We're not going to the police just because someone said that kid was stabbed with scissors. Did you talk to Phoenix about any of this?"

"No."

"All of this was years ago. Phoenix is harmless. He's eccentric. That's all. Now, can you leave me alone so I can get some work done?"

Sherryl got up to leave.

"I won't tell no one," she said. "But if anything like this happens again, we're going to the cops."

Sturgis stared at the closed door after she left. He tapped his pencil on the desk and frowned.

Sherryl can't go to the cops. Not now.

Phoenix crouched behind a trunk. Large leafy fronds concealed him as he peered through the gaps. He saw two people, a man and a woman, about ten yards beyond the tree with the suspended pig. The man lay on the ground, propped on his elbows. The woman stood by him with a worried expression. Bits of conversation, "phones don't work," "can't walk," and "call 911," drifted through the rustling of the leaves. He saw the woman depart, leaving the man lying on the ground.

A feeling swept over Phoenix and his pulse quickened. The urge, but stronger, the same feeling he had experienced the last time he killed a person, when he had taken care of the boat pilot. The man was alone. But there were two people in his playground.

My playground!

His father had told him not to do what he did to the boat pilot ever again. But he had also told him he could play in his playground. He shut his eyes and swayed.

They came into my playground...

Phoenix knew the area. And he knew the man was not going anywhere. He skulked uphill through the trees and went past the man. He could see the top of the man's head through gaps in the foliage. The man held his phone up, angling it in vain to catch a signal. He dropped it into his pocket. Phoenix smiled and pushed forward.

Reaching the clearing before the woman, Phoenix surveyed the area around the parked convertible for an ambush location. The tree was too far, and it was on the passenger side. She might lock herself in the car before he could reach her. He needed to be closer. Then he had an idea.

He slithered under the vehicle and waited.

Minutes later, he heard rustling, followed by footsteps. The woman emerged from the forest, disheveled and frantic, holding the key fob in hand. She squeezed the button, and the car beeped as the door unlocked. She walked to the car and stood by the door for a moment to catch her breath. Phoenix could hear her panting with exertion. Her leg was mere inches from where he lay. Clutching the shears in a firm grip, he drove the implement sideways into the back of her leg, above the ankle.

She let out a shriek of pain as he pulled the shears out and slithered out the other side. She had not seen him yet.

He peered over the window from the passenger side and saw her disappear as she fell to the ground.

He felt the urge wash over him as he stood, moving to the driver's side of the car. She had collapsed against the car, and she jerked her head to see who it was. Bewilderment, fear, pain, all crisscrossed her face as she had not yet realized what happened to her. Then she saw the shears in his hand...

Amy screamed and jumped to the side when something stabbed her leg. She collapsed to the ground, clutching her leg. Through her jeans, she could see a dark patch spreading down the back of her leg. She jerked her head around but saw nothing until a man appeared at the back of her car. She saw a grinning face, blank and expressionless eyes, and a pair of shears.

A wave of panic and terror washed over her. She scrabbled against the dirt as she pushed away. She tried to get back on her feet but staggered on her good leg and fell back on the ground.

The man raised the shears, and Amy saw a glint of sunlight and crimson on the tip. She screamed again.

He brought the shears down hard, and Amy jerked to the side. She felt a sharp pain in the side of her neck, and a warm gush rushed over her shoulder and down her arm. She looked down in horror at herself and then looked at him.

"No!"

The man stepped back, a look of concern on his face. He dropped the shears. Her vision blurred and as she faded out of consciousness, she had one last look at his eyes.

Those eyes...

"Shit!" Phoenix screamed, staring at Amy as she lay on the ground, a pulsing stream discoloring the ground as it soaked into the earth. He clutched the sides of his head and stepped back. He had intended to stab her in the chest and planned to spend some time with her before finishing her off. But she had flinched to the side, and his blow had caught her in an unintended spot on her neck.

"No!" Phoenix let out a scream of rage and disappointment.

He stood, staring down at her limp figure. In a fit of anger, he kicked the car. He collected his shears and leaned against the car, breathing hard, mulling over his next step. He squatted against Amy's body and, with his shears, made a cut on the side of her neck, near where he had stabbed her. For several minutes, the only sounds were his heavy breathing, grunts of effort, and the rasping sound of his shears. His face creased into a smile every time he thought of his next move.

The man in the forest... he's not going anywhere.

THIRTY

The green lawn, a square expanse of about two acres, looked as immaculate as a golf fairway. On one side of the square, the mauka side, Sturgis' house graced the perimeter, its curved lanai denting the square's edge. Sturgis leaned on a patio chaise lounge, swirling a drink with a glass swizzle stick. Bits of green leaves twirled in the liquid.

"Thaddeus is a man of many talents," Sturgis remarked. "This is a damn good mojito."

David Finlayson sprawled on a similar chaise on his left.

"Maybe I'll have one too," he said. "I rarely drink in the middle of the day, but what the heck?"

Almost on cue, Thaddeus materialized at Sturgis' side. Sturgis ordered a second round for himself and one for Finlayson.

As Thaddeus departed to make their drinks, Sturgis gazed at the ocean.

"I love how the lawn looks like the infinity edge of a pool. I feel like I could slide off the edge of the lawn and splash into the ocean."

"It is beautiful," Finlayson agreed. "With the sun almost overhead, the lawn is shimmering and blurring the edge. And the ground slopes just enough so you can't see the tops of the neighbor's trees down below. Even the surface of the pool looks spectacular."

Sturgis sipped his drink.

"So, how's things going in the lab?"

"Fine," Finlayson said. "All the equipment is getting set up, and we should be able to do a dry run in a month. Or maybe I should say 'wet run' because I plan to use all the chemicals like I normally would."

"What are you going to try it out on?"

"Probably a fetal pig. How's things with the surrogate?"

"Good, good," said Sturgis. "She's at a private home in Kona. You said the experiment will run for ninety days, give or take?"

"Yes, depends on my calculations. I think around ninety days will get you fifteen years. That's about as far as I want to push it, since this is all new and I don't know what will happen beyond that."

"So, I'll start with a teenager. That's good. I'm hopeful."

"So am I."

Thaddeus returned with their drinks. They both took a sip as they absorbed the scenery.

"David," Sturgis swirled his drink. "We need to talk about something that came up."

"Sure."

"Remember that day of the beach party at Hokule'a Beach? There was that guy Jick, who said he was a medical consultant."

"Yeah, what about him?"

"He may not be a medical consultant."

"Then what is he?"

"I don't know. Thaddeus says he was here, spying on the house. And he was at the lab the same day."

"What? Really?"

"Yes, we got him on the security cameras."

Finlayson frowned.

"He may be here to check us out," Sturgis continued. "We cannot afford any interruption or interference now."

"What should we do?" Finlayson asked.

"We're going to throw a party and invite him. Then, when he's had a few drinks, we're going to invite him here to have a talk about discussing options to bring more doctors to the Big Island. If he is a medical consultant, he should be thrilled at the opportunity."

"What if he's not?"

"You don't need to worry about that."

"What do you want me to do?"

"I need you to be there and ask him questions. Talk to him. Get a feel for what he is doing here. We don't want him to get suspicious. But I need to know what he is doing here."

"Okay," Finlayson said. "No problem. I don't want to get into trouble either. If he's here spying on us, you and Thaddeus can do... whatever."

Finlayson sipped his drink.

"Are you going to have Pavel at this party?"

"Not sure. I might."

"You should. Pavel can ask him questions about his medical consultant background."

"Yeah, maybe you're right."

"How's Phoenix doing?" Finlayson asked.

"Fine. But I am worried about him. He has these tendencies, these feelings, that sometimes get the better of him."

"What do you mean?"

"Violent tendencies. Which is surprising, given his background."

At the edge of the lawn on the right side of the immaculate fairway, a figure appeared, shimmering around the edges from the glare, as if rising out of the water, carrying an object in each hand.

"Who's that?" asked Finlayson.

Sturgis squinted.

"Looks like Phoenix."

"What's he got with him?"

"I don't know. Maybe a couple of coconuts? I guess he went for a walk. Or maybe he went to his playground."

Finlayson glanced at Sturgis. He knew about the area west of the Sturgis estate that Phoenix referred to as his playground. Phoenix headed toward them, swinging a coconut from each arm. He stopped when he was fifty feet from the lanai, flashed a huge grin at Sturgis, and swung what he carried around.

Finlayson's eyes widened in horror as he rolled off his lounge chair, landing on the ground on all fours. He staggered to the edge of the lanai, collapsed with his head over the edge, and retched. His body bucked and heaved as the few sips of his short-lived mojito spewed out of his mouth like a projectile and sprayed the grass, followed by the remnants of his breakfast.

Neither Phoenix nor Sturgis glanced at him. Sturgis drew his eyebrows together in a frown.

The two "coconuts" were the decapitated heads of a man and a woman.

"What the hell is this, Phoenix?"

"They were in my playground, Dad."

"I have told you many times, only animals!" Sturgis thundered at him. "Who are these people?"

"I don't know. They went past the 'kapu' sign and were in my playground. I... I couldn't help it."

Flies started buzzing around the heads.

Sturgis' gaze swept over Phoenix.

"What happened to your face? And your arms?"

A faint darker hue had appeared like a dusky halo around Phoenix's right eye. Several scratches traced curvy lines on his arms.

He nodded toward the male head.

"It was him. He saw this," Phoenix jiggled the woman's head. "And went nuts. He tried to stop me."

"Shit." Sturgis turned to the house. "Thaddeus!"

Thaddeus appeared. His eyes roved over what Phoenix held. If the spectacle shocked him, his face did not betray it.

"Yes, sir?" Thaddeus' face remained impassive.

"Clean up this mess. There's a lot of work to be done."

"Yes, sir."

As Thaddeus and Phoenix prepared to leave, a piercing shriek came from the house. Sherryl Sturgis stood at the door, fist bunched to her mouth, a look of abject horror on her face. She stared at the sight of her grinning son and his grisly trophies. Her eyelids started fluttering as she leaned against the door frame. Anticipating what was about to happen, Thaddeus sprinted toward her and grabbed her just as she collapsed to the ground. He took her back to the lanai and laid her on Finlayson's lounge chair.

"Get him out of here," Sturgis barked at Thaddeus.

Thaddeus and Phoenix departed.

Finlayson staggered back to a chair and collapsed into it, holding his head as he rested his elbows on the table. He cast a glance at the departing figures of Thaddeus and Phoenix, the latter still clutching his ghoulish trophies. Finlayson's belly twitched again, and he looked away.

"Jesus, George, that kid is a psycho."

Sturgis looked at Finlayson, his face expressionless.

"He's always been like this. I knew this from when he was a kid. It worries me. It has always worried me."

Sturgis knelt next to his wife. Her breathing was shallow, and some color had returned to her cheeks. He patted her cheek.

"Sherryl. Are you okay?"

She responded with a groan as her eyelids fluttered open.

"George," she focused on her husband's face. She tried to say more but continued staring at her husband's face as tears rolled down the sides of her face. She tried to raise herself on her elbow.

"Oh, George," she wailed. "I, I..."

Sturgis massaged her wrists.

"Don't say anything," he said soothingly. "Just relax for a few minutes."

She leaned back in the lounge chair. Then her face reddened.

"No," she said, pushing herself up on her elbows. "This is terrible. We... we need to report this. Right away."

"Let's not do something too hasty," Sturgis said. "I agree we should do something. Let me think about it."

"Think about what?"

She was now awake. And angry.

"George, I've told you for years we needed to get him help and you always refused. And now look at what he's done. He murdered two people. Oh, my God." She hitched in a shuddering breath as the sudden realization of the magnitude of the problem sank in.

"Sherryl, you should go lay down. Let me think about this. I'll talk it over with David here."

Sherryl stared at Finlayson.

"Why talk it over with him? Who is he? Why is he involved in this?"

"He's not. He's just here and saw this. That's all."

With a look of reluctant resignation on her face, Sherryl went inside the house. After she left, Sturgis parked himself in a chair facing Finlayson.

"I hope we're doing the right thing," Finlayson said.

"What are you talking about?"

"The experiment."

"Oh, that. Don't worry about it. We'll be fine."

"What are you going to do about this?" Finlayson asked.

"I don't know. Yet. Maybe what I should have done a long time ago."

Finlayson frowned at him.

"What do you mean?"

Sturgis said nothing. He sat deep in thought, fingers steepled in front of him. He leaned back and, with a sudden jerk forward, jumped out of his lounge chair. He strode into the house.

"What I should have done a long time ago."

Thaddeus and Phoenix headed for the garage building. As they approached the building, Thaddeus pointed to a bin.

"Put them in there," he said.

With some reluctance, Phoenix placed the severed heads in the bin. Thaddeus clamped the lid shut. He opened the door of the shed and drove out a few minutes later, riding an all-terrain vehicle. Thaddeus had placed shovels, buckets, electric saws, and two folded tarps in the back. He stopped next to Phoenix and waited for Phoenix to climb in.

"Let's go."

THIRTY-ONE

Jick slid into his Jeep and set off for the clearing where he had stashed the camera, pulling into the dirt parking lot forty-five minutes later. He slung his pack over his shoulder and made his way to the clearing. The camera perched on the rock ledge as he had left it. Flipping open the waterproof data cover, he did a quick swap with a blank card, pocketing the data card to be analyzed. He made his way back to his Jeep and drove back.

Back at the hotel, he flipped open his laptop and stuffed the data card into the card reader. An application automatically launched and, after a minute, a screen popped up with a summary of the data card's contents.

He clicked on the first picture. He saw a man walking along the breezeway carrying what appeared to be a flat object.

Wonder what it is. I wish this camera had better resolution.

The second picture showed two men in mid-stride heading toward the garage building. One man held an indistinct spherical object in each hand. The picture was time-stamped four hours after the first.

Bowling balls? Kettlebells? Bottles?

The third picture showed an ATV from the back, pointing west. It was time-stamped a few minutes after the previous picture.

The fourth picture showed a man in a different pose, again carrying the same flat object, this time heading toward the house.

There were no other pictures. He experimented with the various enhancing features in the app but could not get much better resolution. The various filters helped to a degree, but the picture was still too indistinct.

Not sure what to make of any of this. Looks like routine activity.

He gazed out his window at the bar and grill.

Then a late lunch and a Mai Tai. Or two.

He studied the pictures again. The camera was a little too far to get good details, but nothing unusual jumped out. There were two pictures of a man carrying the same object, then presumably the same man on an ATV. There was one picture of two men riding in an ATV, and one picture of one man carrying two objects that look like kettlebells. Probably a weight set or workout area in the garage."

He planned to go back to the camera every day to swap out cards.

Maybe in another week or so, if nothing else happens, this wild goose chase will end.

Phoenix pointed to a spot in the forest, and Thaddeus navigated the ATV to the spot. He turned off the engine, and they climbed out. A male body, minus its head, lay on the ground next to where they had stopped. There were obvious signs of a struggle in the bruises around the body's fists. Several puncture wounds were visible around the chest. Two bloody stab wounds were present near the groin and around the broken ankle.

Thaddeus pulled the digging tools out of the back of the ATV.

"Let's get to work."

Thaddeus and Phoenix started digging in the loose soil, using the electric saw to rip through roots. After an hour of backbreaking work, they had dug a deep hole that was about two-thirds of the needed length.

"Screw this, Thaddeus. Let's use the saw."

Thaddeus said nothing. Phoenix grabbed the power saw and started sawing through the lower torso. The saw encountered some resistance around the vertebrae, but Phoenix soon had the torso in two pieces. Wiping sweat off his face, he rolled the halves into the hole.

"Excellent."

Thirty minutes later, they had filled the hole.

"One more," said Phoenix.

They set out in the ATV for the other body. After another forty-five minutes of backbreaking work, they had a hole dug and, like the male body, had sawn the torso in half. As Phoenix pushed both halves into the hole, a loop of intestine spilled out and caught on his shoe. He shook it free in disgust.

"Okay, Thaddeus, fill 'er up."

Fifteen minutes later, the burial was complete.

"What should we do with the car?" Phoenix asked.

"Later, I drive it back down to the highway and around to the house. We park it in the garage. Then I get rid of it. For now, I'll move it under a tree."

"Okay."

Thaddeus climbed into the Mustang, executed a deft three-point turn, and pointed the car toward the gate. He backed it against the tree and shut off the engine. Phoenix and Thaddeus climbed into the ATV and headed back to the house.

Phoenix and Thaddeus emerged from the jungle on his ATV and drove it into the garage. Sturgis stood by the breezeway; he motioned Thaddeus over. They disappeared into the house as Phoenix parked the ATV. He climbed off the ATV and headed to the house. Every major muscle group complained; the digging had been arduous, and he was exhausted.

Time for a shower and an early dinner.

Thaddeus emerged from the house.

"Come with me."

"What's up?" asked Phoenix.

"I need your help."

"What do you need help with, Thaddeus?"

"The heads," he said. "Your Dad say we forgot to get rid of the heads."

"Just take them somewhere and bury them. I'm tired and need to take a shower."

"Your Dad say you need to do it."

Phoenix groaned. "Damn it, Thaddeus. Okay, I'm sure he's still mad at me. Let's get this done quick."

THIRTY-TWO

Jick started his day with an invigorating swim in the ocean, followed by a series of laps in the hotel swimming pool. He pulled himself out of the water and scanned the surroundings for a shower. He saw a carved wooden "Rain Forest Shower" sign mounted on a bamboo post next to a rock wall. Jick looked at it, puzzled. The wall was in a shady corner; although there was a floor drain, there were no obvious showerheads anywhere. A shelf with a stack of crisp white towels stood next to the sign. There were no faucets either.

An attendant noticed his puzzled expression and smiled.

"Take a look at the ground, sir," he invited.

Jick noted a pattern of textured concrete in an earthy red color resembling a field of cooled lava. A pattern of swirls resembling *pahoehoe* lava formed an intricate Hawaiian-themed design. The swirls formed three large circles that lay in an arc along the wall.

"See that pattern? Now stand on any of those circles."

"Uh, okay," Jick said.

As soon as Jick stood in the center of a circle, he heard a click, followed by a soothing jet of warm water. It rained from above, from invisible showerheads tucked among the leafy canopy above. Invisible misters in the surrounding walls also turned on, enveloping him in clouds of rolling mist as the warm water rinsed him from above, creating the impression of standing in a rain forest. Jick squinted as he looked for the source. Tucked in the leafy canopy overhead were discreet black shower nozzles.

This is some shower.

After a quick rinse, he stepped out, grabbing a towel off the stack.

"Clever," he said to the attendant. "Motion sensor?"

"Pressure sensor in the middle of each circle. Nice, isn't it? This is our new rain forest shower. We just installed this a week ago. The sign that explains what to do is not here yet; we're expecting it in a few days."

"I see."

Jick donned his robe and made his way back to his room. As he passed the concierge desk, the woman seated behind the desk cupped her hand over the mouthpiece of her phone and motioned him over. She wedged it with her shoulder as she handed him an envelope.

"Message for you, sir."

"For me?"

"Yes, sir, came in through the fax earlier."

He looked at the envelope. It said "For Jick" on it. No last name. Jick frowned and tore it open. It read:

"Howdy pardner, party Friday evening at six o'clock. Beach near the airport. See the map below. Be there. UG."

A crude hand-drawn map showed the location of the party with an "X" about a mile from the airport. There was a number next to the line leading to the beach.

Probably a mile marker. Why is Uncle George inviting me to a party?

Jick strolled back to his room, deep in thought, wondering about Uncle George's motive in inviting him to a party.

Why didn't he call me about the party? He has my phone number from my earlier wrong number... Or maybe he doesn't. Since I didn't call him on his number.

Jick scrolled through his earlier calls. He identified the wrong number call on the day of his arrival and called it.

"Hello." The voice was familiar.

"Is this Sherryl?" Jick asked.

"It is. Who is this?"

"Jick. We met that day at the party near the Hawaiian Orchid. I stopped by your table. I called George by mistake."

"Oh yes, I remember you now. What can I do for you?"

"Is George available?"

"Why, yes, he is. Hold on."

A minute later, Uncle George came to the phone.

"Jick!" a jovial voice boomed. "Did you get my message? I hope you're coming to the party."

"That's why I called. I was wondering why you wanted me there."

"You're a medical consultant, right?"

"Yes."

"And Hawaii needs doctors, right?"

"Uh, yes."

"There you have it. I figured we need to talk so you can help us."

"That's it? You want to talk to me about bringing doctors to Hawaii?"

"That's it. I figured we would have a party, and if you can help us, we can discuss things further down the road."

"Oh, okay. I guess I'll see you there."

Jick ended the call and stared at his phone.

He wants to talk about bringing doctors here now? This is weird. And I still need to figure out what's wrong with him. Why does he behave like that?

He eyed his breakfast with frank appreciation. An omelet, side of Portuguese sausage, fresh island fruits, coffee, and passion fruit juice.

Ah, perfect.

After breakfast, Jick relaxed with a cup of coffee while searching the internet for information. After searching for symptoms including unexpected or exaggerated crying, weeping, or laughing, one result that appeared was *'pseudobulbar affect.'*

Pseudobulbar affect. That's it!

He found an article cross-referenced with an article from the National Institutes of Health. He read out loud from the informative article.

"Pseudobulbar affect is a condition characterized by sudden and uncontrollable episodes of laughing or crying. The episodes are not necessarily connected to the underlying emotional state. For example, even when experiencing anger, the outward display may be uncontrollable laughter. Or episodes of crying when feeling happy. A mildly amusing joke may provoke several minutes of uncontrollable laughing or crying."

Jick did a deeper search for symptoms of traumatic frontal lobe injuries.

"Hmm, looks like uncontrolled anger and aggression are very possible, not to mention lack of impulse control. But this Uncle George character seems mild-mannered."

He leaned back and recounted his earlier encounter with Uncle George.

"He's certainly an oddball. And I bet his wife has a lot of problems dealing with him since his injury."

Jick read for a few minutes longer. He was certain this explained Uncle George's unexpected and exaggerated giggling the first time he met him.

Poor guy. Probably can't control it. Wonder what he was like before his brain injury. Now he's just a friendly old fart.

Finlayson let himself into his condo. He went into the kitchen and peered into the refrigerator. A half-full bottle of white wine in the door beckoned him. His hand shook as he poured himself a glass. His stomach had settled after the events at Sturgis' house. He noticed Sherwin sitting on the lanai, reading a book. He stared at him, undecided on a course of action. Then, making up his mind, he walked out onto the lanai.

"Hi, David," Sherwin looked up from his book.

"Hi, Sherwin," Finlayson swirled his glass as he sat next to Sherwin. "How's things in the lab?"

"Fine," he replied. "Everything is pretty much set up as you had wanted."

"Good, good," Finlayson said. "Sherwin, I can probably finish up here. There's not much left to do. You should head back home."

"I'm in no rush. We have a little more work to do, and I'm happy to help you finish."

"No," Finlayson said abruptly. "You should go. Now."

Sherwin paused, surprised at Finlayson's tone. He noted the sheen of perspiration on Finlayson's face and noticed his brows knitted together. Finlayson's hand shook as he picked up his glass.

"Everything okay? Did the meeting at Mr. Sturgis' place go okay?"

"The meeting was fine. I..." he paused. "I can't say more, but I really need you to leave now."

Sherwin shut his book.

"David, what is going on?"

"Nothing."

"I asked you before we came here if we were doing something illegal. You said no, and now you want me to leave before finishing the project."

"I needed your help getting things organized in setting up the project. I did not need your help to finish it."

Sherwin studied Finlayson's face.

"You're hiding something, David. Something got you seriously freaked out."

Finlayson opened his mouth to say something. Then closed it. Then opened it again.

"I can't talk about it. It's not illegal. But I need to make it right. And I can't do it with you here. So, go back home. It's for the best."

"Okay, if that's what you and Mr. Sturgis want, I'll go. I'll finish out this week and book a weekend flight out."

"That's fine. For the next couple of days, just hang out here or on the beach. You don't need to do anything at the lab. I'll take care of it."

"You don't want me to go back to the lab at all?"

"No."

Sherwin took one last stab at the problem.

"David, is this something you can go to the police about?"

"What? No, of course not. This is not a police matter."

"Okay, if you say so. I'm going to take a nap. I'll start packing my stuff tomorrow."

Sherwin retreated to his room.

Finlayson fetched his laptop from his bedroom and sat at the dining table. He opened his laptop, opened a browser window, and started searching.

For the next two hours, he searched various websites until he found what he was looking for.

Sherwin emerged from his nap to see Finlayson sitting at the dining table, laptop open, reading. He appeared engrossed in an article and did not notice Sherwin going into the kitchen, pouring himself a glass of water. Sherwin glanced at the screen. It looked like Finlayson had opened an archived newspaper article. Although the text was illegible from this distance, Sherwin could make out the headline: "Murder of Pregnant Woman and Medical Team Shocks Greece."

Sherwin Smith's eyebrows shot up in astonishment.

Finlayson looked up with a start as he noticed Sherwin in the kitchen.

"Sherwin. Sorry, didn't see you there."

"What are you reading? You looked...absorbed in that article."

Finlayson shut the laptop.

"Oh, nothing," he said. "Just something interesting I came across."

He poured himself more wine before opening the sliding door to the lanai.

"I'm going to catch some sun," he said. "Have you booked your flight?"

"No, I was having a nap. I'll do it now."

After Finlayson slid the door shut, Sherwin walked around to the dining table. He opened the laptop. It had not logged off, and the archived newspaper article was still on the screen. Sherwin read the article and shut the laptop. He leaned back into the dining room chair, a frown on his face.

"Shit."

THIRTY-THREE

Jick settled on a cabana lounge chair, sipping a Mai Tai. A plate of appetizers sat on a table next to him. The sun traced a slow descending arc through the sky. As it crossed behind the clouds, dazzling, radiant pink rays radiated like celestial fingers reaching for the sky. His laptop perched on his lap as he clicked through pictures.

He had retrieved the data card from the second day and noted the camera had archived nine pictures. Each showed the same man in different poses, each time carrying the same object. Three pictures showed him walking toward the garage and three pictures showed him heading out on his ATV. The other three pictures showed him heading back on his ATV.

Weird. I can't figure out what that guy is doing. I wish I could clear up the picture.

His phone rang. It was Sam.

"Hi, Jick, got a minute?"

"Sure, what's up?"

Sam got right to the point.

"I need to talk to you about something odd that just came to my attention. It may or may not have any bearing on this case."

Jick waited for Sam to go on.

"A few years ago, there was a murder on the Big Island. A young man who worked at a bar was murdered as he left work. Someone knifed him in the parking lot while he changed a flat tire. They never found the killer."

"Okay, so what's the significance?"

"I get an emailed update once a month from an organization that maintains a database of cold cases. Mostly, it's an update of which cold cases are solved, and which may have had some fresh developments. Yesterday, I received the monthly update, and as I looked through it, one case caught my eye because it was in Hawaii."

"This stabbing case?"

"Yes. When they autopsied this young man, there was one unusual finding. They noticed blood around his mouth. He was stabbed in the chest, and these kinds of wounds often result in bleeding from the mouth."

"Yes," Jick said wryly. "It's very common in the movies and on TV. In real life, mouth bleeding is less common. You have to hit certain blood vessels, and it has to bleed into the bronchial tree for the person to cough up blood."

"Fine, Doctor Jick," Sam chided. "Let's not get too technical."

"So what was unusual about this particular finding?"

"I'm getting there. To get back to my story, the unusual part was the lack of blood in his mouth or the back of his throat. There were also no lacerations in his mouth. That meant the blood around his mouth was from him biting his attacker. Which meant it was the killer's blood. Maybe the killer covered his mouth so no one would hear if he screamed out and the victim bit his hand trying to escape. They fed the DNA into the national database, but there was no match. The case has since gone cold."

"Was there finally a DNA match?"

"You're getting ahead of me, Jick. But yes, there was a match. Here's where things get weird.

"Some twenty-five years ago, in Greece, specifically on the island of Lesvos, there was a murder, or I should say, murders. Plural. When it happened, it was a big deal and made several news cycles in Greece. Outside Greece, there was just a minor splash for a couple of days and then it fell off the radar.

"They found four people murdered in a room that was repurposed as an operating room in a private residence. The residence was owned by someone who had died a couple of years earlier, and the property was tied up in some type of litigation. Anyway, long story short, there was supposed to be no one living there. It was in a remote location.

"Whoever set up this operating room knew what they were doing. A generator supplied the electricity; all the necessary equipment was there to do one specific type of operation, and there were three staff members. We presume they were prepaid a large sum of money for their silence. All of this was done hush-hush, and there was no paper trail. No one knew about this until the bodies were discovered."

"Convenient," Jick murmured. "So, what specific type of surgery were they planning to do?"

"A cesarean section."

"What?"

"That's right. A cesarean section."

"And what happened?"

"All three staff members and the mother were shot and killed. The mother's belly was still open. There was no baby."

"That's no surprise. Someone took the baby. So, what's the DNA connection?"

"I'm getting there. Authorities collected DNA from all four victims. One of those DNA samples matched the person whose DNA was in the mouth of the dead restaurant worker in Kona, Hawaii."

"Really? The DNA from a dead person matched the blood found in this stabbing victim's mouth? That doesn't make any sense. Which one of the victims in Greece did the DNA come from?"

"Don't know. All I saw was the positive match. I emailed Greece. I'm hoping to get more information and maybe even the crime scene photos in the next couple of days."

"Why do you think there's a connection with this Sturgis case?"

"Oh, I forgot to mention the best part. I did some background research into the victim. Turns out he was the guy responsible for Sturgis' brain injury. He piloted the boat that hit Sturgis a few months earlier."

"Oh, that kid," Jick exclaimed. "I heard about this. The waitress at the resort told me the kid who had been piloting the boat that hit Sturgis was killed a few months later. I didn't realize we were talking about the same guy.

"Well, well, well, now this does get interesting. Didn't you say Sturgis was Greek?"

"Yes."

"So, a kid was killed in Hawaii, and the killer's DNA shows up from an unsolved murder in Greece twenty-five years ago...

"I'd like to see the crime scene pictures. Can you get them?"

"Of course. Any particular reason why?"

"Curiosity. It may help. To get an idea of how professional this operating room setup was. Oh, and is there any way you can get the autopsy report of the kid who was killed here?"

"Sure, why? We know he was stabbed to death."

"Curiosity. Sometimes you can tell from the type of injuries, the number of wounds, location, etc., the state of mind of the murderer."

"I'll see what I can do."

Jick hung up and leaned back in his lounge chair. The Mai Tai had become watered down from the melting ice. He swigged it and signaled for another. He jiggled his finger on the touchpad, and his laptop sprang to life. A directory window listed the filenames of all the pictures he had archived since he had activated the camera, each picture date and time stamped, listed in chronological order. He frowned as he stared at the computer, preoccupied by his conversation with Sam.

What the hell is going on here? Except for the hospital equipment logo on that one shipment, I got nothing. None of these pictures mean anything. Now this...

He glanced at the directory window again. The setting sun had dimmed and was now perched on the top edge of his laptop screen. He pulled the screen shut and watched as the sun set between his legs. His toes cradled either side of the sun as it sank toward the waves. He took a few pictures with his phone, captioned one *"Like my orange soccer ball?"* and sent it to Sam.

He stuffed his laptop back into its case.

I'm missing something here.

He stared at the directory window as he zipped his laptop case shut. A nagging sensation fluttered in his stomach.

THIRTY-FOUR

The following two days were uneventful. Jick skipped a day and then went back to retrieve his camera's data. At the hotel, he loaded the pictures onto his laptop and started clicking through them. They were more of the same grainy pictures of the same man carrying a rectangular object back and forth and riding an ATV on multiple occasions.

I need to figure this out. What's that guy carrying? Too bad I can't move the camera closer.

On one occasion, he saw a truck parked against the garage building. The next picture showed a box partly loaded into the truck with about three feet of the box sticking out of the back of the truck.

Another delivery.

Jick's phone rang. It was Sam.

"Sam, how's it going? Got anything new?"

"Good, good. Hope I didn't wake you up."

"No, I was up."

"Believe it or not, we already got some pictures of the crime scene in Greece. The authorities there are just as stumped by a positive match in Hawaii. They're eager to solve this case, as it was a public relations fiasco when it happened. It was an obstetrician, an anesthetist, and a nurse, all gunned down, along with a refugee woman from Africa."

"The mother was a refugee from Africa?"

"Yes," Sam said. "According to the Greek authorities, someone bribed an official at a migrant camp on Lesvos to conduct interviews with several young women. The victim, whose name was Mariama Ndiaye, is the only information we have. She vanished from the camp and disappeared, so someone must have smuggled her out. No one knew she had disappeared until they found her dead. For these refugees, the only information they collected was their name and fingerprints. Few of the refugees had any form of ID, so even the name may be fake."

"Did she have any family in the camp with her? Or was she alone?"

"She had a younger brother, a two-year-old son, and her mother."

"Didn't the mother complain that her daughter was missing?"

"I don't know."

"What happened to them?"

"They were sent back to Senegal."

Jick was silent for a minute as he contemplated what might have happened to this unfortunate woman's family when they were sent back to Senegal. They would have exhausted their savings getting to Greece. With nothing but a glimmer of hope for a better life. Now her son would arrive back an orphan. Would they have been welcomed back in the village? Would they have had the means to support themselves?

I bet the poor mother would have had to raise her son and her grandson. All their dreams of a better life crushed...

His attention returned to the case.

"Was Mariama Ndiaye already pregnant when she disappeared from the camp?"

"I don't know. I emailed the pictures to you. They're password-protected. I'll give you the password. Check your email. We can look at them together."

"Sure."

Jick opened his email. He typed in the password, and the pictures loaded. He clicked on the first one, his frown deepening as he clicked through the series.

It was a standard operating room with the usual operating table, overhead lights on boom arms, an anesthesia machine, a resuscitation table, another table with surgical tools, and an infant warmer. Blackout curtains hung over the window in the background.

Not a hospital. No hospital-grade OR has curtains.

What made this operating room unusual was the position and state of the occupants.

At the base of the operating table lay a man in surgical garb. He was face down in the middle of a blood puddle. The bullet had hit him in the middle of his upper back. By the copious amount of blood, it looked like he had contributed to the blood pooled on the floor from the patient.

Poor guy was facing the patient, closing the uterus. He didn't know what hit him.

The patient lay supine. Jick could see the low transverse incision in her abdomen and what looked like a dried curtain of blood from her pelvis to the floor, adding to the puddle the surgeon lay in. The uterus lay on top of her abdomen. It resembled a deflated football as the obstetrician had almost finished sewing the incision shut. The top of the patient's head was blown off, and a large crimson flower had splashed across the anesthesia machine.

The anesthetist lay in a heap at the head of the table. His face and head were intact, but the front of his neck looked like he wore a dark red scarf. After he had fallen, a towel landed on his neck and soaked up enough blood that it looked like he had draped a scarf around his neck.

A young woman lay at the foot of the infant warmer. She was the only victim whose face was visible. Jick noted the expression of horror. She had been in mid-scream when she was cut down.

Poor kid. She sure as hell knew what was about to happen.

The infant warmer was empty.

"Which of these four victims' DNA matched the Hawaii murder?" Jick asked.

"Don't know yet. I'm expecting another email from Greece any minute. I wanted to share the pictures as soon as I got them. I'll call you as soon as I hear anything else."

"Okay."

Jick hung up the phone.

I'm missing something here. There's something staring at me in the face, and I'm not seeing it.

A short thirty minutes later, Sam called again. Her voice almost bubbled with excitement.

"Jick, you're not going to believe this. The DNA sample did not match one of the four victims. The sample that matched *was from the fifth person in the room.*"

Jick had a sudden realization, and he drew in a sharp breath.

"The baby?!"

"Yes, Jick, from the mother's abdomen. The placenta. The baby's DNA matched the killer's DNA here in Hawaii."

"Makes sense," Jick said. "I should have realized that right away. Of course, the DNA match couldn't have been from one of the dead people.

"So, who was this baby? And how did he end up in Hawaii? Somewhere here on this island is a twenty-five-year-old man who murdered an employee of a restaurant. And he was born to a Senegalese mother in Greece, a mother who was also murdered, along with everyone in the room, when she gave birth to him."

"Here's the other news. *The Senegalese mother's DNA didn't match the baby's.*"

"What?"

"That's right."

Jick leaned back in his chair.

"It's possible she was used as a surrogate. Which makes more sense. No one is going to kidnap a refugee woman, impregnate her, and kill her just for the heck of it. She was used. Used most likely as a surrogate. And she went along with it because they must have offered her something like asylum. But why was she then killed? And why kill the medical staff? What the hell is going on?"

"Good questions, Jick. I guess you're going to stay there and dig deeper?"

"Oh, hell yes. I have to. Whether I find Alicia, this is too good a problem."

"Be careful."

"Sam, I am." He grinned at Sam. "I always am, Sam. And I had green eggs and ham. For breakfast."

Sam ignored the joke.

"Okay, for my next question," Jick said. "Is there any connection at all between this case and the Sturgis case?"

"There has to be. Can this just be a coincidence?"

"Don't know. I'll keep looking around here. Uncle George wants me to go to a party to discuss recruiting doctors to Hawaii. I think I'll go. Wonder if he knew the kid who hit him in the boat accident."

THIRTY-FIVE

Jick had a restless night's sleep, his mind circling the scattered, seemingly unrelated pieces of the case.

I'm going to need three cups of coffee this morning...

He spent the morning lounging by the pool, laptop balanced on his outstretched legs. With nothing else to do until Uncle George's party that evening, he navigated back to the county website to peruse properties in the nature reserve.

Let's see what else is there.

As he flew over the nature reserve with his cursor, he clicked on the toggle that turned off satellite mode and turned on plan view, which displayed boundaries. To his surprise, he noted that all the developed properties in the nature reserve were on only twenty-acre lots, which meant all the land to the west of the subdivision was also unused but not part of the nature reserve.

And probably unusable since there's no access. Unless there were easements across the developed lots, which I doubt the owners would approve of. I wonder if the state has any plans for this land.

Jick noted that all the unusable land was marked as one contiguous lot owned by the state, except for a parcel that adjoined the Sturgis estate on the west and was not marked as state-owned.

Wonder who owns this piece.

He clicked on the property.

"Sturgis Trust," he read. "Wow, he owns a hundred acres of undeveloped forest land on top of his twenty-acre estate. Wonder what he's doing with it."

Jick went back to the satellite view and tried to adjust the view so he could see it in 3-D. Like Sturgis' principal estate, this parcel also abutted the bluffs. Further west of this parcel, the unusual microclimate that gave rise to the forest ended in an abrupt line at the top of the valley edge. The topography changed to the dry, desert-like terrain of the western side of the Big Island. No roads led to the property from the west. As he zoomed down almost to the ground, he could discern vague lines that suggested dirt roads or tracks.

Looks like it can be reached with a four-wheel drive from the west.

He clicked on "Contour Lines" and thin lines of equal elevation overlaid the map. He angled the parcel to get a better three-dimensional feel for the lot. Like Sturgis' main parcel, this one extended from the base of the bluff like a shelf which gradually angled downward. He clicked on "Information" about the lot. Based on tax records, it appeared there had been a dwelling on the lot some thirty years ago, but it had long since been abandoned or demolished. The county had stopped collecting taxes based on property value at least twenty-five years ago. Now the lot was just considered agricultural, with no easement access. The entire lot had an annual tax of one hundred dollars.

Not bad. A hundred acres of pristine land with no access for just a hundred bucks a year. Good thing I have a Jeep. I sense a day of exploration. Maybe tomorrow...

He zoomed in and magnified it as much as possible, but the details were too grainy to identify any structures.

But if I wanted to build a structure on this lot, it would be closer to the cliffs, where the "shelf" is flatter.

He noticed Sam had emailed him the autopsy report of the boat pilot kid and had also included the police report of the investigation, along with some of her narrative notes. He clicked on her notes.

"Caleb Jonathan worked at a restaurant. Some months earlier, he had gone out with a group of friends on a boat that belonged to the father of one of his buddies. They took turns piloting the boat. Caleb had never piloted a boat this large and did not have the experience needed to maneuver a boat. He sped up and down the bay and struck a person from another boat that was anchored some distance away. That passenger was George Sturgis.

"Mr. Jonathan was charged, but in court, his lawyer argued Sturgis had swum too far from his boat and was outside the legal limit defined by the 'Diver Down' statute. The charges were dismissed.

"Sturgis spent a protracted period in the hospital, undergoing rehabilitation. Not too long afterwards, Caleb Jonathan was the victim of an assault outside his workplace. He was knifed to death while attempting to change a flat tire. The investigation showed the flat tire had a deliberate puncture on the sidewall."

He clicked Sam's notes shut and opened the autopsy report.

Most of it was standard boilerplate stuff about the subject's size, general description, size and weight of various internal organs, and results of toxicology samples.

Then he got to the interesting part, the description of the wounds. Caleb Jonathan was stabbed at least twenty times, mostly in his right chest but also in his left chest, over the heart. There was a deep stab wound on the right side of his neck and two on the left side.

"Right-handed killer," Jick surmised. "He must have first punctured the tire, then waited. He must have wrapped his left arm around Caleb's face, covered his mouth, and stabbed him repeatedly on the right side until he collapsed. Then he stabbed him a few times on the left side.

"There was nothing out of the ordinary in Caleb's life, except the boat incident. The owner of the boat, who was quite wealthy, hired a top defense attorney, and Caleb got off.

"I wonder... with Sturgis' known narcissistic tendencies, would he have ordered a hit on this kid? I don't see it. Maybe before his head injury. Now he's just a doofus."

He shut his laptop.

He spent the rest of the day swimming, eating, and napping, interspersed with Mai Tais and chilled whites. By the time five o'clock rolled around, Jick was relaxed and awake.

Nothing beats doing nothing on a vacation. Let's go see what Uncle George wants.

THIRTY-SIX

Jick threw on a pair of shorts with an aloha shirt, sandals, and took off for Uncle George's party. Ten miles south of the resort, Jick approached the designated mile marker and slowed, easing the Jeep onto the shoulder. Spotting a dirt road that led makai toward the ocean, he navigated the short stretch of less than a mile and came to a dirt parking lot. In the distance, he could see a small gazebo tent under which a few people sat.

He parked and climbed out. As he approached the tent, he spotted Uncle George, Finlayson, Pavel, Sherryl Sturgis, and Thaddeus. While Thaddeus stood to one side, arms crossed, the others sat around a table. There was no music to interrupt the sound of the waves. The blue flames of food warmers flickered against the underside of a half-dozen dome-covered pans that sat on a table along the left side. Next to the table, a bartender stood under a tiki bar with a thatched roof.

"Jick, welcome to the party," Uncle George boomed out a loud greeting.

"Thanks for having me," Jick said. "Small group here. Am I early?"

"No, not at all," Uncle George said. "Please. Have a seat."

"No live band today?"

"No, not tonight. Also, this invitation was mostly for us to discuss your medical consultant connections."

"Oh?" Jick asked, settling into a chair. "What did you want to discuss?"

"Later, later," Uncle George said, waving him off. "Let's start with a drink and an introduction."

He swept an arm in an expansive gesture toward the woman sitting at his side.

"Jick, this is my wife, Sherryl."

Jick glanced at George.

"Yes, we've met. My first day here. At your party."

"Oh, of course, of course."

Jick focused on Uncle George's wife. Her hair was once again perfectly styled, but this time, the gray roots were also the same reddish tint. She had chosen a bright crimson shade of lipstick, which matched her nails. Her eyes were not watery this time, but she wore glasses.

Probably getting used to new contacts last time.

Her face looked drawn. Dark circles under her eyes were visible through the makeup.

She looks like she's been crying. I wonder what's going on.

He held out his hand.

"Pleased to meet you again," he said to Uncle George's wife.

"Hello again," Sherryl replied. "I didn't know why you joined us on the beach that day. George says you were destined to meet, yeah?"

"I don't know about that. I just dialed a wrong number."

"That wasn't even his number," Sherryl said. "That was my number you called a couple of days ago, Jick. He took my phone by mistake. When it rang, he answered. A random event. So, you were destined to meet, yeah?"

She had picked up the Hawaiian linguistic mannerism of confirming a statement with "yeah?" at the end.

Jick smiled.

"Sure."

A server appeared at Jick's side with a glass of red wine. He placed a martini in front of Uncle George and a Mai Tai in front of Sherryl Sturgis. The remaining drinks on his tray were a beer for Finlayson and a clear liquid in a chilled glass for Pavel. There was no drink for Thaddeus.

I bet Pavel's having vodka.

Jick eyed Sherryl Sturgis' drink, served in a large Tiki glass with the scowling visage of an imaginary Polynesian god.

Looks like one of those Moai statues. Straight out of Easter Island.

A halo of dark rum crowned the drink. A pineapple slice and maraschino cherry perched on the edge of the glass, speared on a small cocktail sword. With the sprig of pineapple leaf and paper umbrella finishing the presentation, it looked like it belonged in a brochure for an island paradise holiday.

That bartender sure knows how to present his drinks. I think one of those has my name on it. I'll have one later.

"Where's your assistant?" Jick asked Finlayson.

"He couldn't make it tonight. He's packing. We've almost finished our work here, and he needs to return to the mainland this weekend."

Uncle George raised his martini.

"A toast," he announced. "We're going to have a toast for Jick and his medical consultancy company. Here's to its success."

Jick frowned.

"You're having a toast for my job as a medical consultant?"

"Of course, of course," Uncle George said. "Like I said, that's why I asked you here tonight. But before we start, a prayer."

Jick said nothing as Uncle George clasped his wife's hand with his left hand and Finlayson's hand with his right.

"Let's form a circle."

Jick glanced around the table. Sherryl had lowered her eyes, her expression unreadable. Thaddeus maintained his impassive look, looking off in the distance. Everyone else except Uncle George looked uncomfortable. Uncle George beamed at them.

No one seemed to be in a rush to form a circle. Jick caught an expression of anger as it flitted across Uncle George's face. Jick reached for Sherryl's left hand and

Finlayson's right hand. With some reluctance, the group formed a complete circle.

"Heavenly Father," Uncle George cooed, "Bless this man and his business. Our beautiful aina needs doctors, and we have been blessed with the arrival of Jick...," he paused to look at Jick, "last name?"

This is getting really weird.

"Arnold."

"...Arnold. With your blessings, I will help Mr. Arnold bring more healers to the island. Amen."

A murmured "Amen" went around the table. Uncle George released his wife's and Finlayson's hands. Everyone followed suit.

Jick leaned back and surveyed the small crowd.

This guy is nuts. No way he's cloning a human.

"Let's eat," Uncle George said.

The waiter plated a course of Hawaiian-style kalua pork, *lomi salmon*, mashed potatoes, steamed vegetables, and a salad.

Looks delicious. But where's the heat? No hot sauce, no achar, not even some jalapeños?

Jick turned to Sherryl Sturgis as the meal wound down.

"You look a little tired today. Are you feeling okay?"

"Yes, I'm fine," she said. She drew a shaky breath and then continued.

"George told me about you and what you do. A medical consultant who helps young doctors. You're just the person we need to attract new doctors here."

"I'm not so sure," Jick said. "There's a lot that goes into setting up a medical practice and in this state, I think the legislators should consider laws to sweeten the pot to attract new doctors. I deal only in the logistics of setting up the practice. I don't control the reimbursement."

"With George's influence, I'm sure you can work something out, yeah?"

Pavel, a man of few words, chimed in.

"How long you do this?"

Jick glanced at him.

"A few years."

"And what you did before that?"

"Various jobs," Jick deflected. "And how about you? What do you do now? Something in the medical field?"

"No," Pavel said. "I work in the medical field in the past. Perhaps we should discuss together how to bring doctors to Hawaii."

"Uh, sure," Jick said.

"What do you do now?" Jick repeated the question.

"Not too much. I help Uncle George with things. Right now, I am helping David in the lab."

He did not offer any additional details. Jick was thankful he had steered the conversation away from his own experiences. The bartender filled everyone's glasses. Jick declined the wine and ordered a Mai Tai.

Better be careful. I've already had, I don't know, quite a bit of wine.

After dinner, Uncle George leaned back with a sigh of contentment, a glass of port in his hand. He lifted it in Jick's direction. Jick responded with his Mai Tai glass.

"Let's talk about doctors, shall we?"

"Okay, what would you like to talk about?"

"I've used doctors all my life," Uncle George said.

"I bet you used some after that injury," Jick said.

Uncle George caressed his scar, tracing a line with his finger and ending with a flourish as he traced the "C" over the shunt scar.

"I did, I did," Uncle George nodded.

"He had a lobectomy," Pavel said. "That's when they have to take out a lobe in his brain. And then they put in a shunt. A little tube to move his brain fluids to his body."

"Why do they do that?" Jick asked.

He sure talks more now that he's had a few glasses of vodka. I wonder how he knows the jargon...

"To reduce the pressure in the brain," Pavel said.

"What happened? If you don't mind my asking," Jick asked.

"Not at all," Uncle George replied. "I was on a boat with some friends, just a couple of miles off the coast of

Kona. And some kids were zooming around on the water. They didn't see me and ran over me in the boat."

"Do you remember any of it?"

"I remember the first time the boat went past. Some kid was behind the wheel. Then the boat turned and came back. All my friends had climbed back aboard. That's all I remember..."

Uncle George's face took on a dreamy look as he thought back to that day. Then his face reddened. His face contorted into an expression of rage.

"Some damn fool kid. He could've killed me. What a loss."

Then a smile broke out.

"But we let bygones be bygones. Let's enjoy the party."

"Did you know someone killed that kid a few months later?" Jick asked.

Uncle George froze, then turned to Jick with a fixed, blank stare.

Geez, he looks different. What a weirdo.

"Yes, I had heard," Uncle George nodded slowly. "I don't know any details. He probably did something reckless behind the wheel and was in an accident? Or was it drugs?"

"Neither. Someone stabbed him to death in the parking lot of the restaurant where he worked. He had just finished his shift. I heard it was in the news here. I'm surprised you didn't know he had been knifed."

Another blank stare.

Those eyes. Weird how he goes from twinkling and friendly to a blank stare like that.

"The courts should have punished him because of what he did to me. They didn't. And now he's dead," Uncle George said. "Whether it was an accident, or he was knifed, not much of a loss."

Geez, he also sounds different. Wonder what that brain injury did to him...

"Of course it's a loss," Jick said. "He made a huge mistake, and the courts did what the law dictated. He did not deserve to have his life taken from him. I hope you at least sued the boat owners if you felt the courts were too lenient on the boy."

"The courts absolved the boat owner of liability," Uncle George said. "And suing the kid would have been like trying to squeeze blood out of a rock."

Uncle George continued to stare at Jick. Jick noticed his face had reddened.

"I don't want to talk about this anymore," Uncle George said. The blank stare disappeared, and the twinkling expression returned. He broke into a smile.

"Let's talk about doctors, shall we?"

This guy is a weirdo... and Sam thinks he's cloning a human?

Jick's eyes roved over the scars.

Personality changes from frontal lobe injuries are so unpredictable.

"Okay," Jick said. "Let's talk about doctors. What can I do for you?"

"Oh, not here, not here," Uncle George said. "Tonight is just socializing and relaxing. I like you, Jick. I wanted to let you know what I have planned. I would like to provide startup funds to attract more doctors to the Big Island. Tomorrow, I'll send a car around to the Hawaiian Orchid and I would like you to come to my place. I have a formal proposal put together. With a juicy consulting fee for you. I think you'll like it."

Jick drained the last of his Mai Tai and smiled at his host.

"Sounds good. I'll be there."

"Which room are you in?"

"412."

"Excellent. Shall we say around nine a.m.?"

"Yes, that would be fine. I don't have any other plans tomorrow."

"Perfect. See you tomorrow."

THIRTY-SEVEN

The rising sun cast a dim glow over the beach and ocean. Jick had awakened early and wandered down to the beach. As the sun rose, the palette of colors came alive. The grey in the trees faded as vibrant shades of green and gold radiated from the leaves and sand. The ocean sparkled where sunlight struck the wave crests. Jick leaned back on his chaise, sipping his coffee.

This Kona coffee is damn good.

In the clear light of day, with the haze of the previous night's wining and dining having worn off, a mild feeling of unease settled over him.

Wonder what he really wanted me for. No way he arranged a party for me just to bring more doctors here. Even if there is a shortage on this island.

He cast an idle glance to the right and saw a member of the hotel staff heading toward the cottages. She carried a tray stacked with several dishes. As she walked around a corner, a hotel guest arrived from the opposite direction. With a deft pivot, she lifted the tray and did a graceful pirouette around the guest. Jick saw the guest say something.

Probably an apology for the near miss.

From this distance, the cluster of dishes on the tray looked like the outline of a city skyline. The silver domes covering the hot food were a stadium. A carton of chocolate milk formed a peaked building with its sloped roof. A slender vase with an orchid resembled a tree next to the building, and a glass of orange juice looked like a silo.

Looks like the cover of Supertramp's "Breakfast in America."

As she walked toward the cottages, Jick continued tracking her until she was out of sight. The woman's gait, the way she carried the object, and its shape. Flat on the bottom, contoured like a cityscape on top. Something clicked in Jick's brain.

Jesus, it's a food tray.

Jick bounded out of the chaise and hurried back to his room. He sat at the desk, flipped open his laptop, and loaded the pictures from the spy camera. He flipped through them, stopping at a picture of the mystery man and the object he carried. There was no mistaking it. The grainy object the man in the photos carried several times a day was a food tray.

Jick scrolled through the directory of images and reviewed every picture that featured the man carrying the object. The timestamps corresponded to morning, afternoon, and evening. Some pictures showed the man heading west; some showed him returning. On one day, the camera picked up the man heading west and returning. Jick examined the timestamps; forty-five minutes separated the two pictures.

Breakfast, lunch, and dinner. Holy shit, he's carrying a food tray to someone.

Jick leaped off the bed and paced his room.

He carries a food tray out three times a day, loads it into that ATV, and heads west, to the empty hundred-acre parcel Sturgis owns. Then he brings it back about an hour later. Who the hell does Sturgis have out there? Who gets those trays?

Jick contemplated his next step.

"I need to check out that hundred-acre wood."

He called Sam.

"Hi, Jick," Sam exclaimed. "I was about to call you."

"For what? Never mind. Let me tell you about my development, and then you tell me yours.

"I'll get straight to the point. Until a few minutes ago, we had nothing to go on. Now we may."

"What's changed?"

"I'm not sure," Jick said. "That camera picked up multiple pictures of a guy carrying an object that I just figured out may be a food tray."

"A food tray?"

"Yes, and he carries it to an ATV and heads out into a hundred-acre parcel of land that's west of Sturgis' main house. Three times a day. Breakfast, lunch, and dinner. That parcel has no easement to any roads and has essentially very little to no value. It was probably part of the huge state-owned nature reserve, and Sturgis somehow acquired it."

"So, he's carrying food to someone out there. This is getting interesting. Wonder what it means."

"I don't know. All I know is there's a guy who takes food out there every day. I need to find out what's going on."

"Be careful."

"I will. What have you got?"

"I called Greece and talked to one of their detectives. They're eager to send us any information they can about this cold case. Turns out the two murdered doctors were illegally in the country. One was Senegalese; the other was from Ghana. Regardless, Greece has an ongoing problem with illegal immigration from Africa, and this murder created a political shitstorm because two doctors entered the country illegally, months apart, performed a cesarean section, then were murdered. Along with a Greek nurse. It was a long time ago, and it's faded from the public, but it's still a sensitive case, and the Greek authorities would love to solve it."

"Is that it?"

"No, I haven't got to the best part yet.

"I mentioned the connection with Sturgis since it's all we've got, and they did some digging. Sturgis and his parents left Greece when he was very young but guess what? He returned to Greece two years before the murders *and went to a fertility clinic.*"

"What?!"

"A smoking gun, Jick. He goes to a fertility clinic and later, there's a gruesome mass killing during a cesarean section. Then the baby's DNA turns up at a murder scene in Hawaii twenty-five years later."

"Did they have any records? Any idea what he, or they, if he was married, did at that clinic?"

"He was married. But they didn't have much else. I think the Greek authorities may have had to dig through dusty boxes in some hospital's basement. What they found were records of Sherryl Sturgis undergoing hormonal treatment getting ready for an egg harvest. And an appointment notification for George Sturgis, presumably to donate a sperm sample. That's pretty much it."

"They couldn't have children. That's obvious. So, what did Sturgis and his wife do next? Recruit an illegal immigrant from Africa to be a surrogate and then murder her? And the medical personnel? Makes no sense."

"No, it doesn't. But it's all we've got for now."

"But what we're saying is, there is a possibility Sturgis' son is a murderer, right?"

"Possibly. It's still a stretch to connect these dots and say they lead to Sturgis' son. We have three or four incidents separated by time and distance and it seems the only common thread is a connection to the Sturgis family. But we still need proof. I'm still not sure how this ties in with what we began investigating in the first place. Is Sturgis trying to clone a person? If so, why?"

Jick sighed and rubbed his temples.

"I need to explore that hundred-acre wood. Wanna send me a gun?"

"What? Jick, if you think you need a gun, you need to call the police."

"I have nothing to give them. Just a vague suspicion that there's more to Sturgis' estate than meets the eye. Besides, according to some locals, Sturgis is in thick with the cops. And I can't just walk into a gun store here and buy a gun. Isn't there a federal loophole that allows you to send a gun here?"

"There is," Sam admitted. "You'll need to take care of it and surrender it when you leave. Jick, this is making me nervous. You're getting into something dangerous again."

"I'll be careful," Jick promised. "I don't think I need a gun; it's just that I have a vague feeling something is going on, and I need to evaluate all possibilities."

"I can express ship it to the resort via courier," Sam said.

"Amazing what our government can do," Jick quipped. "Even though you don't officially work for the government, right?"

Sam ignored the comment.

"Okay, sit tight. The gun will be there tomorrow. I guess I feel better knowing you're armed. Just don't get into a gunfight like on your last adventure."

"I won't."

Sam put down the phone, deep in thought. A sense of unease washed over her. She picked up the phone and dialed a number.

"Hi, Sam," Quin answered. "What's up?"

"I just got off a call with Jick. There's something going on in Hawaii. He asked me to send a gun via courier."

Quin whistled.

"What's going on there?"

"Not sure. We just established that a DNA sample from a crime scene in Greece a quarter century ago matched DNA found at a crime scene in Hawaii. Jick wants to investigate it."

"Is it related to the reason he's there?"

"Could be. There may be a connection to the Sturgis case."

"And he's worried enough about it to ask for a gun?"

"Yes, which is why I called. How would you like to be the courier?"

"Sure," Quin did not hesitate. "I'll call him when I get there. He'll be surprised."

"And Gaby can stay here."

"Sounds good. I'll leave tomorrow."

Jick hung up the phone and leaned back on his bed. Realizing the man in the pictures carried a food tray, followed by his conversation with Sam about the murders in Greece and the possible connection to George Sturgis, left him both puzzled and unnerved.

I still can't believe this elderly doofus with brain damage is into something nefarious. There has to be a reasonable explanation for this. So why am I feeling jittery?

He glanced at the clock. Eight-fifty.

"Damn. Uncle George's car is going to be here in ten minutes."

A thought popped into his head.

"Will you walk into my parlour?" said a spider to a fly...

I don't know what he wants me for, but it sure as hell isn't to bring doctors to Hawaii. I wonder if he suspects something about me. But how the hell could he? I need to get out of here.

He grabbed the keys to his Jeep as he walked over to his room door. He peered out the peephole. Seeing no one outside, he opened the door and cast a furtive glance in both directions. No one. He sprinted to the stairwell and stood on the landing, out of sight of anyone in the hallway.

Seven minutes to go.

Nine o'clock arrived, and the hallway remained empty. Jick waited a few more minutes, then clattered down the stairs to the first floor. A door opened onto a garden on the side of the building. Jick cracked open the door, cautiously glanced toward the hotel driveway, then sprinted for a thicket of trees nearby. He crouched in the bushes behind a tree to survey the driveway.

A few minutes passed. Bright sunlight filtered through the trees, creating a dappled pattern on the circular drive. Two birds screeched as they strafed each other before settling in a tree. A golf cart trundled by with an elderly couple; two sets of golf clubs clattered in the back as they went past where Jick crouched. Nothing seemed out of the ordinary in the idyllic setting.

Until Thaddeus emerged from the driver's door of a silver Durango parked near hotel registration. He faced away from Jick, standing at the SUV's open door and staring at the lobby. Jick crouched lower in the bushes.

Two men walked out of the hotel, each wearing a colorful aloha shirt. They made their way to Thaddeus. Jick could not hear the conversation, but one man waved his arms and shrugged his shoulders. The other shook his head, pointing at the lobby. Thaddeus stood staring at the lobby for a moment, lost in thought as he contemplated his next move. Then he said something to the two men, and they climbed into the SUV. It looped around the driveway and headed back toward the highway.

Jick emerged from behind the tree and made his way to the lobby. As he entered the building, he saw two security officers approach the concierge desk. A man stood by the desk, speaking to the concierge. Jick parked himself on a nearby sofa.

The security officers and the man started a conversation. Jick craned his neck in their direction, but with the background music and other people chatting, he could hear nothing. He spotted an ATM closer to the concierge desk, and he walked over to it. He fumbled with his wallet as he eavesdropped on their conversation.

"...he said he was here to take me to a meeting with Uncle George..."

"...told them they had the wrong guy..."

"...they kept insisting..."

The security officers and the man strolled in the direction of the registration desk and the rest of the conversation faded.

Jick watched as the man finished talking to hotel security. After the guards left, he strolled over to the man.

"Hi, there," he said. He held out his hand.

"I'm Jick."

The man did not shake the outstretched hand. He squinted at Jick and frowned.

"Are you the guy those men were looking for? Mr. Arnold, they said."

"I think so."

"Look, I don't know who you are, but my wife and I don't want any trouble. We just want to enjoy our vacation."

"Sorry," Jick said. "I don't know who those men were, either. Is it okay if I ask you a couple of questions about them? You don't need to divulge any personal information."

The man eyed Jick with hesitation. Then he held out his hand.

"Richard."

Jick shook his hand.

"What did those guys do that made you want to call security?"

"They knocked on our door. When I answered, one of them said the car was ready to take me to see someone named Uncle George. No greetings, no introductions, nothing. Just come with us to the car."

"What did you do?"

"I said they had the wrong guy. One of them said it was the right room number. Then the other guy eyed my wife and whispered to the first guy that the person they were going to pick up was by himself."

"And then?"

"The first guy said I had to be the guy because it was the right room. He tried to take me by my arm. I pulled away, closed the door, and called security. Who the hell is this Uncle George guy? Some local mob boss or something?"

"No. I don't think so. Thanks for talking to me."

"Hang on a second," Richard pressed. "Who are you?"

"No one," Jick said. "Just a person looking around."

"Are we going to be okay here?" Richard asked. "Do we need to move somewhere else?"

"No, you'll be fine. Enjoy your vacation."

Jick made his way back to his hotel room, deep in thought. He stopped at the door to scan his card. The room number stared him in the face.

5-1-8.

Five eighteen.

He scrunched his eyes shut as he squeezed the bridge of his nose between his thumb and forefinger. Then he stared at the number again.

I think I gave Uncle George my old room number. 412. That's why they didn't come to the room.

The door latch beeped green. Jick pushed open the door and went in.

I may have just saved myself a heap of trouble...

THIRTY-EIGHT

Sherryl Sturgis knocked on the study door.

"Come in."

Sherryl sat in a chair across from her husband and stared at him. Her eyes were bleary and bloodshot.

"You wanted to talk, George? We need to do something."

"Relax," Sturgis said. "I've got it covered. I called Chief Williams and told him we needed to meet with him. We need his advice on what to do next. I told him it was off the record. You realize if we turn Phoenix in, we won't see him again. Except through a pane of reinforced glass and talking to him through a prison phone. He won't survive in there."

"I know, George. But we can't defend him from this. Or hide what happened. I have never set foot in our other lot, Phoenix's 'playground,' as he and you call it, and I never want to. God only knows what he does there. We know he's sick, yeah? But this is too serious. He killed two people. We have to do the right thing and turn him in."

"Okay, if you insist."

Sherryl's head snapped up.

"What do you mean by if I insist? Don't you feel the same way?"

"Yes, of course I do." He softened his voice, almost coaxing. "Tell you what. Let's take a bottle of wine and head down to the beach park. The one up the road. We'll have a glass of wine, talk about it, and then go to Chief Williams' house. I told him we'd be there..." Sturgis checked his watch, "...at four, so that gives us over an hour."

"Okay, that sounds nice," Sherryl said. Her eyes teared as she realized what they were about to do.

"I'm scared, George. And nervous. I wish I knew why Phoenix did these things."

"I don't know," Sturgis said. "This is all... unnecessary."

Sturgis opened the wine cabinet. He fished out a bottle of red wine from the back of the bottom shelf.

"Ooh la la," Sherryl said. "The good stuff."

"Nothing but the best for you. I think this one is good." He studied the label.

"A pinot noir. From Oregon. Willamette Valley. Someone recommended this one. It's supposed to be excellent."

Sturgis put the bottle, two glasses, and a corkscrew in a wine picnic tote.

As they headed out of the house, Sturgis paused.

"Gotta run back to my office for a second. I was doing some financial stuff and forgot to log off."

Sherryl waited in the car as Sturgis ran to his office for a minute. He returned with the wine tote slung over his shoulder and they set off, heading north, away from Kawaihae. A mile up the road, they came to a small parking lot with six spaces. He parked next to a sign marked "Scenic Overlook." A black fence demarcated the parking lot, and a gravel trail wound to the ocean. A blue and white sign with "Shoreline" and "Public Access" separated by a squiggly wave drawing marked the start of the trail. The few houses in the area were scattered far and wide over what must have been twenty-plus acre lots.

Sturgis slung the wine tote over his shoulder, and they set off, crunching their way down the gravel path. In the relentless midday sun, they had the overlook to themselves. At the end of the trail, a single tree provided some speckled shade over a weatherbeaten bench. From fifty feet below, the sound of waves crashing against the cliff wall rolled over the edge of the overlook in a steady roar. There were no clouds in the sky-blue canopy. The overlook sat in a natural depression in the cliff face, which made the view better and amplified the sound of the ocean. It also meant that no one from the nearby houses could see them.

"UV index must be at least fifteen today," Sherryl remarked.

Sturgis pulled the cork out and poured two glasses. They sat under the single tree, listening to the waves as they savored the first glass.

"This is very good," Sherryl remarked. They enjoyed the wine in silence. Neither seemed to want to start the discussion of the important topic at hand.

Sturgis topped their glasses, took a deep breath, and finally began.

"Let's talk about the pros and cons of turning him in," he began. "Versus not turning him in."

"Of course we're turning him in," Sherryl said. "We kinda have to do the right thing here, yeah?"

"But Phoenix is our son, our flesh and blood."

"And he is a murderer, George," Sherryl snapped. "If we don't turn him in, aren't we also guilty?"

"I don't want to see him in jail."

"Me neither."

"If we turn him in, he will go to jail. For life."

"I can't believe you're talking about not turning him in. *George, our son is a murderer!*"

"I didn't say we shouldn't turn him in. I just wanted to discuss it."

"There's nothing left to discuss."

He leaned closer, lowering his voice as if the waves might overhear.

"How about a compromise?"

Sherryl stared. "A compromise?"

"Yes, how about if I have a talk with him and make him swear he will never do something like this again. He's never done this before. I think he just got carried away because someone was in his playground. I'll install an electric fence around the entire area so no one will ever go inside there. Ever."

"Are you serious? George, this is insane."

Sturgis rose from the bench and stood near the cliff edge. Sherryl joined him, holding her glass. The sun was still overhead but angled toward the distant horizon.

"Looks like it's going to be a beautiful sunset," Sherryl remarked. She turned to Sturgis.

"George, remember when I asked you about that TV show I saw? The one where the kid who hit you in the boat was killed. And I asked you if it could have been Phoenix."

Sturgis' eyes narrowed.

"What about it?"

Sherryl's voice faltered, but she kept going.

"He just killed two people. And cut off their heads. Back then, when you got hurt, he was so traumatized by what happened to you. He adores you, George. And he's sick. I think he has done this before. I bet he did kill that kid. And I bet he did it for you. And when he goes through whatever he's about to go through, we have to be there for him."

Sturgis turned away and walked back to the bench. The wine tote sat on the edge, the top flap unzipped. A second zipper inside the tote concealed an inner pouch, designed for various sundries like a cheese cutting board. He unzipped the inner pouch and reached in. He adjusted his waistband and picking up his glass, returned to Sherryl's side, who was now watching the sun.

"So, you don't like my idea of the compromise?"

"No."

"Is that your final word?"

She turned to look at him, exasperated.

"George, what a ridiculous question. Of course, that's my final word. Now let's go to Chief Williams' house."

"It is going to be a beautiful sunset," he said, looking past her. She turned back to stare at the ocean as he glanced around the overlook.

"It is," she agreed. "Still a few hours away, but there are no clouds. Should be spectacu..."

She was cut off mid-sentence by the sharp whip-crack of a gunshot.

Sturgis had pulled a gun out of his waistband, aimed it at the back of his wife's head, and pulled the trigger. The bullet shattered the front of Sherryl's face as it emerged and sailed over the cliff edge. Sherryl's body jolted forward, and she pitched over the edge, still holding her glass.

Sturgis stared after her, his expression blank, eyes staring. He flung the gun as far as he could and watched it sail over the edge. It flashed in the sunlight as it bisected the glowing orb, spinning in the air before splashing into the sea. He looked around the scenic viewpoint. The spent shell gleamed on the ground. He kicked it over the edge.

He peered over the edge. The waves continued their symphony of the gentle rumble and roar as they crashed against the rocks. Nature had swallowed any evidence of recent activities. Nothing betrayed what had just happened.

Sturgis turned to head back to the car. As he trudged along the path with the wine tote slung over his shoulder, his expression was blank, staring.

A single tear rolled down his right cheek.

THIRTY-NINE

Jick arranged a change of clothes, toiletries, his laptop, locksmithing tools, flashlight, snacks, and a water bottle on his bed. He planned to be away from the hotel for a few days, maybe camp out in the Jeep somewhere.

Maybe Uncle George wanted to talk to me about attracting doctors here. But the whole thing is weird. Something is going on here... besides, I need to check out that hundred-acre wood.

And I guess I can't wait for the gun.

He stuffed his backpack with the items on the bed, took one last look around the room, and exited after taking a cautious glance in both directions. No one was in the hallway. He ran down the back stairs and emerged from the fire exit. He made his way to his Jeep, tossed the backpack on the back seat, and climbed in. He closed his eyes for a moment and let out a *whoosh* of relief.

Why do I suddenly feel like I might be in danger?

His nerves were already on edge when he heard a knock on the passenger window. He jumped, startled by the knock, and saw David Finlayson standing outside. Jick looked around the Jeep for a weapon, but there was nothing obvious he could use.

"I'm alone," Finlayson said through the glass. "And unarmed."

After a moment's hesitation, Jick thumbed the lock open and Finlayson climbed in. As he pulled the door shut, Jick glanced around the parking lot.

"I'm alone," Finlayson repeated. "Good morning."

"Sure no one followed you?"

"Yes. I came from my place. No one knows I'm here."

"What are you doing here?"

Jick noticed his disheveled appearance and stubbled face, eyes rimmed with exhaustion. He looked like he had not slept in days. He waited for Finlayson to speak.

"I wanted to talk to you," Finlayson said, his gaze flicking to the backpack on the back seat.

"Going somewhere?"

"I have some exploring to do."

"Around Sturgis' house?"

"Not your business."

Jick prodded. "You needed to talk to me?"

"Why are you here?" Finlayson countered.

"That's a direct question. Why should I tell you? And for the record, I am a medical consultant."

"You're not here to spy on me?"

"No. But if I was, do you think I would tell you?"

Finlayson gave a humorless smirk. "Guess not."

"Finlayson, why did you come here?"

Finlayson sighed.

"Because I need to do the right thing. And maybe face the consequences. Honestly, I hoped you were some sort of government agent here to spy on me."

"Why do you think the government would want to spy on you? Have you done something wrong?"

"I can't tell you. But I can tell you they are on to you."

"What do you mean? And who is 'they?'"

"You know who. And they know you were spying on them. They saw you on a security camera, both at the lab and at Sturgis' house."

Shit. Now I know why they threw the party for me.

"I'm doing the right thing. You need to get out of here. You're not safe here."

"Thanks for the advice, Finlayson. I appreciate the warning. Want to tell me more?"

"I can't right now. Maybe later."

"Is 'they' Uncle George and Thaddeus?"

At the mention of "Uncle George," Finlayson's eyes hardened.

"Uncle George," he said. "What a character. Jovial, cheerful, always throws wonderful parties. He wasn't like this before his brain injury."

"What do you mean? I thought you'd met him just a few months ago. When he offered you this position here."

Finlayson's hand froze on the door handle. Then he pushed it open.

"Please, for your sake, leave now."

"Finlayson," Jick pressed. "Why can't you take this to the police?"

"Because I can't. It wouldn't do any good. I'm going to finish what I started and then get the hell out myself."

"Why wouldn't going to the police do any good?"

"Sturgis has been here a long time. He's close to the chief of police. I'll say it again. You may be in danger. Leave now for your sake."

Finlayson climbed out and shut the door.

Finlayson coming here confirms there's something going on. Still doesn't connect all the dots but getting closer. Time to do some exploring...

He started the Jeep, pulled onto the highway heading north toward Kawaihae, and then on to the highway to Kohala. As he passed the familiar turnoff to the nature reserve, he continued straight and then slowed, waving faster cars by as he scanned the road. After a mile, the forest ended with a somewhat abrupt transition to the more ubiquitous dry, desert-like scrub that dominated the area. A dirt road appeared on the right. He braked and slowed, tires crunching against the gravel shoulder as he negotiated the turn.

This has to be it.

As he turned, he spotted an SUV with a blue light affixed to the roof, going in the opposite direction. It was a police car. It slowed for a moment, then the officer flashed a shaka at him as he drove by. Jick waved back and watched in his mirror as the police car disappeared down the highway.

That was odd.

The road was well-maintained, and he could see a few houses on the hillside. He crept past the houses as he made his way uphill. After two miles, the well-maintained road dwindled into a series of ruts and potholes, eventually ending at a padlocked farm gate. A sign hung on the gate with the word "Kapu" inscribed.

No trespassing.

"But this should be the edge of the hundred-acre wood, so..."

Jick climbed out of the Jeep. There was no one around.

"Hello?" he shouted. "Aloha."

No reply.

"Okay," he muttered. "Better to beg forgiveness than ask for permission, I guess."

He took his locksmithing tools out of the glove box and in a few minutes, the shackle opened with a satisfying click. He swung the gate open.

I knew this would come in handy.

He tossed the tools back in the glove box and drove through. He closed the gate behind him, leaving the chain loosely draped around the post. Ahead, the edge of the forest loomed. He pushed ahead another hundred feet and eased the Jeep into a natural clearing. To his surprise, a Mustang convertible sat tucked behind a tree, half-hidden, like it had been parked there deliberately.

Jick climbed out.

"Hello, hello," he yelled. "Aloha, anybody here?"

Only the sounds of nature replied to his shouts. He surveyed the area around the parked car, but nothing seemed out of the ordinary. Cupping his hands against the window, he peered into the convertible. He spotted a folded piece of paper tucked into one of the cup holders.

Looks like a rental agreement.

Walking around to the driver's side, he peered down through the windshield and thought he could see the edge of a wallet tucked under the front seat. Three bottles out of a six-pack of bottled drinks lay on the back seat.

Tourists.

He ran his finger along the hood and windshield. His finger left a trail in the dust.

This car's been here for a while. Wonder where they went. No phones in the car that I can see, but that looks like a wallet sticking out from under the seat.

Jick contemplated trying to pick the lock on the car door.

Bad idea. I'm sure I could open the door, but that would set off the alarm.

He made a mental note to report the car when he returned to the hotel. He slung a pack over his shoulder with his water bottle, flashlight, and snacks and headed toward the trees. The sun scorched his skin, and he quickened his pace toward the shade. As soon as he stepped under the trees, it felt like he had opened a door and stepped into an air-conditioned room.

Wow, must be at least ten degrees cooler in the shade.

He trudged through the forest, stopping every few yards to mark a trunk.

"A hundred acres is big. Not sure where to start."

He looked around to see where he stood. He could not see the ocean through the thick trees. The ground sloped up on his left, toward the bluff. He knew Sturgis' house lay ahead, several hundred yards away.

The guy with the tray must have a path from the house. To some sort of building, and big enough for an ATV. No way he's staggering through the trees carrying a tray.

He could not see more than a few trees deep, as the foliage was too dense. During his aerial survey of the property on the county tax website, he did not recall seeing any structures.

The resolution wasn't great. Maybe a building under the cover of trees?

Jick realized that exploring these hundred acres was going to be more difficult than he had envisioned. Walking around the property at random would not accomplish anything. He walked a little further, then decided he would head toward the bluff.

I could walk along the bluff line, maybe see if there's a cave or something, and go from there.

As he began his arduous trek uphill, he caught a whiff of something noxious. He stopped and looked around. The smell of rotting flesh was obvious.

Must be some dead animal nearby.

As he turned to his right, the stench thickened.

Then he saw it.

A few yards ahead, an object that looked like a punching bag suspended from a branch. As he approached, he realized it was an animal suspended from a noose. Judging by the number of insects swarming over its body, the animal had been dead for a while. Jick could see a puddle of discharge and droppings staining the dirt under the carcass. Having nothing to wad under his nose, he held the back of his hand against his nostrils as he approached, eyes watering.

"Jesus," he whispered. "Someone tortured this poor creature."

The tips of its paws had been hacked off, and congealed blood clotted the ends. Swarms of flies and ants clung to the stumps in writhing knots. Rows of gashes striped its body and face, each wound alive with movement. As he watched, a drop of something yellow leaked out of the animal and added to the puddle. Jick backed away from the pig and headed for higher ground, away from the smell.

A bird screeched close to him, and he jumped. The forest suddenly seemed hostile, as whoever tortured and killed the pig could be near. He looked around at the dense foliage, but there was no one present. A bird fluttered through the leaves as it flew out of the forest.

Wish I could have waited for the gun.

He snapped a stout branch off and gripped it both as a walking stick and a weapon. He made his way up to the base of the bluff. The last twenty yards were steep, and he paused to catch his breath, chest heaving, as he clambered up the slope. He took a swig of water and wiped his face. A high-pitched whine announced the mosquitoes had discovered him.

This is getting nowhere fast. I need a more organized plan to check this place out.

He decided he would stick to his plan of exploring the base of the bluff and then head back to the Jeep. Then call Sam and see if he could move to a different resort.

I'm still a little spooked about Uncle George. Especially after Finlayson's warning. I'll lie low for a while.

The ground leveled as he neared the bluff. Sunlight pressed hot against his neck. He considered stepping into the open but stayed in the trees, angling along the slope instead. Shade meant slower progress, but he was in the shade. As he trudged through the trees, he did a calculation in his head.

A hundred acres square is about two thousand feet on each side. I'm probably about five hundred feet from the edge of the forest, so there's a long way to go.

Fifteen minutes later, he froze.

A clearing at the base of the bluff sat in front of what looked like a wall. There was a natural indentation in the bluff, and a wall had been built across it. He spotted two doors, flush with the bluff face. A small, square window, each with bars bolted in a tic-tac-toe pattern, was to the left of each door. Another row of bars was fastened from the top of the wall to the bluff, effectively making the rooms behind the doors a cage.

No way to spot those from the air.

Both doors had deadbolts that were in the locked position, but the door on the right was also padlocked. Both doors had a slot close to the lower edge. Jick's eyes widened when he saw the slot. And on the ground by the slot, a food tray.

Oh, shit.

Jick left the tree line and crept toward the building, listening intently. No sound. He scrambled up the slope and approached the first door, the one without the padlock. He sneaked a quick peek through the window.

Jick saw that the space behind the door was indeed a prison. The indentation in the bluff led to a space that was about twenty feet deep. The only furniture in the room was a mattress. In the back corner of the room, a camp shower and toilet sat side by side with a case of plastic water bottles on the ground next to the shower. A single light bulb hung off the cave roof; a wire led to a small solar panel affixed outside the bars. There was no one inside.

His stomach tightened as he crept to the second door. He peered through the window and saw that it was a mirror image of the first room. Same mattress, same toilet, same shower, same naked lightbulb. Except for one big difference.

A woman stood in the room, facing away from him. On an impulse, he called out.

"Alicia?"

The woman jumped like a cattle prod had poked her in the ribs. She spun around and Jick's eyes widened in surprise.

The woman's expression was shock, then horror, as her eyes tracked to a spot over Jick's shoulder.

She let out a piercing scream.

As Jick was about to open his mouth, he felt a crashing blow to the back of his head. He collapsed to the ground as a final thought went through his head before he blacked out.

She's pregnant.

FORTY

Phoenix knocked, didn't wait for an answer as he walked into his father's office and flung himself into a chair.

"Where's Mom?"

"I had to send her away, son."

Phoenix stared at his father.

"What do you mean you had to send her away?"

"She didn't like what you did. She wanted to tell the police, send you away. I didn't want that. I can't have the police here, son, so I had to send her away."

"Where did you send her?"

"Off-island."

Phoenix stared at his father, sensing something in his father's voice that must not have rung true.

"Where is she, Dad?"

"Don't worry about it, son. You can go play in your playground for a while."

Phoenix did not move for a minute as he stared at his father with the same blank expression. Sturgis noticed and shifted in his chair.

"If she had turned you in, you would have spent the rest of your life locked up. No more Mom. No more Dad. No more playground. Would you have wanted that?"

"No."

"Then it's all good. Now go play."

"I don't want to go play. I want to know where Mom is."

"Phoenix, this is your fault. I told you, only animals. After you killed that Caleb kid, I told you never to do that again. You didn't listen. If you had listened, I wouldn't have had to send Mom away."

Father and son stared at each other. Phoenix said nothing for a long moment before abruptly rising to his feet and exiting the study. Sturgis sat at his desk, tapping his pencil, steady at first, then faster.

I hope this works.

The plane touched down at Keahole Airport in Kona with a puff of smoke and a roar of its engine's reverse thrusters. Quin disembarked down the metal stairs, amused as Jick had been days earlier at the airport's old-fashioned method of loading and unloading a plane. He collected his bag and made his way to the car rental shuttle. After obtaining his rental car, he set his phone's GPS for the Hawaiian Orchid resort and settled in for the thirty-minute drive to the resort.

Quin parked his car in the guest parking lot and headed straight to room 518. He knocked on the door.

"Jick?"

Silence.

Maybe he's down by the pool. He wasn't expecting me.

Quin strolled downstairs and surveyed the pool area. No sign of Jick.

He paused for a moment to appreciate the salt air, swaying palm trees, and the view.

Not as good as Jamaica, but sure beats Dallas.

He went to the registration desk and introduced himself with his ID.

"I believe you have authorization to give me the key to Jick Arnsson's room? Room 518," he said.

The clerk checked the reservation and nodded. She slipped a magnetic card into the programmer and handed it to Quin.

"Here you go."

Quin returned to Jick's room and knocked again. Still no answer.

He let himself into the room and surveyed the signs of habitation. The room looked neat. Too neat.

"Wonder where he went," he mused.

He scanned the papers on the desk. One paper was for the delivery of Jick's rental car. A hardtop silver Jeep.

He headed outside to check and to retrieve his bag. There were some Jeeps, but none in hardtop silver. Frowning, he retrieved his bag and carried it back upstairs.

He opened the suitcase and took out the gun he had brought with him. A standard law enforcement spec Glock. He slid fifteen rounds into the weapon with practiced ease.

Now I've gotta find Jick.

He stepped into the bathroom to wash his face. As he reached for a towel, something nagged him. He looked at the basin.

Where's his toothbrush? And the rest of his stuff?

He opened the drawers in the dresser and checked the contents.

No way he came to Hawaii with just two briefs. He left to go somewhere.

He called Jick's number, but it went straight to voicemail. He called Sam.

"Hi, Quin," Sam answered. "Nice flight?"

"Yeah, I'm at the hotel, in Jick's room. He's not here. And his phone goes to voicemail."

"I wonder where he went. He wasn't expecting you, so maybe he had to run some errands."

"His toothbrush is not here either."

There was silence at Sam's end.

"That is... a bit concerning."

"My thoughts exactly. He didn't call you?"

"No."

Quin thought for a moment.

"I guess I'll just wait here."

"Okay, be careful."

"I will."

Quin ended the call. He spent the next hour watching TV. Still no Jick.

He opened his laptop and reviewed his notes on the case. The uploaded files from Jick showed him the location of Sturgis' house and the hundred-acre parcel that adjoined the western side. He zoomed in and spotted the unpaved road that ran along its side. Then he arrived at a decision.

The last thing he said was something about checking out the hundred-acre wood. So that's where I'm headed.

Quin tucked his gun into a bag and headed to the parking lot. He navigated to the highway heading north out of Kawaihae. He slowed as he went past the turnoff to the Wao Kele Nature Reserve.

What an odd pattern of growth. A forest with an abrupt transition to desert.

He drove further until he spotted the right turn into the neighborhood that ended near the edge of the nature reserve. As he drove uphill, the paved road gave way to more potholes until it deteriorated into an unpaved track. He pushed on as the track curved toward the forest. A gate and a sign with 'Kapu' stenciled on it greeted him; the gate was locked with a chain and padlock.

"Forbidden," Quin murmured.

He climbed out of the car to inspect the gate. To his surprise, the shackle on the padlock was open. He studied the open padlock, deep in thought.

Jick did take up locksmithing so...

He opened the gate, drove through, and looped the chain as he had found it. He drove further up the track, his tires kicking up puffs of red dirt. Then he rounded a bend and braked hard at the sight of a parked vehicle.

A hardtop silver Jeep.

As he approached the Jeep, another vehicle, this one parked behind a tree, came into view.

And a convertible Mustang.

Quin parked the car beside the Jeep and climbed out. He tucked the gun in his waistband and scanned his surroundings.

"Jick!" he shouted.

There was no answer.

He peered into the Jeep and saw a backpack on the passenger seat. He tugged the door handle, but it was locked.

That has to be Jick's.

According to the map, he was on the western edge of the hundred-acre parcel. Ahead of him was the sudden transition to the forest as the ground dipped. He could see clouds rolling off the top of the mountain like a giant tablecloth being unfurled. A mist settled on the forest and seemed to evaporate into thin air as the clouds rolled off the edge of the forest.

I bet that's what keeps the forest green. Neat how it rolls off the forest like an irrigation system.

Quin detoured for a quick look at the Mustang, but nothing inside caught his eye. He walked toward the forest edge, marveling at the change in temperature as he crossed into the shade.

Wow, from sun to shade, there must be at least a five, maybe ten, degree drop. Like entering another world.

He pressed forward, stopping every few minutes to survey the foliage. There were no obvious signs of someone else having passed through.

"Jick!" he shouted. No answer.

A sense of unease crept over him. He pulled out the gun and started walking through the trees, pushing branches out of the way. After another five minutes of hiking, he came to a natural clearing. Through the jungle foliage, he could discern a shape on the ground. Definitely man-made. A rectangular shape about the size of a person.

"Jesus," Quin breathed, eyes widening, when he realized what it was.

He staggered down to the clearing and stood by the shape.

This was recently dug.

Clutching his gun in a tight grip, he glanced around the clearing. The only sounds were of birds and insects. He kicked the loose dirt with his shoe and dislodged a clump. He knelt next to the grave and tried to scoop out a handful. He tucked his gun in his waistband and using both hands, scooped out a large handful of dirt.

This is going to take forever. I need to find Jick.

He stood, staring at the grave, so focused he did not notice a figure detach itself from behind the shadow of a tree and approach from behind. At the last instant, perhaps from an atavistic survival instinct that signaled danger, Quin spun around. Too late.

A man had emerged from behind a tree, carrying a baseball bat. He heard a resounding crack and felt a searing pain in his right arm. He screamed and clutched his right arm. The figure swung the bat again, and Quin felt something snap in his arm, accompanied by another surge of white-hot pain. He screamed again and collapsed to the ground. In an instant, the assailant swooped in and pulled the gun out of Quin's waistband.

Quin lay on the ground, perspiration drenching his shirt, gritting his teeth in pain as he stared at the assailant. His assailant studied the gun.

"Nice," he commented.

Quin said nothing. In a nonchalant gesture, the assailant waved the gun toward an imaginary foe as he puckered his lips and made shooting sounds.

"Pew pew," the man said, aiming the gun. He tucked the gun in his waistband with a flourish as he turned to look at Quin.

Quin felt a wave of fear as he stared at the man. The man grinned, but the expression was devoid of emotion. The grin looked more like a rictus, and the eyes were blank and staring.

"Welcome to my playground."

FORTY-ONE

Jick let out a groan. His head throbbed, and everything looked blurred. When he finally regained his focus, he realized he saw the same thing as before. Cave room, camp shower, toilet, naked light bulb. Except he was now inside the room. It was the room on the left, not the padlocked one. As he pulled himself into a sitting position, the room swayed and then steadied. Reaching back, he felt a painful lump had developed behind his left ear.

"Oh, shit."

He stood, braced himself against his thighs as the room swayed again. He walked to the door and tested it. Locked. No surprise.

He pushed against the locked door, but the deadbolt held. He tried to slam against it with his shoulder but stopped when his headache reminded him it was a bad idea. Gripping the tic-tac-toe pattern window bars, he jerked back and forth as hard as he could, but the bars did not budge. He pushed his face against the bars and called out.

"Hey, anyone in there?"

From the next room, a woman's voice floated back.

"Yes, I'm here. You've been out for a couple of hours, at least. Who are you? And how do you know my name?"

"You are Alicia? Alicia Rogers?"

"Yes," she replied.

"And you're pregnant?"

"Yes," the voice seemed to catch. "This guy must be crazy. I've been in hell for months. Who are you?"

"I'm Jick. I came to Hawaii to look for you."

"To look for me? Who sent you?"

"Sam. Samantha Arnsson."

"Sam sent you? After so long?"

"You went missing months ago. They found your car and searched the area. When they couldn't find anything, they figured you might have had a hiking accident. Sam said she felt guilty about sending you to investigate this guy, Sturgis. I guess your mother contacted Sam for an update on the case, and Sam sent me to take one last look before closing the case. What happened to you? Why are you here? And pregnant?"

"I..., I don't know," Alicia said.

"You don't know what happened?"

"No. All I remember is watching Sturgis' house from a lookout on the other side of the valley. It was hot; it must've been around noon. I went to my car to get a hat and then go back to the lookout. When I got back, someone was hiding behind a tree, waiting for me. I felt a little lightheaded; I think a hand clamped over my face, and I blacked out. I didn't see anybody. When I woke up, I was here."

"There was no one else there? You didn't see or hear anyone or anything there?"

"Not that I can remember."

Retrograde amnesia. Wonder what they used to knock her out.

"I've been to the same lookout," Jick said. "Is it that one with the wooden bench?"

"Yes."

"Then what happened?"

"Nothing. I woke up in this cave. I yelled and screamed, but it's too far away for anyone to hear. On the first day, this guy showed up in a mask. He said nothing, just pushed a food tray through the door slot. There was a note that said no one would hurt me and everything would be okay. But I needed to stay here for a few months. When I read that, I lost it and started screaming at the guy that there was no way he could hold me here for that long. He stood outside listening but never said a word.

"He shows up three times every day. Never talks and doesn't answer when I talk to him. He's a big guy, with tattoos on his arms; they look like razors. He's the guy who knocked you out. He must have come back to get the tray and saw you."

"Sounds like Thaddeus," Jick muttered.

"Who's Thaddeus?"

"Sturgis' muscle. His enforcer."

"What? You mean Sturgis kidnapped me?"

"Sure looks like it. You've never met him?"

"No. I haven't talked to anyone in months. Until you showed up. I sometimes yell and scream at that guy when he brings food. No answer. He just opens the slot, pushes in the tray, and leaves. About a half-hour later, he comes back and stands outside the window, looking in. It's creepy, but as soon as I push the tray out, he takes it and leaves."

"He must have orders not to talk to you. What's the story with your being pregnant?"

"I don't know. I have a boyfriend. It could be his, I guess. I don't know. I can't remember that far back."

Jick asked the next question as carefully as he could.

"Alicia, do you feel you were... assaulted?"

"No, I don't think so. After I woke up here, I felt fine. Uninjured. Fully dressed. They bring meals and provide everything else. I didn't even realize I was pregnant until a few weeks later when I started feeling nauseated. I don't know."

Jick mulled over what she said as she continued.

"About three months ago, the tattooed guy brought another letter. By then, I had become hysterical again and scared. I guess he, or they, didn't want me to injure myself. The letter once again reassured me I would not be harmed. And they would let me go after the baby is born. It was signed 'UG.' Why would a random stranger want to hold me here until a baby is born?"

Jick digested this for a moment.

"I don't know. But it proves the baby isn't your boyfriend's. So, whose is it?"

"What is going on here?" Alicia asked. "Who's 'UG?'"

"Probably Uncle George," Jick replied.

"Who's Uncle George?"

"It's what Sturgis calls himself to the locals here. When he's all pleasant and throwing parties."

Jick thought for a moment longer.

"Alicia, you came here to check on Sturgis, right?"

"Yes."

"And Sam thought Sturgis could have been involved in cloning a human."

"Okay, yes."

"And these shipments of items that triggered the investigation..."

"Yeah?"

"And you were spying on his house when you were kidnapped."

"Okay, so?"

"And here you are, pregnant."

Jick could imagine Alicia's expression as she realized what Jick implied.

"What are you saying? You mean I'm pregnant with a clone? A clone of Sturgis?"

"It's a possibility. If Sam's suspicions are correct, your being pregnant would explain a lot. Except for two things."

"What's that?"

"First, the scientist Sturgis hired is still here."

"You mean Finlayson?"

"Yes. I wonder why. Assuming he made a clone, and they implanted it, his job is done. He's not a physician. Why is he still here? And why would Sturgis do this? He already has a son. And Sturgis is no spring chicken. Wanting a baby at his age makes no sense."

Jick shook his head.

"Uhh, that hurts," he groaned.

"What's the other thing?"

"Let's assume Finlayson made a clone. An actual clone of Sturgis. How did they implant it? You can't just put the zygote into a device like a turkey baster and insert it."

"What's a zygote?"

"Oh sorry, that's the term for a fertilized egg. The actual clone is probably a few cell divisions past that, but I don't know."

Jick sat back on the ground. None of this made sense. There was no way Alicia was carrying a clone of Sturgis. Unless...

"Alicia, what toiletries do you have there?"

"The usual," she said. "Toothbrush, toothpaste, soap and shampoo, toilet paper. Why?"

He phrased the next question delicately.

"What about, uh, feminine hygiene products?"

"Yes, those too. Why?"

"I'm not a fertility specialist, but from what I know, you can't just implant a zygote at any time. It has to be at a specific time during your monthly cycle."

"What are you saying?"

"They would need to know when your monthly cycle is."

"There is a sign posted here next to the toilet. It says that every day, I have to dispose of any toilet paper or feminine hygiene products into a bag and push it out with my dinner tray. There's a box of plastic bags and a stack of those brown paper sacks that kids use as lunch bags. I seal everything into a plastic bag and shove that into a paper bag."

"That may explain it. I wonder who's helping them with this. They would need to have an obstetrician's level of expertise. And you've seen no one else except the masked guy?"

"No."

"And they've never taken you out of that cave?"

"No. Although, there was one time many months ago when I woke up in the morning and felt I was wearing something different from when I went to bed. It's so dark in here I just assumed I had made a mistake."

Jick mulled this over.

"Could they have drugged you and taken you out of the cave, done the implantation, and then brought you back? I wonder...

"I don't suppose you remember when your cycle started before that episode."

"No, it was too far back."

"I just thought of a third thing. That last shipment."

"What last shipment?"

"Before I left for Hawaii, Sam said there was another suspicious shipment. A holding tank. Why would they need a holding tank? Something here doesn't add up."

Jick looked around the cave.

"I need to get out of here."

Jick leaped at the wall, clutching at the window's edge to get a boost, trying to reach the top of the wall. He could not reach the top and crashed back to the ground. His headache flared again.

"Ow, shit."

He looked around the room. There was no furniture that he could dismantle as a weapon. Just the mattress on the floor with a pillow and blanket. And the camp toilet.

Which is in the shape of a stool.

He picked up the camp toilet. It was a molded plastic cube, all edges rounded. It would not do as a weapon.

Maybe if it's full of stool... pun intended.

He placed it along the wall. He balanced on it, then sprang toward the top of the wall. His fingers made contact, and he clutched the top of the wall, straining to pull himself toward the nearest bar. He caught one of the bars and held it with both hands, jerking his body back and forth to wrench the bar off its attachment in the bluff wall. A few pebbles dislodged from around the anchor, but it held firm. Finally, unable to hold the bar any longer, he let go and landed on the ground.

"Ow," he groaned.

I'll try again in a few minutes.

When he had regained strength, he tried a second time. The result was the same. The anchor moved a little in its mooring, dislodged a few pebbles, but held. Jick dropped to the ground, swinging his arms around.

"This is impossible."

He went to the back of the cave and peered along the roof. There were no visible openings, not even a telltale breeze from further inside. He gave up as the shadows lengthened, and the solar-powered lightbulb flickered to life. The insects and coqui frogs revved up their nightly crescendo. Jick sat on his mattress.

"Wonder how they knew you were watching them," Jick said.

"The first couple of days, I reconnoitered around the neighborhood. And the house in Kawaihae. Nothing happened there. Then I checked out this neighborhood. I knew which house was his, so I spied on it from above and from the other side of the nature reserve. I didn't see much, so on the fourth day, I snooped around outside his wall. There's a spot on the mauka side where the wall ends and there's a chain-link fence..."

"I know. I snooped around out there too."

"Oh, okay, so you know the spot. From there, I could see the garage and the house. I stayed there for an hour, and nothing happened. Then I went back to the lookout, and you know the rest. I think I must have made a dumb mistake. I bet there was a security camera in the trees. And that's how they spotted me."

"I made the same mistake. I didn't see any cameras. Later, Sturgis tried to invite me up to his house. I thought the request was weird and wondered if they were trying to kidnap me. Then Finlayson stopped by the hotel, warned me I had been spotted. I spied on them from the same spot. I bet you're right about the camera being in the trees."

The high-pitched *"Ko-Kee"* of the coqui frogs was drowned out by the rumble of an ATV. Thaddeus appeared at the window, unmasked. Alicia stared at his face. He leaned down by each door, opened a slot, and pushed a tray through.

"I'll pick up the trays in the morning," he said.

"First time you've ever said anything," Alicia said. Thaddeus ignored her.

"Thaddeus, wait," Jick called out. "What's going on here? I was just hiking around. Let me out of here."

Thaddeus turned to look at Jick for a moment but did not reply. He climbed aboard his ATV and left.

Jick exhaled. "We might as well eat."

As they munched their sandwiches, Jick mulled over his conversation with Alicia.

"Who does your laundry?" he asked.

"They collect the clothes every week and bring them back washed and folded. It looks like they have some kind of catchment tank somewhere higher up. There's a pipe that leads to that camp shower. It's just cold showers, but the water's warm in the middle of the day."

"Hope I won't be here long enough to need a shower. Or to have my laundry done."

After three hours, the solar panel light dimmed and guttered out. They were left in darkness except for the moonlight.

"Guess we'll go to bed. Jesus, Alicia, you've been living like this for eight months!"

There was no sound from Alicia's room until Jick heard a muffled sob. Then he heard her blowing her nose.

"I'm sorry. I shouldn't have reminded you."

"It's okay. I just feel overwhelmed sometimes."

"I promise I'll do my best to get you out of here." His words rang hollow to his ears.

The following morning, Thaddeus returned with two trays. He slipped breakfast under the door, collected the trays from the previous evening, and left without saying a word. Jick resumed his quest to explore the door and window for a means of escape.

"This is hopeless," he muttered to himself.

Later that morning, as he lay supine in bed, arms behind his head, he heard a cautious voice at the window. It snapped him to attention, and he bolted off his cot.

"Jick?"

Finlayson!

FORTY-TWO

"My mother isn't here," the man said to Quin, the rictus grin fading to a blank expression. "Dad sent her off-island because she wanted to send me away, to have me locked up. Is she off-island? I don't know. That's not good, is it? No, it isn't. Do I miss her? No, not really. Well, maybe a little. Is she coming back? I don't know."

Quin stared at the man as he muttered questions out loud and answered himself. He walked away from Quin, stepped into the woods.

"I'm only going there," he said, pointing to a tree a few yards away. "Don't go anywhere, or I'll be very angry." He patted the gun.

As soon as the man stepped behind the tree, Quin scrambled to his feet, cradled his right arm, and took off running. In a flash, the man picked up the backpack he had stashed there and sprinted after Quin. He caught up with Quin in a few steps and tripped him from behind. Quin sprawled to the ground and let out another scream as his broken arm could not support him as he tumbled to the ground. His face planted in the dirt.

The man opened the backpack and pulled out a coil of rope. He jerked Quin's arms together over his head, ignoring his scream, and lashed Quin's wrists together. Dragging Quin to the nearest tree, he tossed the rope over a branch and pulled. Quin let out another shriek, this time even louder than before. He tried to tighten his good arm to hold most of his weight.

The man pulled the gun out of his waistband, aimed it at a spot near Quin's right shoulder, and pulled the trigger.

The bullet tore through Quin's shoulder and emerged from behind, leaving a small, ragged exit wound in its wake. Quin screamed again, his face contorted in absolute agony.

"That was for making me angry," the man said.

The man stopped pulling on the rope when Quin stood on tiptoes. Not being able to pull Quin off the ground, he stopped when Quin's arms extended straight toward the sky. He tied the free end of the rope to the next tree.

"Good enough for now," the man said.

Sweat poured off Quin's face as he stood, staring at the man through the salty droplets. His body convulsed against the rope from the intensity of the pain. Rivulets of sweat snaked through the caked dirt on his face. He blinked a few times to clear his view.

"Please," Quin gasped. "Who are you? Let me go. I'm just a tourist on a hike."

"Tourist on a hike with a gun?" the man smirked. "And you're in my playground."

The man knelt next to the backpack. He placed the gun on the ground and rummaged through the backpack's contents. He pulled out a pair of shears. Quin's eyes widened in fear when he saw the shiny implement.

"Please let me go," Quin felt his voice break. "I won't tell anyone I saw you."

"I know you won't," the man grinned at Quin. The blank expression in his eyes did not change. He tore open the front of Quin's shirt and, in a few deft strokes with the shears, cut Quin's shirt off. Quin stood bare-chested, arms above his head, a trickle of blood down the front and back of his shoulder, sweat glistening on his face and torso.

The man stepped back to survey the scene. He shut his eyes, and Quin could see him take a few slow, deep breaths. A smile played around his mouth. With his eyes still shut, he snipped the shears open and shut in the air a few times. Then he opened his eyes.

"Where should I start?"

FORTY-THREE

"Finlayson! What are you doing here? Hurry, open this door!"

David Finlayson slid the deadbolt back and opened the door. Jick rushed outside. He glanced at Alicia's door, which was still padlocked.

"Alicia!"

"Yes," she answered. "Jick, who is this?"

"David Finlayson," Jick said.

"Listen, I can't open your door. I wish I had my locksmithing tools with me. You're going to be okay for now. Sturgis needs you alive. We're going to get out of here and go for help."

"Yes, yes, please hurry," Alicia pleaded.

"Come on, Finlayson," Jick urged. "Let's get the hell out of here."

"Wait, who's in there?" Finlayson asked.

"Her name is Alicia. She's Sturgis' surrogate for the child."

"There's a pregnant woman in there?" Finlayson looked incredulous.

"Yes. We can talk about it later. Come on, we have to hustle."

Finlayson turned to stare at the locked door for a second. Then he turned and followed Jick through the woods. They crashed through the dense forest on their way back to Jick's Jeep. As they stumbled through the forest, they heard a sound. An unnatural sound. Not native to the forest. It was a scream, loud, anguished, like a person in excruciating pain. The sound came from downhill and toward the left, away from the Jeep.

"What was that?" Finlayson asked.

"I don't know," Jick said. "But it sure as hell isn't a bird or an animal. It's a person screaming."

As they debated their next move, the unmistakable crack of a gunshot echoed through the trees, followed by another scream.

"Shit. Stay here, Finlayson. Don't go anywhere. I'm going to see who it is."

Finlayson melted into the bushes as Jick veered toward the sound.

Jick sneaked through the forest, skulking between trees, ducking under low-hanging vegetation, heading toward the sound. He saw a clearing ahead. At its far edge, a man stood next to a tree, with a backpack at his feet and a gun lying on the ground next to it.

As Jick watched, he noticed something quiver above the man. It was a rope lashed to one of the overhead branches. Jick realized there was something tied at the end of the rope behind the tree. The other end of the rope led to a neighboring tree. The rope quivered again as whoever, or whatever, jerked against the rope.

He's got something tied there. Another pig? This must be the bastard who tortured the other one.

Jick skulked around to the other side of the clearing, measuring each step with care, making sure each footfall landed on soft earth. As the figure came into partial view, Jick noticed with a shock that it was a man tied to the tree. The unfortunate man stood on tiptoes, arms stretched above his head. A ribbon of dried blood had trickled down his chest from his right shoulder. Reddish dirt caked his face, through which rivulets of perspiration had carved dark lines. His right arm appeared to be broken.

Jick's first thought was "*Who the hell...?*" as he stared at him in profile.

I need to get a better look...

Jick noticed the victim squinting and blinking. He skulked along the contours of the clearing to get a better look. Jick's eyes widened in sudden shock as a bolt of recognition hit him. For a split second, his brain refused to believe he was looking at Quin.

Jesus. It's Quin?! What the hell is he doing here?

The man raised a pair of shears, and Jick could hear the metallic rasping as it opened and shut. He saw the man stand motionless for a few moments, saw his chest expand as he took a deep breath. Then he exhaled and Jick heard him speak.

"Where should I start?"

Without another moment's hesitation, Jick burst out of the clearing and sprinted for the man. The man turned, saw Jick charging toward him, and dropped the shears as he dove to the ground for his gun. Jick closed the gap just as the man's hand reached for the gun.

He drove his elbow into the man's side, and the man let out an "oof" as his fingers closed around the grip. Jick grabbed the man's forearm with both his hands. He drove his chin hard into the man's biceps, and the man grunted. He tried to twist the gun to point it at Jick. As he writhed on the ground, he elbowed Jick and pushed him to the side.

The man was now astride Jick, with Jick holding the man's right wrist in a vise grip. Jick had a good look at the man's face. His eyes were blank, staring, devoid of emotion. His mouth was twisted in a snarl as he struggled to seize control of the gun. He fired a shot, which whistled past Jick and embedded in a tree trunk next to Quin.

Jick grabbed a handful of dirt and flung it into the man's eyes. The man yelled in rage as he pawed at his face with his left hand. Jick slammed an open palm into the man's nose. From his position on the ground, Jick could not muster enough force to break his nose, but the jolt stunned the man. He howled and reared back.

Jick twisted away from under him and scrambled to a kneeling position. Jick threw another punch, and the man screamed and fell back as Jick dived for the arm holding the gun. The man squeezed the trigger again, and a shot whistled into the surrounding brush.

Jick was taller than the man and outweighed him by a considerable amount. He twisted the man's arm forcibly until the gun pointed at his chin. Holding the man's right hand, Jick squeezed hard, and the gun discharged. The bullet struck the man on his right cheekbone and exited near his ear. Bone fragments sprayed as the man screamed and let go of the gun.

Jick rolled away with the gun. Now the man faced away from him. Jick staggered to his feet, keeping the gun trained on the man.

The man also staggered to his feet, clutching the ruined side of his face. The bullet had shattered his right cheekbone and torn off part of his right ear. He turned to face Jick.

"Down," Jick commanded. "Stay on the ground."

The man seemed not to hear. He remained standing and mouthed a few words.

"My mother," he mumbled, his words thick and slurred from his shattered cheekbone. "I don't think she's coming back."

He let out a roar and charged at Jick. Jick fired a second round; it caught the man in his chest and stopped him in his tracks. He crashed to the ground and lay still.

Jick grabbed the shears and cut the rope tied to the neighboring tree, helping Quin ease his broken arm down. Quin cradled his broken arm with his left arm and sank to the ground, shaking with relief.

"Jick," he managed to croak. "Thanks, man."

"You're welcome," Jick said, still catching his breath. "Now tell me what the hell you're doing here."

Quin nodded toward the gun.

"That's for you. Sam was worried after your last conversation and asked if I would take it in person. Looks like you didn't need my help after all."

"I was in a tough spot too. Finlayson rescued me. He's hiding somewhere up there. Let me get your arm stabilized, and we'll get out of here."

He rolled the body of the man who had assaulted Quin onto his back.

"Do you know him?" Quin asked.

"No, but judging by his appearance and where we are, on Sturgis' property, this is his son. Looks like him. Same weird facial expressions."

"Is he nuts?"

"The locals say he is. I didn't realize he was this crazy. Before I was caught, I saw a dead pig hanging from a tree. Looks like this crazy kid makes this kind of thing a habit."

As he spoke, Jick stripped the pants off the body.

"What are you doing?" Quin asked.

"Hope you're not squeamish about the dead guy's pants riding on your shoulders."

Quin blinked. "What?"

"Probably better than the dead guy riding on your shoulders."

"Are you kidding me?"

"I'm making you a sling."

Jick draped the pants over Quin's neck and shoulders, so the legs hung down the front. He tied the legs together into a sling. After Quin cradled his arm in the sling, he pulled the open end of one of the trousers' legs over Quin's arm for added stability. He wrapped the other leg around Quin's broken arm and tucked the loose end into the open end of the sling.

"There, now he'll do some good. Good thing his bladder didn't let go when he was shot."

Quin looked at Jick, incredulous.

"You just shot a guy. I'm still shaking."

"Let's get Finlayson and get out of here."

"He's here?"

Jick pointed up the slope.

"Up there somewhere."

"Before we go, look at that," Quin pointed with his left hand at the edge of the clearing. "That rectangular shape on the ground. I think there's a body buried there. Or something."

Jick glanced at it.

"You're right. We know where this clearing is. Let's get Finlayson and we'll come back with reinforcements."

They walked along the clearest path toward the Jeep. After a five-minute walk through the trees, Jick stopped.

"Wait here. Finlayson should be up the slope over there. Let me sprint up to him and get him."

"Okay."

Jick sprinted back toward the caves and, after a short distance, yelled for Finlayson. Almost immediately, he heard a rustling, and Finlayson rose from behind some bushes.

"Is everything okay? I heard gunshots."

"I found someone I know," Jick said, breathless. "I'll explain later. He was tied to a tree and was about to be tortured by some man who I'm guessing was Sturgis' son."

"That's Phoenix."

"Sturgis' son?"

"Uh, yes. How is he?"

"Dead."

"You killed Phoenix?"

"He was about to torture and kill my friend. I ambushed him and we fought. He lost."

Finlayson stared at Jick. He settled back into the bushes, with an expression of shock and disbelief on his face.

"You really killed Phoenix? Did you have to? Was there no other way to rescue your friend?"

"Are you serious? Finlayson, what's wrong with you? Of course I had to."

"If Sturgis finds out you killed his son, he will kill you."

"We can worry about that later. We need to get out of here and rescue Alicia."

"The pregnant woman?"

"Yes, Finlayson, the pregnant woman. I don't think it sank in earlier. She's the surrogate."

"Sturgis said she was staying at a house in Kona."

"And you believed him?"

Finlayson said nothing. He hurried after Jick through the trees.

They raced through the jungle until they saw Quin waiting where Jick had left him. As they rushed through the forest as quickly as Quin's injuries allowed him, Jick made the quick introductions.

"Finlayson, this is Quin. Quin, Finlayson."

They reached the edge of the forest and burst out into the open. Jick's Jeep was visible in the distance.

"Hurry, let's go."

As they crossed the dusty terrain to the Jeep, Jick heard a motor from the makai, or downhill, side of the forest. The sound grew louder.

There must be another trail there.

An ATV crested into view, Thaddeus behind the wheel, with a man sitting next to him. Jick recognized him as one of the two men who had tried to pay him a visit at the hotel.

"Run!"

Jick and Finlayson sprinted for the Jeep, but Quin's slower progress hindered them. As they reached the Jeep, Jick saw the men jump out of the ATV, each armed. Thaddeus pointed his gun at them while the other man sprinted about twenty yards away before pointing his gun.

Shit.

Jick had his gun, but with two guys so far apart, there was no way to shoot them both.

I bet Thaddeus is a better shot than me.

Jick dropped his gun and raised his hands.

"Move away from the Jeep," Thaddeus ordered. "Raise your hands."

Finlayson obeyed. Quin leaned against the Jeep, panting.

"You too." Thaddeus addressed Quin.

"I can't," Quin said.

Thaddeus noticed the sling and dried blood around his shoulder. His eyes roved over the makeshift sling. He did not ask questions as he collected Jick's gun and tucked it in his waistband.

"You," Thaddeus pointed at Jick with his gun. "Get into the ATV."

As Jick walked toward the ATV with his hands still up, Thaddeus shifted the gun to his left hand.

"This one for you, braddah," he said, as he slammed a fist into Jick's face. Jick did not expect the blow, and he did not duck. His head snapped back with the sucker punch, and he crumpled to the ground in a heap. Thaddeus tossed the gun onto the seat. He picked Jick off the ground as easily as hefting a sack of potatoes. He dropped him in the ATV's back row.

"He easier to carry 'em this way, yeah?" Thaddeus grinned at the others.

"You drive," Thaddeus commanded Finlayson.

Finlayson and Quin climbed into the front seat, and the other man climbed into the middle row with Thaddeus. Jick lay motionless in the back.

"You try anything, I shoot," the man warned them.

The ATV jolted into motion as they set off down the trail. They negotiated the trail's twists and turns, Quin grimacing every time the ATV bounced over a rock or dipped into a rut. It emerged at the base of Sturgis' lawn. Finlayson realized it was the same trail Phoenix had used that horrifying day when he ambled into view carrying two decapitated heads like trophies. Finlayson navigated the ATV across the yard, then took another trail that Thaddeus pointed out. After meandering through the forest, it ended at the clearing in front of the caves. They had gone full circle.

Thaddeus unlocked the padlock on Alicia's cell. He forced Finlayson inside, then deposited Jick on the ground. Quin walked in by himself, cradling his injured right arm, as Alicia looked on, despair in her eyes.

"What happened?" she asked.

"We almost made it," Finlayson said bitterly. "I don't know how he knew we were headed that way."

Thaddeus slammed the deadbolt home, the click of the padlock being locked sealing their fate. Alicia looked at the prostrate form of Jick and then at Quin.

"Who are you?"

"Quin," he said in a ragged voice.

"What's your story?"

"I came here to deliver a gun to Jick. I'm Sam's friend. And you are...?"

"Alicia Rogers."

"You're alive!" Quin said in amazement.

Alicia settled on her bed with some effort, one hand bracing her belly. She said nothing; her silence was heavier than words.

FORTY-FOUR

Jick let out a groan as he came to. The headache that had developed after Thaddeus had hit him earlier had abated. Now it flared anew, and his chin throbbed, too.

"Good thing this body is young and healthy," he mumbled.

"What?" He heard Alicia say.

"Nothing. My body wasn't in shape before I started a new workout regimen. I felt like an old man."

He pulled himself into a sitting position. Alicia had wet a towel using the camp shower and pressed it against his chin.

"Thanks."

He felt the bump on his chin.

My head hurts. I'm getting a feeling of déjà vu. That Thaddeus can sure throw a punch.

"Now what?" It was Finlayson.

Jick turned to look at him.

"Finlayson, what are you doing here?"

"What do you mean?"

"How did you know I needed rescuing?"

"You had all your stuff in the back of your Jeep. I figured you wouldn't leave, so I stopped by today. You hadn't returned all night, so I figured you were somewhere here."

"How did you know I wasn't back all night?"

"I checked."

"How did you find this place?"

"Sturgis talked about it at the party they invited you to. I don't know if I was supposed to know about it. I didn't know the exact location, just that it was against the bluffs."

He hesitated, then added, "This morning, Sturgis came to the lab. Thaddeus called him. From what I could make out from his side of the conversation, I guess they didn't get you at the hotel. Then they caught a break."

"What kind of break?"

"One of their contacts on the police force saw you turn mauka on the highway. They told George. I came up here to investigate. I parked on the dry side near your Jeep."

"But why did you feel the need to rescue me?"

"Because of what I saw."

"Not worried about getting into trouble?"

"George won't do anything to me. He needs me to complete his project."

"You already admitted you knew there was a surrogate involved. So, I'm going to take a wild guess. Are you in the process of cloning Sturgis?"

Finlayson said nothing for a moment. Then he took a deep breath and exhaled.

"No point denying it, I suppose."

"What exactly is your project?"

"My new discovery. I've discovered a process, still in trials and only in mice, that can speed up the process of cellular reproduction until we reach a desired target. Then you can stop the process and let nature run its course."

"And what's that supposed to achieve?"

"I should be able to take a newborn baby, put it in a specialized environment, and artificially speed the aging process until we reach a desired target age. In other words, age the organism in a tank to the age of ten, but in a few months. But it's still experimental."

Jick stared at him.

"Are you nuts? Why would you do something like that? And why would Sturgis want something like that?"

"He's getting old, Jick. He can't raise a child from infancy anymore, and he wanted to start with an older child. This process would give him a preteen to start with."

"But why? He already has a son. Why would he want to be cloned? Unless... "

Jick paused in mid-sentence as a thought dawned on him. He said nothing for a full minute as he stared at Finlayson. Finlayson felt uncomfortable enough to venture a question.

"What?"

"How long have you known Sturgis?"

"A few months," Finlayson stammered. "He offered me this one-year deal to clone him. I thought it would be a great way to test my new research. I warned Sturgis it was experimental, but he was adamant. Why are you asking?"

"From some things you've said, I got the impression you knew him longer."

"I didn't. I just met him a few months ago."

Jick studied Finlayson for a few seconds without saying anything. Finlayson seemed to wilt under the gaze.

"Now I know why he killed them," Jick murmured.

"Who?" Finlayson asked.

"Sturgis. But you wouldn't know any of the victims," Jick said. "Although you may know *about* it."

Finlayson said nothing.

"Finlayson, I think Sturgis' 'son,'" Jick put it in air quotes, "is a clone of Sturgis, isn't he?"

The color drained from Finlayson's face as he sank to the floor.

"Why... why do you say that?"

"Deduced it from what you've said. And it explains something else. I think Sturgis murdered the entire team involved in his birth. Did you know that?"

Finlayson mumbled something.

"What did you say?"

"I didn't know that until yesterday."

"What happened yesterday?"

"Phoenix was a murdering psychopath, maybe just like his father. And I think George has known that for years. Phoenix killed two people and cut off their heads. I saw them. He was grinning, swinging those heads like they were a couple of coconuts. He may have killed before, which is why Sturgis wanted to start again with a new son.

"And that's when I realized what a mistake I had made years ago, cloning him in the first place. I was always a little scared of him but didn't know how violent he could be. Then, when I saw Phoenix swinging those two heads...

"After what I saw, it changed things. I found an archived article about an unsolved murder in Greece from twenty-five years ago. I realized it was Sturgis and that I had cloned a psychopath. Maybe I suspected it all along and just didn't want to think about it. I've felt uneasy all along about what I did years ago and unfortunately, my recent research was publicized, and he read about it. That's when he got this idea.

"After what I saw, I wanted to make it right. So, I decided to rescue you."

"Why didn't you just say no when he asked you this time?"

"I don't know." Finlayson looked distressed. He pressed his hands to his face. "I don't know. It wasn't about the money. I guess the possibility of creating an actual adult fractal was too seductive. It was not going to be just a clone like another sheep."

"Finlayson, for a smart guy, you're quite slow on the uptake. First, you can't say no to him, and he pays you to do your crazy shit. Then, you decide nah, this is a bad idea, so you decide to rescue me. You have the moral compass of a wind vane. How do you think Sturgis will reward your disloyalty now that you've been caught trying to rescue me?"

Finlayson stared.

"George would never hurt me. He needs me to finish what I started."

"Really? After you almost blew his entire project apart? You still don't get it, do you? Now he has to make a choice, doesn't he? Push ahead, finish the project, then kill you; or cut his losses and kill you right away. Either way, you're on borrowed time. And with his brain damage, he's not going to make rational decisions. He has a severe frontal lobe injury. That's what makes him have those crying and laughing spells. It's called pseudobulbar affect. It also affects his ability to engage in higher-level executive functioning. In other words, he could decide on impulse to kill you right now, even though it might be detrimental to his plans."

It was clear Finlayson had realized none of this. He got to his feet and moved to the window.

Jick leaned against the wall. His headache had subsided to a dull sense of discomfort. He ruminated about Uncle George, wondering how a jovial and kindly old man could be a murdering psychopath. He thought back to the moments when Uncle George's facial expressions seemed to morph from jovial to cold and staring.

"He would be an interesting case study about what happens to people with severe frontal lobe injuries," he said. "But we need to figure out a way to get out of here."

Finlayson looked out the window.

"There's an ATV approaching. It's Thaddeus."

FORTY-FIVE

Jick peered out of the window to see Thaddeus climbing out of the ATV. He was alone. He unlocked the door, pulled out his gun, and swung the door open.

"You two," he pointed to Jick and Finlayson. "Come with me."

"Where's your buddy?" Jick said. "The other thug?"

Thaddeus ignored him, motioned with his gun for Jick to move. Jick and Finlayson stepped out, and Thaddeus slammed the deadbolt home.

"You drive," he told Jick. And to Finlayson, "You sit next to him."

They climbed aboard with Thaddeus sitting in the back seat with a gun trained on them. Jick felt an itching sensation between his shoulder blades.

He's got his finger on the trigger. I hope he's careful.

Thaddeus pointed to a corner of the clearing where some dead branches had fallen from the trees.

"Move those out of the way. Then go around on the left side."

To Jick's surprise, the fallen branches obscured a trail that was not the trail that led back to the main house. This trail snaked along the base of the bluffs.

The ATV made its way down the trail and the three rode in silence. In a hundred yards, they rounded a corner and came to another clearing. Under a canopy of trees, a dilapidated building stood in the middle of the clearing. An ATV, smaller than the six-seater they rode in, sat parked outside. As Jick turned off the ATV engine, another sound intruded, a rumble from somewhere behind the building.

There's a generator back there.

Thaddeus pointed at the door of the building.

"In there."

Jick led the way, followed by Finlayson with Thaddeus bringing up the rear.

"It's open."

Jick turned the knob, and the door opened with a screech like it belonged in a Halloween haunted house.

"Got some lube?" he asked Thaddeus. Thaddeus ignored him.

He stepped into what appeared to be an old living room. Illumination came from a single light bulb that hung from a wire in the middle of the room. The wire connected to an extension cord that led toward the back of the building. Faded curtains hung at the windows. Except for the single light bulb and the curtains, the room was empty.

Thaddeus pointed to a closed door on the left.

"In there."

Jick opened the door and squinted against a flood of light from the well-lit room. He took in the details of an operating room. A fresh coat of white paint covered the walls, giving the room an airy feel, and a metal operating room table nestled in the corner against the far wall. Twin tracks of overhead lights ran the length of the room, and an anesthesia machine sat in the adjacent corner from the operating room table. A few stools were scattered around the room. A familiar figure perched on a stool in front of the anesthesia machine, a polished wood cane resting across his lap.

"Uncle George!" Jick exclaimed. "What are you doing here? Last time we met, you wanted my help to bring doctors to Hawaii."

An expression somewhere between a smile and a sneer crossed Sturgis' face.

"Uncle George. That's what the kids call me. It is useful having 'Uncle George' because I find it easier to get along with people in the outside world. 'He' does it better than I do," Sturgis said.

Jick stared at him. His eyes roved over Sturgis' scar.

A narcissist and a sociopath. Now with a damaged brain.

"You've always been Uncle George to me," Jick prodded. "May I, uh, speak with, uh, him? Can we talk about bringing doctors here?"

"Forget about him," Sturgis said. He pointed at the stools with his cane.

"Sit."

Finlayson and Jick parked themselves on a stool. Thaddeus leaped onto the operating room table. He placed his gun at his side.

"David," Sturgis said, shaking his head. "Oh, David, I am so disappointed to see you here."

"Wait, George," Finlayson said. "I can explain."

"You don't need to... yet," Sturgis cut him off. "I'll get to you in a few minutes. Just sit there and shut up."

Finlayson opened his mouth to say something, thought better of it, and closed it again. Jick noticed the uncomfortable sheen that had appeared on Finlayson's face and neck.

Stupid bastard. This isn't going to end well.

Jick surveyed the room, looking for a means of escape. There was none. Although the door was not locked, there was no way he could rush for the exit without getting shot. He looked at Thaddeus and the position of his gun at his side.

No chance.

He realized Sturgis was addressing him.

"You came into my parlor," Sturgis said. "You evaded the car at the hotel and then walked right in."

"What is going on here?" Jick asked.

Sturgis smiled. He stared at Jick for a moment as he stroked his chin.

"Jayant Arnsson," he mused. "A very unusual name. Indian, isn't it? The first name. With a Swedish surname."

"What?"

"Your name."

"It's Jick Arnold."

"Don't insult my intelligence, Jick. You left your fingerprints on your wine glass at the party. And the police chief was kind enough to run your prints."

"Chief Williams is in on this?"

"He knows nothing. This is Hawaii. I make strategic contributions to the various police charities and keep in contact with the chief. We get together for social events. He does favors for me."

Jick said nothing.

"But," Sturgis continued. "That name is so unusual that when I ran a search, it turned up only one match. A doctor who was murdered in Dallas a few years ago. In his obituary, it even said his colleagues called him 'Jick.' So, tell me how you stole his identity."

This man is diabolical. If I get out of this in one piece, I need to talk to Sam about my fingerprints.

"I'm just a medical consultant," Jick said, aware that this sounded even more untruthful.

"If you continue to insult my intelligence, I'll have you shot right now."

"Okay," Jick said. "I am a medical consultant, but I was sent here as an investigator to find Alicia. I was told I would be given a temporary identity in case someone looked. I don't know anyone named 'Jayant Arnsson.'"

"That's better," Sturgis said. "But let me see if I get this straight. Our government is using the identities of dead people to send an investigator on this kind of assignment? With matching fake fingerprints? That doesn't add up."

Jick said nothing.

"Assuming it was the government. But it has to be. Whoever sent you would need access and clearance to manipulate a national fingerprint database."

Sturgis fixed a blank stare at Jick.

"Who sent you?"

"I don't know."

"You don't know?"

"I get freelance assignments. Someone, most likely in our government, suspected you were into cloning."

"What's your real name?"

Uh oh, gotta change the subject.

"Does it matter? I'm wondering what you're up to here."

Sturgis was quiet for a moment.

"You know," he began. "You may have signed that girl's death warrant."

"Whose death warrant?"

"Alicia's, of course."

"That's crap, Uncle George. You were never going to let her go."

"Stop calling me Uncle George. And don't be so sure I wouldn't have let her go."

"Like you did in Greece?"

Surprise flickered across Sturgis' face.

"What do you know about Greece? Never mind; don't bother answering. It doesn't matter. And yes, I would have let her go."

Sturgis jumped off his stool and paced the room, the tip of his cane clicking against the concrete floor as he crossed the room. He stopped behind Jick.

"Jick, examine this from my perspective. Unlike the situation in Greece, and I'm surprised you know about it, this is the United States of America. I live here. The last thing I want is a murder investigation landing on my doorstep.

"The girl had never seen me in person. She had never seen Thaddeus without a mask. I kept close tabs on the missing persons investigation by spending time with the chief and discreetly asking for updates. After a few weeks of searching, they found nothing, and the case went cold.

"When it was all over, a month from now at most, we would have dropped her off at the nearest hospital and she would have had nothing to report. Hell, I would have given her a pile of cash for her trouble.

"What would she have told the authorities? An improbable story that she was the victim of a kidnapping, found herself pregnant, gave birth to a baby, and was then returned unharmed. Without the baby. Here, in the land of Aloha.

"And even if the authorities investigated, what would they have found out? That she may have been kidnapped, delivered a baby, and was returned unhurt. They might not have even believed her story. It would have had the same credibility as a 'kidnapped by aliens and returned unharmed' story. You used to see those all the time in the tabloids."

Sturgis paused, and his face turned red. He let out a sudden loud snort as he tried to hold in a giggle.

"What's so funny, Uncle George? Being kidnapped by aliens?" Jick asked.

Sturgis glared at him as he wiped his face. The paroxysm of giggling subsided, and Sturgis said nothing as he collected his thoughts. He took a deep breath and continued.

"I took great pains to tell her all we wanted her for was the baby. Until you came along and interfered."

Jick said nothing.

"I did not, do not, want a murder investigation, but you may have left me no choice."

Jick said nothing.

Sturgis turned to Thaddeus.

"Who's the other guy with them?"

"Don't know, sir."

He turned to Jick.

"He's a friend," Jick said. "He brought me a gun, just in case, and tried to deliver it in person."

"Damn," Sturgis muttered. "He went into Phoenix's playground, didn't he?"

Thaddeus nodded.

"Must have."

"How did your friend get hurt?"

"Phoenix attacked him, tied him to a tree, and shot him in the shoulder," Jick said.

Sturgis looked puzzled.

"How did this other guy end up with you?" he asked Jick. He turned to Thaddeus with an inquiring look. Thaddeus shrugged.

"I rescued him," Jick said.

Sturgis turned a slow gaze toward Jick. Jick felt a prickle of unease. What he was about to say was unavoidable.

"Then where is Phoenix?"

"Dead."

Sturgis' eyebrows rose, but he said nothing.

"We wrestled over a gun, and he lost."

Jick braced himself, expecting Stugis to order Thaddeus to shoot him on the spot. He looked at Thaddeus.

Where's the bullet going to hit?

Jick eased off the stool and planted his legs on the floor, getting ready to feint and charge at Thaddeus. Instead, Sturgis' reaction floored him.

"Good. Shit happens sometimes."

Sturgis broke into a sudden smile. Jick froze, stunned. Whatever reaction Jick expected from Sturgis, this was not it. He stared at Sturgis in amazement.

"You're glad I killed your son?"

Sturgis continued to smile, and Jick could see his face turn red as he tried to stifle a laugh. Then, tears started flowing down his face. Sturgis slammed his fist on the table.

"Damn it," he shouted. He reached for a tissue and dabbed his face.

"No, of course I'm not 'glad' you killed Phoenix. But sometimes killing is... necessary."

Jick's head spun. Instead of rage, grief, wanting vengeance, Sturgis seemed to rejoice at his son's death. He stared at the scar again.

"Phoenix's activities in the playground were becoming too aggressive," Sturgis said, his tone measured now. "And he was becoming more unstable."

"So, it was okay that I killed him? And necessary?"

Sturgis did not answer.

But why was killing Phoenix necessary? And he didn't plan to kill Alicia. All he wanted was the baby... just like in Greece... except for one thing.

FORTY-SIX

It was at this moment, mulling over Sturgis' callous disregard for his son's death, that Jick had a sudden realization. He realized why Sturgis did not care about his son's death.

"Jesus, Sturgis," Jick said. "I think I figured something out. You planned to kill him yourself, didn't you? After all, Phoenix wasn't even your 'son.'"

Sturgis smiled at Jick as his blank eyes stared at him.

"Go on."

"Suddenly, it makes sense," Jick said. "When you said you didn't care that he was dead. And why you hired Finlayson. And why you decided to clone yourself."

Sturgis continued staring at Jick.

"You planned to kill Phoenix after Finlayson cloned you again. But this time, Finlayson planned to add an experimental twist to age your new 'son' to his teenage years. There was no guarantee it would work, but if it did, Phoenix was going to be expendable."

Sturgis' smile widened.

"I won't insult your intelligence, Jick. Yes, Phoenix was a clone. And yes, I planned to dispose of him if this worked. Something I should have done a long time ago."

Jick turned to Finlayson. He paled under Jick's gaze, looking visibly uncomfortable. Jick shook his head at him.

"Finlayson, I don't know what to say. You've always known about Sturgis. I'm amazed you still agreed to do this again."

Finlayson turned to look at Sturgis, then back to Jick.

"I told him it was experimental," Finlayson muttered.

"But he was adamant. A lot had happened in his life. Not just becoming concerned about Phoenix. The boating accident had made him concerned about his mortality."

"Now it's all coming together," Jick said. "You read about Finlayson's recent research and had an idea. The first one was damaged goods, so why not try again? Besides, after your brain injury, you were not capable of rational executive thinking. And becoming concerned about your own mortality. And with Phoenix being so unstable and violent, why not try again?"

"Not capable of rational executive thinking?" Sturgis smiled at Jick. "That's not a very gracious thing to say, Jick."

Jick turned to Finlayson.

"And that's why you're still here on the island. Right? It's not just to clone Sturgis, it's to clone him again, and then do this experimental aging thing."

Finlayson stared at Jick.

"So, why are you here trying to rescue us, Finlayson?"

"Yes, David, answer his question. Why are you trying to rescue them?" Sturgis smiled at Finlayson.

Finlayson stared at Sturgis' blank stare and mirthless smile. He licked his lips.

"I didn't wany anyone else getting hurt. I'm still going to finish the project."

"Finlayson, did you know about those murders in Greece?"

Jick realized he was trying to buy time by changing subjects.

"I swear to you, I know nothing about those murders. Everything I did, I did in California. Yes, I made an embryo that was genetically identical to Sturgis. A miniature, exact replica in nature. The perfect fractal..."

He mumbled the last in a dreamy voice. Jick looked at him in disgust.

"That explains your reaction when you found out I killed Phoenix. He was your creation, and you were proud of him. And when you said Sturgis wasn't like this before his brain injury. You've known Sturgis for years. What happened next?"

"That was pretty much it. Sturgis paid me a lot of money, which helped advance my research and career. I worked with him for a year. He came across as grandiose and supremely confident. Phoenix was the perfect human fractal.

"I knew nothing about those murders then. I knew Sturgis was Greek, and he told me he and his wife couldn't have any children. He said he was taking the embryo somewhere; I assumed it was out of the country, but I wasn't sure.

"All I gave him was an embryo in a cryogenic container. I didn't know what he planned to do with it. I asked him and he told me he had hired a surrogate."

Sturgis smiled at the description of him.

"Grandiose and supremely confident? You flatter me, David."

He leaned forward, eyes gleaming.

"But yes. Phoenix was a clone. Sherryl and I couldn't have any children. We went to a fertility clinic and explored options. All our choices seemed borderline futile and risky. I came across the work Dave Finlayson did and asked him to help me. He did a great job. Phoenix turned out almost perfect. Almost.

"He was just a little different," Sturgis said.

"Maybe he was a replica at the genetic level, but epigenetics is a weird thing," Jick said. "Phoenix grew up in a different era, with a unique set of external influences, and was a different person. He grew up around wealth, probably had every indulgence granted. I bet you and Sherryl got him out of a lot of scrapes. So, there was no accountability as he became worse. Sturgis 2.0 was more violent than Sturgis 1.0, right? Isn't that right, Uncle George?"

Sturgis glared at him but said nothing.

"When I read about the murders in Greece," Finlayson said. "That it was a cesarean section, I had an uncomfortable feeling that it could have been Sturgis. The timing was right, and the location was Greece, where Sturgis was born. But I didn't want to know. I re-read that article earlier this week after all these years, and I was sure it was Sturgis.

"I visited him once after he returned to the States. He had moved to the Big Island. I wanted to see my greatest creation...

"Jick, he was perfect. Bouncing little baby boy. Named Phoenix. After all those years of struggling, Sturgis' faith in my abilities had paid off. I had succeeded, and I had enough money to move ahead with my research.

"I asked him about the surrogate he had hired. He said I didn't need to worry about it. She had done her job, and it was over. He also said he had paid her well, and she was grateful for the opportunity. I didn't want to know any more about things that were best left unsaid. I went on with my life.

"Then he read about my recent research," Finlayson said. "And the rest is history."

"People aren't disposable commodities," Jick said.

"Phoenix was violent. And unstable," Sturgis countered. "Maybe if I had put him in therapy at a young age, things would have turned out better."

"So, you just want to start over with a custom-made replica of yourself, rapidly aged to being a teenager. And that's why you weren't heartbroken when I told you he was dead. As you said, if this works, Phoenix was expendable."

"Things will be different this time," Sturgis insisted. "Intensive teaching and training from a young age, therapy at the first sign of any problems."

"But as long as you don't have any deep feelings for your 'son,' the outcome may not be any different," Jick said. "What does Sherryl think about all this?"

"She didn't know about any of it."

"How did you keep all of this from her?"

"We went to a fertility clinic and went through the motions. Egg donation, sperm donation, everything. After we were done, I told the clinic we were not going to do it and to dispose of everything."

"And all of this?" Jick waved around the room. "Sherryl doesn't know any of this latest venture?"

"She knows this is Phoenix's playground. She doesn't want to know what he does... did, in here, so she stays out. This old farmhouse building was the ideal place to set up shop."

"Wonder what she's going to do when Phoenix doesn't show up. How are you going to explain his absence to her?"

Sturgis smiled an enigmatic smile.

"I may not have to."

"What do you mean?"

"She wanted to turn Phoenix in after he killed a couple of tourists. And I didn't want her to do that. I didn't want the attention."

The blank stare was back. Jick felt the truth sink in.

"You murdered your wife?"

"Not because I wanted to. I gave her every chance to reconsider. But I admit, she had a point about getting Phoenix in therapy from a young age. Maybe if I had, things would have been different. But murder is sometimes necessary."

Finlayson's eyes widened in shock and horror, and his face drained of color.

"You killed Sherryl?"

Sturgis ignored him as he jumped off his stool and paced around the room. He stopped behind Jick.

"I need more information about you. Let's talk some more about why the government felt the need to create a fake identity for you, from an actual dead person, just to investigate me. What do they know? What do you know?"

"I'm nobody," Jick said. "Just an investigator."

"Bullshit." Sturgis' voice cracked like a whip.

"They didn't just send you here to investigate a missing woman. You knew all about Greece. This is something bigger, and I need to know what they are investigating."

He pulled out the knife and circled Jick with slow, deliberate steps. He stood behind him.

Jick felt a sudden searing pain in his right arm as a warm gush ran down his right arm.

"Aaah, shit!" Jick yelled, clutching his arm.

Sturgis had slashed Jick's right arm halfway between his shoulder and elbow. Jick bolted off the stool and spun around.

"Sit. Or I'll have Thaddeus shoot you where you stand."

Jick sat, holding pressure on his arm. He lifted his hand to assess the wound.

Doesn't look like he hit an artery.

"Once again, from the top. Who are you, and what do you know?"

Jick chose his words carefully, deciding to stretch out his answers.

"As I said, one of Alicia's friends asked me to investigate her disappearance."

"And who is Alicia? Is she also an investigator?"

"I think so."

"Who is this friend?"

Jick took a deep breath.

"Maybe not a friend. More like a co-worker. From the mainland. They, and I don't know who 'they' are, were investigating you because of suspicious shipments, followed by Finlayson moving here. That raised alarms you may be engaged in cloning activities."

"Why investigate the disappearance now? She's been missing for almost nine months."

"I don't know. You'll have to ask the coworker."

Sturgis smashed Jick's face with a backhand across the mouth. Jick's stool rolled a few inches from the force of the blow. Thaddeus watched the proceedings from his perch, his gun inches from his right hand, a silent warning. Jick tightened his grip on the stool, unable to retaliate.

"Wait," Jick said, spitting blood. "There's more. I am a medical consultant, but I am not here in that capacity. Alicia's parents were desperate for information, so they agreed to take one last look. This was an informal trip to see if there was anything else left to do. All I was supposed to do was retrace her steps."

"Then why were you spying on my house?"

"No specific reason. Her car was found near the forest reserve. I checked everything nearby."

Sturgis looked thoughtful.

"That still doesn't explain your faked identity. If all they had was a suspicion of cloning, why would anyone go through this effort just to investigate me?"

"Maybe you're more important than you realize."

Jick hoped to massage Sturgis' narcissism. Sturgis did not take the bait.

"You got nothing else?"

Jick shook his head.

Sturgis motioned to Thaddeus.

"Wait, wait. The people who sent me know I'm here. They'll look for me."

"Let them," Sturgis said coldly. "There's no cell phone signal here, and we destroyed your phone."

"I told them I was going to explore this area," Jick tried again.

"They can't come onto my property without a reason. Got anything else?"

"Who's going to help you when it's time for Alicia to deliver?"

"I've made arrangements."

"Like you did in Greece?"

Sturgis' eyes narrowed.

"How did whoever sent you here connect this," he waved around the room, "to what happened in Greece? Oh, never mind, I don't care how you know. It's not important."

Jick had a sudden idea that he could leap off the stool and grab Sturgis, use him as a shield. He glanced at Thaddeus. His hand had moved to his gun.

Damn it. He must have realized what I was thinking.

"I can help you with what you're doing here," Jick said. "I have some medical knowledge. Before I became a medical consultant, I was an EMT."

Sturgis looked undecided as he walked around the room.

"Why are you doing this, Uncle George?" Jick asked. He hoped to goad Sturgis to buy himself more time.

Sturgis glared at Jick.

"Stop calling me that. I needed to start over. And I'm running out of time. So, I took a chance on Finlayson's new research. Without knowing whether it would work...

"Wait," Sturgis clutched his head. "I already told you all this... Shut up."

Sturgis continued his slow pacing around the room. He stopped behind Finlayson's stool.

"George," Finlayson stammered. "I-I'm sorry about what I did. I just didn't want anyone else to get hurt."

Sturgis walked around Finlayson's stool and fixed a blank stare at him.

A chill went through Jick.

Shit. Finlayson doesn't realize what he's done... Sturgis is going to kill him...

"David," he purred. "You disappointed me. You're lucky we can still finish this project. Otherwise..."

"But," he mused. "When you went to rescue them, you didn't know she was there. You went there only to rescue Jick? That's odd. Why would you want to do that? Unless..."

Sturgis stroked his chin. The gesture was unsettling in its calmness. Finlayson felt an involuntary tremble as he stared at the expression on Sturgis' face.

"...you were trying to sabotage the project," he concluded. "You weren't trying to do that, were you, David?"

"N-no," Finlayson stammered again. He jumped off the stool. "I swear to you. I'll help you finish the project."

"Even if it means the man you tried to rescue is to be killed?"

"Y-yes." Finlayson's face glistened in his terrified state. "I'll help you."

"Sit down," Sturgis ordered.

Finlayson parked himself on the stool.

Sturgis resumed his slow walk, circling around Finlayson's stool until he stood behind him.

"Ah, screw it."

In one swift motion, he unsheathed his knife, reached around Finlayson's throat, and pulled the knife back in a vicious motion. Finlayson let out a shriek and toppled off his stool, his neck spurting a crimson arc toward the middle of the room.

He clutched at his neck, gasping, his eyes locking on Sturgis, then on Jick. He tried in vain to mouth a few words. Jick clutched his stool and stared, horrified and helpless, unable to intervene. Finlayson died on the floor, clutching at his neck, staring at Jick.

"I needed a place to sit," Sturgis said with a shrug. He sat on Finlayson's still-warm stool.

"Why did you do that?" Jick asked. "He said he would help you. And you already had your own stool."

"He went to the caves to rescue you, not Alicia. There is only one reason for that. He wanted to sabotage the project."

Sturgis' voice trailed off in a dreamy whisper.

"He didn't want me to live forever. But Sherwin is smart. And Phoenix is still alive, growing beautifully. Sherwin knows how to finish the project. Finlayson is such a great note taker. I'll take my chances with what I've got. Even if Sherwin can't finish, I have that."

He gestured toward the caves.

"Alicia will help me. Help me live forever."

He fixed a stare at Jick.

"Now, where were we? Ah yes, you were going to tell me about your EMT background. Tell me why I shouldn't kill you right now."

"Uh, sure," Jick said. "But how are you planning to smuggle in doctors to help with her delivery?"

"I won't need to smuggle anyone in," Sturgis said. "There are many doctors in the U.S. from foreign countries. Many of them are unlicensed but just needed to get out of their country. They can't get licensed here. Most states have a bureaucratic and onerous licensing process that keeps well-trained doctors in a state of limbo for months or even years. Hell, there's a guy on this island who worked at a convenience store. He was an obstetrician in Russia. It's easier to bring a foreign obstetrician here than it was in Greece. All you have to do is overstay your tourist visa. Or I can smuggle them in here, have them do what they can do, and smuggle them back out again. No one will get hurt, and they'll be happy."

Jick had not thought of that. Sturgis was right. There were many physicians in the United States who were in bureaucratic purgatory, an unlicensed professional limbo, but preferred living here than in their home countries. Easy pickings for him to find someone.

"How did you manage the actual implantation?"

Sturgis did not answer. He smiled at Jick.

"You would need to know the proper time to do it, so you would already need to have someone on your payroll who knows what to do..."

His voice trailed off. Sturgis said nothing.

"It's Pavel, isn't it? The guy who worked at a convenience store. He's the obstetrician from Russia?"

"You're smart, Jayant Arnsson, or Jick Arnold, or whatever your name is."

Sturgis sat on Finlayson's stool. His back was toward the door. Thaddeus sat on the operating room table. Jick perched on his stool between them. Finlayson's body lay in the middle, still oozing blood. There was a lull in the conversation, the air heavy with the iron tang of Finlayson's blood.

I hope I convinced him to keep me around...

Jick looked at Thaddeus sitting on the operating room table, legs dangling a few inches off the floor. The gun was on the table next to his right arm.

Jick looked around for a weapon. There was nothing within reach. Then he looked at Sturgis sitting on Finlayson's stool.

If I grab Sturgis from behind, I can use him as a shield. But if Thaddeus gets off a shot while I'm sprinting, it's game over.

Jick eyed Sturgis' knife. It was sheathed again.

Maybe the element of surprise when I run at him...

"Do you want to know how we knew about your connection to Greece?" Jick asked.

Sturgis jumped off the stool to pace the room.

Damn.

"I don't care, but sure, go ahead," Sturgis said. "Indulge me."

"When your 'son' murdered the guy who hit you with the boat, the victim bit him."

Sturgis looked puzzled.

"Yes, Phoenix's hand was bandaged. So what?"

"The baby's DNA from the murders in Greece matched a sample found on that guy who was murdered outside the restaurant. It was the same kid who hit you with the boat. It wasn't a definite connection, but it was a smoking gun."

Sturgis looked floored by the revelation. He turned red as the shock started another episode of giggling.

"Stop!" He shouted as he pressed his hands to his face.

"Good old-fashioned DNA analysis," Jick said.

Sturgis looked amazed at the revelation.

"That's pretty good," he admitted.

As Jick spoke, he tensed himself, preparing to rush at Sturgis. He opened his mouth to change the subject back to his EMT background to buy a few precious seconds. Before he could put his plan to attack Sturgis into action, a sound interrupted the lull in the conversation.

It was the unmistakable sound of the Halloween haunted house screech from the front door.

FORTY-SEVEN

Everyone froze. David Finlayson's body lay on the floor, still oozing blood in uneven rivulets. The puddle had grown, spreading in an irregular pattern across the imperfections in the shiny concrete floor. Perhaps it was poor David Finlayson's ultimate act of retribution from beyond the land of the living. Or just plain bad luck for Thaddeus. Finlayson's blood had pooled under Thaddeus' feet.

Keeping his gaze locked on the door, Thaddeus grabbed his gun and leaped off the operating room table. His feet landed in the slick puddle and slipped out from under him like he had stepped on a banana peel. His legs shot out from under him and for a comical split second, he was airborne, with an expression of astonishment on his face. Then he landed on his buttocks with a wet splat, dropping the gun.

Jick seized the opportunity. He leaped off the stool and launched himself, diving at Thaddeus as he sat on the ground. With Thaddeus being much stronger, Jick knew he would have to hit vulnerable areas quickly and as many times as he could, before Thaddeus had time to react. He head-butted Thaddeus over his left ear. Thaddeus let out a grunt and toppled over. Jick raised his right arm and, like a professional wrestler, struck Thaddeus with an elbow drop to his throat. He felt something pop, and Thaddeus let out a strangled croak.

Thaddeus and Jick struggled in the gory mess, slipping and sliding as each tried to gain traction. Jick was the first to get the upper hand. He lay on top of Thaddeus. With his left hand, he delivered a vicious chop to Thaddeus' groin as he grabbed Thaddeus' head like a bowling ball, using Thaddeus' left eye socket as the thumb hole. Jick jammed in with all his might, and he felt something pop in the eye socket. Thaddeus screamed.

Jick lunged over Thaddeus and grabbed his right elbow, preventing Thaddeus from grabbing the gun. He rolled off Thaddeus and reached the gun before Thaddeus. Slick with Finlayson's blood, the gun almost slipped from his fingers, but he tightened his grip, pointed the gun at Thaddeus' head and fired. The round punched Thaddeus on the side of his chest. He steadied his grip, aimed at Thaddeus, and fired again. The second round hit Thaddeus above his right ear and exploded through in a brutal spray.

Jick spun on the ground, slipping in the slush as he readied another shot, this time aiming at Sturgis. Then his eyes widened in shock, and he stopped, lowering his gun, as he recognized the intruder who had entered the room.

Sherwin Smith's car idled in the cul-de-sac outside the Sturgis estate as he conducted a quick survey. He drove the short distance to the nature reserve parking lot, got out, and then walked back to the cul-de-sac. Adjusting the object tucked in his waistband, he approached the gate, jabbed the intercom and stepped back. No answer. After waiting a minute, he jabbed the button again. No response again.

As he stood by the gate contemplating his next move, a metallic clank interrupted the stillness. Sherwin ducked into the bushes as the gate whirred open and a car rolled out, driven by a stranger. Timing it perfectly, Sherwin slipped through as the gate swung shut. He jogged up the driveway toward the looming house.

As he approached the main house, a door opened, and a figure emerged, heading in the direction away from the driveway, toward the mauka end closer to the cliffs.

Sturgis.

Sturgis jumped into an ATV and continued toward the forest. Sherwin saw the ATV disappear behind some trees.

There must be a trail there.

No one else emerged from the house. He jogged across the lawn to the spot where the ATV had disappeared. Behind some bushes arranged for concealment, he noticed a trail winding into the forest. Sherwin crept along the path, ready to jump into the bushes if he heard anyone approaching. He followed the tortuous path until he noticed what looked like a dilapidated and abandoned farmhouse in the distance.

Except for the two ATVs parked in front. And the drone of a generator.

Sherwin settled into the bushes and waited, unsure of his next step.

What am I doing here? Should I turn back? No, I can't...

After a half-hour of uncertainty, second-guessing, and fear for his safety, he approached the building from the back and peered into a window. Before he could do a proper assessment, he heard a loud shriek from inside the building. Sherwin caught his breath, eyes wide. Hands shaking, he pulled the object out of his waistband.

An ornate knife with a ceremonial handle glinted in the sunlight. Clutching the knife with a firm grip, afraid it would slip from his damp grip, he approached the door, turned the knob, and pushed.

The front door sounded like he was about to enter a haunted house. The door hinges screeched in protest as he pushed. He thought he heard voices from an inside room, but they ceased immediately.

I need to get out of here. No, I can't...

After the door screeched, his first impulse was to turn and run. But he also knew he could not. He noticed some moldy floor to ceiling curtains hanging in front of a window in the corner. Sprinting to the corner, he stood behind the curtain and waited, his heart thudding in his chest. There was no movement, and no one came out.

Then Sherwin heard a crash, followed a few seconds later by some shouts. The sounds came from behind a modern and recently installed door on the left side. He edged toward it and decided to risk a peek.

He opened the door a few inches and peered in.

A bloody Jick was locked in a vicious struggle with an equally bloody Thaddeus. Sherwin saw Jick jam his thumb deep into Thaddeus' eye socket. The wet pop and Thaddeus' scream made Sherwin flinch. He watched Jick get the upper hand controlling a gun on the floor. Jick fired two shots, and Thaddeus collapsed.

But Sherwin's eyes were drawn to something else, something that was far more important to him. It was Sturgis, sitting on a stool, facing away from him, distracted by the fight between Thaddeus and Jick.

He's here. And now's my chance.

Sherwin Smith grasped his knife with both hands and ran into the room. With everyone distracted by the fight between Jick and Thaddeus, no one noticed his entry. He charged into the room, holding the knife like a battering ram, the handle wedged in a tight fist, and drove the knife into Sturgis' back.

The steel slid into his back all the way to the hilt. Sturgis let out a gasp and looked at his chest. A glistening red triangle had appeared, protruding out of his chest just over his left nipple. A dark halo appeared around the base of the triangle and expanded down his chest. As Sturgis stared at his chest, the triangle disappeared as Sherwin pulled out the knife. He drove it in again, and the triangle reappeared an inch lower. A second halo appeared, merged with the first, as Sturgis stepped off the stool, took a step forward, and turned to face his attacker.

His face frowned in disbelief, then recognition, followed by astonishment. Then his knees buckled, and he dropped to the ground. Sherwin's eyes widened when he realized Sturgis had collapsed on top of David Finlayson. Sherwin saw Jick spin on the ground and stop, stunned when he recognized Sherwin. He lowered his gun.

"Sherwin!" Jick yelled.

Sturgis was splayed across Finlayson's body, his breaths coming in quick gasps. Sherwin knelt and rolled Sturgis onto his back. Sturgis' face was ashen, and his eyes were closed. Sherwin slapped him on the cheek.

"Hey, Mr. Sturgis!"

Sturgis' eyes fluttered open. Sherwin clasped Sturgis' face and came close. The blank expression focused on Sherwin's face.

"Sherwin?" Sturgis mouthed.

"For Mariama," Sherwin whispered, releasing him.

Sturgis' eyes lingered on Sherwin's face before closing for the last time. A final wheeze escaped his lips as his head slumped to the side.

"Sherwin!" Jick yelled again.

Sherwin staggered to a stool and collapsed onto it. His face glistened, and his hands shook. He placed his hands on his thighs as he leaned forward.

"I have wanted to do that for years," he said, his voice raspy. "For years. And the last thing he heard was my mother's name and the last thing he saw was my face. Now he can rot in hell."

"Your mother?"

"He killed my mother."

Jick pulled himself upright, staring at Sherwin as realization struck.

"Mariama Ndiaye was your mother?"

Sherwin looked dumbstruck at Jick.

"You know her name? How do you know her name? Yes, she was my mother."

"I came to Hawaii to investigate the disappearance of Alicia Rogers. Does that name mean anything?"

"No. Who is that?"

"There's a cave about a hundred yards away from here. Alicia Rogers is a pregnant woman. Sturgis was going to use her the same way he used your mother."

Sherwin exhaled hard, eyes cold.

"I'm glad I killed him. May he rot in hell."

"How did you know to find us here?"

"I didn't." Sherwin looked at Finlayson's body.

"Finlayson was super stressed and said he had to go take care of something to make something else right. I was afraid Sturgis would discover whatever Finlayson wanted to do and disappear. I figured now was the right time to do what I had wanted to do my whole life. So, I came to look around. With the dagger. And it finally happened."

Sherwin stared at Finlayson's body.

"You know," he said. "When I first came here, I wanted to kill him, too."

"Why?" Jick asked.

"Because he was part of it."

"You knew about his earlier involvement in this?"

"Yes."

"We need to talk later. You can fill me in."

"Sure."

Jick rolled Sturgis' body over and crouched beside him. The haft of a dagger protruded from his back. The handle was black and smooth, with white banded inlays.

"Looks like it's made of bone. There's a pattern carved into the base of the blade. Wish I could take a picture of this."

"It's a Senegal dagger," Sherwin said. "I got it after realizing we were going to work for Sturgis. I knew all along that he had killed my mother. It was to be the tool of my revenge."

Jick stood.

"Yes, of course. I just need to do one more thing."

Jick searched the room until he found some garbage bags stashed under the sink. He pulled one off the roll. Bending over Sturgis' body and using a towel, Jick pulled the knife out. He soaked some of Sturgis' blood in the towel, wrapped the knife in it, and placed it in the garbage bag.

He dug through Sturgis' pockets and removed his phone.

"What are you doing?" Sherwin asked.

"Collecting DNA. We'll need it to prove what Sturgis did. All right, let's get out of here. You can tell me everything later."

Jick scooped Thaddeus' gun off the floor. He searched Thaddeus' pockets and extracted a set of keys. There were also two sets of car keys. He took Thaddeus' phone, too.

My keys. And probably Finlayson's, too.

They stepped outside and climbed into Thaddeus' ATV. Jick started the vehicle, and they bumped their way down the trail leading back to the caves.

As they approached the caves, he saw Alicia peering out the window. She gasped at the sight of Jick.

"Jick! What happened to you? Are you hurt?"

"It's not my blood," Jick said. He glanced at his arm where Sturgis had cut him.

"Well, most of it isn't, anyway."

"Whose blood is it?"

"Finlayson's. He's dead."

Jick climbed out of the ATV. He picked up the gun and headed for the door.

"You've got a gun," Alicia said. "What happened to Sturgis?"

"He's dead. And Thaddeus too."

Alicia's eyes widened.

"What?"

One of the keys in Thaddeus' bunch opened the padlock.

"Let's get out of here," Jick said. He looked around the clearing.

"I think the coast is clear. There's only one or two other guys I've seen, and I don't think they live here. They're just hired muscle when Thaddeus needed something."

"Did you really kill both of them?"

"No, just Thaddeus." Jick pointed at Sherwin.

"Alicia, this is Sherwin. He was Finlayson's assistant. He killed Sturgis. Sturgis killed Finlayson."

Sherwin gave a sheepish grin as he shook Alicia's hand.

"You killed Sturgis?"

"Sturgis did the same thing to Sherwin's mother years ago that he did to you now," Jick said. "Then he murdered her. Sherwin has been on a quest for justice for years."

Alicia scanned Sherwin's face.

"Thanks," she said quietly.

Sherwin grinned again.

"Don't mention it."

Quin emerged from the cave.

"How are you holding up?" Jick asked.

"Hurts like hell."

Jick studied Quin's shoulder wound.

"Can you wiggle your fingers okay?"

"Sure."

Quin moved his fingers.

"And you still feel everything in your arms and fingers? No numbness or weakness?"

"Nope. Everything is fine."

No nerve injury. But the wound looks like it's getting infected. I need to take him to a hospital.

They piled into the ATV and headed toward the western edge of the hundred-acre wood. Jick's Jeep, the unfortunate Leo and Amy Truong's Mustang convertible, Quin's car, and Finlayson's rental sedan dotted the clearing.

"Nice parking lot of rental cars," Jick said. He stopped next to his Jeep.

Sherwin helped Alicia and Quin climb into the back seat. As they drove away, Sherwin eyed Jick.

"I don't think you can stroll into the lobby looking like that. You're soaked in blood."

Jick flipped the visor mirror open and examined his face and neck.

"Hmmm," he said.

"Let's go back to my condo," Sherwin said. "The entrance is private. You can sneak in through the lanai door and have a shower. We also have a washer and dryer."

"Great idea," Jick said.

As they made their way out of the subdivision and turned onto the highway, Jick glanced at Sherwin. He seemed to have calmed down after the adrenaline rush of what had transpired.

"So, Sherwin, what's your story?"

FORTY-EIGHT

"I was born in Senegal," Sherwin began. "My grandmother told me stories growing up. She told me they had been on an adventure before I was old enough to remember. That we almost died on the way to Greece. She told me they had promised us freedom as refugees if my mother did something for them. Then one day, my mother disappeared. They told my grandmother she was helping a childless couple give birth to a child. Some months later, they told my grandmother she had died in childbirth, and we were to be sent back to Senegal. My grandmother asked them why, if my mother had done what she had agreed to do. They never told her why, but soon afterwards, we were sent back to Senegal.

"We lived in a slum near Dakar. Life was very hard growing up. My grandmother could not manage. She did her best. My mother's younger brother, her youngest, died when I was barely old enough to remember him. He fell sick and was gone in a few days. With both her children gone, her health deteriorated, and she eventually gave up. I don't think she had a choice. She gave me up for adoption.

"The only memories I have of the orphanage are unpleasant. A blur of fear and hunger. I was almost seven when a couple from the States adopted me."

"Seven?" Alicia said softly. "That's an age where you already understand loss. You must've been terrified."

"I was," Sherwin said. "I remember being scared when my grandmother told me she could no longer take care of me. And I was terrified when they told me this couple was going to take me to America. I remember the trip to the airport. My first ride on a plane. Absolute terror, but also excitement."

He was quiet for a moment as he pondered that day.

"But they were wonderful. They were with a church and had an outreach there. Looking back, can you imagine the commitment they made to me? Taking me in when I was almost seven."

Sherwin lifted the crucifix pendant off his shirt and looked down at it.

"This was my dad's," he said. "I wear it in his memory. He passed away just before I graduated college."

"They sound like wonderful people," Quin said.

"They were. Anyway, to get back to how I ended up here. As I grew up, I wondered what had happened to my mother. My grandmother said my mother was smart, well-read, or as well-read as a girl could be, living in a slum in Dakar. She had sacrificed everything to make a better life for us. I started doing research on everything I could lay my hands on about what had happened to her. I couldn't let go of what might have happened to her. Finding out became an obsession.

"For years, I found nothing. It was like she never existed. I couldn't believe there were no records. If someone recruited her to help a childless couple, there should have been some records at a hospital or clinic somewhere. Nothing turned up.

"Until I found an article about an unsolved mass murder in Greece. It happened at the same time we were there. And on the same island, Lesvos. Two doctors, a nurse, and an unidentified migrant woman. I had a feeling deep down inside that the murdered woman was my mother. The story was all over the Greek media because of their local politics. The two doctors were in the country illegally, and one was from Senegal. I figured there had to be a connection. Besides, I had no other leads."

He exhaled and shook his head.

"But nothing. Dead end after dead end after dead end. Whoever murdered those doctors and the migrant woman did a great job covering their tracks. After a few months of searching, I was about ready to give up.

"Then I caught a huge break."

"What happened?"

"I had scoured websites in Senegal about the murders and found nothing. Even less than in Greece. Until I joined a bereavement support group in Senegal for children who had lost their parents. It was a website for Senegalese orphans to post their stories. I too was a Senegalese kid who had lost a parent. I had a hunch that those murdered doctors had families. Maybe I would get lucky. And it paid off.

"I got a response one day when I asked a question on their message boards about the murders in Greece.

"It was Dr. Mbaye's daughter."

"Who's Dr. Mbaye?"

"One of the murdered doctors who took care of my mother. The anesthetist."

Jick's thoughts went to the picture of the murder scene. The murdered anesthetist with the red "scarf" around his neck. He felt a pang of sympathy for a fellow physician. He too had practiced as an anesthesiologist for years. This doctor had a family, and he took a shortcut to enter Greece. It ended up being a terrible decision that cost him his life.

Jick flipped his turn signal on as he swung onto the Queen K highway, heading south to Sherwin's condo.

"Go on."

"I was about to graduate from college by then. As soon as I graduated, I went to Senegal to meet her. She told me that about a year before my mother's murder, two men had paid a visit to the house. They had found out Dr. Mbaye had applied to emigrate to Greece, and they wanted to discuss an offer. But the best part, Dr. Mbaye's daughter had taken a picture of the men with her new cellphone camera. And she still had the picture with her! It was her last picture of her father."

"You have this picture?" Jick asked.

"Yes."

"Here with you?"

Sherwin nodded.

"Hold on a second."

Jick pulled off the highway.

Sherwin scrolled through his phone, and held it up for Jick to see. A tall, black man, whose face could be seen in profile, talking to two men whose faces were angled toward the camera. There was no doubt about their identity.

Sturgis and Finlayson!

"This is great, Sherwin," Jick said. "Keep that picture in a safe place. It proves that Sturgis and Finlayson knew each other years ago."

"Don't worry, it's archived in a safe place," Sherwin said.

"This is a fascinating story, Sherwin," Alicia said. "Go on."

"This picture was my only lead. With more online sleuthing, I found out Finlayson's identity. I joined the same company he worked for and planned all along to kill him. After finding out the identity of the other guy in the picture.

"I couldn't believe my luck when Finlayson asked me to join him in a secret project in Hawaii. I didn't know we were going to meet the other guy in the picture. I was almost floored when Finlayson showed me the picture of him. Older, with a shaved head and a scar across his head, but it was the same guy in my picture. I knew they were going to do something illegal again. I could have left, but I wasn't going to pass up this chance to kill them both.

"Until you showed up."

Sherwin wiped his face and stopped, staring at Jick. Jick merged back onto the highway.

"So, twenty-five years ago, Finlayson clones Sturgis, who uses your mother as a surrogate. Then Sturgis murders everyone to cover his tracks, and Finlayson says he knows nothing about it. Twenty-five years and a serious brain injury later, Sturgis asks Finlayson to do it again, this time with a twist. Then brain-damaged Sturgis murders Finlayson, thinking you will be the one to finish the project. But you kill Sturgis as revenge for your mother's murder."

"What are you going to do with me?"

Thoughts swirled through Jick's head. Like Sherwin, he, too, had taken part in a methodical plan of action to avenge the murder of a loved one. He took a deep breath.

"Nothing. I'm not a cop."

Sherwin breathed a visible sigh of relief.

"Thanks."

He wiped his face again.

"What happened to Finlayson back there?"

"Sturgis murdered him. For his stool. But also because he went up there to rescue me. Which, to Sturgis, meant he was disloyal."

"That's crazy."

"Yes, he was. He had suffered severe damage to his frontal lobe in that boating accident. The normal system of checks and balances in the brain was short-circuited. And he was narcissistic. And a sociopath. Combine that with his brain damage, and his behavior became unpredictable. He was no longer capable of proper 'executive thinking,' so to speak.

"You seem to be a smart kid. Someday, do an online search for a historical figure named Phineas Gage. It describes the profound personality changes that can happen after a frontal lobe injury. And a phenomenon called pseudobulbar affect, which Sturgis suffered from. Those weird giggling and crying fits he used to get."

"Yes, I noticed that."

"I owe you my life for breaking in when you did. Why did you do it at that moment?"

"Something made Finlayson very agitated yesterday. He said he had heard and seen something that made him wonder what Sturgis was up to. I think he turned a blind eye to what Sturgis was doing. I saw Finlayson reading an article about my mother's murder. Maybe he realized Sturgis had planned all along to do the same thing with the surrogate."

"Actually, no," Jick said. "That's not why Finlayson was agitated. He apparently witnessed the murder of some tourists by Phoenix. I guess he had a moral awakening and decided he needed to do something."

"Oh, okay," Sherwin said. "He also mentioned he suspected you were in trouble. So, he went to investigate that land next to Sturgis' house. I spent the night worrying about it because I didn't want Sturgis to become suspicious. I went to his place, let myself in and waited, hoping to ambush him. There was no one at the house, and nothing was going on. Then I saw him on an ATV, heading into the forest. So, I went down the trail leading to the building. I hid outside for a while until I heard a scream. I think it must have been Finlayson, poor guy. When I opened the door to that room, I saw you wrestling with Thaddeus and Sturgis sitting with his back to me. I seized the moment."

"Let me give you a piece of advice, young man. In life, you should always try to anticipate what could happen and plan for it. It can be the key to survival."

"What do you mean?"

"You knew these people were dangerous. And yet, you came to Sturgis' house armed with a dagger. In the literal sense, you brought a knife to a gunfight. If Thaddeus hadn't slipped on Finlayson's blood, you would be dead."

Sherwin said nothing.

"Sherwin, you got away with something. Remember the old saying: Before you embark on a journey of revenge, dig two graves. You were in danger of getting hurt or killed, and you may still end up getting arrested. We won't tell anyone what happened. But promise me you'll never do something like this again."

Am I lecturing this young man about revenge and vigilantism?

"I won't. I had always wanted to kill both but changed my mind about Finlayson. He was just an eccentric man who made some bad decisions. He didn't know Sturgis planned to kill my mother. But killing Sturgis was satisfying, although not as much of a relief as I thought it would be. Oh, turn right here."

Jick turned onto the road leading to Sherwin's condo. He parked in front of the door, waited for Sherwin to unlock the door, looked both ways, and darted inside.

"Bathroom is down the hall on the left," Sherwin said. "Laundry is the next door. Clean towels and robes are in the cabinet in the bathroom."

"Thanks."

Jick undressed and luxuriated in the hot shower. Afterwards, he slipped on a robe, tied the sash around his waist, and then started a load of laundry.

As he walked into the living room, he noticed Quin grimacing as he repositioned his arm.

"Hurting worse?" Jick asked.

"Yeah."

"As soon as the laundry is done, I'm taking you to a hospital. That wound is looking a little weepy."

"Weepy?"

"That's what... doctors call a wound that has a discharge."

"Okay, let's go to a hospital," Quin said.

"Except for one thing."

"What's that?"

"When someone shows up in the emergency room with a gunshot wound, the ER doctors are required to notify the police. I'm not sure we want that. Let's go back to the hotel, talk to Sam."

"I can't thank you enough for coming here to look for me," Alicia began.

"You are most welcome. And please don't mention it," Jick said.

"Jick, who are you? How do you know Sam? Do you do assignments for her?"

"I'm her brother-in-law."

"Her brother-in-law?! Why does she send you on these assignments?"

"It would take too long to explain. She was married to my brother, who was murdered two years ago."

"I am so sorry to hear that."

"Thanks. I helped catch his murderer, and since then, Sam has asked me to help her. This assignment wasn't supposed to be like this. All she knew was that you were missing and presumed dead. Just one last look around before closing the case, mostly for your parents' sake."

After Jick's laundry was done, they climbed back into his Jeep and made their way to his hotel.

"First thing we do, Quin, is get you to a local hospital. I hope Sam has enough influence so we don't report this to the local police."

"Let's call her from your hotel and let her know what's going on," Quin said.

Jick started a video call through his laptop. Sam answered right away.

"Jick!"

"Hi, Sam."

"How are things there? I've been trying to call you and Quin. Did you see Quin? He has your gun."

"Uh, yes, I saw Quin, and there have been some major developments. The case is solved and closed."

He swung his laptop until it pointed at Alicia. He heard Sam gasp.

"Alicia!" Sam exclaimed. "You're alive. But what...?"

Alicia smiled at the camera.

"Yes, Sam, thanks to Jick. Thanks for sending him to rescue me."

"Rescue you?"

Jick pointed the laptop at Alicia's belly. Sam let out another gasp.

"You're pregnant. What is going on there?"

"Just a second," Jick swung the laptop around to point at Quin.

"Quin! What on earth? What's wrong with your arm?"

"There's more to the story, a lot more. But for now, we need to get Quin to the hospital right away," Jick cut in. "And they should not investigate his gunshot wound."

"Gunshot wound?!"

"Yes, I'll explain everything soon. First, the hospital."

"Yes, we can arrange to block an investigation of Quin's injury," Sam said. "The ER physician will have to notify the authorities. We can take over any investigations as this is a federal matter."

"Okay, that's settled. I'll take him in and then call you back soon."

After they hung up, Jick turned to Quin.

"You ready?"

"Sure."

"Alicia, you and Sherwin wait here. It's not too far to Waimea. I'll drop Quin off at the hospital. Be back in about an hour."

FORTY-NINE

After Jick and Quin left, Alicia went into the bathroom. She looked at herself in the bathroom mirror. The ordeal was over, and the pent-up stress followed by the immense relief overwhelmed her. She stood staring at the reflection. Then she turned sideways and observed her protuberant belly. She placed a hand on her belly and shut her eyes, trying to ignore the kick she felt from within. Tears welled up and trickled down her cheeks. Then she sobbed, shoulders heaving. She grabbed a facecloth and pressed it to her face.

Jick pulled into the driveway at the hospital emergency room entrance.

"Thanks for everything, Jick."

"Don't mention it."

"What the hell did we get involved in?"

"Crazy, isn't it? Sturgis *was* cloning himself. And now there's a Sturgis 3.0 on the way."

The realization hit both men at once.

"Oh, shit. We have a problem, don't we?" Jick muttered.

"Damn right."

"Do you want me to go in with you?"

"No, you don't need to. I have my credentials. I'll be fine."

"Okay. I need to get back ASAP and call Sam to discuss this."

They parted ways, and Jick drove back to Sherwin's condo. He noticed the look on Alicia's tear-streaked face as he entered.

"I can guess," Jick said. "Quin and I had a sudden realization at the hospital. You're not just overwhelmed with relief that it's over. Because it's not quite over, is it?"

He pointed to Alicia's protuberant belly.

"It's him, isn't it?"

Alicia nodded. She pointed to her belly.

"I don't want it. I want to get rid of it."

Jick stared at her.

"Let's call Sam back."

Jick flipped his laptop open. He called Sam, who answered right away.

"Jick, did you get Quin to the hospital okay?"

"Yeah," Jick said. "Now we have another important issue to discuss."

"Why is Alicia pregnant?"

"That's the issue."

For the next few minutes, Jick brought Sam up to date on everything that had transpired after he left the hotel to explore Sturgis' one-hundred-acre lot. There were intermittent gasps and "You did what?!" exclamations from Sam as he narrated everything.

"So, our suspicions were true. Alicia is carrying a clone of Sturgis," Sam leaned back in her chair, still absorbing what Jick said.

Alicia's eyes filled with tears as she looked at Sam.

"Sam, I've been through hell and back. The only reason I'm alive is because this wonderful man saved me."

She gave Jick a tight hug.

"But I don't want this baby."

"It's a long and crazy story but we need to get back home ASAP."

"Okay, I'll book you both on a redeye tonight," Sam sat up straight. "I'll email the confirmation in a few minutes and see you tomorrow."

"Sounds good."

Jick ended the call. He looked around the condo.

"Where's Sherwin?"

"He just went to the store to get some things."

"We have a few hours until the flight tonight," Jick said. "There is one more loose end I need to tie off."

"What's that?"

"Pavel," Jick said. "I need to find him. I need to know how involved he is in this."

"How are you going to find him?"

"I don't know."

He opened the bag containing the things he had taken from the makeshift operating room. He took out Sturgis' phone and flipped it open.

"Good thing it's not a smartphone," he remarked. "No password or fingerprint needed."

He scrolled through the contact list until he found Pavel's number.

"Got it," he said. "Let's see if he's home."

He dialed Pavel's number. Pavel answered almost immediately.

"Good morning, George. Is everything ready?"

"This isn't George, it's Jick."

A pause.

"Jick? Why do you have George's phone?"

"It's a long story. We need to talk. Can we meet somewhere?"

Another pause.

"What's going on?"

"It would take too long to explain over the phone."

"Okay," Pavel said. "I live in Kawaihae. There's a seafood restaurant across from the industrial area."

"I can be there in twenty minutes."

"Okay, see you there."

He hung up and studied the flip phone. It looked out of date by many years. He shook his head and dropped it into the bag.

"Alicia, wait here," Jick said. "I'll be back soon."

He picked up the gun Quin had brought.

"Just in case. I don't know how deeply Pavel is involved, and I don't want surprises."

Alicia nodded.

"Just be careful."

The restaurant's door swung shut behind Jick, a blast of cool air rushing over him. At the far end of the dining area, an indoor/outdoor bar stretched onto a covered patio, separated by a clear plastic curtain. He spotted Pavel sitting outside at the far end, a neat vodka before him. Jick perched on the stool next to him.

"Hello, Jick," Pavel said. His eyes roved over Jick with suspicion. "What's going on?"

Jick ordered a beer, drew in a deep breath, and got straight to the point.

"You're a physician. An obstetrician, right?"

"Who told you? And why do you want to know?"

"This is important. What kind of work are you doing for George Sturgis?"

"I work in his lab."

"Doing what?"

"It is not your business. You will have to ask him."

"I can't. He's dead."

Pavel's face drained.

"What? What do you mean he's dead?"

"That's why I have his phone."

Startled, Pavel looked like he was ready to jump off the stool and bolt. He had a sudden, fearful look, perhaps afraid that Jick was a hired killer, perhaps afraid he was the next target. Jick noticed the change in his demeanor.

He doesn't look like someone who knows everything. And he may look like a Bond villain, but he sure doesn't act like one. Perhaps I'll tell him...

"Don't go anywhere," Jick said. "I'm not here to hurt you. I am a doctor too."

Pavel settled back on the stool.

"Who are you? And what happened to George?"

"Pavel, did you do an implantation of an embryo in an unconscious woman about eight months ago?"

Pavel looked like he had seen a ghost. He paled, and beads of sweat appeared on his forehead.

"Are you with the police? Or immigration?"

"Neither."

"Then why?" Pavel stammered.

"I am here to investigate a woman's disappearance. It was the woman you implanted the embryo into."

Pavel stared at Jick. Then he glugged the rest of his vodka and slumped on the barstool.

"Her disappearance? Was she a kidnap victim?"

"Something like that."

Pavel dabbed his face with a napkin.

"Yes, I did an implantation. But I swear I did not know she was being held against her will."

"Really?"

"I worked at a convenience store. I am obstetrician from Russia, and I could not stay there. I came on short-term visa and never left. It was years ago."

"How did you get involved in this?"

"I lived in California. David Finlayson came into my store sometimes. He knew what I did in the past. He asked me why I did not try to practice here. I told him it was too difficult to do more training here and then take exams."

"So, you worked at a convenience store?"

"I have family here. They help me. One day, Finlayson asked me if I would be interested in doing a medical project. He introduced me to George Sturgis. He tell me about the project and how much money I would make. He said I would travel to Hawaii on a private plane, live in a small apartment for almost a year. He said I would need to do an embryo implantation for a woman who wanted a baby but could not afford it. Then I would need to wait around until the end and do a cesarean on her. And to be available if there were any complications during the pregnancy."

"That's all you know?"

"Yes."

"Have you been to George's house?"

"Only once, when I did the implantation. They took me to an operating room somewhere."

"You weren't worried about doing something illegal?"

"I am already doing something illegal. I am here illegally, Jick."

"You have a point."

"And the money was good."

"How much?"

"Fifty thousand."

"Fifty thousand?! To do an implantation and C-section, and to be available just in case? And this for a woman who could not afford to do it? Weren't you suspicious?"

"Yes. But it was the money."

"And you weren't worried they might kill you afterwards?"

"No, why should they? I know nothing."

"I bet that's what Dr. Mbaye and the other obstetrician thought twenty-five years ago."

"Who is that?"

"Pavel, let me tell you something. You may be very lucky to be alive. That embryo you implanted was a clone of Sturgis."

Pavel blinked. "A clone? An actual human clone?"

"Yes, made by Finlayson. Twenty-five years ago, they did the same thing. Sturgis then murdered everyone in the delivery room, including the obstetrician and the anesthetist, to cover his tracks. This time, he did say he did not plan to kill the surrogate but who knows? He was brain-damaged and lacked any impulse control."

Pavel motioned for another vodka.

"I noticed that," Pavel said. "Pseudobulbar affect, right?"

"Exactly. And Finlayson's dead too. Sturgis cut his throat."

Pavel stared at Jick, transfixed, as if unable to believe what Jick said.

"But why?"

"Because he was disloyal and, according to Sturgis, tried to sabotage the project. And because he wanted to sit on Finlayson's stool."

Pavel reached for his vodka glass. He downed it, signaled for another.

"What happened to George?"

"It was Sherwin, Finlayson's assistant. He stabbed Sturgis to death as revenge for what happened twenty-five years ago. You see, the young woman Sturgis murdered, the surrogate, already had a child. It was Sherwin. He was adopted and raised in America."

"What did I get myself into?" Pavel palmed his forehead and squeezed his eyebrows.

"Maybe Sturgis would have let you go. But I doubt it. I suspect he would have killed you because you knew about the embryo implantation, and you knew the surrogate. He took pains to shield his identity from the surrogate, but you knew too much. And you're here illegally, which means you're easier to erase."

Pavel's voice cracked. "What should I do now?"

"Go back to California," Jick said. "You're not getting paid, but at least you're alive. That's something."

"Are you really a doctor?" Pavel asked.

"I was. Retired now," Jick replied.

"Retired at your age?"

"It would take too long to explain."

"What kind of doctor?"

"An anesthesiologist."

"Why do you do this?"

"Also take too long to explain. I do these freelance assignments for a relative."

Pavel downed his last vodka and reached out a tentative hand. They shook hands.

"Thanks, Jick."

FIFTY

With a thump and a roar as it reversed its engines, the plane landed in Dallas. Sam had sprung for two first-class tickets, and Jick had taken full advantage of the lie flat seats, sleeping soundly for most of the flight. Alicia, however, was restless as no position was comfortable. There had been a minor issue at the airport about letting Alicia board because her late-stage pregnancy made them hesitant to let her board. Jick had convinced them it was safe for her to fly.

"What did you tell them?" Alicia asked.

"Just enough to get by," he replied with a smile.

After collecting their bags, they exited the terminal, where Sam waited. After exchanging greetings, they climbed into the car and headed out.

"We'll go to my place," Sam said.

After arriving at Sam's house and settling in, Sam poured coffee for everyone. She brought a plate of croissants and jam.

"Okay, let's talk," she said, eyeing Alicia's belly.

"I want it out," Alicia said.

"What are your thoughts, Jick?" Sam asked.

"This is a real mess, and we can do a thorough debriefing later. Alicia is in her late third trimester, possibly less than a couple of weeks until delivery, of a baby that is a clone of Sturgis. She wants it out. Which brings up a much bigger problem."

"Which is?"

"Sturgis' 'son' Phoenix was a murdering psychopath. We already discovered he was a clone made by Finlayson twenty-five years ago."

"Yes, and...?"

"We'll call the original Sturgis 1.0. We know Sturgis 1.0 murdered several people the first time he cloned himself. And his clone, whom we'll call Sturgis 2.0, was just as bad, if not worse. Now we have Sturgis 3.0. You can see where this is going."

Sam leaned back, thoughtful.

"Yes. We know Sturgis 3.0 will probably have the same violent tendencies. So, we're discussing a late third-trimester abortion, aren't we?"

"As opposed to a cesarean section to deliver a healthy baby, which no one knows is another clone of a psychopath," Jick said.

"I don't know how to begin to deal with this. This clone will be no different, but we don't know for sure. We could do a deep dive into the whole 'nature vs nurture' argument, but we know his brain will be pre-wired for some degree of psychopathy."

"I want it out," Alicia repeated.

"Should we at least talk about adoption?" Sam ventured.

"No way," Alicia countered. "I do not want to go through labor. I would rather be knocked out, end the pregnancy, and go on with my life."

"We've all heard this hypothetical scenario where someone speculates 'If you were alive in the late 1880s and knew what type of person Hitler would become, would you be justified in killing him in his infancy?'" Jick said. "And the answer to that is, of course, an emphatic no. Punishment before committing a crime is obviously not defensible, legally or ethically. Parenthetically, this theme was explored in that movie *Minority Report*. Have either of you seen it?"

Sam nodded; Alicia shook her head.

"But this is a unique situation. We know with absolute certainty that Sturgis 3.0 is going to be mentally unstable and violent. If we put him up for adoption, it is more likely that he will be raised in different and more difficult circumstances. Even Sturgis 2.0, raised in a stable environment, was violent."

"So, are we advocating for a late third-trimester abortion of a healthy baby?" Sam asked.

Alicia's eyes welled with tears as Jick leaned back in his seat.

"Boy, this is a real gut punch," he said. "But I don't think we have any choice."

"Let's say Alicia has a cesarean section under general anesthesia and never sees the baby," Sam said. "We put him up for adoption. In fifteen years, he kills neighborhood pets and eventually works up to killing people. Unlike the Hitler argument, we know this is going to happen. It's already happened twice."

"I want it out," Alicia said.

Jick studied her face.

"Epigenetics is a funny thing. Even though their genomes were identical, Sturgis 1.0 and 2.0 were different. Different people, different era. And even though 2.0 was more violent, we don't know if Sturgis 3.0 will be the same or worse. Or could he be better? Could he be the psychopath who channels his instincts in a positive manner? We don't know. Therefore, I don't think we can justify a late third-trimester abortion of a healthy baby."

Alicia looked anguished.

"I want it out," she repeated. "I don't care if we end the pregnancy."

"Alicia, you haven't had any prenatal checkups. We hope this baby is healthy. We don't know about your health. You will need to be screened for things like preeclampsia or diabetes."

"I feel fine," Alicia said. "I just want it out and for this nightmare to end."

Sam was busy typing on her keyboard. She looked at the group.

"Only a few states allow third-trimester abortions," she said. "The nearest is New Mexico. Do you wanna go back to Albuquerque with Alicia?"

She grinned at Jick.

"No," Jick said. "You're overlooking something important. I don't think this will be as straightforward as we would like. I doubt any state would just grant an abortion on demand. Let's say, for example, that Alicia declares she is a rape victim as justification. She may qualify for an abortion, but to identify the rapist, they would preserve a DNA sample of the fetus. Now imagine the reaction when that sample matches the sample from Greece twenty-five years ago or the sample from Kona a few years ago. *And it doesn't match the mother.* It would be an absolute disaster."

"You're right," Sam said, frowning. "I hadn't thought about that. We could try to get her out of the country. I could discuss it with my superiors. Boy, this is already a disaster."

Alicia let out a gasp and started sobbing.

"What's wrong?" Sam asked.

"I felt this thing kick," Alicia said.

She said 'this thing,' not 'him.' Not even 'it.' Jesus, what a cluster...

Sam excused herself, phone in hand, closing the door behind her. Alicia dabbed her eyes and let out a shuddering sigh.

"Hang in there, Alicia," Jick said, trying to lighten the mood. "Sam will figure this out."

Sam returned thirty minutes later.

"Well, we have some options," she said. "None of them are good, so we should discuss them all and pick the best of a bad bunch. Regardless of which option we choose, we can't do it in the States as it will eventually get out that Finlayson was cloning humans."

"True," Jick said. "So, what are the options?"

"There aren't too many options with countries that allow late third trimester abortions. Mexico does, so does India, but only in very specific and limited court-ordered circumstances. And, they would also keep a record of it, including DNA samples."

Alicia stirred in her seat and winced as she felt another kick.

"So what do I do?"

"There is one other option. Greece."

"Greece?"

"Yes, Greece. They still have an open murder investigation, and they would like to close it as soon as possible. I could call the authorities in Greece and update them on everything, including what has happened here. Greece already allows abortions on demand, and if there are any restrictions based on the estimated age of the pregnancy, maybe a court would issue an emergency override. And they can do a DNA analysis but not upload it into the database. And Alicia could return to the States and put this behind her."

"Okay, when can I go?" Alicia said in a tone of eager desperation.

"Let me call that detective in Greece. I'll let him know we solved the case, but there is a catch, and we will need their help."

Sam left the room again. This time, she was gone for an hour. They could hear her speaking, followed by long periods of silence. When she finally entered the room, she wore an expression of cautious optimism.

"There's a new twist," she announced. Seeing the expression on Alicia's face, she added, "But it may not be bad news. Hear me out."

"Okay."

"The Greek authorities see this as their problem. Although the clone was made on U.S. soil, the crimes of implantation and the murders of the staff were committed on Greek soil. I spoke with a high-ranking official from their Ministry of Justice. She was understanding and offered a solution you might like.

"We will fly you to Greece. There, officials from their health and justice departments will meet you. After a medical checkup, they will perform a cesarean section under general anesthesia. They will make the baby a ward of the state.

"What that means, from a practical standpoint, is the child will be placed in some type of orphanage. A few officials and staff will know just enough of his background to realize he will be there under special circumstances. Eventually, even if he is adopted, he will be kept under close supervision by the state. If he commits any crimes, their judicial system will deal with it. Since Greece does not have capital punishment, if he commits a crime, he will be incarcerated. The official from their Ministry of Justice did not feel comfortable agreeing to a late third-trimester abortion but is agreeable to make the child a ward of the state. Any information about you will be expunged from the official record when you return home. Which means neither the baby nor anyone else can look you up."

Alicia stared at Sam for a few seconds, then nodded.

"Okay," she said. "I'll never have to see it, and that's that."

"You're going to Greece," Sam announced to Alicia. "And Jick, I'd like you to go with her."

"Sure, no problem."

"I'd go too, but I can't."

"Of course, I understand," Jick said. "When do we leave?"

"Tonight. We're chartering a private plane at DFW to take you to DC. There, you'll meet one of my associates who will take you to a different charter to Athens. You'll be met at the airport and taken to a real hospital, not a back-alley experience."

"So, what happened?"

"The detective was flabbergasted by what had happened. He contacted a local judge and, after explaining the situation to him, the judge contacted their Ministry of Justice."

"This solves the problem. The doctors won't have to deal with the ethical dilemma of performing a late third-trimester abortion, and the baby won't be placed in just any orphanage. It sounds like the Greek authorities are willing to help take care of and monitor this kid. All in all, a satisfying solution.

"It was quite an interesting conversation. At first, the Greek authorities were in disbelief that Sturgis had found someone to clone him. I told them we had a DNA sample from George Sturgis, which would match the baby. In ideal circumstances, they would have liked to wait for confirmation before proceeding, but since time is of the essence and Alicia is not having an abortion, they agreed to proceed right away.

"Their files had a report of Sturgis and his wife visiting a fertility clinic and a record of his wife having gone through an egg harvesting procedure. Looks like Sturgis never intended to use his wife's eggs. It was just a cover-up because he wanted to make a replica of himself. And his wife never knew."

"I wonder where she was when he murdered those people," Jick said. "Wasn't she there for the delivery? Maybe he went by himself. I guess we'll never know. After all, this was all about him. Narcissism and psychopathy rolled into one."

"Wonder what would have happened to his wife if she ever found out. I wouldn't put it past him to kill her, too," Sam observed.

"He did kill her."

"He did?"

"Yes, his wife was devoted to Sturgis to the point of enabling him. But even she had a breaking point. From what Finlayson said, Phoenix murdered two tourists and Sherryl Sturgis wanted to report him. Sturgis didn't want his clone sent to prison, so he silenced the only other person who knew about the tourists' murders."

"Wonder what he did with her body."

"Don't know. Quin and I saw a burial site on his land. Maybe it's her; or I guess it could be the tourists."

"Wow," Sam said. "When this is all over, we'll need to make an official report. And those poor tourists' bodies need to be found."

"Of course."

"When I told the Greek authorities Sturgis was dead, and we had the DNA sample, it closed their case," Sam said.

"A Sturgis positive DNA match with the sample taken from Mariama Ndiaye's belly would do it. Even if the media gets hold of it, there will be no mention of the recent events. It would just be a cold case solved."

"And you can bet Sherwin will keep his mouth shut," Jick said.

"The bodies of Sturgis, Finlayson, and Thaddeus are in an abandoned farmhouse on his property. And one last thing. Phoenix's body is out there too, next to a grave where someone is buried. You should get a DNA sample."

"Oh, of course," Sam said. "We'll take care of it."

Sam turned to her keyboard and started typing. After a few minutes, she stopped and looked at Jick and Alicia.

"Oh my God," she said. "This has to be it."

"What?"

"I scanned through some recent missing persons reports from Hawaii. There's only one in the recent weeks. A newlywed couple on their honeymoon, Leo Truong and Amy Truong, née Nguyen. They left one morning from their hotel and did not return. There has been no trace of them or their rental car."

"I bet it's them," Jick said. "And it's a Ford Mustang convertible. It's parked on the west side of the hundred-acre parcel Sturgis owned."

"Okay, we'll follow up on it," Sam said.

"Thanks for organizing all of this," Jick said. "There's only one thing left to do. Come on, Alicia, let's go to Greece."

FIFTY-ONE

Sam waited at the baggage carousel. She waved when she saw Jick emerge through the security checkpoint.

"Welcome back," she said, hugging him.

Jick collected his bag, and they made their way to the parking lot.

"I'll drop you off at home. Hope you're not too tired."

"I'm fine," Jick said. "Those lie-flat seats courtesy of Uncle Sam and Aunty Sam were great."

"You're welcome. Come over to my place after you're refreshed. We can get caught up on everything. Quin's coming too. It's his first visit in weeks."

"How's he doing?"

"Good. He had surgery on both the shoulder and the broken forearm. Today's his last day of antibiotics and rehab starts soon. He's okay to start some activities."

Later that evening, Jick and Sam sat on her patio, watching the sun morph into an orange orb as it sank behind a neighbor's house.

"Quin should be here any minute," Sam said.

"Vikram, Jr!" she admonished, looking over Jick's shoulder.

Vic Jr. turned to look at his mother, grinning as he charged across the yard toward her.

"I kid-proofed the backyard," Sam said. "But he still tries to get into trouble."

Jick surveyed the yard.

"He has stopped putting things in his mouth, so I feel a little better letting him run around. The plants aren't toxic, and I've locked all the yard stuff. I scattered his toys around the lawn so he can get distracted from one toy to the next."

Jick watched his energetic nephew throw himself into his mother's arms. He held still for a moment, then shook free and darted off again, distracted by a butterfly that tantalized him before flying away.

"He needs a dog," Jick grinned.

"I don't disagree. But I'm too busy with him right now. I think when he's about four or five, yeah, we may get a dog.

"Quin already has one," she added with a smile.

"Hmm, he does, does he?" Jick side-eyed his sister-in-law. "And how is that supposed to help little Vic?"

Sam shrugged.

"Dunno. We'll see."

"You said Quin's coming here. Is he okay to drive?"

"No, he's using a rideshare. Later, if you're okay hanging around, I'll drop him off at home."

"Yeah, sure."

"But more about Quin later, when he gets here. So, how did Greece go? Tell me all the gory details."

"Not that much to tell," Jick said. "Alicia was both upset and relieved. I guess it depends on perspective. If you didn't know the circumstances, the whole surreal experience was even mundane. As an anesthesiologist, I did many C-sections. This one was routine, and the baby was fine. Alicia's prenatal checkup, the only one she had, was fine, and she sailed through.

"The operating room was set up just like in that picture of what happened twenty-five years ago. Even the position of the infant warmer. When Sturgis 3.0 was kicking around in the infant warmer, that would have been the exact moment that Sturgis 1.0 burst into the room and massacred everyone. And here we were, delivering another clone of that sick man.

"I couldn't shake the feeling of unease watching the nurse scrub him down and measure his Apgars. The terror on the poor nurse's face from that picture in Greece as she knew she was about to die was a gut punch. And here we were, doing it again.

"I watched Sturgis 1.0 cut Finlayson's throat. We know about the murders Phoenix committed, not to mention the countless animals he must have tortured and killed over the years. I'm sure the dead pig in the forest wasn't his first kill.

"Knowing them in person and then seeing this clone felt weird. It was hard to wrap my head around the fact that this bouncing little baby boy may, and probably will, turn into a killer. In a way, foreknowledge may be a good thing. If Greece keeps him under close supervision, he could make an interesting case study on the genetics, and the effect of epigenetics, on psychopathy.

"But overall, I felt good about our decision. Could I have justified ending this pregnancy, even at this late stage? Sure. There was no straightforward answer, and I think we did okay. All the medical staff were briefed on a need-to-know basis, and the whole thing was professional. When everything was done, they took the baby to the newborn nursery, and that was it."

"And Alicia was knocked out, so she didn't have to see the baby, right?"

"Yup."

"Your first impression of Sturgis was that he was just a doofus, that there was no way he was cloning a person."

"I was wrong. He seemed to have developed a Jekyll-and-Hyde personality after his brain injury. There was the lovable and pleasant Uncle George that he presented to the public, and there was the psychopath, Sturgis. Even when he was the jovial Uncle George, he had moments of anger that bubbled through. I thought he was just weird. Brain injuries can do unusual things to your personality. You can see it after strokes, too. It doesn't have to be a traumatic injury like his."

"Is Alicia still in Greece?"

"Yeah, their healthcare system differs greatly from ours. They wanted her to stay for a while longer than the recommended three days. This is because they knew she would fly back to the States. Higher risk of blood clots with long flights, and all of that. So, she'll be there for probably another week. I'm sure she's eager to see her parents and son."

"Has she called them yet?"

"Oh, I forgot to mention. Yes, she called them after the surgery. I was in the room, so I got to hear their reaction. They were stunned, speechless with shock and relief. Her son was in tears; her mother was bawling in the background. She told them she was in Greece, and something had happened. She'll come up with a story to explain her disappearance, and then she wants to forget this entire ordeal."

"I don't blame her. She was okay with your leaving?"

"Oh, yeah," Jick said. "She already felt she had inconvenienced me enough."

The doorbell pealed.

"I'll get it," Sam said.

Quin and Gaby emerged onto the patio with Sam.

"Jick," Quin exclaimed. "Good to see you, man."

Jick stood, and he and Quin embraced. Jick ruffled Gaby's hair, and she ran off to play with Vic Jr.

After drinks were served, Quin leaned back in his chair.

"I don't know where to start," he said.

"Then don't," Jick replied.

"You are quite something, Jick. I can't thank you enough."

"Then don't," Jick grinned.

"This started with us ordering Indian food that day when I introduced you to this case," Sam said. "We've gone full circle, so let's order Indian food tonight."

"Sounds fantastic," Quin said.

Thirty minutes later, as they tucked into a delicious assortment of curries, naan, raita, and other Indian delicacies, Quin lifted his beer over his head with his right shoulder.

"Feels good. Here's a toast to Jick."

Everyone clinked glasses.

"Got any plans?" Quin asked.

"Just one. Probably plan on not accepting any more missing person assignments from Sam," Jick grinned with a wink at her.

"Probably a good idea," Sam said.

"I might re-explore the whole traveling around the country bit," Jick said. "I'm getting a little antsy staying here in Dallas, anyway. Time to see what else is out there."

"May fortune favor the bold," Quin said.

"Or, in my case, the foolish."